SUSANA *and the* SCOT

SABRINA YORK

St. Martin's Paperbacks

This is a work of fiction. All of the characters, organizations, and events portrayed in this novel are either products of the author's imagination or are used fictitiously.

SUSANA AND THE SCOT

Copyright © 2016 by Sabrina York.
Excerpt from *Lana and the Laird* copyright © 2016 by Sabrina York.

For information address St. Martin's Press, 175 Fifth Avenue, New York, NY 10010.

ISBN: 978-1-250-06970-2

Printed in the United States of America

St. Martin's Paperbacks edition / January 2016

St. Martin's Paperbacks are published by St. Martin's Press, 175 Fifth Avenue, New York, NY 10010.

10 9 8 7 6 5 4 3 2 1

This book is dedicated to all my readers who are fearless Scottish lasses at heart. May you find an untamed Highlander of your own!

ACKNOWLEDGMENTS

My deepest appreciation to Laura Jorstad for her copy-editing genius, to the St. Martin's Art Department for such a beautiful cover, and to Alexandra Sehulster for all her guidance.

Thank you, Monique Patterson, for giving Susana and Andrew this chance at love.

My sincere thanks to my fellow writers for their support along this journey. Especially Cherry Adair, Pam Binder, Sidney Bristol, Delilah Devlin, Tina Donahue, Laurann Dohner, Sharon Hamilton, Mark Henry, Desiree Holt, Cat Johnson, Elle James, Jennifer Kacey, Gina Lamm, Delilah Marvelle, Becky McGraw, Rebecca Zanetti, and so many more.

And of course a shout-out to my amazing support team: Linda Bass, Crystal Benedict, Stephanie Berowski, Crystal Biby, Kris Bloom, Monica Britt, Kim Brown, Sandy Butler, Carmen Cook, Celeste Deveney, Tracey A. Diczban, Shelly Estes, Natalie French, Lisa Fox, Rhonda Jones, Denise Krauth, Barbara Kuhl, Angie Lane, Tracey Parker, Laurie Peterson, Iris Pross, Tina Reiter, Hollie Rieth, Pam Roberts, Regina Ross, Sandy Sheer, Kiki Sidira, Sheri Vidal, Sally Wagoner, Deb Watson, Veronica Westfall,

viii ACKNOWLEDGMENTS

and Michelle Wilson, as well as the shy ones, Christy, Elf, Fedora, Gaele, Lisa, Nita, and Pansy Petal.

To all my friends in the Greater Seattle Romance Writers of America, Passionate Ink, and Rose City Romance Writers groups, and the Pacific Northwest Writers Association, thank you for all your support and encouragement.

CHAPTER ONE

July 1813
Reay Parish, Caithness Shire, Scotland

"You probably shouldna ha' kissed her."

Andrew Lochlannach tightened his hands on the reins and frowned at Hamish. Bluidy hell. Did he need to bring it up *again*? He shot a look over his shoulder. They were riding ahead of their company on the dusty track, so none of the others could hear, but that didn't stop the sudden roil of mortification. "That is *not* why he sent us here."

Maybe. Probably.

Hamish threw back his head and laughed. The sun glinted off his red beard. "Really? Your brother catches you in the arms of his wife's sister—her baby sister, over whom she is ferociously protective—and now here we are. Exiled."

Something riffled in Andrew's gut. "We havena been exiled."

"Have we no'?" Hamish threw out his hands. "Here we are, in the wilderness—"

"Reay is not a wilderness." It was, however, nearly so, tucked away on the western border of Caithness County. Though as isolated as it was, it was one of the more prosperous baronies, even more so than Dunnet.

Andrew tried to ignore the trickle of trepidation, the curiosity that had been teasing him since he'd set out on this journey. He'd known a girl from Reay, once upon a time, loved her. Lost her. And now he would see the land from which she'd hailed. The knowledge tugged at his heart, but he thrust that familiar ache away.

"Far from hearth and home, charged with protecting the denizens of Ciaran Reay from . . . cattle thieves." This last bit Hamish offered with a sniff, as though it were beneath his prowess. Then again, it was.

But their mission was much more than that. At least, it was to Andrew. His brother, Alexander, Laird of Dunnet, had trusted him with his charge. He was counting on Andrew to prevail. That faith meant the world to him.

The lands his brother had gained through his marriage had been beleaguered with an influx of miscreants and vagabonds, stealing cattle and robbing the castle stores. Several outlying crofts had been burned to the ground. In addition to the thievery of wandering bands of men made homeless by the Clearances of land to the east, there were indications that the local lairds had their eye on the parish and, with the Baron of Reay's illness—and a recent attempt on his life—they obviously had plans to claim it for their own.

They would not. This land belonged to Alexander now, and Andrew would do everything within his power to protect it. It was the reason Hannah had married Alexander, after all. To assure the security of her people.

"I canna blame him, though. For banishing you."

"I havena been banished!"

"Imagine finding your wife's sister swooning in the arms of a rakehell."

"She wasna swooning." Lana was hardly a swooner. In fact, she hadn't seemed all that interested in Andrew's kiss, which was, all things considered, a surprise. And a trifle lowering.

"And not just any man. A master seducer."

Well, yes. This, he could not deny.

"And to make matters worse, his own brother. His suave and handsome brother known for kissing every woman he sees—"

"Not *every* woman."

"Enough of them." Hamish chuckled. His gaze narrowed on Andrew. "And how many kisses did that make?"

Andrew shifted in the saddle. Shrugged.

"How many?"

"Ninety-nine." A mutter.

Hamish's nose wrinkled. "Och. That many?"

"Aye."

"I dinna realize you were so close to winning our bet."

Andrew grimaced. Aye. Only one away. How he regretted that bet. It had been a stupid bet, made under the influence of far too much whisky. Most of his bets with Hamish were. Stupid, and made under the influence of too much whisky. He hoped one day he'd learn his lesson, but he doubted he would.

It had been this way with Hamish since they were boys. One quest after another to outdo the other in all things.

If he was being honest, Andrew had to admit, he'd accepted this particular wager because he'd hoped . . .

Ah, well. It had been a foolish hope.

He'd kissed ninety-nine women and not one of those kisses had ignited so much as a flicker. Not a fragile hint of the feeling he'd been searching for. In all likelihood, he would never find it again.

"I shall have to be more diligent," Hamish said, and then he fell silent, but only for a moment. There was laughter in his voice when he added, "It's a pity you made that vow."

Bluidy hell. He should never have told Hamish about

that vow. He should have known the blighter would never let him hear the end of it.

Again, too much whisky.

Perhaps he should have vowed to avoid spirits instead of women.

Beyond his brother's vehemence when he'd discovered Lana in Andrew's arms, in that moment Andrew had had an agonizing epiphany. No matter how many women he kissed, he never would find *that* feeling again. Mairi was dead and gone, and with her, a part of him had died, too.

And now, because of a momentary desire for a kiss and a stupid bet, he'd been exiled—probably. He'd certainly lost his brother's trust, or at least a crumb of it. He swore to himself, he would never, ever allow himself a casual flirtation again. They were far too dangerous.

However, whether it was exile or not, Andrew was determined to prove himself to his brother on this mission and maybe, if he was lucky, pay back a little of the debt he owed. Alexander had sacrificed so much for Andrew—very nearly his life. If he found peace with Hannah, if he found passion and acceptance and love, it was only fitting.

The burn of envy at the thought was beneath him.

"Then again," Hamish continued, oblivious to Andrew's inner turmoil. He often was. "If you are out of the race, that means more women for me to kiss."

Andrew forced a grin, though it probably came out as more of a grimace. He really did wish Hamish would stop talking about that bet. He was done with all that.

"Of course, I only need three. Three more women and I will finally beat you."

"You've beaten me before." They were well matched, he and Hamish, in all things. More often than not, their bouts on the lists ended in a draw. They both rode, shot, and drank with equal skill. And until that kiss with Lana, and his subsequent oath, they had both excelled at seduction, too.

"Ah, but I would verra much like to beat you in *this* challenge." Hamish winked. "I imagine there are many bonny lasses in Reay, if Hannah and Lana are any measure." Hamish's eyes glimmered. He'd taken a particular shine to Lana, the youngest Dounreay sister, who had accompanied Hannah to her wedding. In fact, all the men in the company—including Andrew—had been attracted to her ethereal beauty. But they'd all been warned off. Even Andrew.

Perhaps, especially Andrew.

His brother's admonishment still irked him.

True, he had a reputation for seducing women, but he wasn't a beast. He could control himself. He wasn't so base that he would fall on the first attractive woman he saw. He hardly needed Alexander to remind him that Lana was his sister-in-law. His relation. Aside from that, Andrew had already reached his gloomy realization. Already made his vow.

There would be no more women in his life, in his bed.

"Ach, well," Hamish sighed gustily, shattering his darkling thoughts. Hamish did that. It was probably why they were still friends. Everyone needed someone who could banish darkling thoughts. "I do hope there are some bonny lasses, bet or no. I doona fancy spending the next few months living like a monk."

Andrew tried not to snort, and he failed. Hamish hadn't lived as a monk a day in his life. "Fine. But do keep in mind our true reasons for being here." They were here to secure the lands and provide a military presence that would deter further mischief. They were not here to chase skirts.

"I shall have to ask Rory for . . . suggestions." Rory, one of the men who had escorted Hannah to Dunnet, rode with their company of soldiers, returning home. "Surely he will know which of the Reay lasses are, shall we say, more amenable."

"Shall we at least meet with Magnus Dounreay first, to determine what needs to be done to shore up the defenses, before you launch your seductions?"

Hamish fluttered his lashes. "I would never allow the pursuit of a woman to interfere with my duties." A blatant lie, but Andrew fobbed it off. They rode in silence for a moment and then Hamish said, "You know, even though you've conceded the wager—"

"I havena—"

"Nonsense. If you've vowed to avoid women, you canna very well kiss them. And therefore, you have surrendered to my prowess."

Andrew snorted.

"My point is, even though you've conceded the wager, I still expect you to pay up when I win." His eyes danced.

Bluidy hell. He would have to pay. The thought annoyed him.

Perhaps he should have waited to make his vow. He was only one woman away, after all.

But no.

Andrew firmed his resolve. Wager or not, it was advisable for him to stop kissing women. It had not turned out well for him.

The memory of one girl—one with bright shining green eyes and hair like a waterfall of fire—danced through his mind, but he pressed it away. He thought of Mairi often, daily, hourly perhaps. And each time, he forced the yearning for her back down into the dark well of his soul.

She was lost to him forever and no matter how many women he kissed, it wouldn't bring her back to him.

He stared ahead at the long lonely road. Restlessness pricked him. There was a hill to their right, a verdant rise of green. Quicker than following the dusty track around its base. The urge to break free nudged him.

"I'll race you to the top of that hill," he said. Without waiting for Hamish's response, he kicked Breacher's sides and his mount leaped forward. He tried to ignore the sneaking suspicion that he was really trying to run from his past.

Naturally, Hamish followed.

Naturally, Andrew reached the crest first. Breacher was unbeatable in any race. As he waited for Hamish to catch up, he gazed down at the parish of Reay, which would be his new home for the time being. He didn't know how long he would have to stay, but he already missed Lochlannach Castle, his brother, his bed.

Despite his disgruntlement, he had to allow that Reay was lovely from this vantage point. The crofts and the fields spread out in a patchwork of green. The sea sparkled, a deep sapphire, in the distance. The rose-colored turrets of Dounreay Castle were just visible beyond the woods. In the lea below, a farmer led a shaggy cow along the rutted track with a rope.

It was all very peaceful. Very bucolic.

Hard to believe the parish had been besieged by brigands.

Hamish rode up to his side and gusted a sigh. "Ach. Beaten again."

Andrew cocked his head to the side. "You should be used to it by now," he teased.

Hamish growled at him, but there was very little heat in it.

The two shared a chuckle as they surveyed the land they were sworn to protect.

Even as they watched, a cloaked figure astride an impressive stallion charged from the woods and closed in on the farmer. When the fellow leaped down from his mount, it became clear how small he was—probably a boy—so it was a surprise when he tossed back his cloak and pulled up a bow, pointing it at the farmer.

The two exchanged words and, while he was too far away to hear what was said, Andrew could read the belligerence in the boy's stance. The farmer backed away from the cow, and then, upon the other's command, lay down on the grass with his hands above his head.

Bluidy hell. Were they witnessing a theft? Here and now? Within moments of their arrival on Reay lands?

Excellent.

The ride from Dunnet had been long and uneventful. Andrew ached for some excitement. Exhilaration flooded him.

Ach, aye. How triumphant would it be to arrive at the castle, victorious, with a captured thief in tow? Trussed up like a pig and tossed over his saddle?

Andrew grinned to Hamish. "I'll take this one," he said, and then he set heels to Breacher's sides and pounded down the hill toward the robbery in progress.

ᑤ

Turf flew beneath Breacher's hooves as Andrew pulled up to the scene. It pleased him to see the robber's nostrils flare in awe at his approach. The boy's mount was impressive, to be sure, but Breacher was far more so.

And he himself was impressive, he imagined. A large and looming warrior, bursting as he had onto the scene. No doubt the boy was quite intimidated.

Andrew flung himself from the saddle and unsheathed his sword; the scrape of metal rang through the field with an ominous shiver. He took a moment and added his trade-mark twirl, flipping his sword up and over his head before pointing it at the brigand.

It was clear the farmer was duly cowed. He *eep*ed and covered his head, peeping out between his fingers. The boy . . . not so much. He propped his fists on his hips and glared as Andrew finished his routine. And then he snapped, "What the hell are *you* doing here?"

Ach, aye. A boy. A lad. His voice hadn't even dropped yet. Andrew decided to take it easy on him. "Never ye mind," he said in a silky tone, before assuming his bat-tle stance. It was a fearsome stance, indeed. "Drop yer weapon."

The boy's eyes narrowed, spitting emerald fire. Slowly, he turned his bow from the farmer to Andrew. "Drop *your* weapon."

Andrew blinked. He'd never been defied quite so bla-tantly. Certainly not by a boy half his size. Men trembled before the might of his sword. Women swooned. He was rather daunting, if he did say so himself.

And he did.

Maybe he wouldn't take it easy on the lad after all. Maybe this boy needed to be taught a lesson. He stepped closer, brandishing his sword. "I said, drop your weapon," he boomed.

In response, the boy lifted his bow, pulled back on the string and let fly.

Andrew nearly flinched, but by the grace of God did not. The arrow whizzed by his head—far too close—and while it didn't nick him, it sliced off a lock of his hair. He watched it fall in a gentle drift, that silver swath, to land on the green grass of the lea.

Something rose within him, not fury so much as deter-mination.

Well, perhaps a touch of fury. He rather preferred his hair attached to his head.

Even as the boy whipped another arrow from the quiver, Andrew charged, swinging his sword and cleaving the bow in two. It shattered in the boy's hands.

The lad snarled and reached for his dirk.

Andrew didn't give him time to find it. He encircled the boy with the strong bands of his arms. It occurred to him that in addition to being far too young for this kind of pursuit, the boy had no muscle whatsoever. In fact, he was almost soft.

Aye. The lad needed guidance. A firm hand.

A spanking, perhaps.

He was far too undisciplined.

Indeed, the lad went wild; he thrashed and fought against Andrew's hold, even though there was no possible way he could break free. His screeches of outrage were earsplitting and the invectives spilling forth far too foul, so Andrew clapped his hand over the boy's mouth.

"Go on," he grunted at the farmer, nodding his head down the track.

The farmer scrambled to his feet and dashed off, so traumatized by this to-do, he forgot to take his cow.

"So you think to steal cattle from Reay?" Andrew hissed into the thief's ear.

The boy turned and stared at him over his shoulder. They were face-to-face. Close. Their gazes locked and something snaked through him. Andrew wasn't sure what it was, and there was no time to interpret it . . . because all of a sudden, pain sliced through him as the villain's sharp teeth bit into his palm. At the same time, the boy gored him with a pointy elbow. Andrew, perforce, released him.

The boy spun around and his hood fell. A shock of burnished red hair tumbled out in a shimmering fall.

Andrew froze as a chilling realization washed through him.

The thief wasn't a boy. It was a woman.

And holy hell . . . what a woman.

That red hair, flittering in the breeze? That soft body writhing against his? The burn of her glare? And aye. That feeling? The one that had flickered by too quickly for him to capture it?

Arousal.

It had been a long time since he'd felt it, far too long, but he should have known. He should have known she was a woman. The moment he spotted her. The second he touched her.

Certainly when she'd shorn off a lock of his hair.

A man would never have done something so vindictive. A man would have simply skewered him.

But vindictive or not, she was magnificent.

It occurred to him, it was a damn shame he'd just sworn off casual flirtations, because this armful of curves was—

She hauled off and smacked him.

It barely registered because she was such a tiny thing, and because he was so befuddled. But he noticed at least.

"You idiot!" she howled. "You buffoon. You brute! Look what you've done!" She stormed over to the shards of her bow and gathered them up.

There was no reason for him to grin, faced with her wrath as he was, but he did.

It irritated her more. She smacked him with the bow as well. Or what was left of it. "This was my favorite!"

"Your favorite bow?"

She gored him with a furious glare. "What the hell are you doing here?"

"Isn't it obvious?"

She crossed her arms. "Not precisely."

"Protecting Reay cattle from thieves."

Her expression soured. "Really?"

"Aye."

"You're not doing a very good job at it."

"I caught you."

She leaned in, her expression fierce. "What on earth made you think I was a cattle thief?"

"You came barreling out of the woods, alone, brandishing a weapon on an unarmed farmer—"

"He wasna unarmed. And he wasna a farmer. That man has been stealing our cattle for weeks—"

Andrew gulped and set his teeth. "It was only natural to assume *you* were stealing the cow."

"How can I steal my own cow?"

"*Your* cow?"

"Of course it's my cow, you dolt."

"The cow belongs to Magnus Dounreay."

She growled at him. *Growled.* "I am his daughter."

Andrew froze. *Fook.* This was Hannah's sister? But then, now that she mentioned it, there was a haunting familiarity about her. Hannah had the same frown. He was certain of it. He'd seen it often enough.

"We've been tracking the thief for days." She glanced over at the spot where the farmer had been. "And look what you've done. After all that work finding the blighter, you let him go."

"He left the cow," Andrew offered.

It didn't help.

She poked him with a sharp finger. He felt it, even through his leather breastplate. "You, sir, are a nuisance. Keep away from me."

Keep away from her? Not a chance. In fact, all of a sudden his assignment in Reay looked all the more intriguing. Andrew tipped his head to the side and grinned at her. "I canna do that," he said.

"And why not?"

He waved at the troop of men just joining Hamish on the crest of the hill. "Because we've been sent here by the Laird of Dunnet to oversee the defenses of Reay." His grin broadened as her dismay blossomed. "In fact, I'll be here for quite some time."

∞

Susana Dounreay's heart lurched.

It had been bad enough to see *him* pounding down the hill like an avenging angel, racing toward her—all her bad dreams and nightmares combined. The one man she never wanted to see again.

It had been bad enough that he'd smashed her favorite bow.

Bad enough that he'd *touched* her, wrapping her in his arms and pressing her against his hard hot body, releasing memories and regrets and hungers so long caged.

On top of all that, he didn't remember her.

After everything, after all they'd shared, after all he'd done to her . . . he didn't remember her.

She should be happy. She should be delighted. Thrilled beyond words. She had no idea why the thought nearly crushed her.

But even that wasn't the worst of it. Because then Andrew—the man she never wanted to see again—had blithely announced that he was here to stay.

Acid churned in her belly as the prospects and probabilities flickered through her mind. Panic seared her.

He couldn't stay. She couldn't allow it. She couldn't bear to see him, talk to him, suffer his presence every day.

She crossed her arms and studied him, searching for a weakness perhaps. To her annoyance, she did not find one.

He was much taller than he had been when they'd last met. And broader. And his muscles were . . . Her gaze strayed to the flex of his chest. Och, aye. He'd not had such spectacular definition as a boy.

He'd always had the most beautiful hair. White-blond and flowing and long. All the girls in the parish in Perth had swooned over it. Susana suppressed the urge to grab her dirk and slice it all off. His eyes were still as blue, though they seemed shadowed. His face was sculpted perfection, from the long blade of his nose to his broad forehead . . . to those damn dancing dimples she wanted to slap.

Rage swept through her. Rage and frustration and . . . something else she would not name.

How on earth was he even more handsome?

Clearly the years had been friendly to him—which for some reason infuriated her more.

Ach, she didn't want him here.

"You might as well turn around and go back home." She thought she'd invested the suggestion with the appropriate tone of authority, but apparently she had not. He grinned at her. Those dimples, the ones she remembered so well, rippled. Her gut rippled along with them.

"I willna. My brother is counting on me to secure these lands—"

A cold hand clutched at her chest. "Your brother?" A horrifying suspicion arose.

"Dunnet. Alexander Lochlannach is my brother."

Ah. Bluidy hell. He was a Lochlannach.

Her brother-in-law.

No matter what she said or did, no matter if he left or stayed, they were tied together, forever, by the bonds their

siblings had forged. It was a pity that, with all the heart-
ache he'd given her six years ago, he hadn't bothered to
mention his family name. Had she known, she would never
have encouraged Hannah to marry into the family. In fact,
she would have advised her to run.

He leaned on his sword and proffered an arrogant
smile. "I'm Andrew," he said, and her stomach clenched.
Ach. She knew. She knew his name far too well. She'd
cursed it often enough. "And you must be Susana?" he
said in a silky voice. "Hannah told me you were lovely,
but I had no idea how lovely you were."

Was he even cockier now than he'd been as a boy?

Was that humanly possible?

She glared at him. "Why are you here?" she hissed.

He misunderstood the true meaning of her question
and answered it at face value. "Because, Susana, you
need our help. The raids on your lands have been increasing, and the neighboring lairds are getting more aggres-
sive."

Susana nearly growled. For one thing, the way he rolled
the *s*'s in her name sent a ripple of displeasure over her
skin.

For another, she was damn tired of men and their pos-
turing. From Stafford, the laird to the east who had been
launching raids on their land, to Scrabster, the laird to the
west, with similar outrages.

But the most galling by far, was this man. This
cocky, smirking, arrogant peacock. A man who was far
too handsome for his own good. A man who'd always had
things his way. A man who took what he wanted and then,
when he was done, tossed it aside for the next best thing.

Infuriating.

He took her silence as an invitation to continue, although it most certainly was not. "No doubt Stafford and

Scrabster see your father's illness as a weakness, an opportunity—"

"My father isna weak," she retorted. She didn't have much patience on a good day and this was proving, already, to be a very bad day. Aye, Papa was ill. He'd been ill for a while and was recovering from an attempt on his life—most likely orchestrated by Stafford's minions. But he wasn't a weak man.

"When they see that Dunnet has taken charge of the land and has the strength to hold it, they will have no choice but to back down . . . unless they want an all-out war."

It aggravated her that he was right. With the ramparts bristling with Dunnet's men, Stafford would think twice about staging another incursion on Reay lands. And the good lord knew she desperately needed the help. Since Hannah and Lana had left, all of their duties had fallen in Susana's lap, along with her own. What she wouldn't give for the luxury of handing this weight over to someone. Someone competent. Trustworthy.

But not him.

Susana didn't want Andrew Lochlannach here. In her home. Under her roof. Near her daughter.

Her soul howled at the thought.

He had to go. There were no two ways about it. He had to turn tail and hie back to Dunnet. The sooner the better.

But if he did, indeed, come to Dounreay, and if he did, indeed, try to take over her duties of protecting her home, she was going to make his life a living hell.

This she vowed.

She would send him packing or die trying.

CHAPTER TWO

Susana Dounreay's glare darkened as she stared at him; her displeasure was clear. Andrew was fairly certain she was annoyed that he'd interfered with her capturing the criminal, but he suspected there was a deeper displeasure there as well. A pity he didn't know what had spurred it.

If there was ever a woman he did not want to displease, it was this one.

What an irony that only minutes ago he'd been so certain he would never meet a woman who sparked a fraction of his interest. And now here she was. A woman who fascinated him. It wasn't just the red hair or the snapping green eyes. It was more than that. It was the way she'd felt in his arms, her warmth, her scent perhaps. Something had unlocked the flood of need he'd worked so hard to contain.

Granted, the reason for his fascination could be that she reminded him of Mairi. Mairi had hailed from Ciaran Reay. No doubt they were kin, which would explain the undeniable resemblance. The urge to ask rose within him, but he pushed it down. Judging from Susana's expression, this was probably not the time to ask.

And while she might look like Mairi, she wasn't. Though her hair was red, like Mairi's, Susana's was a deeper, richer hue. Her eyes, though the same glimmering green, were sharp, like a predator's. Mairi's had been softer and dewy. And filled with love.

And then there was Susana's form.

As delectable as Mairi's had been, this woman was far more lush with a trim waist and flared hips. Breasts that made his mouth water. Long legs encased in those provoking breeks . . .

Breeks, for God's sake.

His thoughts stalled as he studied the unbecoming display. He'd never seen a woman in men's attire and he wasn't sure what he thought about it, although he was certain it made him uncomfortable. It should not be attractive in the slightest.

Should it?

Mairi had been a lady, through and through. A gentle soul with a soft voice and sweet smile. She would never have bounded about the countryside brandishing a bow and wearing breeks.

Mairi wouldn't snap and snarl and . . . *bite* him.

She most definitely would not have shot at him.

Aye, Susana Dounreay might look like the girl he'd once loved, but the two were hardly the same. It was almost a disservice to Mairi's memory that he wanted Susana.

But God help him, he did.

She was still scowling at him wordlessly when his men rode up on them. Hamish, who had witnessed the entire scene, was grinning like a loon. Andrew felt the urge to smack the grin from his face. The urge only swelled when his friend turned his attention to the enticing redhead.

He slipped from his saddle and sauntered over, easing off his riding gloves.

Andrew had known Hamish his whole life. He didn't know why he'd never noticed until now—until he stood before Susana Dounreay, smiling down at her—just how tall he was. How damn handsome.

That interest flickered in Susana's eyes as she perused

him made something slightly acidic slither through his veins.

"Well, hullo there," Hamish purred.

Andrew's hackles rose.

Hamish shot him a smarmy glance. "It was rather impressive how you foiled that robbery," he said. "Aren't you going to introduce me to this . . . miscreant?" His eyes danced as he said it, making it clear he was mocking Andrew, not Susana. She was quick to pick up on this and served Andrew a superior smirk.

He ignored the heat rising on his cheeks. Aye, she hadn't been a robber at all, but it was a mistake anyone could have made.

He was certain of it.

"Hamish Robb, this is Susana Dounreay."

Hamish blinked. And then he smiled. And then he threw back his head and laughed. "Sus-Susana Dounreay?" he said through his chuckles. He sobered, fixing a sincere expression on his face, but it was a poor attempt at sobriety. The lady's identity was clearly of great amusement to him. "Miss Dounreay, it is a pleasure to meet you." He took her hand and to Andrew's utter revulsion, in an overblown display of chivalry, kissed it.

And she allowed it.

In fact, she smiled. "A pleasure to make your acquaintance, Hamish Robb. Please tell me you are in charge of Dunnet's men."

Andrew frowned.

"Ach, alas. I am not. Andrew is our fearless leader." He gestured in Andrew's direction but it was a gesture of exclusion, not inclusion. It made a prickle of displeasure dance on his nape.

Susana huffed a disgusted breath. "Andrew? The man who just let the thief I've been tracking for weeks escape?"

She glowered at him, though it was wholly unnecessary. Her displeasure with him was hardly a secret. "Lovely," she spat. And with that, she spun on her heel and made her way over to greet Rory—who was, apparently, an old friend and who, apparently, needed a hug. *A hug.* Then together, chattering like magpies, they went to examine the purloined cow.

Andrew had never been a jealous man, but he recognized the feeling, the dark swirl of frustration and need. The anger that another man, any other man, had captured *her* attention.

It hardly signified, he reminded himself as he attempted to rip his gaze away from her. He was here for one reason and one reason only.

It irked him that it took him longer than it should have for him to recall what that reason was.

"Well," Hamish gusted. "That was interesting." He watched Susana mount her horse with far too much attentiveness. Though Andrew couldn't blame him—it was a rather fascinating sight, considering the fact that she was wearing breeks. He quelled the urge to clout his friend. But then Hamish murmured, "I never thought I would find number ninety-eight so quickly."

Andrew's stomach knotted. The thought of Hamish kissing Susana Dounreay was not a pleasant one. He made a sound that was something like a snarl. "Remember why we're here."

"Och, I remember." Hamish's eyes twinkled as he pulled his gloves back on and swung into the saddle. Andrew followed suit. "Protecting the puir souls of Dounreay from brigands. You're off to a wonderful start, I might add."

"Shut up."

Hamish waggled his brows. "I'd like to protect *her* . . ." He nodded at Susana Dounreay as her stallion launched into motion. She rode at the head of the company, her back straight, her hair flowing free in the breeze. "I've never seen a woman as . . . captivating."

Andrew's fist curled tighter around his reins. There was no reason for that squall of discontent to whip through his veins. He had no claim on Susana; indeed, he wanted none. But Hamish had no claim on her either.

He clearly wanted one. His eyes gleamed as he studied Susana's backside, cupped as it was by the saddle. It occurred to Andrew it was far too alluring a sight. A woman should not be allowed to sit a saddle like that.

A woman should not have hips that swayed with every step of her mount. She certainly should not be seated astride. The thought made his skin clammy.

"She's not a maid," Hamish said in a contemplative tone and Andrew glared at him. He wasn't sure why.

Och, he was.

"How do you know that?"

"Rory mentioned she has a daughter."

This bit of news made something bitter tickle the back of Andrew's throat.

Of course she wasn't untouched. She was a gorgeous, glorious, fearless woman. Men would be pursuing her in droves.

Just not *him*.

"She's married then?" Surely there wasn't a thread of desolation in the question.

"A widow."

"Ah." Andrew fell silent and studied Susana, the cant of her head, the slope of her shoulders, the taunting sway of her hair. Not married. Not a maid. Probably available.

Hamish grinned. It was an evil grin. He excelled at evil grins. "It's a pity you've sworn off seduction."

Damn. He should never have mentioned the vow to

Hamish. Again, in retrospect, he should never mention anything to Hamish. Especially not after he'd had far too much whisky.

Because here, now, was a woman he very much wanted to . . . pursue.

It pricked at him, this sudden swelling of excitement at the sight of her, because his vow was still very new. One would think his resolve would have lasted longer.

Of course, she did remind him of Mairi. That was probably it. And nothing more.

"You *have* sworn off seduction, haven't you?"

Andrew glared at his friend, though it was hardly Hamish's fault that now, so soon after consigning himself to a life of celibacy, he should meet *her*. "Aye." Sworn off. Completely. No matter how tempting the swing of her hair night be. No matter how alluring her form, her glower, her scent . . .

His gut heaved at Hamish's next question. "So you're certain you doona intend to seduce the lovely Susana?"

"Nae." He didn't intend his response to be so sharp. Or perhaps he did.

"Are you *certain*?"

"Aye," he clipped. Nearly a snarl.

"So . . ." Hamish nudged him again. The look in his eyes was a familiar one. It had never before caused such cold dread to crawl through him. "What do you think? Should *I* seduce her?"

Andrew set his teeth. He didn't know why the thought of Hamish and Susana made him feel ill.

His soul screamed *Nae!* But his reason spoke more stridently. "If you wish," he muttered, but the moment the words left his lips, he regretted them. Which was ridiculous.

He had no claim on her.

He didn't want one.

It was inconvenient, the seething desire he had for a prickly warrior princess with arrows that were far too sharp . . . and barbs to match.

He wasn't here to seduce a woman. Indeed, he'd vowed to himself to give all that up.

And she was his sister-in-law. Surely that complicated any seduction immeasurably.

But as they made their way through the flower-spattered meadow toward the seaside town of Ciaran Reay, he couldn't help thinking about it.

He couldn't help thinking about it a lot.

Susana fumed as she rode back to the castle, still reeling from her confrontation with Andrew. It was hard to believe he was here, solid, real.

In her life, once more.

And damn. Why could she not eject from her mind the memory of just how solid he was?

The sight of him barreling down that hill, his white-blond hair flowing out behind him, that fierce expression on his too-beautiful face was burned on her mind. Her heart had fluttered, then thudded. And then—when she'd realized he wasn't some figment of her imagination, but here, really here—it had plummeted.

He was the last person she ever wanted to see.

She'd been a stupid girl when she'd traveled to Perth six years ago to visit her mother's people. She'd allowed herself to be cozened by dancing dimples and a charming grin. She'd believed the tripe he'd fed her about how she was special and wonderful and the love of his life.

She'd been seduced.

That in itself was humiliating enough.

But then she'd learned it was all lies. That she hadn't been the only girl the handsome boy had seduced. When she'd been faced with proof, when she'd seen him kissing Kirstie Gunn, she'd been devastated.

Kirstie had bragged about it too. Mocking Susana as a fool for thinking a boy like Andrew would really want *her*. They'd laughed about it, Kirstie told her. *He'd* laughed about it.

Unable to bear the heartbreak and the mortification, Susana had left, fled Perth without a word to anyone. She'd come home. Where it was safe. Where men treated her with the respect she commanded. Where no man would ever hurt her again.

She'd spent the intervening years strengthening her spine and carving out a place in this world.

She hardly ever thought about that faithless boy anymore.

And now he was here.

For an indeterminate period of time.

It was a horrifying prospect.

When she reached the stable yard, she ignored her visitors and threw herself from her horse, tossing the reins to Ian. She stormed into the castle and up to her father's study, filled with rage.

For one thing, Dunnet had already sent a company of men upon his marriage to Hannah. Why did he need to send more? Without warning? And to *take over* the defenses of Dounreay without so much as a by-your-leave?

Worse than that, he had sent *him*.

Papa was at his desk, surrounded by work, but he wasn't working. He was sleeping. His snore rippled through the room.

Susana crossed her arms and tried very hard not to snort. Still she did. Loudly enough to wake him.

He grunted and his lashes fluttered open. When his gaze lit upon her, he smiled widely. She was not mollified. "Susana, darling. Ye've returned. Did you find any brigands?"

Any brigands? Hah!

"Papa, did you ask Dunnet to send more men?"

"What?" He rubbed his eyes in an attempt to appear innocent and surprised. Susana wasn't duped. She saw that flicker of guilt.

"Did you? Did you ask Dunnet to send more men?"

"I sent him a letter telling him about the last attack. About that bastard Keith."

Susana set her teeth. Och, how she would like to get her hands on Keith. That he'd tried to poison her father—*poison* him—made her see red. Lucky for him, he'd escaped before she could rain down her wrath upon him.

"Did you ask Dunnet to send more men?"

"I might ha' mentioned it."

"*Och!*" Susana whirled around and paced the room. "Papa, you know we have things well in hand."

"Do we?"

Her stomach clenched at her father's words. She was the one in charge of defenses. She couldn't help but feel as though she'd failed. She'd doubled the men on watch since the last attack and set an investigation in motion searching for other traitors the enemy might have slipped into their ranks.

She'd been appalled to discover they'd been betrayed . . . by men they'd taken in, given shelter. To learn that Keith and Heckie and Jock for God's sake were not the braw upstanding men they'd seemed to be, but vipers sent in to undermine their security, galled her.

Worst of all, her father had been attacked. *Her father.* He'd very nearly died.

That bitterness rising in the back of her throat was probably not terror.

She could not let it happen again. She could not. And the only way to assure his safety, assure all their safety, was to maintain absolute control. To be on top of every situation, to orchestrate every element.

She finally felt as though she and Keir, her captain of the guard, had devised a system that worked. Everything had been going well. She'd been satisfied with their efforts. That satisfaction was absolutely shattered with the advent of Dunnet's reinforcements. She was certain it had little to do with *him*. Any other man, attempting to worm his way in and take control of her dominion, would have annoyed her all the same.

Or perhaps not.

"Susana, lass. Doona look like that."

"Like what?"

"So distraught. Dunnet's men will augment our forces, not weaken them."

"We doona know that." Andrew had already gotten in the way. Set her investigation back weeks.

"Stafford will know it. He isna a fool. He'll see our added forces and realize we are nae longer all alone."

"That isna what I'm worried about." She tuned and paced the room again. "The men who caused all those problems were not from Dounreay. They were strangers. Men we took in. We placed our trust in them and they betrayed us. The last thing we need right now is more strangers on our land."

"Dunnet's men will be trustworthy. They are loyal to their laird."

Her nape prickled. "Are they?"

"Of course they are."

Susana froze as Andrew's deep voice flooded the room.

Had he *followed* her? She whirled and fixed him with a glare. His response was a blasé smile, which made her want to spit nails.

He stepped into the room—uninvited—and thrust out his hand. "Magnus Dounreay? I'm Andrew Lochlannach, Alexander's brother. He asked me to lead a contingent of men here and take over the fortifications."

God, he was large. He nearly filled the room. His heat, his scent, his *presence* dominated her senses. How aggravating.

It exasperated her when Papa took the offered hand and shook it. When he studied Andrew with far too much curiosity, something snaked through her. It felt like panic. "Andrew. Ah." Papa glanced at Susana. She set her chin and stared him down. He hardly flinched at all. His lips firmed and he turned back to their guest. "Yes. I see. So . . . You're Dunnet's brother?"

"Aye, my laird."

"Sent to take over the fortifications?" Papa's tone, the far-too-curious look he sent Susana, irked her. Tension fizzled between them. She ignored it.

"Aye, my laird. I would love to speak with you about it. To get an idea of the measures you already have in place."

Susana tried not to bristle. *She* was in charge of that. She always had been.

"Ye'll be talking to Susana about that, my boy. Have you met my second daughter?"

Andrew's expression warmed, and not in a good way. "Aye. I have."

Papa shot a look at her and chuckled in a manner that caused Andrew to follow his gaze. Perhaps her expression was telling, because the buffoon winced.

"Please, have a seat." Papa waved at the chair on the far side of his desk.

Anxiety riffled at Susana's nape, sending a hot tide creeping through her. She didn't want these two men talking. Not about the defenses of Dounreay. Certainly not about . . . other things. "Papa. I'm sure . . . our guest is tired from his journey." She couldn't bring herself to call him by his name.

Andrew's expression could only be described as obnoxious. That it came with a wide grin only provoked her more. "Nonsense. I would love to chat with you . . . both." He folded his long body into the chair and nudged the other toward her with a toe. It scraped across the wood floor with a provoking screech. His brow quirked. The challenge in his eyes was blatant.

Though it piqued her to do so, Susana sat. It wouldn't do to leave these two men alone. If she stayed, she could steer the conversation away from any dangerous waters. She folded her hands in her lap and fixed her attention on her father's face. He was staring at Andrew with a queer expression, one that made a pulse tick in her left eye.

"So you hail from Dunnet?" Papa asked.

Ah, a simple question. A logical question one might ask a visitor from Dunnet. But Susana sensed the undercurrent, the perturbing thread of import in the query.

"Aye."

"Have you always lived there?"

Ah, fook! It took some effort, but Susana untangled her locked fingers.

"Aye. Always."

Papa's brow furrowed. He opened his mouth to ask another question and Susana did the same, to redirect the conversation, perhaps, but Andrew spoke before either of them could.

"Although I did attend school in the south for a few years."

Papa's expression made her pulse thud. "In the south?"

"Perth, actually."

Papa's chuckle reverberated in the room, low and pernicious and—*shite*—*knowing*. But he only said, "Perth is quite lovely." His glance at Susana sent a shiver through her. She reminded herself to relax. And breathe. But she could not. Her nerves were screaming for action.

She stood in a rush that wasn't reflective of her desperation to separate these two in the slightest. "We really should get our guest and his men situated."

Andrew leaned lazily back in his chair and folded his fingers over his belly. "I would like to begin assessing the defenses at once. I'm certain there is much that needs to be done."

"First, we must settle your men."

Their gazes tangled and Susana did not imagine the challenge she saw in his. It was probably a tactical mistake to meet it with one of her own, but she couldn't resist. And she could not back down. She couldn't pretend to be something she was not.

His smile was nothing but a ploy to charm her into submission. This she knew without a doubt. Probably because of the glint in his eye. "Fine," he said. "And then we can discuss the defenses?"

She fixed her lips into something resembling a smile. "I would be delighted. Please, come with me." Roiling with apprehension and perhaps a hint of fear, she led Andrew out of Papa's study, down the stairs, out of the castle, and across the bailey.

Oh, she would situate Andrew Lochlannach and his men.

In the stables.

With the rest of the dogs.

&

From her perch atop the mill, Isobel Dounreay MacBean gazed down at her kingdom. It was lovely from up here. The busy castle denizens bustled about in their daily work, utterly unaware she watched their every move. To her right, the town of Ciaran Reay spread out before her; beyond, the sea sparkled in the sunshine. Farms and crofts stretched out for miles in a blanket of green. Though, as the summer continued to warm, it was turning a trifle brown.

She could probably see the whole of the world from this vantage point. She glanced at the turret tower and tapped her lip in contemplation. The view was probably better from there, though.

Regardless, up here she was truly the queen of all she surveyed. She loved the feeling of being high above it all, the teasing gusts of the breeze and the sight of the wheeling gulls in the sky. Mostly, she loved the freedom. There was no one up here to order her about. It was wonderful.

A clatter rose at the castle gates and she turned in that direction and blanched as her mother barreled across the bridge.

Isobel quickly scuttled behind an eave. It wouldn't do to have Mama see her up here again. The last time there had been quite a scold.

Her grip on the shingles slipped a bit, and she readjusted her bow and found better purchase, and then peered around the eave.

While it didn't surprise her to see Mama barreling over the bridge—she often barreled—it did surprise Isobel to see her followed by a company of men, all in Highland battle dress and riding impressive destriers. They were men she did not know.

Mama tossed herself from her mount and stormed into the castle. Isobel could tell she was vexed from the way

she walked—as though she had someone to scold. Her
hands were clenched in fists and her expression was fierce.
Isobel had seen that expression often enough.

Mama was often cross.

Siobhan said Mama wouldn't be so cross if she had a
husband, which made no sense to Isobel. But lately she'd
been thinking that if Mama had a husband, perhaps she
would be distracted. Perhaps she wouldn't watch Isobel
with such an eagle eye.

It would be nice to have more freedom. And come to
think of it, it really would be nice to have a father, too.
Siobhan had a father who took him hunting and fishing and
taught him to ride and fight. Having a father like that would
be very fine indeed.

As a result, of late Isobel had been toying with the idea
of finding a husband for Mama—though it would have to
be someone who suited *her* as well. The trouble was,
Mama was picky and prickly and had turned each man
away in no uncertain terms. Aside from that, there were not
many eligible men in Reay—and most of those were very
old.

How providential that now, new men had arrived.

A gust whipped up and danced her hair around her
face and she impatiently pushed it back so she could see.
She trained her attention on the largest of the men. Something about him fascinated her. It probably wasn't the way
he sat his horse, or his commanding posture. It probably
wasn't his hair, which flowed around his shoulders in a
white-blond fall.

Nae. It was most likely his sword.

It was a splendid sword.

He looked like a knight with that sword. A valiant
knight.

He eased from his mount, shared a word and a laugh

with one of his men, and then, with a lazy lope, followed
Mama into the castle.

Aye, Isobel thought. He was a fine man. Perhaps he
would do . . .

Then her gaze settled on his friend, and her heart stuttered. He was as tall, as broad, as valiant as the white
knight. He had a sword as well, though it was nowhere near
as impressive.

But glory! His hair was a shock of red curls.

Isobel's lips curled into a grin. Mama had red hair, too.

Clearly that meant only one thing. *This* man was perfect for her.

With a humming anticipation, she turned and made her
way off the roof.

And she hardly slipped at all.

୬୬

Susana was annoyed. There was no doubt about it. The
swish of her hips as she led him across the bustling bailey was a dead giveaway, that and the dark glowers she shot
over her shoulder. But Andrew couldn't help but be amused.
For one thing, she was damn alluring when she was annoyed.

Hell, she was damn alluring altogether. The curve of
her waist alone could drive a man insane, much less that
silky tumble of hair. He wanted to wrap it in his fist, wind
it around his body. A certain part of his body.

At the thought, his cock rose.

It was difficult to remind himself that he'd vowed to
eschew seduction. Try as he might, he couldn't banish the
fantasy of stripping those breeks from her lovely body and
laying her down in the heather. Visions of that twitching
backside—bare before him—danced in his head.

But he'd made a vow. A sacred vow. And as tempting

as she was, he would control his baser urges. He could. Probably.

She led him into the stables, past his men—who were unpacking and seeing to their horses—and through the kennels. Though he was perplexed, Andrew followed. He would probably follow anywhere she led. It was a fact that should have scared him to death or at the very least, concerned him. But it didn't. However, when she started up a staircase at the very end of the long hall, he had to stop her.

She glared at the hand he set on her arm. He tried to ignore the sizzle raging through him at their first touch. It was ridiculous how much that touch affected him. And how much he enjoyed her glare.

He edged closer. "Where are we going?" he asked in a purr.

Judging from her frown, his tone irritated her. He rather enjoyed irritating her, he found.

She ripped her arm away and continued up the stairs. He followed and found himself in a narrow loft that ran the length of the kennels. It was dim and a little dusty. Motes danced on the air. The roof was so low he had to duck his head to miss the rafters.

"Your men will stay here," she said.

Andrew gaped at her. The room was swept clean and empty. A thin shaft of light from the far window illuminated it with a murky light. But the yipping from the kennel and the stench of excrement wafted up from below. For some reason, all thoughts of alluring backsides dissipated. Disbelief gushed through him. "*Here?*"

She crossed her arms and offered what could only be described as a smirk. "Here."

He tipped his head to the side. "This is a kennel."

"I am aware of that."

"I have twenty-five men."

"The room is quite large."

"There are no beds."

She blew out a breath. "We'll bring in pallets."

Andrew blinked. He set his teeth and tried to remain calm. His men were warriors. They did not sleep on pallets. In a kennel. "This will not do." Surely she saw that. Surely she understood . . . He caught a glimpse of her smug expression and it dawned on him.

She did. She did understand. She knew damn well what she was doing. Her response only verified his suspicions.

"I'm sorry, but you've descended upon us with no warning whatsoever with a large group of men. I'm afraid this is all we can offer you at this time." Her smile was deferential, but hardly sincere. The light dancing in her eyes lit a flame in his belly. "Of course, if our accommodations are unacceptable, you can always return to Dunnet . . ."

Oh, she'd like that, wouldn't she?

The minx.

Rather than the exasperation her self-satisfied look should have sparked, Andrew found himself filled with another emotion entirely. Anticipation. Exhilaration. The thrill of a challenge.

For that was what she was, Susana Dounreay. A challenge.

And it appeared she reveled in provoking him.

A pity she didn't understand he was a dangerous man to provoke.

The tumult her presence sparked within him flared again, burning the edges of his resolution; an inconvenient lust blossomed, and with it an unruly resolve.

He wanted, very badly, to kiss her. He wanted to wrench her into his arms and cover her sweet mouth with his. He wanted to taste her, consume her, possess her.

And he would.

Clearly he wasn't the kind of man who could swear off women. Clearly he wasn't the kind of man who could keep a vow.

So be it.

Damn to hell his ridiculous vow.

Damn to hell the fact that she was his sister-in-law.

He was going to seduce this vixen, and he would start right now.

Desire, like a snarling, snapping beast, rose within him, and he stepped closer.

CHAPTER THREE

Susana's eyes flared as Andrew advanced on her like a hungry fox that had spotted a plump rabbit. She didn't mean to retreat, but she had to. She'd seen that expression in his eyes before and she knew what it meant. Something within her howled: *Run.*

Perhaps it was the expression in his eyes, or the knowledge that she was playing with fire, or the sudden realization that she'd foolishly come here, to this deserted loft, with the most dangerous man she'd ever met, but she couldn't still the urge to whirl and pace to the far end of the room to peer out of the smudged window. She was aware he followed. She felt his presence like a fire in a forge.

Desperation prompted her to continue their conversation, to put some space between them, to raise a shield. "The room is perfectly habitable," she proclaimed. "And once we have pallets brought in, it will serve you well."

"Will it?"

His voice was low in her ear, a whisper almost. And far too close. She wanted to turn, to confront him, but she knew, if she did, they would be face-to-face, perhaps lip-to-lip, and she could not allow that. She could never allow that.

The last time he'd kissed her, it had been her undoing.

A pity he didn't remember.

"My men willna like being housed with the dogs." *Holy*

God. Was that his hand on her hip? His thumb tracing her waist? "Nae doubt they will all want to find . . . other beds to welcome them."

Susana stilled as his words sank in. The threat was clear. And it was rather horrifying. A horde of randy warriors set loose on the innocent maidens of Dounreay? That his hand slid over to toy with the small of her back, to tangle in the skeins of her hair, didn't help.

Her pulse thudded and her knees went weak. She couldn't have it. She couldn't have this man *touching* her. She sucked in a breath and slipped to the side, out of his grasp. When she was far enough away for some measure of safety, she turned to face him, a reproachful look fixed on her face. "Are your men so lacking in discipline?" She hoped her frown, her reproving tone, would bring him to heel. She should have known better.

He grinned and stepped closer. His eyes glinted, as though needling her was an amusing sport. "They are verra disciplined . . . when their needs are met."

She crossed her arms, as though that could protect her, and pretended to study the room. Pretended she wasn't aware of his thrumming presence, his heat, his intent. "Well, I shall hold you responsible for any . . . improprieties." She took a step toward the staircase, only a tiny one—surely not an attempt at escape.

He chuckled—*chuckled*, the bastard—making it clear he recognized her cowardice for what it was. And he paced her.

"They're all good men. They all volunteered to come with me. Each and every one of them is dedicated to the cause of protecting Reay from the villains who have been plaguing you. However . . ."

The way he trailed off derailed her retreat. She stilled. Glared at him. "However, what?"

"However, they do have . . . needs. Surely you can find better lodgings."

She blew out a breath. "In time." In time.

In time, he would be gone, God willing.

He stepped toward her again, although nonchalantly, as though he were not chasing her across the room. It occurred to her they were engaged in something of a macabre dance. It set her nerves on edge. She hadn't realized what a long room this was, or how far it was to the stairs.

"Doona leave it too long." His smile was heinous. It made all kinds of shivers dance over her skin. "My men are . . . restless." She had the chilling sense he was talking about himself.

"I shall . . . do my best." Like hell. "And now, if you will excuse me, I have things to do."

His brow quirked. She tried not to notice what a perfect brow it was. "Ah, but I thought you and I could . . . talk."

"Talk?" She didn't intend to squawk, but she could tell from his predatory stance, a conversation was not the primary urge on his mind. At least, not one with words.

He nodded. Though his features were patently earnest, the sincerity was patently affected. "About the defenses you have in place . . . so I can decide what needs improvement."

Aggravation rippled. It displaced her concerns about being here, with him, all alone. Fury did that, she'd often found. Overrode common sense and led one into dangerous waters. Her hands curled into fists. She strode toward him until they were nearly nose-to-nose. "Nothing needs improvement," she snapped. They didn't need him. Or his men. Or his stupid ideas.

"Nonsense. Now that we're here, we intend to make a statement to Stafford, or whatever miscreants are lurking out there thinking Dounreay is an easy target. But before I set my plans in motion—"

"Your plans?" *He already had plans? Och!* He was so exasperating.

She barely noticed that he stepped closer . . . until their chests brushed. He was hard and hot; the touch made her tingle. His voice, low and luring, made her tingle as well. His gaze skated over her face, then stalled on her lips. "Let's meet and discuss—"

Her pulse skittered. "I doona have time to meet with you. Not today." She took a step back. He followed.

"Nae?" A whisper. And his caress over her shoulder, that was a whisper as well. Like a panicked fawn, Susana eased back again. And again. He matched her, step for step.

She swallowed heavily. "I . . . You have descended upon us with no warning—"

"My brother sent a letter."

He was too close. Far too close. She swallowed heavily. "Twenty-five men that now need to be housed and fed. On top of that, I have many other duties that need attending."

He cocked his head to the side. "Which duties?"

"*Many* duties." She frowned and glanced toward the staircase. Ah, lord. It was so far . . . He was too warm. Too broad. Too alluring. Though she didn't intend to, she took another step back and—

Oh, hell. He'd backed her against the wall. That he couldn't stand straight in the low-ceilinged room was a small consolation.

"Susana," he said as he leaned closer. His breath was a tantalizing trail over her face.

An unholy thrill snaked through her. Surely that wasn't anticipation? Hunger? Need?

She could not allow him to kiss her. She could not—

Her knees nearly melted at the touch of his lips. His warmth, his taste, his scent made her mind whirl. Thank God he had his hands on her waist and was holding her steady, or she might well have collapsed.

It occurred to her that she should push him away, fight him, but she couldn't. Something, something deep within her resisted. Something deep within her needed him. Needed this.

And ah, it was glorious. As glorious as she remembered.

His lips were soft, gentle, questing as they tested hers and then, with a groan, he pulled her closer, melding their bodies together. He deepened the kiss, sealing his mouth over hers and dancing his tongue over the seam.

She opened to him. She couldn't resist. He filled her senses with his presence, his heat. With tiny nibbles, sucks, and laps, he consumed her, enflamed her. All sanity fled. All logic and resolution and anger flitted away as Andrew tasted her, tempted her.

His hands were not still. They roved over her body from her shoulders down her arms to her waist. They tangled in her hair and stroked her cheek and chin.

Heat blossomed, danced through her veins. Her body softened, melted, prepared for him.

She should not have responded the way she did. She should not have pressed against him, rubbed against the hard bulge on his belly. She should not have explored the muscled flesh of his back, cupped his nape, raked his silken scalp. She should not have moaned.

Surely all these things would only encourage him.

He lifted his head and stared at her, an odd mixture of befuddlement and awe in his eyes. His tongue peeped out and dabbed at his lips, snagging her attention. Surely she didn't lean toward him in a mute plea for more.

Was she truly so weak?

Aye. She was.

His head lowered, as though he intended to kiss her again.

Her heart thudded. Her muscles locked. Her lips parted.

"Ah. There you are." A deep voice floated across the abyss of her sanity, shattering the spell he'd woven around her. Andrew's head jerked up at the interruption; it banged against a rafter and he *oof*ed. Susana took her chance and slipped from his arms.

Oh, hell. Had she really let him kiss her? This man? *This* man? Knowing what he was, had she let him so close with hardly any resistance?

"Hamish." Andrew brushed down his tunic and turned to his second in command.

Hamish, a very handsome man—who also needed to stoop—ripped his contemplative gaze from her and glanced around the loft. "What are you two doing up here?"

Susana fought to control the blush rising on her cheeks. Surely that was a rhetorical question. Surely he didn't want to know the truth.

Andrew opened his arms to encompass the loft. "These are our new quarters."

Hamish blinked. His attention flickered from Andrew to Susana and back again. "You canna be serious."

Andrew nodded. "Miss Dounreay was just explaining to me that she wasna notified we were coming—"

"I thought your brother sent a letter."

"So did I." His beautiful lips twisted. "But apparently it dinna arrive before us. So for the time being, we'll be sleeping here."

Hamish's nose curled. "It smells."

"Indeed." Andrew shot her a sultry glance. "Miss

Dounreay assures me she will find other quarters for us as soon as possible."

"I see." Hamish tapped his lips. No doubt he did.

"I'm certain she will find something more suitable right away. Will you no' . . . Susanna?" His tone was weighted with intent. His meaning was clear. Obviously he was convinced he'd charmed her with that kiss. Charmed and befuddled her to the extent she would bow to his bidding. Hie off and find him some palatial chamber in which he could lounge.

Bluidy bastard.

She affected a blinding smile. Fluttered her lashes even. "Of course, my laird," she murmured, affecting a curtsy. "Right away, my laird."

Perhaps he caught the bite of her tone, perhaps he recognized her submission as the ruse it was, for his brow wrinkled.

"You . . . ah . . . are going to find us better lodgings?" he asked.

Other than a pointed grin, she didn't bother to respond. She spun on her heel and left him standing there in the murky kennel loft like the dog that he was.

❧

Andrew stared after Susana, his emotions in turmoil.

Ah, God, how could he explain it? How could he explain how her kiss had affected him? That it had filled him with such glory? Such elation? That with one taste of her he'd known—*known*—that *this* was what he had been searching for, for six long years?

At the touch of her lips, he'd been engulfed in a stupefying enchantment, a singing in his veins, a lightness of spirit. It had felt like coming home, holding Susana Dounreay in his arms. It had felt . . . right.

It was a bluidy shame they'd been interrupted. He very much wanted to kiss her again. To see if he'd imagined it, that staggering . . . familiarity.

Hamish strolled toward him, tucking his fingers into the pocket of his jerkin. His grin was wicked. "I hope I didn't interrupt anything . . . interesting," he said.

Andrew raked his hair. Hamish had no clue. He had no idea what he'd interrupted. That kiss had shifted his world on its axis. Even now, he spun.

His friend pinned him with a sharp glance. "Because it seemed like you were very close to winning our wager."

The wager? Who gave a good goddamn about the wager?

Hamish ignored his gaping stare. "I met a charming milkmaid as I was brushing down my mount. I thought she would be number ninety-eight, but clearly she will have to wait." He winked. "I wouldna want you to slip in with a win. Looks like I shall have to turn my attentions to the lovely Susana and steal her kiss before you do."

Andrew opened his mouth to tell his friend to bugger off. That he'd already kissed Susana, already won the bet, but something stilled his tongue. He didn't want to share this, share her, with anyone.

Besides, Hamish was joking. Surely he was joking.

Still, Andrew's hands curled into fists.

Which was providential.

Or he might have throttled his best friend right then and there.

ᕳᕲ

Susana stormed from the loft and made her way to the captain of the guard's office in the battlements. At one time, the small stone chamber had been the lookout post atop the castle walls, but now it was Keir's center of operations.

At the moment, it served as her sanctuary. She needed

to collect her thoughts. To regain her footing. To remind herself who she was . . . and who she had been.

She'd sworn—*sworn*—never to be seduced again. Never to let a man have a hold on her. Never to let someone hurt her the way that boy once had. She'd come perilously close to succumbing to his charms. With hardly any provocation.

It had been a kiss.

A mere kiss.

And she'd been ready to give him more. Everything. Anything.

The thought appalled her.

Keir glanced up from the papers he was studying when she entered and sent her a grin. "Back already?" He hadn't approved of her riding out on her own to investigate the loss of yet another cow, but Susana had insisted. She was determined to carry her share of the load. Keir couldn't do everything on his own, and their men were spread woefully thin. She'd certainly not expected to catch the thief in the middle of a robbery.

She plopped down in the chair by the desk. "Aye."

"Find any trouble?"

Any trouble? "Plenty."

His grin faded and his muscles bunched. He was a typical warrior male, ready to leap into the fray. Though it was obvious to her he had an interest in her, he'd always kept his distance and behaved like a gentleman. More than that, he'd treated her as an equal. Which was probably why, even though he was younger than some of her men, he was the captain of her guard. Though they may be more experienced, the older men tended to pat her on the head and try to send her on her way. Keir did not.

He sat back in his chair and pursed his lips. "What was it?" he asked.

"I caught the thief."

"Excellent."

She frowned. "Not so. He escaped . . . thanks to Dunnet's men."

Keir stilled. "Dunnet's men?" He fingered his quill. "I sent them all to patrol the southern crofts."

"Not *those* men." Susana leaned forward. "Did you know my father wrote to Dunnet, asking him to send *more* men?"

His jaw tightened. "I dinna."

"Apparently, since our fortifications havena been strong enough to deter Stafford, or the other miscreants roaming the hills, my father decided we needed a more powerful presence. So Dunnet sent more men. They arrived today."

Keir's throat worked. "How many?"

"Twenty-five." This she spat. Though in truth, there was only one of those men that irked her. Susana lurched to her feet and paced the room. "Can you believe that? And the leader of these men has announced *he* is taking over the defenses . . . altogether."

"What? But . . ." His lashes flickered. "That's your job."

"I know. How annoying is that?" She pinned Keir with a glower. "We doona need them."

"We most certainly do not."

"I am so aggravated."

He almost smiled. "I can tell."

"I've housed them in the loft over the kennel."

Keir tipped his head to the side. "But there's plenty of room in the east wing of the castle."

The smile she offered was sweet. "I'm aware of that. Can we find twenty-five pallets?"

"Pallets?" A conspiratorial light danced in his eye.

"Lumpy ones?"

"I'm certain that can be arranged."

"Verra lumpy."

"I'll speak to Tamhas at once."

She whirled and made another pass of the room, tapping her lip as she thought. "And weren't we planning to make some repairs to the privy in the kennel?"

"I, ah . . . Yes. I do believe we were." He cleared his throat. "We were also planning to fix the leak in the kennel roof . . ."

Her smile turned vicious. "*That* can wait."

"It's going to rain. In the next day or two," he said in a warning tone.

She affected a shrug. "They are warriors. They can take a little rain."

He bowed mockingly. "As you wish, my lady."

"Oh, and make sure our men are made aware that if they're approached by Dunnet's minions, they're to come to me. I doona want strangers skulking about asking questions about our strategies."

"Good idea."

"Who knows who these men really are? Where their loyalties lie?"

"Indeed."

"There are far too many strangers in Dounreay. Any one of them could be reporting back to Stafford."

Keir nodded. His expression hardened. "Stafford is not our only concern."

Susana nodded. "The raids . . ." Recently, with the upheaval of the Clearances in the Highlands, more and more people had been displaced and lost their homes. Many had moved to the cities in a desperate search for work, but others had turned to raiding and outright villainy to keep their bellies filled. Within the past month there had been six raids on Reay crofts.

"Beyond that . . ." Keir pursed his lips. Something in his voice captured her attention.

"There's more?"

He sighed and scrubbed the back of his neck. It occurred to her—and not for the first time—that he was a very handsome man. His features were bold and strong and his eyes were a dark sleepy brown. His shoulders were broad and his neck thick. His body was roped with muscle. Aside from that, he was loyal and fierce in the protection of Dounreay.

If she were in the market for a husband—which she most decidedly was not—Keir would be an excellent candidate. *He* would probably not forget a woman he'd kissed. It was a pity she had no interest in him. It was a pity a certain silver-haired Lothario had ruined her for other men.

He blew out a breath and looked up at her through the fringe of his lashes. "I heard a rumor about Scrabster."

Susana winced. She must have made a face, because Keir chuckled. He was no stranger to her rants about their revolting neighbor to the east. Aside from the fact that Scrabster encouraged his tacksmen to incite squabbles with Reay crofters and frequently made claims on land and cattle that didn't belong to him, the worm had been relentless in his pursuit of her. Rarely did a week pass by when her father didn't receive another request for her hand. Even though Susana had turned him down flat every time.

"What did you hear?"

"He's gathering men on the border."

Susana ceased pacing and dropped into her chair. "Gathering men?" *Bluidy* hell. Whatever for? He wouldn't dare attack. Would he? Then again, it was Scrabster. He was capable of almost anything. If he thought he could overrun Dounreay and claim the land as his own, he might just try.

For the first time, she felt a flicker of relief that Dunnet had sent more men. Though their overlord the duke didn't care about the fate of his far-flung crofts, at least Dunnet did. Then again, securing their safety was why Hannah had married him, poor thing. A flicker of pity for her sister needled her. Pity . . . and guilt. Hannah had sacrificed everything—walked right into the wolf's den—to keep her people safe. And here Susana was, resisting that help.

But it wasn't Dunnet's help she resented. It was his brother's presence. Here. In *her* world.

"My lady?"

She thrust the inconvenient pang of guilt aside and focused on the captain of her guard. "Aye?"

"Shall we increase patrols on the border?"

She nibbled her lip. Reassigning the men meant the crofts to the south and the western borders would have fewer patrols. But if Scrabster truly was up to something heinous, it was better to be safe than sorry. "Aye, Keir. Shift the bulk of our men to the eastern border."

His smile reassured her. This was, indeed, the wise choice. "Aye, my lady. I will see to it at once."

"Excellent. And Keir?"

"Aye, my lady?"

"Keep Andrew Lochlannach and his men busy, will you?"

His chuckle rumbled through the room. "Ach, aye, my lady. I shall. I shall, indeed."

She grinned at him. It was good to know there was one man she could count on.

And as for Andrew and his enthralling smile, his seductive looks, and his too-tempting lips . . . well, she would avoid him like the plague.

CHAPTER FOUR

If Andrew thought he was going to find Susana and perhaps get another taste of her that afternoon, he was bound for disappointment. After their altercation, she'd disappeared. He and his men settled themselves in the fragrant loft to the tune of yipping hounds with the help of one of her minions. Then, when he went for a stroll with Hamish, taking in the lay of the land, she was nowhere to be found.

Andrew found this a trifle frustrating, because he was anxious to begin. Anxious to study the current plans and assess where he and his men could help. He hoped to pin her down in a conversation about her defenses at dinner, for which he'd received an invitation.

The invitation had come from Magnus, but Andrew was certain she would be there. Anticipation bubbled through him. The thought of seeing her again sent fire licking in his veins.

He probably wouldn't be able to kiss her again—at least, not at the table, with her father and his best friend looking on—but maybe later . . . Maybe he would invite her for a walk in the garden after dinner. Maybe he would kiss her there.

The castle did have a lovely garden. In the moonlight it would be quite romantic.

Though she was a warrior princess, she was, still and all, a woman. She would like to be romanced.

Wouldn't she?

She would like a kiss in a moonlit garden.

And maybe, if she liked it enough . . . there could be more.

Buoyed by such hopeful thoughts, there was a spring in his step when he and Hamish arrived at the castle that evening. They were escorted by Tamhas, the factor, into Magnus's library, where the Laird of Reay was enjoying a whisky.

It was a remarkable library with shelves reaching from the floor to the ceiling of the two-storied chamber. A railing ran around the second-floor gallery, and a curling staircase connected the two floors. Each shelf was jammed with books, some of which, for some incomprehensible reason, sported tiny arrows. The ground floor was scattered with divans and thickly cushioned chairs.

Andrew scanned the room, looking for Susana. His mood dipped when he realized she was not here.

"Ah! My boy!" Magnus heaved himself from the chair by the fire and made his way across the room, greeting both men effusively. He had, perhaps, been at the whisky for a while. "Come in. Come in. Take a seat." He waved them toward the companion chairs by the fire. "I canna tell you how delighted I am to have company." He shot a glance into the shadows—though there was no one there but the three of them. "Manly company," he whispered. "I think this calls for a drink." He headed for the whisky and poured each of them a generous serving of the amber liquid. He topped off his glass as well.

Andrew gusted a sigh as he sipped. It was excellent whisky. It sent a warm burn trickling down his throat and filled his chest with a sense of well-being.

"Not that I doona enjoy having daughters. I do. But a man needs to have manly conversations." He pounded his fist on his chest. In a manly manner.

"I understand, sir," Andrew said, though probably only because it was the polite thing to do, agree with one's host. He couldn't help looking at the door. "Will, ahem, Susana be joining us?"

Hamish snorted into his glass; Andrew nearly kicked him.

When he turned back to his host, he was stunned by the sharpness of his stare, though Magnus hurried to mask it with a smile. "Nae. She sent word that she is too busy for dinner."

Andrew's smile dimmed. He took another sip.

"Too busy for dinner?" Hamish asked. Andrew nearly kicked him again.

"Och, aye, that girl. I doona know what to do about her. She works her fingers to the bone from dawn till dusk. She took on Hannah's duties when she left for Dunnet. And with all that, the recent raids and attacks . . . her burden is even more onerous. It's one of the reasons I am so verra glad you are here. To take a little of the weight from her shoulders. It's not right for a woman to have such worries."

"We're happy to help," Andrew said. He had to add, "Although . . ."

Magnus pierced him with a querying glance.

"Although she doesna seem . . . delighted with the help."

The old man issued a damp snort. "She's always been far too stubborn for her own good. If you ask me, her resistance lies in the fact that she doesna want to relinquish control. If you want to make progress with her, take my advice . . . let her win every argument."

Andrew leaned forward. "She wants me to leave, sir. That is an argument I canna allow her to win."

"Bah. She doesna want you to leave."

Andrew lifted a brow. Magnus hadn't witnessed their recent exchange in the lea . . . or in the loft. Thank God.

"She just wants to be in control."

"Of the defenses?"

"Of everything, perhaps." Magnus chuckled and though it wasn't really very funny, Andrew chuckled as well. Magnus took another sip, discovered his tumbler was empty, and refilled it. Then he refilled Andrew's as well. "I find the trick to dealing with women is to let them think they're having their way, when they are really having *your* way."

Hamish laughed. "Sounds simple enough."

Ah, but it wasn't.

"Doona fash yerself, my boy. Susana will come around. She just needs time to think things through. She'll realize how much we need your help. You'll see."

"I hope so." Hamish helped himself to another drink. "I doona fancy sleeping in the kennels for long."

Magnus blinked. "The kennels?"

"Aye," Andrew said. "She's housed us in the kennels."

His laugh was a sharp bark. "What the hell did you do to annoy her so quickly?"

Andrew ignored the prickling on his neck. "She said there's no other space."

"Balderdash. The castle has empty rooms."

"We have twenty-five men."

"We've a full wing of empty rooms." Magnus narrowed an eye. "So what did you do? To annoy her?"

Andrew and Hamish exchanged a look. Hamish bit back his grin, but his expression was telling. This time, Andrew did kick him. It was probably the whisky's fault.

When he glanced back at their host, he was studying him again with a sharp interest that Andrew found a trifle befuddling. Maybe it was the whiskey causing that stare.

Or the befuddlement. Still, he didn't resist when his tumbler was refilled.

When Magnus finally spoke, it was with an odd query. "So . . . how long ago were you in Perth?" he asked.

Andrew blinked. "I beg your pardon, sir?"

"Oh, do stop calling me sir. I'm Magnus, my boy." He clapped Andrew on the hand and squeezed with alarming strength. "How long ago were you in Perth?"

"I . . . ah." He frowned at Hamish. "Six years ago?" Six years, two months, and seventeen days. That was how long it had been since he'd last seen Mairi. Not that he was keeping track.

Hamish nodded. "Sounds about right."

"And what were ye doing there?"

Was it his imagination, or was Magnus a little too curious?

Andrew took another sip. "Studying. My brother . . . You do know Alexander?" At Magnus's nod he continued. "Alexander thought it best if I . . . left Dunnet for a while."

Magnus nodded. "Ah, yes. Dermid."

Andrew didn't wince at the name, but barely. How mortifying was it that Magnus knew exactly what he'd meant? But then, everyone in northern Scotland probably knew the name of Dermid Lochlannach. He'd been a legend. And a monster.

When Andrew's father had died, Dermid had become guardian of Dunnet . . . and the Lochlannach brothers. He'd made their lives hell from the moment he'd taken the reins.

Alexander had always done what he could to protect Andrew, often at great cost. After one truly horrific altercation, where Dermid had nearly killed Andrew, Alexander had braved his uncle's fury and secretly sent Andrew away.

Alexander had paid, and paid dearly for that act, but it had probably saved Andrew's life. And it was there, in Perth, that he'd met a woman, one who had stolen his heart. She'd made him forget the darkness and reach for the light.

For a brief, shining moment, he'd been happy.

And then the light had faded.

Oh, he still kept up pretenses. He laughed and joked and pretended to be untouched by grief, unaffected by the great hole within him. Alexander expected as much. Everyone expected it of him. He was the blessed one, the brother who'd had an easy life.

He owed it to them, to them all, to play along.

But it was nothing more than a mask. A role.

Somewhere deep inside, something was missing.

He'd felt a flicker of it when he'd kissed Susana. He desperately wanted to feel it again. He tried to ignore the fear that if he did get the opportunity to kiss her again, he might discover it had been his imagination. Or a fluke.

Regardless, if he got the opportunity again, he would kiss her—

"I never did like Dermid," Magnus grumbled. "He drank too much."

"Aye. He did." Andrew set his glass on the table. He'd had far too much already.

"Fell off the battlements, did he?"

Andrew nodded. "Aye. That's what they say." He'd been in Perth when his uncle had met his maker. He could not grieve for the man. With Dermid's death, his exile had ended. It had been a joy to return home. And with Mairi gone, there had been nothing in Perth to hold him.

"Och, well, Alexander is a fine laird."

"Aye, sir. He is."

Magnus squinted and speared him with a one-eyed stare. "And how is he as a husband?"

Andrew blinked. "I, ah, wouldna know."

The old man snorted and leaned closer. "Ye know what I'm asking. Is my Hannah happy there?"

"I believe so, sir." When last he'd seen her, she'd been gazing into Alexander's eyes, and he, gazing back, besotted, the both of them. Aye. He would wager she was happy. He pressed down the flare of envy the memory ignited. Alexander *deserved* any happiness he found. That Andrew might never find the same did not signify. "They seem to be a good fit together."

"Ach. Aye. I thought as much." Magnus tapped his cheek with a gnarly finger. "I have a sense for these things."

"Do you?"

"It comes with my years, I suppose." He stared out the window for a moment and then sighed heavily. "It is my dream to see all my daughters wed before I die." This he said softly, but with a passion that could not be ignored.

"I'm certain you will, sir."

"Will I?" Again he studied Andrew with a curious intensity, and then he blew out another sigh. "I'm not so sure. They are a stubborn lot."

"Women often are." This from Hamish, who had obviously had too much to drink as well. He tipped a little to the side in his chair.

"Not as stubborn as the Dounreay woman, I'll warrant," Magnus said. "I have four of them now." He glanced at Andrew and stroked his lip.

"Four?" Andrew blinked. "I thought you had three daughters." He'd met Hannah and her younger sister, Lana, when they'd come to Dunnet for Alexander's wedding . . . and Susana here.

"They're all verra lovely," Hamish offered, his eyes aglint.

"Aye. They are lovely," Magnus said. "But stubborn.

And aye. I have three daughters. The fourth is my grand-daughter, Isobel." The way he said her name made clear his adoration and pride. "She's probably the most stubborn of them all."

"More stubborn than Susana?" He wasn't sure what made him ask, some imp deep within his soul.

Magnus rolled his eyes. "My boy, you have no idea."

"Does she take after her mother, or was her father stubborn as well?" Andrew wasn't sure what drove him to ask the question. Surely not the desire to discover more about the man who had conquered Susana Dounreay.

Magnus's brow rumpled. "Gilley?"

"Gilley?"

"Gilley MacBean. Her husband, God rest him. I couldna say he was stubborn. Nae. Not an obstreperous bone in his body. He was a . . . pleasant man."

Andrew bit his lip to hold back his retort. Susana with a *pleasant* man? He couldn't visualize it.

"Pleasant and quiet. A simple man. He wasn't the kind of man I would have chosen for her. He wasn't the kind of man I would ever expect her to fall in love with, but they were verra happy. And he loved Isobel greatly. It was a damn shame he died the way he did."

Andrew stilled. "How . . . how did he die?"

"Drowned in the loch, a year or so back." Magnus shook his head. "He'd gone out fishing . . . one of his favorite things to do. Apparently his boat overturned and, well, there you have it."

"That is a shame."

"Susana was beside herself. She loved him verra much."

Andrew tried to silence the howl in his soul. "I'm sure she did."

Magnus took another sip and then stared into the crackling fire for a long while. "A damn shame, it was," he repeated. "A damn shame."

Andrew opened his mouth to say something, change the subject, perhaps even bring up the castle defenses, when Magnus continued on, nearly mumbling to himself. "Thing was, Gilley couldn't do much, but he could swim."

"I beg your pardon?"

"He could swim. Better than any man I knew. Odd that he should drown. In a loch he knew like the back of his hand."

"Accidents do happen," Hamish offered.

Magnus sighed. "Aye. They do." He scrubbed his face with a palm and of a sudden, his fatigue—and his illness— were apparent.

Andrew exchanged a look with Hamish. If their host was ailing, it was only good manners to make their excuses and leave. No doubt they could find a meal in the kitchens—Hamish had already found a very pretty cook he reported was . . . amenable. But before he could say a word, Magnus's eyes lit up. "So tell me, Andrew. Do you hunt?"

"Hunt?" What man didn't hunt? "I love to hunt."

"Och. Excellent." The old man rubbed his hands together. His fatigue, miraculously, melted away.

The rest of the evening consisted of one tale after the other, all revolving around Magnus's hunting prowess.

Neither Hamish nor Andrew was able to get a word in edgewise.

❦

After she left Keir's office, Susana filled her day making the rounds of the crofts, overseeing the schedule for the fall planting season and meeting with the tacksmen. It wasn't difficult to avoid Andrew. Thoughts of him, however, were harder to excise.

No matter what she did, his specter haunted her.

He was a magnificent man . . . in every way. The thought only annoyed her more. And that kiss? Every time the memory rose in her mind, she was flooded with a prickling heat, a hunger, a craving . . . for more.

Which was ridiculous. She didn't want more. She didn't want him to kiss her again. She wanted him to do one thing and one thing only.

Leave. Hop back on his horse and hie off to Dunnet. And leave her in peace.

She had to admit—as she reviewed the salt production reports, and met with her factor about the repairs that needed to be made in the mill, and conferred with the leader of the fishermen's guild—it would have been wonderful to turn over the defenses of Dounreay to someone else. It was yet another duty she had to juggle in her busy day. Aye, she would have loved to turn them over to someone else. Anyone else. Anyone other than *him*.

It irked her beyond belief that he didn't even remember her, when she'd never been able to forget him.

And today . . . ah, today, the memories, the regrets were even sharper.

They'd met for the first time on a beautiful spring day. She'd been visiting family who lived in a little village outside Perth. She'd been so young then. So foolish. So when she met a handsome boy while on a walk in the woods, she'd allowed him to talk to her, charm her. She'd even flirted.

The next day, when she'd gone for another walk—hopeful perhaps that she might see him again—he'd been there. This time he'd taken her hand and held it as they strolled through the woods.

The next day, he'd kissed her.

Everything had been so simple back then. Susana had been thrilled that a boy as handsome as this was interested in her. She'd been helpless before his dazzling grin, unable to resist his wiles. Indeed, she hadn't wanted to.

She'd fallen in love with that boy in a space of days. Fallen in love and given him everything.

It had nearly destroyed her.

Because one day, she went on her hopeful walk and she'd found him . . . but he hadn't been alone.

Nae. He'd been there in the woods, in *their spot*. With Kirstie Gunn in his arms.

Susana had been devastated.

She'd left the next day and she'd never returned.

She'd never expected to see him again.

She'd given him everything. He hadn't even given her his full name.

How could she ever have expected it was Andrew *Lochlannach*? That he was the brother of the man Susana had encouraged her sister to marry?

Ah, well, she thought as she headed up the stairs, exhausted after a long day of running from the past. It was all for the best. She'd learned to be cautious. She'd learned of the true nature of men. They were all faithless and selfish and led by their cocks.

There was great relief in having learned that lesson. Because she would never be fooled again.

She turned the corner and headed down the hall to her rooms; she'd known it would be a busy day and she'd known her father would invite *him* to dinner, so she'd given orders for her meal to be served in her suite. All she wanted to do was collapse in a chair and not think about anything. To curl up and close herself in. Perhaps shore up her defenses.

The echo of deep male voices stalled her steps. Holding her breath, she tiptoed over to the door to the library gallery.

The gallery formed the second floor of the grand library, ringing the room. As young girls she and Hannah had nested up here, spying on their father and his cronies. They'd learned a lot from this vantage point. Perhaps things young girls should not know.

One of the men down below laughed, and Susana's blood went cold. Of course Andrew Lochlannach would be having drinks with Papa. Men did such things. No doubt he was attempting to strengthen his position as the interloper.

It was bad form, at her age, to eavesdrop, but Susana couldn't help but creep closer.

Before she had the opportunity to settle in though, a flicker of movement to her left captured her attention. She narrowed her eyes and peered into the shadows. A small bundle with downy, white-blond hair was crouched at the balustrade, fisting the rails and peering down at the assemblage below with an expression of absorbed fascination.

Susana's stomach rippled. A hint of horror dribbled through her.

"*Isobel Mairi MacBean,*" she hissed.

When her daughter didn't respond, she scuttled closer, bending low so the men wouldn't notice her. She grabbed her daughter's arm.

"What are you doing here?"

Isobel flashed a smile, one that was far too charming, far too dimpled for comfort. Her bluer-than-blue eyes danced. "Listening."

"It's rude to eavesdrop."

Isobel tipped her head to the side. "Then why were you doing it?"

Susana ignored the heat crawling up her cheeks. "I most definitely wasna doing it. And I doona want to hear that you are. Now come along. It's time for dinner."

Isobel sighed and stood, though Susana noticed she took the precaution of scooting back so she would remain out of view to the men below. They were sharing hunting stories at the moment, and, judging from the warbles of laughter, drinking as well. Tugging the imp through the door, she closed it with a decisive, though quiet, click.

She whirled on her daughter and took the precaution of propping her fists on her hips and frowning so Isobel would understand the fullness of her disappointment. Isobel often had difficulty understanding such things. She opened her mouth to begin a lecture on propriety and privacy and probably some other motherly things, but Isobel spoke first.

"Who were those men?"

Susana blanched. "Those men?" She put her hand on her daughter's shoulder and guided her down the hall, away from danger. Or temptation. "Visitors. Shall we have supper in my rooms? It will be like a picnic." Isobel enjoyed picnics . . .

She wrinkled her nose. "Why will we no' have supper with Grandpapa?"

"He has guests. We doona want to . . . interrupt. What do you say? To a picnic?"

Isobel shrugged. "All right."

Susana pushed into her room and tugged the bell pull. Isobel tossed herself into the chair by the fire. She propped her legs up on the arms in a terribly hoydenish pose. Susana frowned. Isobel sighed and settled herself into a more ladylike arrangement.

"Why were those men talking about Hannah?"

Susana's pulse thudded. She sat down in the companion chair. "I . . . ah. Were they?"

"Aye."

"What . . . what did they say?"

Isobel fixed her with a reproving frown. "I thought we werena supposed to eavesdrop."

"We are not." She stiffened her spine. "But since you've already done so, you could at least tell me what they said." Surely that was not bad parenting?

"Well, Grandpapa asked if she was happy and the knight said aye, she was—"

Relief scudded through her, but it was quickly replaced by irritation. "The knight?"

"The tall one."

"They're both tall."

"The one with the long hair." Isobel flicked her curls. "Like mine."

Susana tangled her fingers in her lap. "That man is no knight."

"He seems like one. He seems verra valiant."

"He's not valiant in the slightest." He was cocky and arrogant and far too aggravating for words. "He's a buffoon."

"He had a sword."

Susana blinked. "In the library?" How rude.

"This afternoon. I saw him in the yard. He had a sword." Isobel shot her a challenging glance. One far too like her father's for comfort. Susana suppressed a shudder.

"Stay away from that man. And you know how I feel about swords."

"I like his sword. It is verra shiny. Do you think he would teach me how to use a sword?"

"Darling. You must stay away from that man. From all those men. They are warriors and they doona want to be bothered by little girls."

Isobel tapped a plump lip. "The one with the red hair is verra handsome, do you no' think?" When Susana didn't respond, she continued. "He would probably make a good husband for you."

Why that made a curl of displeasure ripple through her, she didn't know. "Why do you say that, darling?"

"You have red hair, too."

"That is hardly a reason to marry."

Isobel nodded. "He also has a sword." This she said in a hopeful tone, as though the fact that he had a sword was, indeed, an excellent recommendation.

"I'm not looking for a husband," Susana felt compelled to mention.

As usual, Isobel ignored her. "Did Hannah send them?"

She stared at her daughter. "I . . . what?"

"That's why she went away, isn't it? To find men to protect us."

"Wherever did you get that idea?"

Isobel fluttered her lashes. "You doona want to know."

"I most certainly do."

"You told me you dinna want to hear that I'd been listening in . . ."

Oh, dear lord. "Were you? Listening in?"

She nodded. Her curls tumbled. "When you and Hannah and Grandpapa were talking about Hannah going away. You said we needed more protection."

Oh, lord. She had said that.

"And Hannah said Dunnet could provide more men. And make the bad people stop burning down crofts and stealing things."

Susana's heart sank. She hadn't realized her daughter had heard all that. A child should never be burdened with adult worries.

"Aye, darling. They are the men Hannah sent." Susana's chest ached. God, she didn't want Andrew here. She desperately did not. But Hannah had sacrificed everything for this. So Isobel and Papa and, aye, even she could be safe. It was childish and selfish and foolish of her to reject that gift.

Isobel gusted a sigh and plucked at a seam. "I miss Hannah."

"As do I, darling."

"And Lana. It's not the same here without them."

No. It was not.

"Do you think they will visit soon?"

"I hope so, darling. I miss them verra much as well."

Isobel put out a lip. "If these men are Hannah's friends, they must be nice."

Not necessarily. "They're here to do a job, dearest. We shouldna get in their way. Promise me you will stay away from them."

Isobel's response wasn't gratifying. She nibbled on her lip for far too long.

"Isobel? Promise me?"

"All right. But I willna promise to stay away from the kennels. I like the kennels."

Susana's stomach heaved. "I . . ."

"Why did you put them in the kennels, Mama?"

She sprang to her feet and paced the room. "How . . . Where did you hear that?"

"The knight mentioned it." Susana forbore correcting her again. "Then Grandpapa laughed and asked what he did to make you mad." *Oh, dear lord.* Isobel fixed her with a disturbingly curious look. "What did he do to make you mad?"

"Nothing, darling. He did nothing to make me mad." She would go to hell, no doubt, for lying to her daughter. "It's just that there are so many of them. There wasn't time to arrange rooms for them all."

Her daughter's expression made it clear she wasn't buying this explanation, and even to Susana's ears it sounded thin. Isobel's tiny nose wrinkled. "The kennels smell."

"They're men, darling. Warriors. They doona care about comfort."

"They doona?"

"Nae. Men are very different from women."

Isobel sighed. "I suppose you are right. Grandpapa seemed verra happy to have manly company."

"Did he?"

"Aye. He even said as much."

"Hmm." Though it sent a lick of resentment through her, she could hardly blame her father for cleaving to his own kind. No doubt it had been a trial for him being surrounded by strong-willed women for the past twenty-odd years. It was probably a treat for him to have other men around who were not his vassals.

Though she shouldn't ask, her curiosity prickled. "What else did they talk about?"

Isobel tipped her head to the side. "Boring stuff mostly. Though Grandpapa seemed very interested in Perth."

Her heart stopped. Froze right there in her chest. "P-Perth?"

"Aye. He wanted to know why the knight went there and when and how long he was there." She shrugged. "That kind of thing. It was much more interesting when they were talking about hunting."

"Oh, yes, of course. What did they say about hunting?"

Isobel babbled on, sharing the details of the time when Papa had tracked and bagged a five-point red stag, but Susana really wasn't listening. For one thing, she'd heard the story countless times before. For another, her mind spun.

Papa had been asking about Perth.

That meant only one thing.

He had definitely figured it out.

She could only hope to God he would keep his mouth shut.

CHAPTER FIVE

Andrew woke with a weight on his chest. He hadn't slept well—Hamish had snored all night long and the dogs had been restless and, frankly, the smell in the kennel was drilling a hole in his nasal cavity—so he was groggy. He didn't even want to think about the dreams that still teased his consciousness. Dreams of torrid kisses.

Without a doubt, he'd had far too much whisky.

It took some effort to rise from that miasma to full consciousness and realize . . . there was definitely a weight on his chest.

He cracked open an eye and found himself staring into a crystal-clear blue orb. It blinked. It took a moment for him to realize the eye belonged to an impish face, which in turn belonged to a young girl, which in turn belonged to the elbow pressing down on his chest. It was very sharp, that elbow.

"What are you doing here?" he sputtered. Probably not the most cogent question, but it was the first that came to mind when one woke to find a strange child on one's chest.

The girl leaned closer and set her forehead on his, to better survey him, he supposed. Her eyes crossed as she studied him up close. "I wanted to see what one looked like," she said. Her voice was chirpy and blasé and for some reason he found it disturbing.

Andrew set his teeth and put his hands on her tiny

shoulders to gently edge her back. Something about her delicate features set his nerves on edge. The cut of her chin, the slant of her eyes, the quirk of her lips. The dimples that rippled when she tried to hold back her grin. "One what?"

"A buffoon." He found her smile bothersome, too. It was far too dismissive for his liking.

"A buffoon?" What the—"

"Mama said you were one and I've never seen one before."

Andrew narrowed his eyes. "Mama?"

The girl didn't clarify, but then she didn't need to. Of a sudden, Andrew realized why her tiny face made something unsettling curl in his belly. But for her hair, which was a silver blond, she was the spitting image of Susana.

He pushed her farther away. "You shouldna be here," he croaked. His men were used to living in billets with other men and hunkering down on the hard ground for a night's sleep. They were rarely politic in their behavior . . . and most of them slept in the nude.

The thought of this young girl—what was she, five?—getting an eyeful and running back to tell tales to her mama was horrifying.

Indeed, just then Hamish sat up and stretched. His blankets slipped down to pool in his lap. When he finished his yawn, and realized he was being studied by this imp from hell with eyes that were far too sharp, he *eep*ed and clutched his covers to his chest like a virgin.

It was a little amusing, but only a little.

"You really should go," Andrew whispered. "The men are . . . waking up."

"Are they all buffoons, too?" This, she asked with her curious gaze fixed on Hamish, who, for some reason, flushed.

"None of us are buffoons. We have come here to help your mama."

"She doesna want your help."

Aye. That much was clear. "We are here to help, nonetheless."

She made a dismissive sound, something like a sniff, and lifted a shoulder. "Mama says you willna be here long anyway."

That caught his attention. Andrew sat up—being sure to clutch his covers to his chest as well. "She does?"

"Aye." The girl turned her attention on his sword, which, along with his scabbard, lay on the wood planks beside his pallet. She traced the hilt.

Andrew frowned. "Doona touch that," he barked.

She fixed a glare on him. It was rather fulminating for such a small face. "You're not the boss of me," she said. "I can touch what I want."

She proceeded to touch things around his person, at random. His blanket, the wall behind him, his nose. She continued to do so for far longer than was necessary to make the point. He allowed this, because he really didn't know what else to do. He wasn't used to children, never having had one himself, and her insolence befuddled him.

Glory sake, he was a man, a warrior, and she was a child. Yet still, she defied him.

Then again, one must consider the mother.

"What is your name?"

"Isobel Dounreay MacBean. What's yours?"

"Andrew Lochlannach."

"From Dunnet?"

"Aye."

"Ah." Her eyes narrowed.

"What?"

"You're the cretin."

"I most certainly am nôt. I'm a fearsome warrior."

Why this caused her to spurt a laugh was a mystery. He was. Fearsome. When he wasn't trapped in his covers by a five-year-old terrorist.

"Go away."

"I will go away when I like. Mama was right. You really are a beast."

"I'm not a beast. I—"

"You are. I doona like you at all." She riffled her fingers through his hair, measuring the lengths and studying it in the shafts of sunlight.

"What are you doing?" he asked.

She wrinkled her nose. "Your hair is stupid," she said.

"What?"

"It's stupid. It's a dumb color."

He snorted. "It's practically the same color as yours." They were both blond. Hers was a little lighter and a lot finer, but there wasn't much difference. Besides, he liked his hair. And women loved it.

Isobel rolled her eyes. "I'm a *lass*," she said, as though this made any difference. "Men should have red hair."

"And?"

"That's all. Your hair is stupid."

"You woke me up to tell me my hair was stupid?" And what was wrong with his hair?

"It's not my fault you woke up."

Andrew sighed. "You really shouldna be here."

She grinned. Dimples erupted on her cheek. "That's what Mama said."

"Which is exactly why you're here." He shifted farther away. "You really should listen to your mother."

Isobel shrugged. "I *listen*."

"But you do what you want."

She tipped her head to the side and gazed at him as though she really didn't understand his point. Or didn't care to.

"Go. Away."

She stood with a huff and glared at him again and then, with a toss of her head, sauntered away. Dear God. She even sauntered like her mother.

She made her way along the line of pallets with cheeky insouciance. As she passed, one by one, his men leaned up and stared after her in bemused disbelief. When she disappeared down the staircase, Andrew collapsed with a gusted sigh.

"Well, that went well," Hamish said on a chuckle.

"Shut up."

"She's a charming lass."

"Charming isna the word for it."

"Does she remind you of anyone?"

Anyone? Her mother. "She's Susana's daughter."

"Ah, aye." Hamish's grin was bothersome. "That's probably it then. How unsettling is it, meeting the daughter of the woman you plan to seduce?"

"I doona plan to seduce her."

Hamish tipped his head. "It dinna look like that was the case when I came upon the two of you yesterday. Where was it? Ah, yes. Right here in this room."

"Shut up."

"Have the . . . two of you . . ."

Andrew glared at him. "What?"

Hamish swallowed his chuckle. "Have the two of you ever . . . met before?"

"No. Of course not. Why would you ask?"

"Just curious." He pulled on his tunic and breeks and Andrew followed suit. But he couldn't help wondering over Hamish's pensive glances.

୧୨

Breakfast was dismal—a platter of oatcakes and a pot of gruel delivered to their loft by a kitchen boy. It didn't take a genius to work out who had arranged that feast. Andrew should have been annoyed; he had no idea why her maneuvers amused him.

Clearly, this was yet another volley in his game with Susana.

If she thought she was going to drive them away by making them uncomfortable, she had a lot to learn about men. Warriors in particular. His troop of men had trained for much worse than this.

Oh, they were indignant, and cranky, and not pleased by the fact that they had to sleep on dusty pallets and hike out to a privy in the stables to relieve themselves, and bathe in the horse trough, but Andrew knew they had the fortitude to make do. Especially when he told them, in no uncertain terms, what was really going on.

The fact that a woman was trying to drive them away only made them more determined to prove themselves.

So after they all ate, and cleaned up as best they could—in the horse trough—he sent his men out, with smiles plastered on their faces and assignments to review and assess the varying elements of the castle defenses. It was to be a subtle reconnaissance, implemented through casual conversations and anecdotal queries. No doubt Susana had coached her men not to give anything away.

He and Hamish headed for the castle to beard the lioness in her den. As it were.

They found Magnus in the morning room, surrounded by a breakfast buffet that made Andrew's mouth water. There were eggs, bacon, slabs of meat, and all manner of delicious baked goods. He eyed it greedily.

When Magnus chuckled and invited him to partake, he didn't delay. Susana could show up at any moment and he wanted to fill his belly before that happened. No doubt she wouldn't balk at smacking a cake from his hand.

He and Hamish filled their plates and joined their host at the table.

"I must say," Magnus said, as he and Hamish took their seats. "I enjoyed last night verra much."

"I did as well," Andrew said. Although he would have enjoyed it more with less whisky.

"What a wonderful evening . . . I have so missed having men around." His host's sigh was wistful.

Hamish buttered a honeyed scone and bit into it with a moan. "Well, we shall be here for a while. Especially with food like this."

Magnus chuckled. "Aye. Aye. And I canna tell you how thankful I am for that. But sooner or later, you will all return to Dunnet and then I will be the lone male in the castle once more."

Hamish's eyes twinkled. "Susana is verra lovely."

Andrew glared at him.

"Perhaps she will take a husband."

"Och. I've long given up hope on that." Magnus's chin drooped. "She's decided she doesna need a man, you see. She's rejected every suitor. The last one limped away with an arrow in his arse."

Andrew swallowed. "In his arse?"

Magnus nodded solemnly. "She has excellent aim." He shrugged. "Of course I'm assuming she was aiming for his arse. It could have been his apples. She usually hits what she shoots for. But she was verra angry. Shaking with it. That could have thrown off her aim."

Andrew poked at a sausage. "Why was she angry?"

Magnus snorted. "I doona know. All she said was he

was a buffoon." *Ach*. Not promising in the least. "I suspect he tried to kiss her."

Hamish's knowing smirk was an annoyance. "Does she shoot every man who tries to kiss her?"

Magnus nodded. "As far as I know."

"I shall consider myself forewarned." Hamish cleared his throat. "Shooting one's suitors does tend to, ahem, clear the field."

"Aye. Hasna had a suitor since." Magnus sighed. "I just want her to be happy. I canna believe she is truly happy as she is. A woman needs a husband. Do you no' think?"

Why he addressed this question to Andrew was a mystery. Still, he nodded.

"I doona know how I got such stubborn daughters. Probably on account of the fact that their mothers died when they were young. I raised them the best I could . . . but I fear I raised them as boys. They are all rather hoydenish."

"Lana is not a hoyden." Andrew wasn't sure why he felt the need to rush to her defense, other than the fact that, of the three sisters, Lana seemed the most biddable.

Magnus tossed back his head and cracked a laugh. "Clearly you dinna get to know her well. Lana may seem like a sweet, demure lass, but there's a wild seed in her. God help the man who thinks to tame her. And Hannah? Hannah was mulish, too. She probably never would have married if she hadn't had to."

Hamish tried to hide his grin. "Well, maybe one day Susana will *have* to get married, too. And then you shall have male company all the time."

"Hah!" Magnus waggled his brows. "I canna imagine the circumstance that would force Susana Dounreay to wed a man she doesna want. She's independent and

single-minded and tenacious. She is far too fierce to sub-
mit to . . ." His eyes widened. His throat worked. He lurched
back and fixed a pained smile on his face. "Susana!
Darling. There you are."

Andrew should have known she'd entered the room.
He'd felt the warning sizzle of energy in his bowels. He
turned slowly and glanced at her over his shoulder. As
always, the mere glimpse of her stole his breath. In the
morning light filtering through the east-facing windows,
her hair was aflame around her shoulders. Her skin was
smooth as silk and her curves, cupped in a formfitting
gown, delectable.

She frowned at the three men at the table. The glower
should have detracted from her beauty, but it did not. It
caused her eyes to snap and a curtain of pink to rise on
her cheeks. Andrew shifted in his chair as something uncomfortable rose within him.

He was certain it wasn't lust.

"What are you doing here?" she said. Although it was
closer to a snarl. Or a growl. Something feral, most certainly.

Andrew forced a cheery grin. "Your father invited us
for breakfast."

Her glare whipped to Magnus, who shrugged. "There
is plenty of food . . ."

"Plenty," Hamish grunted around a cake.

"Enough for an army," Andrew added with a wink.

Her bristling made clear the barb had hit home. Ach,
she'd thought to starve them out? They would find food.
If nothing else, Hamish was seducing one of the cooks.

Without a word, Susana marched to the buffet and surveyed the damage. He and Hamish had made quite an
incursion. "All the cakes are gone," she muttered.

Hamish stealthily covered his plate—of cake crumbs—

with his serviette, and upon reflection Andrew did the same. "There's plenty of other food," he suggested.

He should not have suggested. She whirled on him and scowled.

Magnus cleared his throat. "She can eat something else today," he said.

Susana turned her ire on her father. "Are you suggesting she have *eggs* for breakfast?" Judging from her tone, in this instance eggs were tantamount to eels or possibly maggots.

"She canna have everything she wants every day. She needs to learn to eat what is available."

"There *were* cakes available." Susana eyed the camouflaged evidence. "*Someone* ate them all."

"She can have something else. We have guests."

Susana snorted. "*You* have guests." This she muttered under her breath, but Andrew heard. But then, he was intended to.

Magnus surveyed her for a long while, his fingers a'twitch. "Susana . . . Has it ever occurred to you . . . ?"

"What?"

Magnus adjusted his collar, which appeared to be a wee bit tight. "Has it ever occurred to you that she might be . . . ?"

"Be *what*?" That Susana picked up a knife in one hand and a fork in the other and wielded them something like weapons bespoke her agitation.

"Might be . . . spoiled?"

Those beautiful lips parted. Those sparkling eyes snapped. The lovely pink blush turned a deep red. Something truly chilling roiled through the room. It was, without a doubt, Susana Dounreay's outrage. "*Spoiled?*"

"It happens, you know. When a child doesna have a firm

hand." Magnus fluttered his lashes. "When a child doesna have a father." Why he glanced at Andrew was a mystery.

"She doesna need a father. She doesna need any man." Susana stabbed her egg with a fork. The yolk bled.

"Every child needs a father. And you canna deny, she is . . . something of a hellion."

"She isna a hellion."

"Yesterday she used the apiary for target practice."

"I'm sure the hives were tempting targets."

"The bees were not amused."

"Isobel is simply . . . adventurous."

"Ah. *Isobel.*" Hamish nudged Andrew's foot under the table. "Isn't she the girl who woke you up this morning?" *Bastard.* He knew damn well it was. He was just trying to stir a pot that was already on boil.

Susana leaped from her chair. "She *what*?"

"Aye. She came to our . . . lodgings and woke Andrew up. What did she say she wanted to see?"

Andrew quirked a brow. "A buffoon."

It was gratifying to see Susana pale. He decided to wedge the barb deeper. "She nearly got an education." He leaned closer and whispered, "Most of my men sleep in the nude."

"Oh, dear God." Susana clutched at her breast. "I told her not to go there. I forbade her . . ."

"You forbade her?" Magnus chuckled. "There was your mistake. Since when has Isobel ever obeyed anyone?"

"I'm her mother. She obeys me."

The chuckle became a bark of laughter. Susana glowered at her father and tossed her serviette onto the table. "Where is she? Where is that girl?"

Magnus shrugged. "I think she said something about hunting rabbits."

Susana blew out a breath. In a nod to decorum, she forced something like a smile at the men around the table and said, "Please do excuse me. I must go find my daughter."

Seeing his chance, when she stood, Andrew did as well. "I'll accompany you," he said.

When Hamish leaped to his feet and parroted, "Yes. We'll come with you," Andrew nearly kicked him.

Susana's face scrunched up. "You doona need to come."

"Nonsense. We were hoping to tour the castle and the outlying lands with you today anyway. We'll help you find your daughter and then, perhaps, you can show us around."

She placed her hands flat on the table and leaned in. "I doona need any help from you." That she nearly spat the words didn't dissuade him. In fact, it spurred him on. Ach, she was a maddening woman. He wanted nothing more than to spend the day in her company.

And, if he was lucky, steal another kiss.

∽

He was not lucky.

As Susana stormed from the castle, he and Hamish scuttled to keep up. She gusted a sigh when she saw a tall man passing through the bailey. He had the look of a warrior about him; Andrew recognized the well-honed muscles, the swagger in his walk, and the predatory expression on his face.

He also recognized the intensity in his eyes when they lit on Susana. And Andrew didn't care for it.

This man was obviously interested in her.

Then again, what man wouldn't be?

She seemed far too pleased to see him. "Ah, there you are, Keir," she warbled.

He bowed. "My lady."

"Have you met Hamish Robb and . . . Andrew Lochlannach?" She waved in their general direction although, Andrew noticed, she didn't bother to look at him. "They've come from Dunnet to oversee our defenses." She attempted a cheerful tone, but failed. "Keir is my captain of the guard."

Keir greeted them with a friendly smile, but Andrew could detect the reserve behind the mask. When his gaze landed on Andrew it stalled. His eyes narrowed and his scrutiny intensified. For some reason, he frowned. He flicked a glance at Susana and then forced another smile, although this one wasn't friendly in the slightest. "Welcome," he said.

"They were hoping for a tour of the grounds," she said meaningfully.

Keir pressed his lips together. "Och, I would love to offer you a tour," he said. "Perhaps later?"

"Why not now?" A simple question.

Keir blanched. He glanced at Susana. "I . . . ah . . ."

"We're busy," she said.

"Aye. Verra busy."

Andrew crossed his arms. "Perhaps we can help with your . . . busy."

Hamish leaned in with a grin. "We're trained men. We're quite accomplished at . . . busy."

"Naturally." Keir's tone was dry. Clearly, he wasn't impressed by this boast. "However, you've come at a verra busy time. Perhaps tomorrow?"

Aggravation gored Andrew. It was clear they intended to put him off—perhaps indefinitely. This would not do. Not at all. He was determined to learn as much as he could, as quickly as possible, so he could analyze their defenses and make the necessary changes. He was determined not to fail his brother in this.

Perhaps it was time for a little prevarication of his own. "Ach, I understand," he said. He clapped Keir on the shoulder. "Not to worry. As you are too busy, my men and I shall . . . explore on our own."

Susana blanched at that. Her gaze flew to Keir's.

His lips flapped. "Well . . . I suppose I could arrange a *brief* tour today."

Andrew tried not to smirk, but failed. "A brief tour would be helpful. And then, tomorrow, we can discuss the defenses in more detail." He offered this to Susana. Her only response was a frown.

"Of course." Though Keir appeared all things genial, a muscle ticked in his cheek.

"Well then," Susana gusted. "I leave you in good hands." She whirled and headed for the stables. Without a word, the men watched her retreat, escape perhaps. Andrew could only hope the others weren't thinking the same thoughts whirling in his head.

How much he would enjoy turning her over his knee and smacking that lush bottom.

∽

Keir's tour of the castle was brief indeed. One could call it cursory. One could also call it a waste of time. But Andrew took from it what he needed. He and his men would fill in the rest of it on their own.

They began with a tour of the bailey, though it was very much like the bailey at Lochlannach Castle and Andrew had figured that much out for himself. What interested him were the things that were different, and disturbingly so.

"This is the armory," Keir said, waving in the vague direction of a long low building set against the castle walls. "And the training grounds." The lists were old, but in good repair, with archery butts and a fenced area for battle practice, much like the one they had in Dunnet. There were, however, no men training. "And these are the battlements." Keir gestured to the ramparts. Again, much like those in Dunnet, and again unmanned.

"Do you not have men stationed up there?" It seemed to Andrew there should be at least a pair of them in the turret, where they could see far and wide.

Keir frowned at him. "They're on rotating shifts."

Andrew and Hamish exchanged a glance. For a castle that had recently suffered raids and betrayal, they seemed woefully unprotected. And where were they? All the men under Keir's command? Andrew didn't see much evidence of them anywhere.

"Tell me about your troops," Andrew asked.

"Our troops?" Why Keir frowned so, he had no idea.

"How many do you have? What is their training level?"

"They are verra well trained," Keir said.

"Are they dedicated to defense?"

"Well, no. They are tacksmen and blacksmiths. Farmers."

"Hmm." Hamish stroked his beard. "So during the planting season and the harvest your defenses are down?"

It was exactly what Andrew was thinking. No matter the season, there needed to men dedicated to the watch. Trained men.

Keir forced a smile, but it didn't meet his eyes. "Naturally we have a plan to backfill during the harvest." He didn't elaborate on what that was, and Andrew didn't ask because he knew the answer would be unsatisfactory. He made a mental note to include increased training and rotations in his plan.

Once they had reviewed the castle strategies, they set out to tour the land surrounding the castle. Keir showed them the apiary and the orchard to the west and the bustling town of Ciaran Reay to the north. He shared bits of information here and there, but nothing truly useful, and he danced around far too many questions altogether.

By the end of their tour, Andrew was mightily displeased.

"Well, what did you think of that?" Hamish asked as they made their way back to the kennels.

Andrew frowned. "A waste of time."

"My sentiments exactly. Either Keir doesna know what he's doing, or his goal is to weaken the defenses, not shore them up."

"Or—and this is the most likely explanation—he was simply wasting our time."

Hamish chuckled. "I got that feeling, too. It doesna make sense, though. Why would they fob us off when we've come to help them?"

Andrew had a clue and it all boiled down to the resentment of a certain redheaded virago . . . who didn't want to give up the reins. What he needed to do was show her how much more effective their fortifications could be if she allowed men who knew what they were doing to design their plan of defense. "I doona think working with Keir will be verra useful."

Hamish narrowed his eyes. "What are you suggesting?"

"I'm suggesting we do just as we threatened earlier, and explore on our own. And in the meantime, I think I'm going to have a little chat with Magnus." If Susana wasn't going to work with him, he was going to have to work around her. No doubt her father would be more than happy to provide him with the information he needed.

With a grin, he made his way to the castle to find the laird of the manor.

CHAPTER SIX

Susana stared at her inventory list and then studied the stores. She tried not to grimace. They had plenty of mutton and ham in the smoke room, but with the influx of men from Dunnet, they would need more. Especially if they would be staying for any length of time. She sighed and made a note for Tamhas. They'd need to bring more vegetables up from the root cellar as well.

She set her teeth as she thought of him, the stone in her shoe, the niggling gnat who wouldn't leave her in peace. It had probably been cowardly of her to pass Andrew off on Keir. Keir hardly deserved such punishment. But she'd had one conversation with that impossible man that morning and had reached her limit.

Her day hadn't gone any better after she'd left him. There was a leak in the roof of the smithy, the wheel at the mill had cracked, and two of their crofters were embroiled in a feud over a pig. To make things worse, she hadn't been able to find Isobel.

This was hardly something new. Isobel was known to disappear for hours on end, either hunting with her friends or running amok in town. But today it was an annoyance, because Susana really wanted to talk to her daughter and remind her to stay away from Andrew.

The thought of the two of them spending any time together made her stomach churn.

She shivered. The storeroom was beneath ground and

cool, but that was probably not what sent a shiver through her.

Damn the man, he was exasperating.

"Susana."

She started as his voice surrounded her, as though she had summoned him with her wayward thoughts.

She spun, clutching her list to her chest, though it couldn't protect her. Nothing could.

He leaned against the doorjamb—so tall he blotted out the light—and crossed his arms over his chest. His grin was annoying. Everything about him was. The way the muscles in his arms bunched, the way his chest flexed, the taper of his waist . . . "What are you doing here?" she snapped.

"Just looking around."

She stepped deeper into the room—away from him—and pretended to count ham hocks. "You already had a tour."

"It was not . . . satisfying."

"Wasn't it?" She forbore a sniff. Likely Keir had taken her meaning and given them a perfunctory tour.

"Nae. It wasna." He stepped closer. She could feel him, smell him. She pretended to count faster. "You werena there."

She blew out a breath. Though he came around to her side, she didn't look at him. "You dinna need me there."

"Nae. But I wanted you."

Her heart clenched. Those words, those words alone, scuttled all thought.

She forced her spine to stiffen; forced her defenses to rise up. He was irresistible, aye, but she needed to resist him. She had to. That kiss, yesterday, had nearly swept her back six years in time, nearly made her stupid and naive once more. She couldn't allow herself to be seduced again.

Especially by a man who obviously seduced so many women, he couldn't remember them all.

Still, his presence at her side befuddled her. His gaze on her face burned. She cleared her throat and fought for distance. "Keir is verra thorough."

His chuckle rang through the room.

She whirled on him. "He is."

"I'm glad you have such faith in him."

Something in his expression caught her attention. She frowned. "Why do you say it like that?"

"Like what?"

"As though my faith is misplaced? Keir is a loyal and dependable man. He's served Dounreay for years."

Andrew's expression firmed. "I'm sure that is the case. And I'm also sure the tour was anything but thorough. However, even given that, Hamish and I found some elements seriously lacking. I have some suggestions I would like to present to you."

God he was irritating. The tilt of his head, that pretense of deference. As though he had any intention of letting her retain any power whatsoever. "Suggestions?"

"For one, I think there should be men on the walls at all times—"

"We need the men for patrols. We doona have enough to assign them to the walls."

"You do now." He stepped closer. "With my men. And your troops should be training regularly, in a designated rotation, not just when they wish to do so."

"We hardly have time for that."

"You should make time. Keir explained that many of your fighting men are farmers and tacksmen. Merchants."

"And?"

"And, if those men find themselves in a battle with hardened soldiers, they will appreciate the extra training."

Damn it. She wasn't sure what enraged her the most, the fact that he was presumptuous enough to tell her how to defend her land, or the fact that he was right. "Can we discuss this later?" She gestured to the mutton. "I'm busy."

"I see that." His eyes glimmered.

"I need to figure out how I'm going to feed all your men."

"They can hunt."

She glowered. "I canna have our forests decimated."

"According to your father, the forests are teeming with game. However, if you are concerned, I will send a letter to Alexander asking him to send supplies. We had no idea you were in such dire straits." He glanced meaningfully around the room, filled to the brim with meat.

She frowned at him. Tapped her foot. "They *are* his men."

"Aye." He said nothing more, merely stared at her, which she found mildly disturbing. Or not mildly.

"Is there anything else?" A bark.

She didn't know why her stomach plummeted when he turned to leave.

But he didn't leave . . . He kicked the door shut with his foot and came back to her.

Her pulse leaped. "I . . . What are you doing?"

He stepped closer. The light of the lamp cast his face in shadows, gave him an ominous demeanor. "I canna stop thinking about it," he said.

Her belly rippled. "About what?"

"That kiss."

Something sizzled through her womb. She looked around, searching for an escape. There was none. Certainly no escape from the desire that suddenly curled through her.

"That–That . . . kiss?"

He smiled. "It was delicious. But there was something about it . . ." He stepped closer and though she stepped back, there was nowhere to go. Once again, he had cornered her. She placed a hand on his chest, probably to keep him away. His heart thudded beneath her palm.

She gazed up at him, unable to move. "Something about it? What?"

"I'm not sure." A whisper. No more was necessary because he was already as close as he could be. His heat scalded her. "I need another taste."

Before she could react, before she could slip away, his lips touched hers, scraped across them, across her sanity. A mere hint of a buss, but it was enough. It was enough to fill her with his essence, his taste, his scent.

Her knees locked and she wobbled. His arms surrounded her, holding her up. His hand pressed against her back, pulling her closer. He groaned and deepened the kiss, covering her, smothering her with his mouth. Washing her with a tide of desire. It was a sea in which she could gladly drown.

As had happened yesterday, with the mere touch of his lips on hers all her reservations, all her pain, six years of resolve, crumbled.

She could hate herself for this weakness. She should. But not now. Tonight she would regret this.

For the moment, she would only glory in the feelings he ignited in her hungry, aching body.

It was as though, in his arms, she was alive again. Ah, but for a moment, surely. Soon she would curl up and turn to stone again, but for now, for this moment, she was alive.

His lips moved over hers; his tongue dabbed in. Susana shook at the sensation. She opened to him, allowed him in, sucking on his tongue. He reared back, his nostrils flared, his eyes wide. Then he fisted his hands in her hair and yanked her closer and kissed her again.

No gentle exploration this. No tender tasting. He consumed her whole with the savage desire of a man long starved.

It was wild and passionate and glorious and . . . folly, but she sank into it.

As he kissed her, his hands roved, dancing over her back, her hips, cupping her bottom. He pressed against her and pulled her into him. The outline of his aroused cock was unmistakable.

The thought flickered through her head, a foolish thought, an injudicious one.

They were alone here in the cellar. It was likely no one would intrude.

Her body was ready for him; her womb ached for him. How difficult would it be to raise her skirts and lean back? How insane would it be to taste that glory . . . just once more?

Aye, she might regret it. But she would survive. She had before.

But before she could act on such an imprudent and rampant desire, he lifted his head. He stared at her, his damp lips parted. His brow furrowed and he whispered, "Susana?"

She swallowed heavily. "Aye?"

"You taste . . ."

Her pulse pinged. "Aye?"

To her frustration—nae, to her relief—he eased back. Surely she imagined that flicker in his expression, that flicker of . . . recognition. He didn't remember her. Did he? She forced down the vexing surge of hope; it was an annoyance. Besides which, she didn't want him to remember

her. She didn't want him to remember anything. There
was too much at stake.

"You taste . . . wonderful."

She forced herself to relax. A mistake. Because he
kissed her again. But this was not an enflamed and seductive kiss, it was . . . a sample. Another tiny nibble of a dish
he was trying to decide if he wanted to eat. It was delicious and far too brief. But it was followed by another, and
another.

The befuddlement in his expression deepened. His
Adam's apple worked. "Have we ever . . . kissed before?"

Something nasty rippled through her. She wasn't sure
if it was rage, relief or disappointment. She pushed him
away and he allowed it. She stalked across the room. This
time, he did not follow. "Do you no' remember the girls
you've kissed?" She tried for a civil tone. And almost
achieved it.

"Of course I do."

"Then why do you ask if you've kissed me? For heav-
en's sake. We've never even met." A bold-faced lie, and one
twined, perhaps, with a hint of desperation. But it was a
necessary lie.

"You taste . . . You seem . . . familiar."

Dread arose in her. She fought it back down. "Oh, for
pity's sake," she said with a snort. "How many women
have you kissed?" Sometimes offense was the best defense.

He winced, but didn't answer. For some reason, his ret-
icence reignited her anger, even when silencing him had
been her aim.

"Do you even remember the name of the last girl you
kissed?"

"Of course I do!"

"What was it?"

He paled. His lips worked. He didn't answer. Then again, no answer was answer in itself.

He didn't remember. He never remembered.

He never remembered anything.

And as memorable as this kiss had been, he would forget it as soon as another girl passed by, capturing his eye.

He would forget her as he'd forgotten her before.

She glared at him, all of her fury, all of her pain, all of her desolation plain on her face for him to see.

Likely he would forget that as well.

"Susana . . ."

"Go on. Admit it. You doona remember."

"I do. I just . . . canna say."

"You canna say?" She blew out a breath, investing in it every ort of her disdain.

She'd been right to distrust him. She'd been right to keep him at arm's length. She'd been right in her desire to punish him and make him pay for her broken heart.

He was a bastard. A faithless philanderer, a heartless Lothario who seduced women, used them until he tired of them, and tossed them aside. And then forgot them.

Oh, what a fool she'd been. Then, and now.

She was right in her determination to resist him, to avoid him.

All he had to do was kiss her and her thoughts scattered, her determination shattered; insanity reigned.

Without a word, she pushed past him and ran from the room.

It was a good thing he didn't follow her, or she might have gutted him.

∾

Andrew leaned against the ramparts and stared out at the picturesque town of Ciaran Reay, nestled against the sea like a jewel. The view from the turrets was superb. He could see far in the distance in all directions. Stafford's land to the west and Scrabster's to the east.

He couldn't see all the crofts to the south through the thick woods, but if they set up a system of signal fires, it would be easy for the soldiers posted here to spot the smoke and send help to the far reaches.

Why there were no men stationed here was befuddling.

That wasn't the only befuddling thought twining in his brain.

After that debacle with Susana, he'd thrown himself into his work. Never had he regretted a kiss as much as he did that one.

Oh, not the kiss with Susana.

The kiss with Lana.

When he'd refused to name her and Susana had stormed out of the storage room, he hadn't been able to move. He'd stared after her, his mind in a tumult.

He hadn't wanted to let her go. He probably shouldn't have. He probably should never have let her go. He should have kept kissing her, maybe taken more of what she'd seemed so willing to offer. He should have ignored that insistent urge to *speak* to her. Because when he'd lifted his head and burbled the question ringing in his mind—well, that had ruined everything.

And her challenge? To name the last woman he'd kissed?

Fook. How could he tell her? How could he admit the last woman he'd pulled into his arms and kissed had been . . . her sister?

That would have bollixed everything up but good.

He gusted a sigh and turned to head back down the stairs but a scraping sound over his head captured his attention. He glanced up. And froze.

A tiny figure scrambled across the slate shingles of the turret's slanted roof, a bow slung over her shoulder. He recognized her at once. That blond hair was unmistakable.

Horror curled through him.

What the hell was she doing there? *On the roof?*

He opened his mouth to call to her and then clamped it shut. The last thing he wanted to do was startle her and cause her to slip. The walkway ended at the turret tower; beyond the low wall, there was nothing to stop her from plummeting to the cobblestones far below. The fall would be fatal.

Dear God.

But his silence mattered not. Even as he watched, one of the shingles shifted beneath her and her foot slipped. She fell.

Time slowed down. The tiny bundle skittered down the steeply slanted roof scrambling to catch herself. She managed to do so. Just inches from the lip. Just inches from utter disaster.

"Oh, my God." His unintended gust captured her attention. She glanced at him over her shoulder. Unaccountably, she smiled.

"Oh, hullo there," she said. She grunted and found a more secure handhold. Moving slowly, he edged around to the side so that if she slipped again, he could catch her. Maybe.

His pulse pounded in his throat. "Jesus God, Isobel. What are you doing on the roof?"

"Hunting."

Hunting? On the roof? He burned to know why, what, but he didn't dare ask.

She grunted again as her fingers slipped. Her confident expression crumbled, washed away by a sudden wave of fear.

"Stay there," he commanded. "I'm coming to get you."

Swallowing his own fear of heights, he balanced his foot on the low wall and levered up to the battlement.

He knew, if she fell, the impact might knock him off, too, but he couldn't do nothing. He couldn't just let her tumble to her death.

"Can you ease down?" he asked. "Slowly?"

She nodded.

Carefully, cautiously, slowly, she shifted down one inch, two, until her feet dangled over the edge.

Balancing on his toes, Andrew reached up and took hold of her ankles. He didn't allow himself to look down. He planned to catch her as she slid off the roof, and throw his body toward the narrow walkway of the battlement. If he angled his body correctly, they would fall on the battlement and the girl would land on him.

If God was with them, they wouldn't go tumbling the wrong way.

"All right. Are you ready to let go?"

"Mmm-hmm." Her voice was wobbly.

"Doona worry. I'm going to catch you." *Please God. Please.* "Ready?"

"Aye."

"Let go."

A moment of complete and utter panic scoured him as she did as she asked, trusting him with her life.

Please God.

Please God.

As her body slid off the roof, he grabbed her, trying like mad to stay balanced, to not tip over the edge into oblivion. And then, using every ounce of his concentration, every ort of his strength, he launched himself backward.

He landed on the stone walkway with a thud that forced

the air from his lungs. But he didn't need it. Not really. There was no need to breathe.

The moment hung over him, a sharp shard of time. And then she landed. On top of him. Whatever air was left in him exited in an *oof*. Every muscle ached and he hit his head hard when he fell, but he didn't care.

Her body was a welcome weight on his.

They were both alive.

He lay still, willing his heart to calm, trying to force his lungs to work.

Something pried open his eye. A finger. And a sticky one at that.

"Are you all right?" she asked.

He nodded. Words were beyond him.

"Oh, good."

"What on earth were you doing on that roof?" he asked when he finally recovered himself—though his pulse still raged in his veins.

Isobel blew out a sigh. "I told you. Hunting."

"Hunting what?"

"Birds, probably."

"You nearly died."

She frowned at him.

"What if I hadn't been here to catch you?"

She didn't seem inclined to answer.

"Have you done this before?"

She snorted. "I do it all the time."

His breath caught. "*What?*"

"Never this high, though. Mama said I shouldna."

"Your mama might have had the right of it." He glanced up at the roof. "Do you think that was a good idea?"

She put out a lip. "Probably not. But I doona like being told no."

He would have rolled his eyes, but everything hurt too

much to move. "No one likes being told no. But sometimes there's a damn good reason for it."

"You really shouldna swear."

He frowned at her. "Do you think you will be doing this again?" If so, he should probably warn Susana. Maybe help her build a cage.

Isobel considered the question at length. A flicker of apprehension crossed her face as she likely relived what had just happened . . . and what had almost happened. "Nae," she said, far too cheerily in his opinion. "I doona think I shall."

Andrew sat up and rubbed his head. There would be a goose egg tomorrow. "You are verra wise."

She tipped her head and studied him. "Do you really think I am wise?"

"In this? Aye. I do."

Her smile was blinding.

His heart thudded.

Dear God.

The girl was a menace.

She definitely needed a cage.

She was very much like her mother, Andrew decided. Both were intransigent and reckless and probably in need of a spanking.

Thoughts of Susana . . . and a spanking claimed his thoughts and he thrust them away. Obviously, there was no point in mooning after her. No point in attempting to pursue her. Not given the way she'd rebuffed him. Not given her undeniable fury with him. Not given her determination to scuttle his every effort to protect her and her people.

From here on out, he needed to focus on one thing and one thing only. His mission. He would launch into it full force, without her cooperation if need be. He and Hamish had already developed a plan and were prepared to set it into motion.

Susana would not be pleased.

He tried to pretend it didn't matter.

CHAPTER SEVEN

Susana leaned against a tree and stared out at the garden. It was beautiful in the rose light of sunset. She loved coming here to watch the evening fall, and after a day like today she sorely needed the simple peace. But as beautiful as it was, it didn't calm her soul.

Memories of the kiss in the smoke room and her subsequent fury kept intruding.

Damn the man, for kissing her again, for leading her back to that place where she felt alive and feminine and . . . vulnerable. As exhilarating and frightening and agonizing as it was . . . she wanted more.

She needed to make a vow to never let him get close to her again. To never let him kiss her again.

But she didn't think she could. If she was being truthful, if he so much as crooked a finger at her, she would follow.

That was the most bothersome part of all.

She'd thought she'd taken charge of her life. She'd thought she'd built a wall that protected her, but it was all a flimsy facade. All it took was a look, a wink, a smile and her defenses crumbled to dust.

Though she'd convinced herself she was over him, that he was a dim memory from her past, she'd never forgotten him. Not really. She'd never gotten over the heartbreak. The pain in her chest was a testament to that.

The worst part of it all was the knowledge that even

though he was a faithless philanderer, a seducer of legions . . . she still wanted him. She still became a malleable lump of hungry flesh in his arms.

Since she couldn't resist him, her best bet was to avoid him.

Even that was a painful thought. Some small hidden part of her being rejoiced in the fact that he was here. That they might have a second chance. That was the foolish part of her being, she decided. Because the only second chance his presence here represented was a second chance to break her heart. It was—

"Susana . . ."

She resisted the urge to roll her eyes at the deep voice behind her, intruding on her melancholy. She ignored the flicker of disappointment that it wasn't Andrew.

"Hamish." With a sigh, she turned to greet him. Ach, he was bonny and braw. He seemed to be a nice man. Why couldn't she have met a man like him before her heart was shattered?

He tucked his hands into the pockets of his jerkin and strolled toward her. The expression in his eyes gave her pause. It was far too predatory for her liking. "Lovely evening, isn't it?" He didn't seem interested in the evening in the slightest. His gaze was locked on her. To be precise, on her lips.

What was it about men and their fascination with lips?

"It's going to rain."

He smiled. It was a charming smile, but it lacked . . . something.

It was probably wrong to compare him with Andrew. Though he was an extraordinarily handsome man, he would never measure up. Those sparkling eyes, not quite as intent. That grin, not cocky enough.

But then, she compared every man with Andrew on

some level. She had for six years. And no man ever measured up.

"I find I like the rain." He set his palm on the tree behind her and leaned in.

Oh, dear. He was far too close. She tipped up her chin to study him.

"I find I like you." He tangled his fingers in her hair.

She resisted the urge to laugh. His seduction was far from subtle. "Do you?"

"Aye." He stroked her cheek with a thumb.

"Surely you doona intend to kiss me."

He blinked. "I do. I've been thinking about kissing you from the moment we met. Have you thought about it?"

"No," she said truthfully. She hadn't been able to think of any other man, any other lips since she'd set eyes on Andrew.

Hamish set his palm to his chest. "You wound me, Miss Dounreay."

She did laugh then. "I'm sure you shall survive."

His eyes twinkled. "I love your laugh," he whispered. His gaze intensified as he bent his head. His lips brushed hers, lingered. She allowed it, but only because he was gentle and sweet. And because he needed to realize there was no reason to continue this pursuit. When she didn't respond—whatsoever—he lifted his head and sighed. "Nothing?"

"Nothing."

He offered a sheepish grin. "I thought not, but I had to try."

"Of course." He was a nice man, and comfortable company. She never felt *at ease* around Andrew. Around Andrew, everything was a tumult. Susana found she rather liked Hamish's tranquil companionship.

He stepped back and stared out at the sea, now painted

in reds and pinks. "Aye. A lost cause from the beginning, I suppose, this seduction."

"Is that what this was?" A simple kiss, a testing kiss?

He chuckled and raked his fingers through his red curls. "Perhaps not. But . . . I wanted to know."

"Know what?"

"If there was a chance."

Poor man. A chance? There hadn't been a chance for any man with her. Not for six years. Not since a tall, charming boy with silver locks pulled her into his arms and kissed her.

"I couldna help noticing . . ."

Susana didn't like the shift in Hamish's tone; it went from playful to contemplative in a heartbeat. She frowned at him. "Couldna help noticing what?"

"The way you look at him."

Her nape prickled. "Him?"

"Andrew. Are you interested in him?"

"Nae." The word came out of its own accord. Probably force of habit.

Hamish's eyes glinted. "And I couldna help noticing the way he looks at you."

She stepped away and crossed her arms, ignoring the trill of excitement his words evoked. "Really?"

"Quite curious, those looks. Considering . . ."

"Considering what?"

"Considering the fact you both deny an interest in each other. Yet when you are together, the energy between you is palpable."

"Nonsense."

"I also couldna help noticing something else." Like a playful boy, he used the tree limb as leverage to swing around and face her. "Something verra interesting."

She stilled. "What?"

"How much your daughter resembles him. Curious that, considering you both proclaim you've never met before."

Her heart froze. She frowned at him.

"Same smile. Same eyes. And those dimples?"

"Doona be ridiculous."

"I've never seen hair quite that color . . . except in the Silver Lochlannachs."

"Many people have blond hair."

"Not that exact color. And then there's the odd fact that the both of you were in Perth six years ago. And your daughter is . . . what? Five?"

"Lots of people were in Perth six years ago. Besides . . . ask him. If he and I ever met, he doesna remember."

Hamish tipped his head to the side and grinned. "Ah. Is that what it's about then?"

"What?"

"Your resentment of him?"

"I doona resent him."

"Liar." There was no heat in the word. "The two of you met in Perth, had some torrid affair. You found you were with child and fled home . . . and now, when you meet him again, he doesna even remember."

He was far too clever. And observant. "Doona be daft."

"Deny it if you will, but *you* know the truth." He offered another grin. It was tinged with something that might have been sympathy. "And so do I."

"Did you really come here to kiss me? Or to try to uncover all my secrets?"

"Both." He winked. "I believe I've accomplished both."

Susana sighed. She couldn't deny it. In fact, she no longer wanted to. "Are you going to tell him?"

"It's not my place."

"Isn't it? You're his friend."

"Aye. But it's not my place to tell him. It's yours."

"Bluidy hell."

"He deserves to know. It would be better coming from you. I know Andrew can be rather oblivious sometimes, but he will figure it out. At some point. It would be better if you told him first. And he does . . . deserve to know."

"Does he?" She fisted her hips. "He's a faithless seducer. He flits from woman to woman. He canna remember the name of the last girl he kissed."

Hamish laughed, threw back his head and howled. "Is that what he told you?"

"Nae. He said he remembered but couldna tell me for some strange reason."

"He couldna tell you because it would have made you furious."

She narrowed her gaze on him. "Why?"

"Because the last woman he kissed was Lana."

Her stomach lurched.

"Oh, doona glower so."

"Why are you laughing?"

"Because Alexander saw the kiss." He threw out his arms. "It's likely why we are here. Exiled. It's really rather funny, if you think about it."

She would not think about it. "I believe it proves my point. He is a faithless philanderer."

"He isna. I know for a fact, while he's kissed many women . . . he hasna been in a relationship for a long time. Since . . ." His eyes narrowed. "Since he returned from Perth, in fact. Something happened there that changed him."

Aye. He fell in love with Kirstie Gunn. "Why are you telling me this?"

"Because you need to know. You need to give him a chance."

Hah! She gave him a chance six years ago and he nearly destroyed her.

Hamish's expression firmed. "He's a good man, Susana."

She snorted.

"He needs this."

Something in his tone captured her attention. "He needs this?" This . . . what?

"He needs a chance to prove himself to his brother. He feels he owes Alexander a debt. It's been a heavy weight on his soul his whole life. He sees this opportunity as a chance to . . . pay him back."

"For what?"

"For saving his life. A man has to feel like a man, Susana."

She frowned at him.

"Take my advice. Take the time to get to know him better. You'll find he's not the man you think he is." He turned away, and then stopped. "And Susana?"

"Aye?"

"You need to tell him the truth about Isobel."

Ach. He was right. Damn him to hell. He was right.

A pity she didn't have the courage to do so.

She sighed as she watched Hamish make his way toward the castle.

She was tired of it all, of this battle between Andrew and herself. Or perhaps it was her inner battle she was tired of. She wasn't a fool. She knew her resistance stemmed from her fear of being used by him; her desire for just that annoyed her mightily. It created in inner turmoil that kept her awake at night.

Or perhaps that was simply hunger. For him. Spurred by the parade of memories from that enchanting affair so long ago, and the kisses they'd shared so recently.

Her logical mind advised that she avoid him like the plague, but her body wanted something else entirely.

A tantalizing thought bubbled in her brain. It wouldn't be silenced.

She leaned back and stared at the panoply of colors that was the waning day, a kernel of an idea sprouting in her head.

What if *he* wasn't the one doing the using? What if she seduced him? Took what she wanted? How would she feel about it then?

The more she thought on it, the more convinced she became that it was an excellent notion. Why should *she* not take what she wanted? He would surely give it.

She was a grown woman. With a child. Hardly a maiden. Hardly a green girl who would fall in love with a man just because he'd kissed her. Seduced her.

Surely she was stronger than that. Surely she'd been through enough to know better than that.

If she wanted to seduce a man, she could.

And as for the fear that he could take what he wanted and walk away . . . Well, so could she.

She could be heartless, too.

∾

Andrew decided to spend the time remaining before dinner with Hamish in Magnus's study, scouring maps of the castle and outlying grounds, making note of where he'd seen weaknesses in the defenses. Alexander was counting on him. And as far as that went, Andrew had no doubt he could prove himself worthy. He was nothing if not skilled in battle strategy.

After his realization yesterday that he would be a fool to wait for any support from Susana, he'd met with Hamish and his men, including the men Alexander had previously sent to Dounreay. Using what little information they had gathered, and what he'd learned from Keir, Andrew had formed an estimation of the current defenses. It was not impressive. They had developed a preliminary plan of action and set those changes in motion. Now it was time for a deeper assessment.

As they entered the study, Hamish grinned at him; the mischief in his expression was difficult to ignore. "What?" Andrew clipped.

Hamish stroked his beard and shrugged. "Nothing."

"I know that look. It's not nothing."

"I just had an . . . interesting conversation with our hostess."

Andrew snorted. She was hardly hospitable. And then curiosity prickled. "What did you talk about?"

Hamish's grin only widened. He picked up a quill and toyed with it in a truly annoying fashion. "She's rather attractive." She was. "Are you sure you doona intend to seduce her?"

Heat rose on his neck. *Blast*. He didn't want to talk about this. Not in the least. And certainly not with Hamish. "Are we going to review the maps?"

"Of course. But I'm curious. About whether or not you intend to seduce her."

"The woman cannot stand the sight of me." The truth of it burned in his belly.

Hamish chuckled. "Since when has that ever stopped you?"

True. It never had. He'd always been able to charm away any resistance. Then again, he'd never felt this sense of futility before. Or this sense of determination.

Would he attempt to kiss her again?

The moment he saw his chance.

"I think she likes you."

He gaped at Hamish. "Where on earth did you get that notion?"

"Just a hunch."

Aye, now the smirk was exceedingly irritating. "What did the two of you talk about?" Curiosity jabbed him like a lance.

"This and that. The weather. Games of chance. Her´ . . . daughter." Hamish's expression was inscrutable.

"It sounds fascinating indeed."

"Susana Dounreay is a fascinating woman—"

Hamish stilled as a muffled snort sounded from behind the desk. He shot a perplexed glance at Andrew and headed over to investigate the source of it. Peering over the back of the desk, he chuckled. "What are you doing here?" he asked.

"Hiding," a high-pitched voice responded. Andrew flinched. He knew that voice. And bluidy hell, Isobel had heard their entire conversation. He quickly thought back, trying to remember what he'd said.

Hamish held out a hand and lifted her up. As she emerged, she fixed her blue gaze on Andrew. Her nose wrinkled.

"You're hiding?" Hamish brushed the dust from her skirts. "From whom?"

"Torquil."

"I see. And who is Torquil?"

"The beekeeper. He's cross." She tossed herself into Magnus's chair and swung her legs.

"And why is he cross?"

She shrugged.

"Any idea at all?" Hamish asked gently.

"I . . . might have used the hives for target practice again." When Hamish gaped at her, she felt the need to add, "But only a little."

"Ah."

"The bees were verra angry," she confided. "They chased Torquil into the loch. And then he chased me. So I hid here. No one ever comes here." This, in an accusing tone.

"You are a menace, you know," Hamish said fondly . . . because he had no clue what a menace she really was.

Isobel responded with a grin. It bothered Andrew, watching their casual exchange, seeing the admiration in her eyes for his friend. He didn't know why.

"What are you doing here?" she asked.

"Plotting our strategies."

"Huh," Isobel said. "Where's Mama?"

Hamish shrugged. "Who knows?"

"Mama willna like that she's not helping."

"Hush," Hamish said.

The sudden fury on her tiny features was amusing. Mostly because it was leveled on Hamish. Why her expression reminded Andrew of his brother when he was vexed, he didn't know, but it did. "I was just trying to warn you," she muttered. "And I doona like when people tell me to hush."

Hamish affected a mocking bow. "A thousand pardons, my lady."

Isobel wasn't mollified by his mocking apology. She glared at him. "I doona think I like you after all."

Hamish blinked. "Did you? At one point?"

"I thought you would be a good husband for my mama."

"Did you?" Hamish smirked at Andrew; it was a challenge not to smack him. "Why did you think I would be a good husband for your mama?"

"Because you both have red hair." Ah. Logical. "But now I'm not so sure."

Andrew couldn't help but add to the conversation. "In

case it has escaped your attention, your mama doesna want a husband."

Isobel put out a lip. "I know that. But she needs one. Sometimes we doona want things we need. Or at least that's what she tells me when it's time to eat my vegetables."

Something in her expression spoke to him. "Do you want a father, Isobel?" he asked. He didn't know why. This was a rhetorical conversation at best. A ridiculous one at worst.

She toyed with the twill on her gown. Shrugged. "I'd like a brother or sister I suppose. And someone who could teach me things."

"Your mama can teach you things."

"She's a *girl*!" she huffed. "I want to learn the things boys know."

"Magnus then—"

"Too old. And he creaks when he walks. And when I ask him some things, he just frowns at me and mutters under his breath about the good old days when women knew their place."

"That would be exasperating, I suppose."

"You have no idea."

"Well, you can ask me things, if you like." He didn't know why he offered, but he was glad he did when she fixed her attention on him and smiled. It was a beautiful smile. Pure and sweet and filled with gratitude. In a sudden epiphany, it occurred to him that having Isobel on his side might help in his hopeless pursuit of her mother.

The thought was beneath him, but it was still there.

Her lashes fluttered. "Can I ask you *anything*?"

"Aye. Anything."

"And you willna grumble and mutter and pat me on the head and tell me to run along and play?"

He was aware that Hamish was staring at him with something akin to horror, but he pressed forward nonetheless. "I wouldna dream of it."

"Excellent." She folded her fingers in her lap and tipped her head. "First off, what does *seduce* mean?"

His confidence deflated like a bagpipe that had been skewered by an arrow. A similar sound might have wheezed from him. "I . . . ah . . ." He glanced at Hamish, whose expression made it clear that Andrew had made this particular bed. Now he could lie in it.

His lips flapped. His mind spun. He could fob her off, but that would ruin this fragile camaraderie. Or he could lie to her, which would hardly be fair to her when she got older. Or he could tell her the truth in which case Susana would have his guts for garters.

He decided a combination would be wise.

"*Seduce* means to try to get someone to do something you want them to do."

"I see . . ." She tapped her lip. "Such as?"

Fook.

"Ah . . . Kiss you?"

Her eyes narrowed. "Is this about kissing?"

Andrew swallowed heavily, nodded lightly.

"So, do you?" she chirruped.

"Do I what?"

"Do you intend to seduce my mama?"

He gaped at her. His lips might have flapped.

"Because you never answered when he asked." She jabbed her thumb at Hamish, who had the gall to bat his lashes. "Do you want to kiss my mama?"

Andrew scrubbed his face with a palm. Why on earth had he offered to be honest with her?

"Well, do you?"

"If I tell you, will you run and play and leave us in peace?" At her vitriolic glower, he added, "I'm asking you, not telling you."

Her frown melted away. "In that case, aye. If you answer my question, I will *run and play*." Although she did spit the words.

"All right, then. Aye. I would verra much like to kiss your mama."

Her smile was smug and her expression was far too contemplative for his liking, but she did leave them then.

Although it was hardly in peace.

CHAPTER EIGHT

"My lady!"

Susana stilled at Keir's call. She waited for him to cross the bailey. He strode quickly and there was a furious expression on his face. "What is it?" she asked.

"My lady, did you give orders to remove the men from the eastern patrols?"

She gaped at him. "Why would I do that?" They'd agreed they needed to keep an eye on Scrabster's men.

Keir scrubbed his face. "I just saw Marcus in the stables. He told me he's been reassigned to patrol the castle. And the other men—but for one patrol—have been ordered to return as well."

Susana gaped at Keir, barely able to swallow her fury. "Ordered by whom?" But she knew. She already knew.

"Lochlannach."

"How dare he?" She clenched her fists. "How dare he go behind my back and give my men countermanding orders without my approval?"

"He is a cocky bastard," Keir muttered.

Cocky! Keir didn't know the half of it.

"Where is he?"

"I believe he's in your father's study. Going over the maps."

"The *maps*?" Susana narrowed her eyes with a ferocity that made Keir take a step back. "Who gave him access to the study?"

Keir swallowed. "Um, I believe your father did."

Och! That traitor.

And she wasn't referring to Andrew.

Susana stormed up the stairs and blew into the study. The heavy door thudded against the wall and the two men at the rough-hewn table looked up. They stared at her, but her attention was trained on one man and one man only.

He was far too handsome. Seemed far too well rested and certainly too well fed. Someone in the kitchen was going to pay for that.

"Lochlannach," she clipped.

To her absolute irritation, he smiled. "Good day, Susana."

"We need to talk." This, she spat. She didn't intend to, but civility was beyond her.

"Certainly." He waved a hand to Hamish, but it took Susana's glare to banish him. When he was gone, Susana kicked the door shut and rounded on her nemesis. She propped her hands on her hips and fixed him with a dark glower.

"You canna countermand my orders."

"Countermand your orders?" Ach, how could he look so innocent? He wasn't, and they both knew it.

"You pulled the men off the eastern borders."

"Ah. That."

She bristled, because his tone made it clear he hadn't been sure which countermanded orders she was objecting to—which meant there were more. *More.*

"I sent those men there for a verra good reason."

"You are overextended to the east. Your western borders are virtually unguarded and the greater threat lies to the west."

She nearly snarled at him. "Aye, but there's talk that our neighbor to the east is massing men."

He sobered. His face took on a serious mien—the first she'd ever seen. "I dinna know that."

"How could you know that? You dinna consult with me before pulling the men."

"My scouts havena reported any activity at all to the east. Besides which, I've been trying to talk to you since I arrived. You are the one who has been avoiding me."

Aye. And for good reason. But still, a flush of mortification rose on her cheeks. She ignored it. She was the one in the right here. Not he. "That does not signify—"

"It most certainly does. I wouldna countermand your orders, if you would work with me."

"I doona *want* to work with you."

He snorted. "Aye. That is clear. But know this, Susana . . ." She didn't like the sibilant tenor of those *s*'s. They sent a ripple over her nape. Like a caress. "I'm here. And I'm dedicated to my mission. I'm determined to keep you and your people safe, whether you want me to or not."

"I doona."

"Again, I'm not surprised. But may I ask . . . why?" His voice was so soft, almost wounded, it gave her pause. She thrust that weakness away. This was battle. There was no room for tenderness. Certainly not for one's opponent.

"Why?"

"Why do you no' want us here? Why would you turn down assistance from a powerful laird? One, in fact, who's charged with the defense of this land? Why would you try to scuttle every strategy I put in place? Why would you resist what we're doing when it's for your benefit? For God's sake, Stafford, or someone, has Dounreay in their sights. Your outlying crofts are being attacked in a methodical manner. Someone is making incursions, driving your tenants away. We need to discover who that is, and what they hope to accomplish. And we need to bluidy work together."

She crossed her arms over her chest, not to protect her heart, surely. "I have always been in charge here. I doona like you coming here and taking over."

"I'm not taking over! When your sister married my brother, her lands became his. He is the laird. And he sent me here to oversee the defenses."

She narrowed her eyes. "I have always been in charge. My men trust me. They follow me."

"As do mine."

"We canna have two separate forces following orders from separate leaders."

"Agreed." She didn't like the twinkle in his eye.

"If we are to be effective, our men must follow one leader."

He nodded. "Aye."

"There can be only one."

"Only one."

"Well," she huffed. "There is only one way to settle this."

His eyes narrowed. "What is that?"

"I propose a duel."

Andrew blinked. "A . . . duel? With swords? At dawn? Aren't those illegal?"

"As though that would signify." She smirked at him. "I'm proposing an archery competition. Winner becomes the commander of both forces. Winner has the final say in all matters."

He crossed his arms and studied her. No doubt, judging from his smirk, he felt he had some skill with a bow. Then again, so did she. He nodded. "All right. An archery competition it is."

"Three heats. Winner is best of three."

"Agreed." He thrust out his hand.

"Agreed." She took it.

As his palm closed on hers, warmth scudded up her arm and wedged in her chest.

"Tomorrow?"

"Tomorrow."

Satisfaction snaked through her. Tomorrow it would all be settled. Tomorrow she would trounce him. Tomorrow he would be so humiliated, he would turn tail and leave.

Why that thought sent a sharp pain lancing her chest, she didn't want to explore.

∞

Andrew didn't sleep well that night. For one thing, his pallet was extremely lumpy. Aside from that, he was tormented by memories of Mairi and haunting dreams where she came to him and kissed him. Only somehow, it wasn't Mairi in the dream, it was Susana.

He woke long before dawn and lay on his pallet staring up at the ceiling, battling a fierce arousal. It was aggravating and cloying and incited visions of a rounded bottom cupped in a saddle, of snapping emerald eyes and a glorious tumble of red curls. And urges . . .

With a sigh, he threw back his covers, dressed, gathered his weapon, and then headed out into the morning.

The loch wasn't far and a frigid swim was just what he needed.

If nothing else, it would cool his ardor for a woman who tasted far too luscious to forget. A woman who wanted nothing to do with him at all. A woman who thought him a buffoon.

He stared at the loch, wreathed in morning mist. Gloomy and shadowed, it matched his mood. Without a thought, he tugged off his tunic and kicked off his boots and breeks and waded in.

The cold caress of the waters made his breath lock, but he didn't stop. He forged deeper, reveling in the prickling chill as it consumed his calves, his thighs, and his belly. And then, filling his lungs, he submerged. The water closed over his head in a frosty fist. He needed this. This pain. This distraction.

He launched himself into a crawl, slicing through the waters to the far side of the loch with bold sure strokes. He forced his thoughts away from the woman who had haunted him for six years, away from the woman who tormented him now, and tried to focus on his mission, but he ended up strategizing ways to get Susana alone.

He knew he was a fool but he also knew he had to try.

While he was looking forward to their duel—beating her, to be specific—he did wonder if trouncing her was the best tactic. He knew he couldn't deliberately lose the duel. For one thing, he respected her far too much to offer her less than his best. If she won, she should win of her own accord. Aside from that, he couldn't afford to lose. He could not fail Alexander. But perhaps he should go easy on her.

It occurred to him that he'd missed a brilliant opportunity by not introducing another wager, a far more personal one. How delicious would it be to win not only the control of the defenses, but a kiss as well?

He turned and began the long swim back to the bank. His muscles were tiring and his chest hurt. But it felt good. It felt good to clear his head as well, and reach solid conclusions on how he should proceed with her. But when he reached the bank, they didn't seem solid at all. Especially when he stepped out of the water and tossed back his hair and wiped the water from his face . . . and saw *her*.

A woman with dancing green eyes and hair like a waterfall of fire stood on the shore in a heather-green kirtle that clung to her curves.

So beautiful. So exquisite.

It took a moment for him to realize she wasn't a dream. That she was really there, the woman who'd occupied his thoughts and dreams all night.

It struck him again just how much she resembled Mairi—no wonder the two had tangled together in his dreams. Unlike Mairi, Susana stood tall and bold, her eyes blazing at him, raking him and not shying away from parts south. Parts that, with his perusal of her, rose.

Hope flickered that she'd gotten over her annoyance with him. That she'd followed him here in a blatant attempt to kiss him again. Ah, but then his hopes were dashed when she yanked her gaze from his groin with a sniff and lifted something . . . something that chilled Andrew to the bone.

A bow, nocked with an arrow. And it was pointed at him.

To be precise, it was pointed at his crotch.

Aye. She was likely still annoyed.

"What are you doing in my loch?" Her voice rang through the clearing, a strident melody. It sent a shiver through him. Although, to be honest, that could have been a drizzle of fear. She did have an arrow pointed at his most treasured possession, after all. And he knew, from experience, she wouldn't hesitate to shoot.

He forced his heart to calm. Attempted to cool his ardor. But failed. She was so stunning, standing there in the shafts of pink sunlight, and threatening stance or not, he wanted her. He couldn't deny it. The evidence was there, between his legs. "I see you found a new bow."

Perhaps his tone was too cocky for the circumstances.

She prickled like a hedgehog. "I said, what are you doing here?"

"Swimming?" he quipped. He tipped his head to the side and offered her his trademark grin. It was charming and boyish and always made women soften and smile back.

Not this woman. A red tide rose on her cheeks. Her nostrils flared.

Andrew swallowed heavily.

Holy hell, she was magnificent.

But she was clearly still furious with him. And possibly deranged. It occurred to him that he should probably get dressed. Not that his breeks could protect him from another arrow, should she deign to shoot at him again, but it would certainly make him *feel* safer.

She tracked him as he splashed out of the water and, keeping one eye on the warrior princess, tugged on his clothes. It took some doing, because his skin was still wet, and his breeks clung to places they shouldn't, but it made him feel less vulnerable.

He'd never met a woman who made him feel vulnerable before. He was certain he didn't like it.

He noticed that she watched his every move with avid attention. And while he appreciated the gleam in her eye as she studied the outline of his cock in his damp breeks, her hold on that bow was concerning. When he was clothed she spoke again, barking, "Well? What the hell are you doing here?"

"I dinna fancy washing up in the horse trough." He braved the bow and stepped closer. Lord, she was lovely in the hint of dawn. The urge to pull her into his arms and kiss those pouty lips racked him.

When her gaze once more flicked down to his groin, and stalled there, and her tongue peeped out, heat sluiced through him. He glanced around the clearing. They were utterly alone. No Hamish to interrupt. No villagers to wander upon them. No one to see.

It was the perfect scene for seduction.

Or murder.

He hoped she wouldn't murder him, but even if she did gore him with one of her sharp arrows, it would probably be worth the agony to kiss her again. He stepped closer and closer still.

"Did you sleep well?" he asked.

Her frown firmed. "No."

"Ach. Neither did I. I couldna stop thinking about you."

Her brow rumpled, then lowered a tad. "Me?"

"Your kiss."

He advanced on her and her eyes flared. She took a step back and he followed, followed until he backed her into a tree. Her lips parted with surprise when she hit the bark, found herself caged between the trunk and his body.

Or perhaps it wasn't surprise. Perhaps it was invitation.

Given a choice between the two, he chose the latter.

"Susana." He cupped her cheek, stroked the soft skin with a thumb. Nudged her plump lower lip. "Tell me you dinna think about it. Dream about it—"

"I dinna!" she huffed, but the rise of pink on her cheeks, the flutter of her throat, gave her away.

"Tell me you doona wonder . . ."

She swallowed. "Wonder what?"

"What it would be like. Between us."

She made a little *eep* as his head descended and then, when their lips touched, she moaned. The sound incited him, enraged him. Or perhaps it was her scent, her taste, the soft scintillating velvet cave of her mouth. Or all of it, combined and twined.

"Ah, God." He groaned and leaned against her, pinning

her between his aching body and the tree. The pressure on his cock was maddening. As the kiss deepened, she rubbed against him. Which maddened him more.

As he kissed her, he caressed her shoulder, her arm, slowly making his way toward those captivating breasts. His palm itched to test their weight.

But he teased her. Teased himself. He continued his exploration down her flank to her waist, and then further, to her bottom.

Ah, lord. What a sublime bottom. He squeezed and she shivered.

Though her mouth was alluring beyond bearing, he yearned for more. He tipped his head and kissed his way over her jawline to nuzzle her neck, just below her ear. Her scent engulfed him and his head spun.

She issued a guttural groan and laced her fingers in his hair, holding him there.

He tried to hold back his smile, but couldn't.

Aye, she might fight him at every turn, but she wanted this. She wanted him.

Unable to resist any longer, he seized her breast and squeezed gently. Her nipple gored his palm and he shuddered. Ah, yes. A body didn't lie. It couldn't.

He raised his head and stared at her. Her lids were heavy, her mouth damp. Her features were etched with a hungry expression.

Ach, he wanted more. Desperately. But he also wanted to hear her admit she did, too.

"So have you?" he murmured, thumbing her nipple. She flinched and made a sound at the back of her throat.

"H-Have I what?"

"Wondered." A pinch.

Her jaw went slack. Her eyes glistened.

She was so close. So close to admitting it. A thrill ripped

through him as she opened her mouth to speak. To speak the words he longed to hear. That she wanted him. She wanted this. And then . . . he would take her. Here. Now. On the forest floor.

"We—We shouldna be doing this."

The denial howled through him, even though her tone was tremulous and tentative, even though it sounded as though she was asking for his agreement.

Frustration rose. "Nae. Probably not." He nested in her neck again, and nipped.

Her response to this wasn't tremulous or tentative in the least. She buried her nails in his shoulder and raked him.

Andrew wasn't a green lad. Though it had been a long long time for him, he'd had women before. He fancied that he understood their psyches. And he knew how to read a woman's response. She wanted this, but couldn't admit it. Something within her held her back.

Though he ached for her to admit it, that need could wait.

For now, he had her in his arms, warm and willing and ready. Determination lanced him.

Holding her gaze, he fisted her skirts, working his way to the hem. Thank God she'd worn skirts and not those damn breeks. A savage howl of delight and excitement and agonizing lust washed through him as his fingers grazed her thighs. She flinched.

"Tell me to stop." A challenge. If she told him to stop, he would. But he didn't think she would.

Her lips parted. Not a word escaped.

He set his palm to her skin, reveling in its warmth. He eased it up, closer and closer to home. "Tell me to stop."

Again, no response, none other than a flicker of her lashes.

He stilled as he found the crux of her thighs, downy soft

and sweet . . . and wet. Lust blazed through him at this proof of her arousal. Aye, lips could lie, but a body never did. He stroked her gently, just a tease.

She sucked in a breath through her teeth.

"Tell me."

She pressed her lips together.

Need churned in his gut. Not just a blinding need to bury himself in her willing body, not just the need to lose himself in her. But need to make her passion, her hunger, meet and match his.

He wanted her weeping for him.

He wanted her to beg.

Slowly he circled her nub, that bundle of nerves, now swollen and tender. She clutched at him as a shiver took her. Her eyes fluttered closed. A whisper escaped. It might have been his name.

Nae. Nae. Nae. He wanted more.

"Tell me," he hissed as he stroked faster and faster still, dancing around her tiny head, scraping her sanity.

He longed to lay her down in the dewy green grass, to cover her, to complete her, to give her what she was panting for, but he would not. Could not. This was a challenge, not a race. He wanted to win, but he wanted to win it all, not just the moment.

"Tell me."

He set the heel of his palm directly over her pearl and pressed down in a circular motion, at the same time, toying with the mouth of her sheath. She trembled, moaned.

She was so wet, so ready, it made his eyes cross. He set his head on her shoulder and forced himself to breathe as he worked her. Steeled his spine. Ah, he wanted her. So badly. But it was far too early for that.

He eased a finger inside her and shuddered as her tiny muscles quivered and quaked and sucked at it. He couldn't

resist nudging deeper and deeper still. Then he ripped his
finger out—she wailed—and he shoved in two.

"Tell me."

"I canna!" she cried, and she came. Released. Surrendered, there in his arms.

It was agonizing, watching her come, and enthralling,
too. As her body closed on him, squeezed and clenched
with maddening frenzy, he could only imagine how delightful it would feel if it were his cock buried deep. But
though his body ached, though his mind screamed and his
cock throbbed, he didn't do the thing they both craved. He
didn't rip down his breeks and spread her thighs and plant
himself in her, there against the tree.

Surely she would have let him.

But he did not.

Perverse though it might be, he wanted more from her
than a quick tup. He needed more. *Craved* something far
more profound.

And though this might be his only chance to claim her,
it was worth the gamble to wait.

He hoped to God it was worth the gamble to wait.

He held her as she recovered, shaking and moaning and
refusing to meet his eyes.

That was all right. He couldn't meet her eyes, either.
Though he was hard and throbbing and definitely unfulfilled, this had been one of the most rewarding encounters
of his life.

Because he'd made Susana Dounreay admit that she
couldn't ask him to stop.

CHAPTER NINE

Susana stared at Andrew as she struggled to reclaim her breath. It seemed to have escaped her. Ripples of delight danced in her veins and her body felt heavy and liquid.

Ach, she hadn't felt such an amazing release since . . . well, since the last time he'd touched her. She wanted, ached for more.

Her hand, surely of its own accord, slipped down and caressed his cock. He was hard. Huge. A shudder racked her. She wanted him. She wanted him in her. She swallowed heavily and licked her lips. And squeezed.

To her dismay, though his nostrils flared, he stepped back, dropping her skirts.

His expression made his intention clear. Though he wanted her—and his need was patently clear—he would not take her.

"Not here," he murmured. His voice rumbled on the air.

Confusion whipped through her; tangled with it was an errant ribbon of frustration . . . and pain.

Why? Why would he not take what she so blatantly offered? She yearned to know, but she didn't know how to ask.

She frowned as she brushed out her skirts and bent to pick up her bow. She hadn't even been aware of dropping it. That in itself should have been warning enough. She avoided his gaze as she arranged the quiver over her shoulder.

At his chuckle, her head snapped up and she glared at him.

"Arming yourself again, Susana?" Surely his smile was a smirk. And why not? He'd gotten what he wanted. He'd gotten her to admit she desired him. But if it was his intention to make her beg for it, he would be sorely disappointed.

"One should always be prepared to defend one's honor."

He missed the barb, or pretended to. Then again, he had no honor. "May I escort you back to the castle?"

She glanced back at the tree, where they had almost . . . Where she had almost succumbed. A ripple of regret nudged her. She forced it away and tossed her head. "Perhaps I shall escort you."

"As you wish."

She started down the path, at a healthy clip. He paced her. They had emerged from the woods and passed through the lea and entered the stable yard before he spoke. "Why did you follow me to the loch?" he asked.

Her heart fluttered. She gaped at him. "Follow you? I dinna follow you."

His expression made it clear he considered this a bold-faced lie.

She hated that he could see through her so easily.

"Were you hoping for another kiss? For what we shared? Maybe more?"

"You are an arrogant ass."

"Why are you angry?"

She walked faster.

"Is it because you wanted more? Are you disappointed?" He took her arm, stopping her in her tracks. "Are you? Disappointed?"

She was furious. That was what she was. She glared at him.

His jaw clenched, ticked. "Do you think I dinna want you back there? Do you think I dinna ache with need?"

"If you were so desperate, you should have taken what was offered."

"Perhaps I shall."

"It willna be offered again."

His eyes glinted. "Oh, I think it will. You canna deny what's between us, Susana. You canna deny how splendid it is."

"Then why did you stop?" God, she hated herself for asking.

"Do you not know?"

"Nae," she spat.

He leaned closer, so close the caress of his breath teased her cheek. "I doona want our first time together to be rushed. I doona want to take you against a tree. And I doona want our first time to be our last. And mostly, I want you to know, beyond a shadow of a doubt, that you want me. As wildly, as hungrily, as passionately as I want you. Do you understand, Susana? Do you?"

He did not wait for her to respond; he spun on his heel and stormed toward the kennels, leaving Susana staring after him.

He'd been so passionate, so sincere, so . . . anguished. She almost believed him.

She would be a fool to believe him.

Most likely, he was toying with her. Most likely, he planned to take what he wanted and then walk away.

What he didn't realize was that she planned to do the same.

ᘓᓫ

It was probably cowardly of her to order breakfast in her room when she returned to the castle, but Susana couldn't take the chance that Andrew might show up in the morning room. She didn't think she could face him across the table.

Not yet.

Blast, but the man befuddled her. One moment she was railing against him, furious and wounded and enraged, and the next she was a puddle of weakness and want. She needed to strengthen her spine, rediscover her balance before she faced him again.

She needed to figure out what to do with him.

On the one hand, she wanted him beyond bearing. On the other hand, he frightened her to death. He held far too much sway over her emotions. And did he but know it, over other things as well.

It delighted her when Isobel opened her door and peeped in without so much as a knock. Normally she would frown and scold her daughter, reminding her of the importance of manners, but this morning she could not. She was far too needful of the distraction of her daughter's cheerful chatter.

"Good morning, darling," she said, waving her in. Isobel grinned at her and kissed her cheek, then surveyed the tray Cook had sent up, licking her lips. Susana chuckled. "Help yourself."

"Och, I'm starved," Isobel said, taking a cake without the bother of a plate.

Though she tried not to, Susana couldn't help but frown. She handed her daughter a plate, which, with a gusted sigh, Isobel proceeded to fill.

"Did you sleep well?"

"Aye." Isobel said, although her attention was on her food. She took the seat across from Susana and tucked in. "Where were you this morning?"

Susana's nerves sizzled. "This morning?"

"I came by earlier and you werna here."

"Ah. I went for a walk."

"Before the sun came up?"

"I do like the dawn." And from her window, she'd seen a certain Viking-like man striding toward the loch.

"Hmm." Isobel took another too-large bite of her cake. It crumbled onto her lap. "Did you walk with *him*?"

Susana stilled. "Him?"

Isobel eyed her with a cynicism far beyond her years. "The knight. I saw the two of you in the courtyard."

"Did you?" Susana swallowed.

"Were you fighting?"

Oh, dear. "Wherever did you get that idea?"

"Every time I see you talking to him, you're frowning."

"I wasna frowning."

"You were. Like this." She made a horrendous face.

"I doona frown like that."

"Aye. You do." Isobel licked a finger. "So, do you no' like him?"

"Like him?" How did one explain the feelings she had for him? She had no clue, but *like* was not one of the words that came to mind.

"Do you?"

"Of course I . . . like him." She took a sip of tea to wash down the lie.

Isobel stabbed a sausage with a fork. "Well, I like him."

"You . . . do?" Her pulse fluttered.

"I told you he was a knight. He rescued me yesterday."

Susana's heart clenched. "He what?"

"Rescued me."

"From . . . what?"

"I was on the roof . . ."

"Isobel Mairi MacBean! I told you not to go on the

roof!" How many times had she told her daughter the mill was far too high for her to climb?

"I know." She swung her feet nonchalantly. "But I wanted to hunt birds. And the view is much better up there."

Her pulse slowed. Up *there*? "Up where?"

"On the turret tower."

Susana gaped. She was capable of nothing more. Her daughter. On the turret tower . . .

Holy God.

Oh, holy God.

"I was climbing and I slipped . . ." The vision played out in her head. A cold hand clutched at her chest. Prickles of sweat erupted on her brow. "But he caught me. He's verra strong."

"Oh, Jesus."

"And verra brave. He climbed up and waited there and when I fell—"

"Mother Mary."

"He caught me."

Susana swallowed. Gulped a breath. Forced a calm, unpanicked tone. "Darling. That sounds . . . verra dangerous."

"That's what he said."

"Did he?"

Isobel wrinkled her nose. "He also said I should listen to you when you tell me no."

"Thank God for that."

"I thought you would like that part." She grinned. Her smile was so like his, it made Susana's heart ping.

"You should never ever do that again. Never. Ever." Dear God. Her mind spun.

Her daughter put out a lip. "I already decided I probably wouldna."

Thank heaven for small favors.

And then, "Probably?"

She shrugged. "You never know. The view is verra fine up there."

"Isobel . . ."

"Yes, Mama?"

Oh, what to say? What to say to a child who didn't like to be told no, one who was incited to rebellion by restrictions?

She covered her daughter's hand with her own. "If anything ever happened to you . . . I couldna . . . I wouldna . . ."

"Mama? Why are you crying?"

"I'm not crying."

"Your cheeks are wet."

"I'm not crying. It's just that you've frightened me verra much."

"Nothing happened."

"You could have been killed."

"But I wasn't." Isobel grinned. "He saved me."

Aye. He had. As much as he annoyed the hell out of her, she couldn't deny that in this, she was very glad he'd been here. That he'd been there. That he'd saved her daughter.

And damn it, that annoyed her, too.

Isobel shot her a superior look. "I told you he was a knight."

This time, Susana did not disagree.

∽

Isobel sat on the garden bench petting her bunny, though it tried very hard not to be petted. In fact, from its struggles, it seemed to want to get away. She tightened her hold and petted harder.

She glanced up as a movement in the corner of her eye caught her attention. The man named Andrew with the silver-blond hair—the man who had vowed not to pat her on the head and tell her to run and play—strolled along the path, though he wasn't looking where he was going. He seemed very pensive indeed.

When he spotted her, his jaw tightened and it seemed as though he was going to turn and stroll in another direction, but he didn't. After a moment's reflection, he continued toward her and took a seat at her side.

"Good morning," he said.

"Good morning."

He peered at the furry bundle nestled in her skirts. "What do you have there?" he asked, although he must have seen one before.

"A bunny."

"A bunny?"

She nodded. "I was going to kill it and then . . ."

"And then what?"

She huffed a sigh. "And then it looked at me."

"It looked at you?"

"And wiggled its nose." She petted its fur. It was soft and smooth. And the bunny hardly quivered at all. "I just couldna do it."

"I understand."

"I couldna help thinking, maybe it's a mama. Maybe it has babies."

"I'm sure the bunny appreciates your mercy."

"And the babies."

"Aye. Them, too."

Isobel's glare was sharp. "Just doona tell my mama. She doesna like weakness."

He huffed a laugh. "Nae. Mercy is not one of her fortes."

He was quiet for a moment. A butterfly flittered by. A bee landed on a flower nearby and explored it. "Though I have to say, Isobel, mercy is not a weakness."

She nodded and petted the quivering bunny again. Then she opened her arms and released it back into the wilds of the garden. It scooted away with the flash of a white tail. She sighed again. "Grandpapa would have liked rabbit stew."

Andrew rubbed her back in a soothing manner that was very pleasant. "I'm sure he'll be happy with mutton."

She wrinkled her nose. "Do you think so?"

He made a face and she laughed. "Nae. No one is really happy with mutton."

They stared out at the garden for a while before she spoke again. Asked him the question that had been nagging at her. "So . . . did you do it?"

His brow wrinkled. It occurred to her he really was a fine-looking man. And he was strong. And he had a sword. He was probably a much better choice as a father than the other one. "Did I do what?"

"Did you seduce my mama yet?"

His face went a little green. His lips worked but he couldn't seem to come up with an answer. She didn't understand his consternation. Either he had or he hadn't.

"A simple yes or no will do."

"Ah, no."

She grunted, wholly unimpressed with him, and wished she hadn't let the bunny go just yet. "Do you think you will?"

"I have to say, Isobel, this conversation makes me uncomfortable."

"Why?"

"It's rather a private matter."

"But you promised to answer all my questions."

"I did. But can you understand that sometimes there are things a person doesna want to share?"

She thought about the turret tower and the beehives and the tiny little fire she might have set in the mill. No one knew about *that*, thank heaven. She certainly didn't want to share it. "Aye. I understand." She tried not to put out a lip. He seemed sincere. He didn't seem to be trying to fob her off. She liked that. And though he hadn't precisely answered her question, he had tried. Aye, she might like him as a father, indeed. If she could convince Mama. "Do you think she's pretty?" she asked.

He blinked. Again, his lips worked. But this time he answered. "I do. Verra much."

"Are you fond of her?"

His throat worked. "Aye."

"Then you should kiss her." She shrugged. "Otherwise she willna know."

He nodded. "Verra wise advice."

"She probably willna like it, though." It was only fair to warn him. He did seem nice and she didn't want to see him pummeled with arrows.

Why he chuckled, she didn't know.

"You should probably sneak it in. From her right side."

"Her, ah, right side?"

Isobel tried not to roll her eyes. For a warrior, he didn't know *anything*. "So she canna reach her bow."

He seemed to pale. "Ah. I see. I shall keep that in mind."

They sat together on the bench and watched the bees flitting from flower to flower. Their soft drone was like music. After a while, she asked, because he really needed to be warned, "Are you going to fight my mama today?"

His gaze was sharper than it should have been. "Where did you hear about that?"

"Everyone is talking about it."

"Are they?"

"Aye." She pinned him with a knowing look. "You're going to lose. Mama is quite skilled with a bow."

He laughed. "I'm quite skilled with a bow as well."

"Perhaps." She sniffed. "But you're going to lose."

It really was a pity, because Mama had no patience for weakness. She would never kiss a man she'd beaten in the lists. She certainly wouldn't *marry* one.

Aye, it was really very sad, because Isobel found she liked Andrew. A lot. He was kind to her and he kept his word, and answered her questions . . . even when it made him uncomfortable. He was handsome, too.

And he had a very impressive sword.

He would have made a good father. Much better than the red-haired man.

It was a shame that after Mama beat him in the lists, she would never ever let him kiss her. Not in a hundred, thousand years.

∽

The competition had a fairlike atmosphere. While Susana had probably not shared the terms of their deal, it was clear she wanted everyone in Dounreay to witness their battle. The archery butts were set up in the bailey against the western wall and as Andrew strode over from the stables, tugging on his glove, he was stunned by the sheer number of people milling about.

Magnus met him at the entrance to the lists. "Is it true?" he asked. "Did you really challenge Susana to a duel?"

Andrew blinked. "Actually, she challenged me."

"But you agreed?" His eyes were wide, his expression perplexed.

"Of course I agreed."

"She's the best archer in this parish."

"And I'm the best archer in mine." He invested his tone with a healthy dose of assurance, but Magnus wasn't convinced. He nibbled his lip.

"What was your wager?"

Andrew checked the tension in his bow and added a little chalk. "What makes you think there was a wager?"

The old man grunted. His eyes skated over the assemblage as though he was searching for someone. His gaze landed on Susana and he nodded. "Because I know my daughter."

Ah, she was breathtaking in a dark-green gown. It brought out the red of her hair and made her alabaster skin gleam.

"Does she often wager with men?"

"Not anymore." Magnus grimaced. "No one is fool enough to take her on."

Andrew's gut shifted. He swallowed. "She's that good?"

"Better. What did you wager?"

"Control."

Magnus's expression made his dismay clear. "Control over what?"

"The defenses."

He rolled his eyes. "Ach, bluidy hell. Ye should have asked me first."

"There wasna a chance." And, in truth, his blood had been running high. Her challenge had only spurred him on. And frankly, it had seemed a good idea at the time.

"She's going ta win."

"You doona know that."

"I'm pretty sure. But good luck." Magnus patted him on the shoulder, shot him a pitying glance, and then he joined the others in the viewing area.

Andrew stiffened his spine and made his way to where Susana stood at the rail, flexing her bow. He tried to ignore

the sinking sensation that he was heading for a dismal
fate.

If he lost, and he had to defer all decisions to her, he
might as well return home with his tail between his legs.
Regardless, none of his men would ever respect him again.

Simply put, he had to win. He had to.

CHAPTER TEN

He didn't win.

Oh, he came close. He hit the center of the target on his first shot. He should probably not have grinned at her then, because she grinned back and her grin was far more arrogant than his.

She lifted her bow and took aim and let fly. He stared in shock as Susana's arrow sliced through the air . . . and then sliced through his, cleaving it in twain. A roar went up in the crowd. He resisted the urge to glare at them, but barely.

Through the entirety of the first round, they were neck and neck, each executing a nearly perfect shot. If he shot first, she impaled his arrow. If she shot first, he flayed hers. The butt was beginning to resemble a hedgehog.

It wasn't until the final arrow of the first round that disaster struck. Susana had the first shot, which she executed with perfection.

Andrew lifted his bow and drew in his breath, carefully sighting along the length of the arrow. Just as he let fly, a gust of wind whipped through the yard and his missile went wide, landing an inch from hers. Dismay curled in his gut as he realized he'd lost the first heat.

Susana turned to him and fixed her features in something resembling sympathy. She patted his arm. "Bad luck, that," she whispered. "Better luck next time."

He attempted not to growl. Instead, he gathered all his

determination and focused on winning the second bout. The arrows were quickly cleared, fresh butts set up, and they were at it again.

It was obvious they were well matched. Arrow after arrow flew true, landing in the butt just where it should, with a satisfying thud. The onlookers were silent, all watching in an awed hush. Andrew glanced up at the sky. Dark clouds had begun to gather, but no one on the grounds moved a muscle.

When another breeze rose up just as Andrew was about to shoot, he dropped his bow and waited.

"Well?" she prompted.

He simply grinned at her, which seemed to irritate her. *Excellent.*

When the breeze died down, he lifted his bow, sighted it, and let fly. His arrow landed perfectly.

Susana frowned at him and took her place.

Just as she released her arrow, a fat raindrop landed on her hand. It must have startled her, because she jerked, and the arrow went high.

The crowd groaned.

Well, it was nice to know who they were rooting for.

Her dismay was evident. She stared at the butt in disbelief. Andrew patted her shoulder and offered a sympathetic smile. "Bad luck, that," he whispered. "Better luck next time."

Her response was a glower. "One more heat," she snapped and whipped a hand in the air, ordering the men to clear the butts.

But just then the sky opened up and the sprinkle of rain became a deluge.

The onlookers squealed and covered their heads and ran for shelter.

Andrew, however, did not. He turned to Susana—

ignoring the spatters of rain on her the bosom of her gown, although they did rather lure his attention. "What do you say?" he asked. "Shall we continue?"

"I'm not afraid of a little rain."

"Nor am I."

When lightning sizzled through the sky, followed by a tremendous clap of thunder, they both flinched.

"Later, perhaps?" he suggested.

He was relieved when she nodded. "Aye. We shall finish this later." She spun and headed for the armory.

Naturally, he followed.

The armory was dimly lit by the watery shafts of light trickling in through the high windows. Susana headed for the back wall.

"Your aim is verra impressive," she said as she set her bow on a rack littered with other bows and rafts of arrows.

He set his beside hers. "As is yours."

She sighed and raked her fingers through her damp hair, shooting a look up at him. It was tinged with a grudging respect. "We are well matched."

"Aye. We are."

Their gazes tangled. He was fairly certain neither was taking about their shooting skills. Not really.

The room was close, musty and dusty, and it smelled of their damp clothes. But Andrew was aware of another scent on the air. He knew it and he knew it well. Their battle had aroused her.

Hell, it had aroused him. A woman who could stand up for herself? A woman who could stand up to him? Who could meet his challenge? Best him? The urge to kiss her scoured him. Although if he was being honest it was, truly, the urge for something more.

"I havena been able to stop thinking about it," he said.

Her brow quirked. "You keep saying that," she muttered on a sigh.

"It's true."

And she knew. She knew what he meant. He could tell from the glint in her eye, the tinge of pink on her cheeks . . . she knew.

He stepped closer and though her nostrils flared, she allowed it. He cupped her cheek, holding her still, though he suspected he didn't need to. His thumb traced the soft skin of her neck. She shivered.

His pulse thrummed as he lowered his head, homing in on those pink and slightly parted lips. He knew their taste, their feel. He ached to possess them again.

"What are you doing?' she murmured, though there was no heat in her words. She trembled before him like a hummingbird.

"Kissing you."

She frowned but didn't step away.

When his lips met hers, that familiar sear of heat raced through him along with a welling excitement. Her taste, her scent, engulfed him. When her mouth parted beneath his, encouraging him, inviting him in, a flame flared in his chest, sending shafts of heat to his groin. His cock, never quiescent around her, rose. The urge to press against her, feel her body melded to his, scorched him.

With a growl, he pushed her back, against the low table. He'd intended to be gentle—probably—but he was not. They hit the table and it banged against the wall. Several arrows fell with a clatter.

He ignored them.

As did she.

She wrapped her arms around his shoulders and twined her fingers through his hair. Tipping her head to the side, she deepened the kiss. It moved from a tender exploration to a scorching demand in a heartbeat.

Glory and exhilaration rang in his heart and soul. There was such perfection in this damp, heated exchange. Such promise.

Arousal rose within him.

Her fingers tightened on his shoulders; his sought and found the dip of her waist, then slowly rose until he claimed the delectable curve of her breast. As his hand closed on her, on the soft, warm weight of her flesh, he moaned. It was delicious. He took her acceptance of this caress as an encouragement to continue.

He'd only intended to steal another kiss. He'd only intended a flirtation, but now, now with her in his arms, warm and willing, with her belly pressing, rubbing against his cock, he was incited to greater daring.

Oh, certainly, this was Susana Dounreay, and there were far too many weapons within her reach. But judging from her sighs and moans, she would probably not skewer him if he tried for more.

Then again, he didn't care.

He leaned her back on the table and she shifted up so she sat as he stood before her. He let his lips wander over the line of her chin and down to her neck. There, her fragrance nearly unmanned him. It was musky and sweet and scented with rain. Soft and silky and heavenly to taste. To nip. To suck.

"Oh!" she cried as he rubbed the spot below her ear with his teeth, even as he found and scraped her nipple. It was hard, that nipple. Swollen and engorged and, apparently sensitive. She wriggled against him; the pleasure was so sharp, he couldn't stop himself from making another pass, and another. And then he took her tender flesh between his fingers and pinched. Oh, gently. Gently for certain.

Her response wasn't gentle in the slightest. She reared back and glared at him, though her eyes were misted over and heavily lidded. Her nostrils flared. She growled. And then she yanked his head back and kissed him again, wildly.

At the same time, she tugged at his tunic, her crazed fingers searching for his skin beneath the leather. When she placed her palm flat on his belly and dragged it over his chest, she groaned.

He wrenched up the hem of her skirts and skated over her silken thigh. His pulse pounded, his muscles shook. Higher and higher he rose, closer and closer to the downy nest at the juncture of her thighs.

When he touched it, when he found it beaded with dampness, his vision went red.

"You're wet," he said in a low rumble.

"It's raining."

He shoved a finger in, deep into her channel. She hissed a sigh and closed about him. The sensation, velvety smooth, yet tight as a vise, sent fire licking through his veins.

Ah, yes. He had intended a flirtation. A kiss.

But hell. He was having more.

She was wet and ready. She was splayed before him, panting and hungry.

Be damned, he was fucking her now.

ᏬᎲ

How he did this to her, she didn't know. Merely a kiss, the exchange of a few words, a wayward caress . . . and she was wild for him. Afire.

She couldn't ignore the hunger that rose within her. It

had been too long. Far too long. Too long since she'd had him. Had any man.

Need raged within her. She knew it was probably a mistake. It was probably an enormous error. It was likely something she would regret come morning, but she wanted him.

If she was truthful, she'd never stopped wanting him.

Her fingers trembled as she unfastened his breeks, but when they closed around his hard, hot length, her surety grew.

Something in his eyes, in the tenor of his groan told her he wanted this, needed this as much as she.

Ah, yes, she might regret it tomorrow, but today's hunger was far too savage to be denied.

She spread her legs and leaned up, offering him entrance. His eyes flared and he took his cock from her keeping, from her tight grip, and eased it in.

Susana nearly swooned as the fat head slipped inside. Long-starved nerve endings screamed their delight. He pressed deeper, wedging inside her, filling her, completing her.

God, it was delicious. Why had she waited so long?

She lifted her legs and wrapped them around his waist and pulled him closer. He drove in with one sure thrust.

As he hit *that* spot, so deep within, her every muscle clenched.

He hissed a groan as she closed on him and then, tightening his hold on her hips, yanked out.

Everything within her rebelled. The emptiness was an aching void, but he didn't torment her for long. He thrust back in, harder this time, deeper. New shivers took her.

"Aye," she muttered. "More."

He complied. His hips picked up speed, and he fucked

her, sluicing in and out in an ever-increasing frenzy. Harder, faster, tighter, he pummeled her, with each lunge, sending greater and greater pleasure through her. Her breath caught, her heart raced, her body burned with an internal flame. It was far too intense, far too exquisite, far too raw. She didn't think she could survive this. She didn't think she could bear it. The tension increased, closed down on her, threatened to shatter her sanity.

She clasped him tightly, holding him close, savaging the flesh of his back with her nails in her frenzy to urge him on. "More" she huffed into his ear. "More."

And ah, he gave her more.

The sounds of flesh slapping flesh ringed the small, shadowed room. Their grunts and groans twined.

His movements became shorter, sharper. His cock swelled, filling her completely. Each slide drove her higher and higher into the ether. Each thrust sent shards of indescribable delight sluicing along every nerve, making her mindless and mad.

Helpless, hopeless, battered by bliss, she broke. Mind spinning, soul wrapped in exquisite pleasure, she released.

He wasn't far behind. Indeed, her crisis incited his. As she clenched him, barraging him with a hellish raft of shivers, he tossed back his head and hissed, "Susana," and he flooded her. Flooded her with a delicious heat.

When his body stopped shaking and the shudders had quieted to mere ripples, he relaxed against her. She could feel the thrum of his heart through the layer of his tunic and her dress. His weight was warm and delicious and she couldn't help wishing they were melded, skin-to-skin.

She kissed his neck, reveling in the gruff scratch of his beard against her cheek, and sighed. He murmured something unintelligible and eased back, but she locked her legs. Holding him in. She didn't want it to end. Not yet.

The connection, the closeness was far too enjoyable and she'd been alone for too long.

He chuckled and lifted his head. "I told you we were well matched."

"I dinna disagree."

His grin was provoking.

"What?" she muttered, but there was a lightness to her tone, one she hadn't tasted in a long long time.

He raised and hand and cupped her cheek. Thumbed her lips. "It is only . . . that's the first time you havena disagreed with me," he said.

"That's hardly true."

"It is."

She narrowed her eyes. "Are you trying to start a quarrel?" Seriously? At a time like this? When he was still buried deep within her?

"Nae," he blurted. And then he repeated himself, more softly, in a low rumble. "Nae. I'd rather not quarrel. I'd rather do this."

His lips touched hers, teased them. He sucked in her lower lip and she felt her desire stir again. Could it be that, even though he had sated her completely, she still wanted him?

But in truth, she didn't want to quarrel, either. Not when she had him in her arms. Not when his body was warm against hers and his tongue danced delight on her neck. Ah, she was weak and she knew it. At the moment she didn't care.

"In fact . . ." He lifted his head and stared at her and while she was annoyed that he'd stopped that delicious drizzle of exploration, she liked the look in his eyes.

"In fact . . . what?"

"What if we never have the third heat?" he said softly.

Susana's pulse fluttered. "Never have the third heat?"

"What if we call it a draw? Right here and now. What if we agree . . . to both be in charge."

She gaped at him. "Both of us?"

"Working together. Do you no' think, with our combined brilliance, we could outstrategize any villain?"

She tipped her chin to the side. "Are you saying I'm brilliant?"

"I'm saying you are verra brilliant. And clever and beautiful."

"You're . . . not so bad yourself."

He chuckled. "Doona overwhelm me with compliments."

"I wouldna dare." He did ease away then, slipping from her; she quivered as yet another shower of delight rippled through her at his passing. She pushed down her skirts as he fastened his breeks and she tried not to dwell on the mortifying fact that neither of them had bothered to undress for this mating. Then again, there had been no time. One kiss and the frenzy had consumed them.

It should frighten her, the ease with which he seduced her, but she was woman enough to admit that her need had been powerful and his allure had been strong.

And she was woman enough to admit she'd missed this. Missed him.

No other man made her feel like this. Ever.

She'd never *wanted* another man. She'd married Gilley upon her return, aye, because she knew she was with child and couldn't bear to dishonor her father's name, but also because she knew Gilley wasn't the kind of man who would ever demand *this* of her.

And he never had.

She'd lived the past six years untouched. Unloved. Alone. Though surrounded by family and friends and beset with the business of her life, she'd walked each day in utter isolation.

When the desire rose—and it often did, as she was a passionate soul—she would force it down, back down into the deep dark well of her soul.

It only stood to reason that when *he* resurfaced in her life, the one man she craved, it was only a matter of time before this happened.

And she couldn't regret it. It had been wonderful.

Joy and fulfillment bubbled up. When Andrew glanced at her and their gazes tangled, and he offered her that boyish grin, the one that had stolen her heart all those years ago, she had to slip into his arms and kiss him again. "Thank you for that," she said. "It was lovely."

It surprised her that he frowned. "It wasna lovely . . ."

"What?" She glared at him. Disappointment and discontent twined in her chest.

He ran his fingers through his hair and blew out a sigh. "It was. It was lovely. Susana . . . it was perfect. But . . ."

She narrowed her eyes. "But what?"

He threw out his arms, gesturing to the swords and bows and spears arranged along the walls. "This is hardly the place I would have chosen to seduce you for the first time."

It was hardly the first time, but she wasn't telling him that. Instead she sent him a minxish grin. "It is the perfect place. For a woman like me."

He stilled. Perhaps noticing the coquettish tone in her voice. Or her fingers trailing along his muscled thigh. And damn, it was muscled. She wanted to see it, touch it, taste it, bare. "A woman like you? A warrior princess?"

"Is that how you think of me?"

"Aye. How could I not?" He adjusted the angle of her

bodice, which had somehow become rumpled. "A room like this arouses you?" He posed it as a question, but it was not.

He stepped closer and pulled her into his arms again. She recognized the glimmer in his eye. She certainly recognized the rising bulk of his passion.

He was ready for another go.

For that matter, so was she.

"I would much prefer a bed," he murmured against her lips. "A soft bower with . . ." He tapped one of the arrows. "Fewer pointy things."

"Perhaps that can be arranged." The words were whispered, but he heard. His lips on hers quirked. His body firmed.

"Tonight, perhaps—"

The door slammed open and they flew apart. Susana quickly bent to pick up the arrows he'd knocked to the floor in his passion to get at her. She glanced up, pretending surprise when she saw Keir in the doorway. He stood with his hands on his hips and a frown on his face. His gaze flicked from Susana to Andrew and back again.

"Perhaps a soft bower without . . . interruptions," Andrew said in an aside.

Susana nibbled her lips to keep back an inappropriate smile.

"There you are," Keir said. He stepped into the armory, ducking his head to avoid a row of crossbows hanging from the low rafters. "I was wondering where you'd gone." He shot a look at Andrew. "The rain has stopped. Are you ready to finish the duel?"

"Ah . . ." Susana set the arrows back in their quivers and leaned them against the wall. When they slipped again, Andrew helped her right them. "We've been talking, Keir . . ."

"Talking?" He said the word in a sharp tone, as though he suspected, or perhaps smelled, what had really happened here.

"We're calling it a draw," Andrew said, taking her arm in a message stronger than any words. "We'll be working together from now on."

Keir's features closed into a tight ball that looked a little like petulance, but he recovered quickly, arranging his expression into something bland and unreadable. "Very good, my lady." He gave a curt bow, spun on his heel, and left the building.

Susana stared after him. She'd suspected he'd had a tendre for her, but their relationship had never been anything more than cordial. She'd absolutely never given him cause to think she had *that* kind of interest in him. She could only imagine that his pique stemmed from his displeasure over being replaced as the man in charge of Dounreay defenses. She hoped he wasn't too upset with her decision, but really, it was for the best.

She turned to Andrew and found him studying her solemnly, as though he could read her emotions. Which was silly. Just like every other man, he was oblivious to much. A muscle ticked in his cheek. "Are you all right?" he asked.

She forced a smile. "Keir will come around. Doona worry. If I command my men to work with you, they will."

∾

It was probably inappropriate to feel like a conquering hero as he emerged from the armory with Susana on his arm, but Andrew couldn't quash the feeling. Exhilaration, joy, and utter satisfaction swamped him.

It was more than the thrill a man felt when he chased and caught his prey. It was more than the contentment in the lingering pleasure of an extraordinarily satisfying fuck. It was far beyond that.

Because it was Susana.

Not only had she allowed him to make love to her—in an armory, no less—she'd encouraged him. Incited him.

The gratification hit him deep, where he lived.

The woman he wanted, more than he wanted his next breath, wanted him, too.

And beyond that, this had been but the first foray of their relationship. He could only hope for more.

When he'd mentioned a next time, she had not demurred. Nae. She had smiled.

He glanced down at her as they emerged into the bailey. She wiggled her shoulders until he realized she meant for him to drop his arm and his mood dipped, but only slightly. Of course she didn't want anyone to see his arm around her. Didn't want anyone to witness their affinity. This was far too new.

But damn, he didn't want to stop touching her.

What he wanted was to kiss her.

What he really wanted was to find that secluded bower . . . and fuck her again.

But he merely smiled and bowed and said, "Will I see you at dinner tonight, my lady?"

He invested a low thrum in his tone and while on the surface, the invitation seemed innocent enough, he could tell from her flush that she had divined his true meaning. He didn't give a good goddamn about dinner. He only cared about seeing her again.

Her lashes fluttered. "Aye."

"Excellent."

Her smile flickered again and then she turned to make her way back to the castle through the puddles in the bailey. He couldn't rip his gaze from her and was rewarded when she looked back, not once, but thrice.

He didn't stop watching until she disappeared from sight, and even then, it was difficult to turn away.

It helped that Hamish sidled up next to him and nudged him with his shoulder. "Well," he gusted. "That was an interesting duel."

Aye. It had been, indeed. But not a duel so much as a dance. A frantic, impassioned, exhilarating dance.

"When are you going to finish it?"

Andrew blinked. "Finish it?"

"The duel."

"Oh, it's finished." The battle between them was finished, but the war wasn't over. Not by a long shot.

"And who won?"

"We both did, I think." He nibbled at his triumphant smile, then added more soberly, "She and I agreed to work together."

"Did you?" He didn't like the contemplative light in Hamish's eyes. "Interesting."

"Indeed. It was a successful . . . negotiation."

They both chuckled as they made their way up into their loft. As they rounded the corner of the staircase, Andrew's steps stalled. Though it had stopped raining, the damage to their rooms had been done. The pallets lay in fat puddles, and drops still pooled from the ceiling.

"The least you could have done was negotiate better sleeping arrangements," Hamish murmured.

Andrew couldn't help but bite back a grin. "Believe me, I'm working on it."

CHAPTER ELEVEN

Susana stared at her reflection in the mirror as she read-
ied herself for dinner. The smile teasing her lips concerned
her a little, but she couldn't banish it. Her mad passionate
tryst with Andrew in the armory had been nothing short
of glorious.

Oh, she still knew she was a fool for feeling the way
she did about him, for allowing him to kiss her, to touch
her. But all that was eclipsed by complete and utter satisfaction.

She'd seduced him and he wasn't even aware *he* was the
one who'd been used.

Beyond the physical pleasure, there was a deep contentment curling in her soul. He'd wanted her as much as she
wanted him. And that tryst wouldn't be the last one. The
glimmer in his eye was a testament to his intent.

A quiver walked through her. She would see him again.
And soon. Perhaps after dinner, they could go for a walk.
The armory was deserted in the evenings . . .

With a smile on her face, she made her way down to
the library, where Papa usually enjoyed a drink before
dinner. Her pulse surged when she entered the room to see
that Hamish and Andrew had already arrived. Keir was
there as well. It wasn't a surprise. Before the troops from
Dunnet had arrived, he'd often dined with the family,
though the conversation frequently revolved around their
defenses. It would be interesting to watch the interaction

among the men, but it would be a good opportunity to underscore her decision to support Andrew's efforts, and nip Keir's reservations in the bud.

Isobel was there, too, which caused Susana a momentary flare of panic. She and Andrew sat across from each other at the table by the window, and he was instructing her on the various uses of chessmen.

Seeing the two of them so close together, their nearly identical faces nose-to-nose, caused a pang in her chest.

Papa believed Isobel needed a father and Susana had always insisted she did not, that no woman *needed* a man. But now, in this moment, she questioned her resolve. Had it been naught but a reflection of her own pain? Had she robbed her daughter of something precious?

When the men saw her enter the room, they all stood, all but Papa, because his hip was paining him. He did, however, lift his glass to her.

"Good evening," she said.

"Susana." Keir bowed. "You look lovely."

Susana blinked. Keir had never made mention of her appearance, for good or ill. That he did so now, with a determined gleam in his eye, was surprising.

"Verra lovely," Hamish chimed in.

"Aye," a deep voice from the window rumbled. "Verra lovely." She couldn't stop her attention from swinging that way. Her gaze clashed with Andrew's. His burned, lighting a flicker of desire in her womb. Though to be honest, it was still burning there, that ember he'd stoked this afternoon. Likely it wouldn't take much to set it ablaze again.

Hopefully not at the dinner table.

A shiver shot through her and she turned away. "Thank you."

"Look, Mama!" Isobel chirped. "I'm learning chess."

Susana tried not to sigh. How many times had she

attempted to interest her daughter in the game of strategy? She'd shown no interest whatsoever. Apparently Andrew's allure knew no age limits.

Isobel held up the horse. "This one is called a knight." She waggled her brows in a meaningful manner.

Susana grinned and sauntered nonchalantly to the window. Hopefully no one noticed her eagerness to stand by his side. To feel his warmth. To breathe his scent. "Ah. The knight. I assume that one is your favorite?"

"Aye." Isobel winked and galloped the knight over the board.

"I prefer the queen, myself," Andrew murmured. Hopefully, Susana was the only one who noticed the evocative way he fondled the piece. And his scorching expression. And the telling way his tongue dabbed his lips.

Honestly, they needed no wetting whatsoever. They were quite tempting as they were.

"Mama?"

She blinked and ripped her gaze from Andrew's. Surely she hadn't been gaping at him? "Yes, darling?"

"Did you know there's a hole in the roof of the kennels?"

"I . . . what?"

Isobel nodded. "A huuuge hole." She spread her arms wide apart to illustrate the hugeness of the hole.

"Surely it is not that large."

"It is large enough," Hamish chuckled from behind her, and Susana spun to face him. "Our billets are flooded."

She glanced at Andrew—why, she didn't know—and he nodded with a chagrined expression. "Our pallets are soaked through."

"A pity that." Hamish sighed in a decidedly melodramatic warble. "We loved those pallets."

She nibbled her lip. "Did you?"

"Aye."

"Well, this is terrible news," Papa boomed. Surely he didn't need to boom. They were all in the same room. "We shall have to find some other place to house the men. What do you think, Susana?"

She was used to this. Papa pretending to ask her advice when he really just wanted her to give him what he wanted. He'd been badgering her to move the men into the castle since they'd arrived. She couldn't have, of course. It would have been tantamount to admitting defeat.

But now . . .

But now it didn't feel like defeat at all. She and Andrew had decided to work together. It was only right that his men should be comfortable. In rooms with real beds. With an actual roof over their heads. A mocking voice in the back of her head added that if he were staying in the castle, he would be far more accessible. She ignored it.

It made sense to move the men into the castle. But she had no intention of making her acquiescence easy . . . on any of them. It simply wasn't in her nature to do so.

She tapped her lip. "Aye, Papa. You are right. We canna allow those men to stay in ruined quarters."

Andrew and Hamish exchanged triumphant smiles, but to her right Keir bristled.

"I believe we have a lovely space beneath the mill," she said.

Hamish *eep*ed and Papa snorted, but Susana ignored them and continued on.

"Aye, it's filled with sacks of grain and supplies. But it shouldna take long to move them." She sent Hamish a playful wink. "There are hardly any bugs."

"My lady. Please." Hamish held out his hands. "Show mercy."

"There are some lovely hallways beneath the ramparts. Of course, the men will have to sleep head-to-toe, but they are valiant warriors, are they not? Used to such conditions? Oh, and for that matter, the orchard is lovely this time of year." She flicked a look at Keir. "Do we not have some tents in the stores?"

Keir nodded, with a determined expression on his face. Clearly her sarcasm had escaped him.

Not so Andrew. It was evident from the glimmer in his eye, the reluctant twist of his lips, and the blossom of dimples in his cheeks, he knew she was only teasing.

Isobel patted Andrew on the hand. "You can stay with me," she whispered.

Susana blanched. Dear lord. Enough teasing.

She sighed heavily. "Ah, well. I suppose the east wing would be the best place for them."

Papa, clearly relieved, grunted.

"I shall see to it . . . after dinner."

Keir leaped to his feet, his brow drawn tight. "My lady?"

"Aye, Keir," she said with a smile to soften his disgruntlement. It didn't help. "If we are to work fist in glove with these men, it is best if they are well rested."

"And dry," Hamish murmured in an aside.

And when Andrew added, in a whisper, "In a secluded bower . . ." a shudder racked her. She shot him a reproachful glare, but then ruined it with a smile.

Tamhas entered the room and announced that dinner was served, and they all headed for the dining room. As she made her way down the hall, Isobel threaded her fingers in Susana's. She peeped up and, eyes wide with innocence, asked, "Mama, what's a secluded bower?"

୨୦

It was an excellent start to the evening.

Not only was Andrew able to see Susana again, and flirt with her quite subtly, she had relented on the matter of their ghastly lodgings. He was very happy for his men's sake, but truth be told, he was happier for himself.

Now he would be near her. Possibly just down a hallway.

That meant—possibly—a full night in her arms. Maybe many.

For the first time since his exile here, he was truly delighted with his fate.

What were the odds? He'd come here empty-hearted and discouraged. He'd been sure he would never find that feeling he ached for. And now, not only had he found a woman who ignited his soul, she shared in his desire for an exploration between them. With this move from the kennels, the opportunities for seduction were boundless.

As she took her seat on Magnus's right, he sat across from her. He couldn't help but notice Keir's frown. No doubt he thought this seat his spot. Andrew didn't care. He wanted to sit across from Susana, so he could stare at her all evening.

It only irritated him a little that, with a huff, Keir took the spot by her side.

Isobel slid into the seat beside him. She peered up at him and fluttered her lashes. Something uncomfortable curled through him. She was a beautiful girl, though something of a termagant. And she'd taken a liking to him. He wasn't sure if that was good or bad, but he knew if he wanted to make headway with Susana, a good relationship with her daughter couldn't hurt.

Hamish, faced with the choice of sitting beside Keir or Isobel, chose the latter.

As he settled in and the footman approached with the wine, something nudged his foot. He glanced across the table at Susana and she sent him an innocent look. Behind that look, though, there was a wicked intent. His pulse leaped.

The minx! Was she teasing him beneath the table?

Indeed, her toe, her luscious—from what he could gather, *bare*—toe, crawled up his ankle. A quiver rippled through him at the light in her eye, the way her lips quirked in a challenging way. He kicked off his shoe and reciprocated. He loved the way her features softened as he made his way up her calf, beneath her skirts.

It was damn annoying that the table was too wide for him to reach past her knee. He probably could, if he slouched, but he didn't dare.

As they made their way through the first course, he played with her, stroked her, and she did the same, causing a cauldron of lust to boil within him. Damn, she was a tantalizing piece of froth.

Conversation flowed around them, a desultory discussion of the weather and the crops and the recent influx of herring. Or something like that. Andrew was hardly paying attention.

All the while, Isobel, between bites, stared at him. He tried to ignore her as well, but it was far more difficult.

"I doona like soup," she announced, apropos of nothing. Andrew could only ascertain that she'd been feeling left out of the conversation. She peeped at him. "Do you?"

With a glance at Susana, he removed his foot, which had been dancing over her delightful instep. As much as he was enjoying their play, it just didn't seem right to continue . . . while he was discussing the merits of soup with her daughter. That Susana put out a lip at his retreat was gratifying.

"I do like soup. I suppose." He took a spoonful to illustrate his point.

Isobel wrinkled her nose. "It seems so pointless."

"Pointless?"

She leaned closer and whispered, "It's mostly broth."

"It's verra healthy," Susana suggested.

"I'd much rather have cake."

"I'd much rather have cake as well," Hamish confided, although this was hardly a secret. He'd recently made friends with the castle baker, a lovely and plump morsel named Saundra who, apparently, reveled in the opportunity to provide him with . . . sweets.

"Well, perhaps we can have dessert . . . after dinner." Susana's foot found his again, nudging him with an unmistakable intent. Andrew nearly came out of his chair.

"I should verra much like dessert . . . after dinner," he murmured, catching her gaze. Though he thought he was being subtle, he most likely was not because Hamish snorted, and Keir glared at him.

Magnus simply took another sip of his whisky. "Of course there will be dessert after dinner," he grumbled, motioning for a refill. "But since we have you all together, we should perhaps talk about your thoughts on our defenses?" He shot a meaningful look at Andrew.

"Aye. Of course . . ." As the subsequent courses came and went, and everyone enjoyed a delicious repast—all but Isobel, who complained that each dish was not cake— Hamish and Andrew shared their observations on where the fortifications were lacking.

As the litany continued—as they had found many weaknesses—Keir's demeanor soured. Clearly the man felt Andrew's critique was a criticism of his work. Andrew made every effort to compliment him where accolades were due, but it didn't seem to help.

Probably because there wasn't much room for praise.

Keir seemed to be an intelligent man, and seemed to

have experience in this, so his errors and omissions were confounding.

In fact, if he didn't know for a fact that Keir was loyal to Susana—possibly enamored of her—Andrew would suspect he was deliberately trying to undermine their security.

For her part, Susana listened to his arguments with an intent and increasingly concerned expression. When Andrew mentioned there were no men stationed in the tower, and no warning system in place in the event of attacks in the far-flung crofts, her considering gaze flicked to her captain of the guard. When he caught her studying him, he flushed and tightened his jaw.

As Andrew and Hamish finished their report, Magnus sat back in his chair and drummed his fingers on the table. "I canna tell you how much we appreciate your assessment," he said. "Although I do find it eye opening to realize how vulnerable we are."

"Aye." Andrew nodded. They were, indeed vulnerable. "But Hamish and I have a slate of ideas, easily implemented, that will fix matters."

Susana leaned forward. "Please tell us more."

God, he loved that expression on her face, the gleam in her eye, the rapt focus of her attention—on him. It wasn't sexual in any way. In fact, her playful mood had been replaced by her concern for her people.

It didn't matter.

In fact, it pleased him that she wanted, needed something more from him than just kisses. It pleased him that he could offer her more of himself.

As the mutton and beef courses were served, followed by a syllabub, he and Hamish outlined their plan. With each idea, Susana nodded. With each suggestion, Keir's frown darkened, but the man said nothing.

When he and Hamish finished sharing the last of it, Susana blew out a breath. She exchanged a look with her father. "It appears we have much work to do," she said.

"Aye." Magnus nodded. "First thing tomorrow we should all meet again and finalize our plans." He nodded at Andrew. "Your men are ready?"

He grinned. "Aye. Even more so if they get a good night's sleep." He couldn't resist a glance in Susana's direction. He wasn't sure if her flush stemmed from chagrin that she'd been trenchant in her resolve to keep his men from sleep, or if it was a shy confirmation that she intended to keep him from it tonight. In a secluded bower somewhere . . .

He hoped for the latter.

"Excellent," Magnus huffed. "But first . . ." He gestured to Saundra, the plump baker, who entered with a platter of cakes. "Dessert."

"Ah . . ." Hamish murmured, his expression far too sultry for the dinner table. "Dessert."

Isobel slurped her lips. "Yum."

Saundra rounded the table, having the good sense to begin with Hamish, or possibly Isobel. As she leaned between them, displaying her bosom to his friend, Susana's foot nudged him once more.

Ah. *Dessert.* He smiled and nudged back, then snaked his toe up the back of her thigh. Even as he realized her leg was at the wrong angle, he also realized it was far too muscled.

His attention whipped to Magnus to find the man gaping at him. His eyes narrowed—swung from Andrew to Susana and back again—and then he jerked his leg away.

A red tide crept up Andrew's neck as he realized he'd been playing footsie with his host.

Magnus grumbled something beneath his breath about needing more whisky, and he turned away, but not before Andrew saw his pointed glance at Susana. In response she plastered an innocent mien on her face and folded her fingers on the table.

When Saundra offered her a cake, she demurred. Gazing at him through veiled lashes, Susana murmured, "I think I'll have dessert later . . . in my room."

Hopefully no one but Andrew caught her meaning.

Hopefully no one noticed his flush.

Hopefully no one realized his cock was hard and straining in his breeks.

At the dinner table, of all places.

∽

Anticipation sizzled through Susana as the meal ended and they all stood. She tried very hard not to glance at Andrew, not to stare, but damn, he was alluring, with that seductive look in his eye.

She knew—*knew*—they would be together tonight, and the thought made her knees weak.

It was frustrating that first she had to oversee the move of his men from the kennels into the east wing of the castle. Who knew how long that would take? She prickled with impatience.

It was also frustrating that Keir caught her arm as she headed off to attend to this duty.

"A word, my lady?" His tone was low, as though he didn't want anyone to hear.

"Aye?" She tried not to snap, but exasperation railed her. She knew he wasn't pleased with the recent developments. He probably resented having outsiders come in and critique his work—and find it wanting. He'd certainly bristled with every suggestion the men had made.

Granted, she had urged Keir to flout their mission, to delay and interfere wherever he could—and she felt the sting of remorse for that. It had been childish at best and foolish at worst. The gaps in their defenses Andrew and Hamish had outlined had horrified her.

He nodded toward the study. "In private?"

Susana sighed and glanced back at Andrew. He was chatting with Isobel and Papa. She sighed. "All right."

He led her into the study and when the door closed, he spun on her. "My lady, we canna allow them to take over the defenses."

"Keir—"

"We doona know these men. *You* doona know these men. You canna trust them."

Her brow rumpled. "Dunnet sent them."

Keir leaned closer and whispered, "I've heard rumors."

"Such as?"

His eyes narrowed. "Such as Dunnet is in league with Stafford. That he married Hannah with the sole purpose of gaining her lands . . . and then turning them over to the marquess."

Something cold clutched at her chest. The thought— that Hannah had married a man, was bound to a man, who would use her so, betray her heart—was sickening. But upon consideration, such a plot hardly made sense. "Why-ever would he do that?"

"There are rumors that Stafford is soon to be named the Duke of Sutherland."

Bile rose. "And?"

"We all know the Duke of Caithness is weak. An absentee laird at best." Aye. Their overlord had never even set foot in the Highlands, as far as Susana could tell. "Dunnet is working to undermine his hold on the county."

"How can a baron undermine the power of a duke?"

"Inciting treason. A group of barons are working together to rally the parishes against the duke."

Her stomach tightened. If Dunnet did such a thing, he could be hanged. And then where would Hannah be? "How on earth would that benefit him?"

"If he can succeed, if the barons of Caithness rise up against the duke, the Prince Regent will have to take note."

Susana shook her head. At what cost to Hannah's husband? To Hannah herself?

"Do you no' see? Dunnet hopes to discredit the duke. If Caithness is removed or replaced, Stafford is the obvious choice. There are already rumors that the prince is inclined to hand all the lands in the county over to him."

Susana shook her head. It all seemed so Machiavellian.

Keir sighed. "Dunnet is in league with him. With Stafford. The man who burned out our crofts and has tried on numerous occasions to claim your land. He couldn't claim Reay through Hannah . . . and now that she's married to Dunnet, the only way Stafford can gain the lands he so desires is by working with Dunnet." His gaze intensified. "I warn you, my lady. Watch Andrew Lochlannach. Watch him like a hawk. I'm convinced he's working for our enemy. He and Dunnet are determined to bring us down."

Susana swallowed heavily. This was, indeed, an appalling prospect.

And also odd.

Though Keir was adamant and spoke with conviction, the facts didn't add up.

Something beyond her innate sense that Andrew, while cocky and arrogant and handsome beyond what was good for him, was not an evil man. Or manipulative. Or sly.

She hadn't gotten that sense from him, or Hamish, in any interaction they'd had—even when she'd been convinced Andrew had come to her from the very bowels of hell itself.

Keir, on the other hand, had good reason to lie to her. Good reason to foment her fear. Especially if he was worried he might lose his position as the captain of the guard. Indeed, his focus on her face was far too intent.

She forced a smile, though it wobbled. "I will think about this, Keir."

"Do." His response was nearly a snarl, so ferocious, it startled her. "And my lady?"

"Aye?"

"Keep away from Andrew Lochlannach."

"I beg your pardon?"

"I've seen the way he looks at you."

So had she. She rather liked it.

"The man has designs on you."

Hopefully.

"He cannot be trusted."

"Keir—"

"I know I've never said anything, but . . ."

Oh, dear. He stepped close, far too close. His gaze locked on her mouth.

She placed a hand on his chest, to halt his advance. It did not. He pressed her against the door, pinioning her there with his muscled body. "Keir?"

"I've always wanted you, Susana," he murmured, just before his lips covered hers.

It was a harsh, desperate kiss and there was little passion in it, which was fine. She hardly wanted passion from Keir. It complicated her life immeasurably. Her captain of the guard was jealous of her and resentful of Andrew and willing to spin a web of lies and fears to maintain his control of her.

She liked this man, and respected him. She didn't want to reject him outright, but she couldn't tolerate this kind of liberty.

"Now, Keir," she said, pushing him away. He allowed this, but begrudged every step. Forcing a lighthearted smile, she said, "You know how I deal with suitors." It was a blatant reminder that she had a tendency to shoot them in the arse.

He studied her for a moment. His eyes narrowed, as though he was searching for something—her conviction, perhaps—and then he nodded.

"Aye, my lady." He tugged down his jerkin and affected a bow. "I'm sorry, my lady. But . . . I just couldn't let it go unsaid. I have . . ." His throat worked. "Loved you for a long time."

Susana blinked. Well, this was a surprise. He'd been protective and attentive, but never loverly in the slightest. She didn't know what to say. She had no interest in him. No interest whatsoever, especially since the advent of a tall, muscled man with white-blond hair and the devil's dimples. "I so appreciate that, Keir. I do. And I appreciate your service. Your willingness to share the information you hear with me."

"You will be wary of him?"

"Him?"

"Lochlannach. Mark my words, he means trouble for us all. We must watch his every move with a vigilant eye."

"Of course I shall be vigilant," she said, and then she turned and left the room, left Keir standing there with a brooding frown on his face.

Oh, she would watch Andrew's every move with a very vigilant eye.

Starting tonight.

CHAPTER TWELVE

Why Andrew felt like a criminal as he slunk through the drafty castle halls, he didn't know. Probably because he was slinking. Probably because he had mischief on his mind. Probably because he really didn't want to be caught before he reached his destination. Whatever the reason, Andrew's heart thudded with exhilaration and anticipation and perhaps a touch of trepidation as he neared Susana's chambers and tapped on her door.

She could very well kick him out.

Hell, she could very well toss him in the dungeon—this was Susana—but he didn't think she would. She had, after all, whispered directions to her rooms as the dinner party had broken up.

She didn't greet him as he'd expected, imagined—with a scalding kiss. As he entered her room, she crossed her arms. "Did you get settled in your new accommodations?"

"Aye." He stepped toward her; she retreated. His unease rose.

"Are they satisfactory?"

"Aye." He advanced on her again. Again, she retreated. Concern rippled through him. He didn't like the way she eyed him. So he stopped in the middle of the room. Though he wanted nothing more than to leap on her and kiss her . . . and more, he restrained himself. Something was bothering her, and he intended to soothe her mind before he began his seduction.

"Where did you go after dinner?"

"Keir wanted to talk to me."

"I can imagine he did."

"He doesna like relinquishing control."

He quirked a brow. "Sound like anyone you know?"

She smiled, though it was clear she hadn't intended to, as she nibbled it away. She turned to the window and threaded her fingers together. He studied her reflection. Concern riffled her brow. Obviously there was more to it than Keir's obstinacy.

"What else did he say?"

She blew out a breath and spun to face him. "He did share some concerning thoughts." Her lashes flickered. "May I ask you a question?"

He spread his hands. "Anything."

"Your brother . . ."

Andrew blinked. Why would she want to talk about Alexander?

"Is he . . . a loyal man?"

"Aye." The most loyal man Andrew knew.

"Would he ever . . . consider . . . treason?"

"Treason?" Andrew's pulse lurched. "Is that what Keir said?" He would pound him to a bloody pulp for maligning his family name.

"Would he?"

"Nae. Never." He could no longer stay still. He stalked across the room and folded her into his arms. "What did Keir imply?"

"That Alexander was plotting against the Duke of Caithness."

Andrew blew out a breath on a laugh. "Oh. That."

Her head jerked up. She gaped at him. He couldn't help kissing her brow. It was wonderful having her in his arms again.

"He is resisting an order Caithness gave him."

She backed away, her eyes wide and filled with suspicion.

Andrew sighed. "It was the order to clear the land, Susana. Caithness ordered Alexander to clear Dunnet and he refused." Of course he refused. It was a heinous order, exiling the crofters to import sheep.

Susana's nose wrinkled. "Those Clearances are a nuisance."

"Aye. That's how Alexander feels about it. And, aye, he's willing to defy even the Duke of Caithness on this point."

"And Keir's supposition that your brother is in league with Stafford?"

Andrew gaped at her. Then he barked a laugh. Keir must truly be desperate to create such a fiction. "Stafford? The man who wanted Hannah to wed his son?"

Susana tapped her lip. "Aye. It didn't make any sense to me, either. But it did make me worry for Hannah."

"Hannah is fine." He stepped toward her again, and this time she nestled into his arms. Where she belonged.

"Are she and Dunnet happy together?"

"I believe they are." He tucked his chin and gazed down at her. "They seem to be quite besotted with each other."

"Do they?" Did she sound cynical, or hopeful? "I do worry about her."

"Know this, Susana. He will protect Hannah with every ounce of his energy. With his every breath. It's the kind of man he is."

"It eases my heart to know that. She is so verra dear."

"She is a wonderful woman." When Susana's brow rippled, he hurried to add, "Perfect for Alexander."

"Perfect?"

"She's just what he needed. She's . . . verra good for him."

"Good for him?"

"He's had a difficult life. Challenges. She accepts him for the man that he is. She strengthens him." He stroked her arm and let his fingers trail down to her waist. "It is how it should be between a man and a woman. Each gives the other something of themselves. Each bolsters the other." She seemed to realize he was no longer talking about Hannah. Her hands began to wander as well.

It was a tentative time between them, a fragile time, as they explored each other—really explored each other. The tryst in the armory hardly counted. It had been a mad frenzy of lust, not this gentle examination. Though it wasn't her body he studied, nor she his. It was something deeper. Something more. Their gazes tangled; it felt as though their souls tangled, too.

"I enjoyed dinner," she murmured.

"As did I."

She lifted her foot and stroked his.

"You are a naughty girl," he said.

"You are a naughty boy."

He couldn't hold back a chuckle. "I thought your father was going to come out of his skin when I accidentally found his foot instead of yours."

Her eyes widened. Her body shook with laughter. "You dinna!"

"Aye. I did. He nearly yelped."

"Puir man."

"He likely willna sit between us again."

"That would be wise."

They shared a smile, which made his attention drift to her mouth, her lips. Her tongue as it peeped out in an undeniable invitation.

"Ach, Susana," he muttered. "It's been far too long."

"Mmm." She tangled her fingers in his hair, scraped his scalp with her nails, and drew his head down. "Far too long."

And then, she kissed him.

∾

Ah, how wonderful it was to taste him again. All through dinner, his touch, his glances had enflamed her. His scent had tormented her.

It had been difficult to concentrate on their discussion, though it had been an important one. He'd eased her mind, answered her concerns. Convinced her that Keir's accusations were the nonsense she'd thought them to be.

The poor man was clutching at straws and worried he was losing his place at her side. She would need to reassure him tomorrow. But tonight?

Tonight was for Andrew.

And her.

She pulled him closer and brushed against him. It thrilled her to feel the thrum of his body, especially where it thrummed against her belly. He was hard, insistent, ready. But then, so was she.

Their impassioned tryst in the armory had been rapturous, but only a sampling, a brief tangle compared with what she had in mind.

Taking the lead, she walked him backward, toward the bed. He allowed this, though his hands roved, and he did chuckle. But then when his legs hit the mattress, his grip on her waist firmed and he spun her around, tossing her onto the feather tick.

She squealed as she landed; her skirts whipped up, revealing her legs. His eyes flared as he stared at her exposed skin.

"Ach, Susana." To her surprise, he knelt beside the bed and took her foot in his hand, easing her slipper off. "Do you have any idea how much I've been anticipating this moment?"

She wiggled her toes and grinned at him. "This moment?"

"Aye." He took her ankle in his firm hold and then drew his finger up her arch. A sizzle of sensation burned through her, and she lurched away. He didn't allow it. "You were verra naughty at dinner, my lady. Teasing me the way you did." He dipped his head. Oh, dear. Was that his tongue? On her toes? She very nearly squealed again. "I think I need to return the favor."

She wriggled to escape the torment, but it was a wasted effort. Aside from which, though it tickled, she really did enjoy the torment. "Re-Return the favor?"

He caught her gaze. His burned. "Punish you."

Oh, Mother Mary. "P-Punish me?"

"Aye." He yanked her nearer and held her foot with both hands, tracing the curves with his fingers and his tongue in a provocative symphony.

Susana gritted her teeth and forced herself to hold still as the delicious torture continued. She very badly wanted to know what he planned next.

Ah. What he planned next was the other foot. Now he held them both and he alternated from one to the other, laving, exploring, and—dear God—nibbling his way over her feet, up her ankles, and to her calves.

His touch burned her, ignited her. It caused ripples of delight and agony to dance over her nerves. She hadn't been touched for a long while. Not really touched. To have this, to have him, reveling, licking, exploring every inch, was delightful. And annoying.

Because he was far too thorough. She knew where he was heading with this, and she wanted him there.

Now.

She squirmed lower on the bed and he chuckled. Then he explored her knees. She had no idea her knees were so sensitive. No idea his enticing touch there could arouse her so. He continued higher, to her thighs. She stilled, barely daring to breathe as he crept closer and closer to the weeping core of her being.

And then he rose up and wrenched her legs apart in one fierce move until she was open to him, bare, vulnerable.

He stared at her for a long, long while, as though memorizing each line, each minute curl. Hand trembling, he touched her, softly, a whisper of a caress, drifting his fingers through her down. He caught her gaze as he pressed in.

She arched as he scraped that bundle of nerves, humming there, nestled there in a secluded bower. Sensation whipped through her, and glory and rain. She wanted to collapse into it, melt into it, dissolve. But there was more. Much more to be had.

Panting, she studied the tight lines of his face as he explored her cleft. Each stroke was dizzying. Each caress sublime. He drew a circle around her pearl and then another, each nearer to the aching tip. Before he reached it, he stopped—which frustrated her to no end—but then he slipped his finger between her swollen lips.

"It's not raining now," he mumbled.

She had no clue what he was talking about and she hardly cared.

Snarling at him, she thrust her hips forward. Their eyes locked. He made a feral sound himself, something like a growl, and buried his face between her thighs.

And, ah! Glory!

He sucked and suckled her, laved and lapped. Nibbled and nipped. His tongue, so talented, drove her to insane heights. Crazed and mindless, she fell back on the mattress and spread her legs wider and urged him on. When he slowed, when it seemed as though he was about to stop, she buried her nails in his scalp. He grunted against her and shifted and then . . . ah, and then he slid a finger into her. Nae. Two.

Her body closed around him and she shuddered. He made another sound, a moan perhaps, and then eased out.

She panted, aching, writhing in anticipation as he hovered there, at her entrance. Toying with her. "Do it," she commanded.

To her dismay, he did not. To her dismay, he lifted his head and smiled at her with damp lips. "Beg me." A whisper. An insidious snaking whisper.

"What?"

"Beg me, Susana. It's a simple word, please. And you know you want it." Mockingly, he thumbed her pearl until she whimpered, quailed.

"Do it."

"Say please."

She glowered at him but she knew, he knew, she wouldn't resist for long. "Please." Reluctant and gritted out, but well worth it.

He didn't hesitate. He shoved his fingers into her and filled her and stroked her. He sought and found a spot, deep within, something magical and manic, and he strummed her there like a lute, creating music in her head, a heavenly song.

Tension rose. A ball in her belly grew and swelled and then released. With a cry, she reached her crescendo, her delirium, her doom.

He continued to toy with her as she recovered herself,

keeping her roused, wanting. The smile on his face was one she would expect, cocky and triumphant.

Ach, he was irresistible, this man. As aggravating as he was, he was irresistible.

While she didn't like being made to beg—she never had—she was thankful he had turned their play in this direction.

Because, in her estimation, it was an engraved invitation to do the same to him.

She smiled at him as she rose up. Took his head in her hands and kissed his be-dewed beard, his cheeks, his lips.

It was a pity he didn't have any clue what she was about to do to him.

Then again, if he had, he would run.

Susana kissed him with a ferocity he hadn't expected, but definitely liked. It had been a joy, tasting her, lapping her, bringing her to orgasm. He'd especially loved the way her body closed around him, clenching and sucking and quivering as she lost all control. Her moans and cries had enflamed him.

He was burning to take her, to mount her, to bury his hard cock in her velvet sheath. He met and matched her kiss with his own, consuming her, dominating her. He levered up with the intent to press her back down onto the mattress, to kick off his breeks, or at least open the placket, and claim her.

She didn't let him.

With a fist to his hair, she yanked him back, unsealing their mouths and staring at him with a resolute expression. It sent a ribbon of heat licking through him. "Susana," he growled. "I want you."

Her smile was far too sweet, far too innocent for the

moment. It threatened to concern him, but he was far too befuddled for the warning to seep through. "Of course you do, darling," she whispered. She set her hands on his shoulders, stroking the column of his neck. Then her palms skated to his chest . . . and she pushed.

It took a moment for him to realize she was pushing him away; his soul wailed.

With a taunting smile, she stood and sauntered to the hearth, leaving him perched by the bed on his knees. He watched her, tracking the sway of her hips, the knowing quirk of her smile. She stopped next to a large chair by the fire. And then she crooked her finger.

He didn't know much in this world, but he did know one thing. When a woman like Susana Dounreay crooked her finger at a man, he came.

Hopefully . . .

Not breaking with her gaze, he stood and made his way to the chair. He had no idea what she had in mind. He didn't care.

Especially when she reached down and traced his cock.

It was heavy and full and pressed uncomfortably against his breeks. But God, it felt good, that caress. She edged closer and palmed him and murmured, "Mmm."

Heat flared. Lust howled. He wanted to grab her and bend her over the back of the chair and fuck her like a stallion fucks a mare in heat. But he didn't. Because he desperately wanted to know what she had in mind.

He was certain he would enjoy it.

Ah, yes. With sure fingers, she unbuttoned the placket of his breeks, allowing his cock to spring free. She murmured again as she grasped him, encircled him. The blood left his head in a rush, making him dizzy. It pooled—all of it perhaps—in his groin.

He hissed as agony swelled.

She released him far too soon. His eyes fluttered open and he stared at her. Hunger simmered, burned.

Her lips quirked. She pointed at the chair. "Sit." Her tone was sharp, commanding, irresistible.

Naturally, he sat.

"Put your hands behind you."

He blinked. His lips parted but she silenced the unspoken word with a finger.

"Do as I say, Andrew."

Oh, holy God.

He whipped his arms behind him and clasped the legs of the chair.

"Do not move or I shall stop."

Stop? Stop what?

But ah! He didn't have to wonder long. She set her hands on his thighs and knelt between them.

His breath locked in his lungs. His pulse pounded. *Oh God, oh God, oh God.* Was she going to . . . ?

Jesus, Mary, and Joseph. She was.

She hissed in a breath and took his cock in her hands, double-fisting him. Her fingers were gentle and soft, but firm. She stroked and he nearly lost consciousness.

That it was this woman, on her knees before him, clutching his cock, nearly unmanned him. He grit his teeth and tightened his fingers and forced himself to suffer her torment.

Bluidy hell, he knew what this was.

She was going to pay him back.

While he didn't mind paying—didn't mind in the slightest—he filed away a mental note that Susana Dounreay was a woman who would meet every assault with one of her own. And hers were ever so much more heinous.

She dipped her head and lapped at the head of his

cock—he nearly sprang out of the chair at that, but somehow managed to stay put. Then she parted her lips and
encased the mushroom head in her sweet mouth. The
sight, the sensation lashed him. He shuddered. Ripples of
bliss and agony danced over his nerves as she explored
him with an untried tongue.

She nearly drove him mad with that untried tongue.

When this was finished, when she'd had her revenge,
as clearly that was what this was, he would need to show
her, school her on how to—

Fook!

She sucked him in, and his thoughts scattered to the
winds. His hips heaved as she took him deeper, making
him ache to drive deeper still. He tried to control himself,
but he was beyond cogent thought, beyond gentlemanly
restraint. Far beyond manners of any sort.

"Ach, aye," he said. "Suck it."

He shouldn't have said anything. She lifted her head,
releasing him with a plop. She tipped her head to the side,
stroking him slowly, dandling her finger in the damp slit
where a salty tear beaded to replace the one she'd stolen.
"Do you like it when I suck your cock, Andrew?"

"Ach. Aye." He lifted his hips, a suggestion, perhaps,
that she please continue.

"Do you want more?"

Oh, Jesus. "Aye."

A wicked grin blossomed on her beautiful, beautiful
face. It occurred to him, in that moment, she might very
well be the most evil being on the planet. Because she put
out a lip and said, in a pouty voice, "Say please."

Shite!

He very nearly released his hands and buried his fingers in her hair and yanked her mouth back where it be-

longed, but he didn't. He'd set the rules for this game and he would abide by them. Bluidy fook.

"Please." No doubt it was easier for him to say it than her, because there was hardly any hesitation at all. But then, he didn't give a flying fook about the word. It was just a word. And saying it would get her mouth on him again. Thank God she didn't realize that.

Or . . . maybe she did.

Her brow rumpled and she sat back on her heels. She released his cock altogether, which was a tragedy of monumental proportions. Nibbling her lip—oh, that she were nibbling *him*—she studied him.

"Susana?" He thrust his hips. His cock bounded, but not much. It was stiff as a pike. "I said please."

"Aye. You did. But so quickly. It makes me wonder."

"Wonder?" Lord preserve a man from a woman who wondered.

"Wonder if you are sincere . . ."

He glanced down at his little warrior and then glanced at her. "Does this look sincere to you? Does this look fooking sincere?"

She shrugged. "I doona know." She affected a grin. "Men are a mystery to me."

"Let me clue you in. When it's like this"—he nodded to the thick shaft, with the angry crown and bulging veins—"a man is always sincere. Especially when he says please."

"Do you really want me?"

"Ach, Christ, woman. Yes."

She seemed inclined to lean in again, but then she frowned. "Me? Or would just any woman do?"

He gaped at her. His first thought was that she was playing with him, trying to get him to say something that might be more difficult than a simple *please*, but then he realized her question was genuine. She really wanted to know.

He swallowed. "Most of the time, honestly, any woman would do."

There was a flash of pain in her eyes, but she nodded and acquiesced. She took him in her hands again.

He released his hold on the chair and cupped her chin. "But Susana, that is not the case now."

She blinked. Her eyes were wide. Her lips parted. "It isna?"

"Nae." And God help him, it was true. Since he'd met her. Since he'd kissed her, tasted her, gloried in her scent. "No other woman would do for me." He kissed her gently. Their lips melded, meshed for a long moment. When she pulled back, there was a sheen of tears in her eyes. Or perhaps he was imagining things, because she forced a frown and, with a remonstrating *tut tut*, arranged his arms behind him once more. "I told you not to let go."

"Aye, mistress."

He was joking, but she seemed to like that. Her eyes glowed. But then she said the most perturbing thing. "I think you need to be punished.

"What?"

"Och, aye."

He watched in shock as she lifted her skirts and straddled the arms of the chair. Thusly situated, she hovered above him. He could feel the heat of her core on his cock, imagined he could feel the drizzle of her arousal. Reaching beneath her, reaching between them, she took hold of him. "Now," she said in the tone of pedantic instructor. "Let's begin again."

She edged lower and rubbed the head of his cock against her damp folds. His eyes crossed. "Tell me what you want?"

"I want to fuck you."

"Just me?"

"Och, aye."

"Doona let go of the chair."

"Nae. I willna." This, he hissed through his teeth.

And ah, God. She slipped lower and lower still until the tip was sheathed in her hot wet embrace. She wrapped her arms around him, bracing herself more securely. "Now," she whispered in his ear. "Say please."

"Ah, Susana." A groan. A desperate entreaty. "Pl—"

She dropped. Impaled him, before the word even passed his lips. And God, was it exquisite. Her weight, the grip of her sheath, the slow, slick slide of her body on his.

He couldn't stay still. His hands came around and cupped her ass, glorying in the feel of her supple globes filling his palms. He held her still and thrust up, once, twice, three times. With each maddening lunge, her breath huffed out, and with it, her groan. Her eyes glowed. Her lips parted.

"Do you like this?" he growled.

"Aye. Oh, aye."

"It would be better on the floor."

A desperate suggestion, perhaps, but he needed to make it. This was delightful, but he burned for leverage. He wanted control. He needed to cover her.

"Och, aye," she gasped, and in a heartbeat, without even disengaging, he had her flat on her back on the carpet, her legs high over her head and spread. With a snarl he yanked out and then thrust in again. Like a wild beast he took her, but she gave it back to him with equal measure. Lunging up into him, grasping, clawing, savaging him as he savaged her. He wanted, needed, to see her breasts, so he yanked at her bodice. It came away with a rip and she laughed. Her laugh rippled through her body and into his, but he barely had time to enjoy the vibrations, because her breasts stole all his attention. They bobbled as he moved, as he pounded away at a faster and faster pace. He had to pause, though, to suckle a nipple, because it would be a shame not to do so and because he'd spent so much time wondering what they—

Ah. Raspberries. They tasted like raspberries.

He found he couldn't release her. So he shifted position, so he could nuzzle her delicious breasts and still maintain a mounting frenzy.

As he nipped a nipple she gasped, cried out, and closed around him.

The bliss was blinding.

Heat coiled at the base of his balls. Tension in his cock, in this spine, in every muscle, mounted. A great pressure closed around him, a dizzying delirious torment he knew well and welcomed.

"Susana . . ." he gasped as he neared the precipice. Mad to take her with him, he nudged her pearl, circled it, pinched.

And, aye. Aye.

As he succumbed, so did she, dissolving in his arms in a series of excruciating quakes that sent him over the edge and tumbling into the abyss. In a wild tumult, he flooded her, filling her with jet after jet of surging seed.

It was an abyss of delirium and delight, so he welcomed the fall.

༺༻

Susana stared up at the ceiling, her mind in a whirl. Andrew's weight on her was a delicious burden. She loved the feel of him, his warmth, his scent.

He'd mated with her like a wild animal in heat. It had been magnificent.

He groaned and eased out. She winced at the loss of his presence within her. But then he took her face in his hands and kissed her thoroughly. With a chuckle, he rolled to the side, but she didn't mind, because he took her with him, settling her on his chest.

He held her close and teased his fingers through her hair. "That was . . ." He shook his head, at a loss for words.

"Aye." She kissed him. "It was."

"One of these times, we shall have to get undressed."

She chuckled. "If we can wait that long."

A light glimmered in his eye. "Doubtful." He pulled her closer and kissed her again. "I just seem to lose all rational thought around you."

"And I you." She propped her hands on his chest and set her chin on her hands. "You'll have to leave, you know."

He blinked. "What?"

"You'll have to leave. You canna stay here."

It was adorable the way he put out a lip. But, reminded of rational thought, this was a very important point.

"Why?" He traced her cheek, her chin. "I was hoping we could . . . explore more."

She sighed. "I canna let my daughter find you here. You have to go."

"Your daughter?"

"Aye. Sometimes she comes to my rooms at night. It could be . . . awkward."

"We could lock the door."

"We could. Or you could leave."

"Ach, so you take what you want from me and then kick me out?" His outrage was feigned. She was almost sure of it.

She chuckled and kissed his beard, then pushed up and away. "Doona pout. I will see you in the morning."

It was hard letting him go, but she had to. She was a mother. And her daughter did indeed have a habit of appearing in her room at all hours.

It was a pity she'd never thought to restrain the habit before.

"Aye. All right." He stood and fastened his breeks then reached down to help her to her feet. His attention stalled on her bodice and she realized that, as he'd ripped her garment asunder, her breasts were bare.

A light flickered in his eyes. He caught her gaze and pulled her closer and kissed her with unmistakable intent.

It was a long time, indeed, before he left.

CHAPTER THIRTEEN

Andrew woke in a dreamy fog. His body hummed with pleasure . . . and arousal. Memories of the night before flitted through his mind. Though he was ensconced, not in a smelly kennel on a lumpy pallet, but in a luxurious bed in a finely decorated room, dissatisfaction rippled through him. Because he was alone.

Though he'd spent most of the night with Susana—and though she was not far away, perhaps still sleeping in her room in the next wing—her absence now was a gaping hole in his soul.

Then again . . . perhaps she was still sleeping in her room.

A flare of excitement flickered. He glanced at the window. Though it was raining—and thank God he wasn't sleeping in the kennel—he could see that the sun was just rising. If he hurried, maybe he could wake her with a kiss. With that thought, he pulled on his breeks and tunic, ran his fingers through his hair, and headed for the west wing.

He was almost to the grand staircase, which separated the wings of the castle, when an odd sound, a dull thud, captured his attention. He knew that sound, and it had no place in a castle.

It sounded again, followed by a warbled cheer.

Perplexed, he pushed open the door from beyond which the strange sounds emanated, stepped inside, and stared.

It wasn't often that one saw a small girl, perched on the

second-story rail of a library, shooting unsuspecting books with a bow and arrow.

Isobel drew back and sighted on a shelf across the room. She teetered precariously and then tightened her legs around the rail . . . and then let fly. The arrow screamed across the room and landed in the spine of a tome with a dull thunk.

"Woo-hoo!" she cried. And then, in her exhilaration, she loosened her hold on the rail and wobbled again.

Andrew's heart lurched. What the hell was it with this girl and heights?

Rather than call out to her, and possibly startle her and cause her to topple to the floor far below, he rushed in and grabbed her by the waist and tugged her from her precarious perch.

She screeched. Her bow tumbled from her fingers; it whipped down and down and clattered onto the hardwood floor below.

"What are you doing?" This they both demanded of the other as he set her safely on the ground.

Andrew sighed. "You were going to fall."

"I wasna going to fall. And look. You made me drop my bow." She peered over the edge, a petulant frown on her face.

"The bow suffered the fall rather well. You, my lady, wouldna have."

She blew out a damp breath. It sounded like *Pffft*. "I've never fallen before. I'm verra practiced at this."

And aye. About that . . . He gazed across the room to the prickling bristles of arrows deeply embedded in what appeared to be the drama section. Shakespeare would not be pleased. "Why are you shooting books in the library anyway?" What had they ever done to her?

She shrugged. "It's raining."

How that signified, he didn't know.

Her nose rumpled and she added, "I was bored."

"Do you often shoot books in the library?"

"Only the ones I doona like to read."

He gulped. Stared down at her diminutive form. "You read?"

"Hannah taught me. I thought it was stupid at first, but you can learn interesting things in books, I've found."

"Such as?"

Her only response was a truly chilling smile.

"Surely there are other things to do that are no' so . . ." Dangerous? Destructive? Discombobulating? "What would your mother say if she knew you were perched on the railing, risking life and limb to defeat an army of books?"

"She does encourage me to practice."

"In the library?"

Isobel grinned. It was an unsettling grin. Far too mischievous. Far too familiar. "She would probably say the same thing she always says."

"Which is?"

She bunched her hands into fists and scrunched up her face into a moue of ferocity that looked very much like Susana's indeed. And then she bellowed, "*Isobel Mairi MacBean!* What on God's green earth are you thinking?"

His breath stalled. "Isobel *Mairi*?"

"Isobel Mairi is my *I'm in trouble* name."

"Your *I'm in trouble* name?"

"It's what my mama says when I'm in trouble."

"Mairi?" An odd mélange of emotions swirled in his gut. He reminded himself that Mairi was a common name. And his Mairi had hailed from Ciaran Reay. There were probably many Mairis here.

"It's my middle name. Mama's, too."

"Ah."

She peered over the rail again and sighed heavily. "Now I have to go down there and get my bow."

"So you can continue shooting? I think not. Why do we no' go to the morning room and have breakfast?"

This snagged her attention. She peeped up at him. "Do you think they will have cakes?"

"I imagine so." There seemed to be cakes every morning. "If Hamish hasn't eaten them all."

Her eyes widened in horror. "Oh. We'd better go at once."

"An excellent idea."

Though she seemed inclined to leap over the rail to the library below, he was able to induce her to use the curling staircase. She did, however, slide down the banister like a hoyden. At the bottom, she paused to collect her bow. He didn't miss the quick glower she sent him as she swung it over her shoulder. He didn't mean to chuckle, but he did.

The morning room was just down the hall from the main floor of the library. It faced east and offered a view of the charming garden. The sideboard was covered with tempting offerings . . . but none of that captured Andrew's attention as much as the woman sitting at the table.

His heart lurched as he saw her. And then, when she glanced up and caught his gaze, it thumped.

She was so beautiful in the morning light with her alabaster skin aglow, her green eyes sparkling and that naughty twist to her lips. "Good morning," she said. It might have been his imagination, but her tone seemed infused with a sultry drawl.

"Good morning." He offered the same.

A delightful pink crawled up her cheeks. To hide it—although it did no such thing—she turned to her daughter. "And what have you two been up to this fine morning?"

"Nothing," Isobel mumbled, hooking her bow on the chair and heading for the buffet.

"Target practice," he said.

Isobel shot him a quelling glare so he didn't elaborate. Oh, he would have to warn Susana about her daughter's antics, but he would prefer to wait until they were private. If he remembered. Once they were private. He did distract easily.

The look she sent him created a roil of hunger in his belly. And it wasn't hunger for cakes. No doubt, once he got her in private, all thoughts of Isobel's shenanigans would waft away in favor of shenanigans of their own.

The thought made him grin. He took the seat next to her and nudged her foot with his. Her blush blossomed. She tipped her head closer. "You were having target practice?" she murmured.

He rolled his eyes. "Isobel was."

"Lord." She glanced at her daughter, who was filling her plate with cakes. Apparently, all of them. "Do I want to know?"

"Probably not."

Her leg relaxed against his. "Did you . . . sleep well?"

"Not at all."

She quirked a brow.

"I was verra distracted . . . for some reason."

"For what reason?" a cheerful voice chirped. He started when he realized Isobel had seated herself to his other side.

Susana muffled a chuckle. "Probably the patter of the rain," she suggested.

Good enough. "It did rain all night. I was verra glad I wasna sleeping in the kennels." For more than one reason. He and Susana shared another long, lingering look.

"I thought you were hungry," Isobel said. "Aren't you going to get breakfast?"

He studied her full plate, then snagged a cake. Though she screeched in outrage, he could see the smile behind it. "Mmm," he murmured, taking a big bite. "Delicious."

"You will need more than cake to sustain you," Susana said in a motherly tone. It was rather off-putting to realize it was directed at him. "We have much to do today, if we're to go over your plans and set the new campaign in motion."

Ah, yes. The reason he was here to begin with. While he was gratified that he was finally making progress on his mission, he was swamped with the desire to launch a different campaign altogether.

Last night had been extraordinary. He was ready for another go.

Very ready.

Still, he stood and dutifully headed for the buffet and filled his plate with fluffy eggs, sausages, and bannocks. No cakes, though. They were all gone. As he retook his seat, Hamish entered the room, looking bright-eyed, well rested, and very pleased with himself. No doubt his bed had been very warm last night as well. "Good morn to you all," he boomed. He headed for the buffet and surveyed it. Then he glanced at Isobel's plate and frowned.

At his predatory surveillance, she picked up a cake and licked it. Then, in succession, licked them all.

Hamish blew out a sigh that might also have been a laugh and filled his plate with much less delectable choices. He took the spot across from Isobel. "It appears as though I slept too long," he muttered.

"You have to be an early bird to get any cakes," Susana said, nibbling back her grin.

"Aye." Hamish's eyes brightened as Saundra entered . . . carrying another platter of cakes, which she set before him with a dreamy smile. "Or make friends with the baker," he said with a wink.

Saundra, still gazing at him with mooncalf eyes, bumped into the table as she exited the room.

Hamish leveled a triumphant grin at Isobel and then, as a precaution, he edged the platter out of her reach. In the case this wasn't precaution enough, he picked up a cake. And licked it.

Isobel narrowed her eyes and made a sound like a growl, but Andrew could tell she was mightily entertained by his antics.

Before Hamish could lick all the cakes, she stole one.

They were very good cakes.

As they ate, they chatted about their plans for the day. The three adults had a full slate ahead of them, of course, but Isobel mentioned she planned to do more target practice and, when Andrew sent her a warning frown, she added it would probably be out of doors. If the rain stopped.

"If you go hunting, be sure to take Siobhan with you," Susana said.

Isobel put out a lip. "He's a boy."

Susana frowned. "I doona want you out and about alone. Not until I know it's safe."

"Of course it's safe," Isobel sniffed, taking another bite of cake. It was amazing how much she could eat in one sitting.

Susana's brow rumpled. "I dinna like the things I heard last night." It was gratifying that his warnings had finally sunk in.

"I have my bow," Isobel said with a shrug.

Susana sent Andrew a pleading look, though what that was for, he didn't know. The girl certainly didn't listen to *him*.

Still, he should probably say something. That pleading look and all. He cleared his throat. "I think your mother has a good point," he said. At Isobel's rebellious glower, he realized his mistake. "Granted, you are an excellent shot." This seemed to mollify her, but not nearly enough.

Hamish shrugged. "If there are bands of ruffians camping in the woods, I would want another excellent bowman with me." He tapped this lip. "This Siobhan, is he an excellent shot?"

"He's fair."

"Fair isna good enough if one needs protection. I would be happy to go hunting with you. Once our work is done." Ah. That was an excellent tactic.

Pity it didn't work.

Isobel rolled her eyes. "You're *old*."

The expression on Hamish's face was priceless. "I most certainly am not old."

"You are."

Susana huffed a breath and sent them both a glance, which made clear her disgust at their puny efforts to manage her daughter. "Isobel, take Siobhan with you if you go into the woods. Or stay on the castle grounds." Her tone left little room for dissent. Unfortunately, Isobel was a master at finding room for dissent.

She muttered something beneath her breath.

Susana narrowed her eyes rather fiercely. "I beg your pardon?"

"Oh, all right."

While Susana seemed satisfied with Isobel's apparent acquiescence, Andrew wasn't convinced in the slightest. Perhaps it was the way she nibbled her lip, or the wicked gleam in her eye, or the way she swung her legs under the table.

Clearly, Isobel was going to do whatever the hell she damn well pleased, no matter what anyone said. He made a mental note to check in on her regularly, no matter how busy they were today.

∽

After breakfast, her daughter went her merry way, scuttling off with a concerning enthusiasm. Susana tried not to fret. Short of keeping her daughter by her side at every moment of the day, she couldn't completely control her. Though she did take the precaution of asking Peiter to keep an eye on her. She hated assigning a guard—she knew Isobel would hate being watched—but with all she'd learned from Andrew about the holes in their defenses, and all the unsettling things that had happened in Reay of late, it made her feel better.

After sending Peiter on his mission, she joined Andrew and Hamish in the study to begin a thorough analysis of all the plans. Keir was supposed to meet them there, but he was late.

They began without him.

It surprised Susana how much she enjoyed the morning, talking strategy and tactics with Andrew. He had many clever ideas, and had insights she'd never considered. They found themselves engaged in long-winded debates about this option or that and as often as she acceded to him, he acceded to her.

In fact, he treated her as an equal.

More than that, he seemed to genuinely respect her opinion.

This was not new to her—she demanded respect from her men. But with Andrew, it was freely given.

Hamish, on the other hand, was annoying.

Not just because he was there, hovering, interjecting random observations into the conversation, and glorying in playing devil's advocate. Susana couldn't help noticing the way he watched them both with far too much interest.

Not that she felt she needed to keep her relationship with Andrew a secret—if, indeed, there was one—but knowing Hamish might be on to them made her uncomfortable. Especially when, at one point, Andrew unconsciously set his hand on her hip as he showed her a spot on the map, stroking her with his thumb. Hamish's gaze locked onto the caress and he shot Susana a smirk.

She endeavored to ignore him.

Once they all had a firm grip on the changes they planned to implement, and were all in agreement on the critical points, Andrew suggested they ride out to review the spots that might be particularly troubling, as well as the locations they'd identified as good points to station patrols.

It had stopped raining and the air was cool, damp. It made her hair curl around her nape, but Susana gloried in it. She gloried in riding next to Andrew, too. As they made their way from the castle and through the fields, she pointed out landmarks and shared stories of her childhood.

At one point, she caught Hamish and Andrew exchanging what could only be described as a smirk.

She frowned at them, though there was no heat in it. "What?" she demanded.

Andrew shrugged. "It's just that, hearing these tales of your adventures as a child . . ." He let the sentence dangle.

"What?" she clipped.

Hamish chuckled. "It's just that . . ."

Andrew nodded. "Aye."

"What?"

Andrew leaned in with a wicked grin. "It's easy to see where Isobel gets it from."

She bristled. "Gets what? From where?"

Hamish's chuckle became a laugh. "She's an unmitigated hoyden. Just like her mother."

"She is not a hoyden." And then, with slightly more bite, "And neither am I."

They both eyed her dubiously, though there was a hint of humor and fondness in both the infuriating glances.

A week ago she would have skewered a man for suggesting her daughter was a hoyden. She certainly would have skewered Andrew for it. Now she couldn't summon the outrage. Partially because they were probably right. But only probably.

"Did you climb the turret tower as a child?" Andrew asked. "Or hunt for books in the library?"

She ignored the heat rising in her cheeks; she'd done worse. Not that she'd admit it.

"Hoyden or not," Andrew said, "she's adorable." That warmed her heart. Thawed her a little more, which was a lovely feeling, after being encased in ice as long as she had been. But it was likely not very prudent.

Still, she admitted, "She is, perhaps, a little undisciplined."

"A little?" Hamish nearly choked on the words at her glower.

Susana sighed. "Papa insists it's because she doesna have a father." She resisted a glance at Andrew. "But I think that's ridiculous. She has me and Papa . . ."

"Every child should have a father," Hamish said.

Andrew stiffened in his saddle. "Not every child has a choice."

Hamish glanced at his friend and grimaced. "I'm sorry, Andrew. I didn't mean—"

Andrew waved his apology off. "I know it, Hamish. While it would be wonderful if each child had a father and a mother, life doesna always work out that way. We all just do the best we can with what we have. And I think Isobel is. She's trying the best she can."

Oh, lord, though his words supported her and her decision and her choices, though they defended her, how they hurt. Isobel could have a father. Should have a father. Did have a father.

All it would take was the courage to tell him.

But she wasn't sure she had it.

She didn't know what she was afraid of, but it was certainly something fierce and looming and dark. Aside from that, if she told Andrew the truth about Isobel's parentage, it might destroy this fragile thing they'd built.

Then again, it might not. It could possibly launch them into a new direction, one she might find very satisfying indeed.

She fell silent as they continued on, down the track to the loch, mulling things over in her head. She knew she needed to tell him at some point. It was the when and the how and the consequences that froze her tongue.

That Hamish sent her speaking glances as they rode didn't help.

❦

They were nearly to the loch when a shrill scream rang in the air. Susana's heart lurched painfully. She knew that voice. "Isobel," she breathed. She sat straighter in her saddle, put her heels to the mare's belly, and pounded down the path.

The vision she beheld as she rounded the last curve sent a bolt of cold lightning down her spine. Her bowels churned.

Isobel stood on the banks of the loch, surrounded by a coterie of beefy, burly men—who clearly hadn't washed in some time. They each had weapons, pointed at her wee daughter, and they were closing in. That she had her bow raised and—even as Susana watched—let an arrow fly did not calm her mother's heart. There were six grown men and only one small girl and she could only point her arrow at one at a time. It wouldn't be long until one of them rushed her.

One man lay on the bank moaning and clutching at the arrow in his thigh. Clearly Isobel had found her mark on that bastard.

Fury raged within her and she pulled an arrow from her quiver. But before she had a chance to fire, Andrew launched himself from his steed with an enraged bellow. He and Hamish barreled into the clearing and, unsheathing their swords in a practically choreographed motion, they advanced on the scene in a trice.

Susana wasn't far behind, with her bow and quiver in hand.

At Andrew's cry, the men surrounding Isobel whipped around to face this new threat, but it was a mistake. Isobel let her next arrow fly. It landed in the larger one's backside. He howled and whirled back on her, but she already had another arrow nocked.

Pride blossomed in Susana's chest. She was only five, but her daughter was fierce. Not fierce enough to fight off six grown men, but fierce enough to try.

Andrew and Hamish advanced with their swords at the ready and engaged the uninjured men, drawing them to the left and away from Isobel. When she saw an opening, Susana ran to her daughter's side.

"Mama," Isobel cried, and launched herself into her arms. Susana held her tight. Thank God she was all right—

The villain Isobel had shot in the thigh crawled closer and attempted to seize her ankle. Susana halted him, brandishing an arrow at his face. The man paled and eased back, but his narrowed eyes spat vitriol. She tugged Isobel toward the horses and safety, skirting around the melee, balancing her daughter and her bow with a practiced finesse.

But her bow wasn't necessary.

Andrew and Hamish fought the four men who were still on their feet with astounding skill. Her eye was drawn to Andrew, the elegant swing of his sword, the clever ripostes and lunges. It was almost as though he were one with the battle, as though he anticipated his opponent's every move, as though this were a well-practiced dance.

It was mesmerizing to watch. The ripple of muscle, the bunch of his thighs as he lunged, the ferocity of his expression as he battled to protect her daughter.

Something hardened in her chest and cracked a little.

It might have been six years of resentment. Or her childish desire to make him pay for his crimes. Or her unholy fear that he would break her heart again.

As unwise as it might be to let all that go, she couldn't help but do so. At least a little.

"He's verra good," Isobel whispered in her ear.

Susana tightened her hold. "Aye. He is."

They both were, but there was no doubt, Andrew was better.

It didn't take the other men long to realize they were outclassed. One by one, they disengaged and ran into the woods. When Hamish charged after them, Andrew called him back. "We have these bastards," he said, gesturing to the wounded men. "Let's take them back to the castle and interrogate them. We can send patrols out for the others."

Isobel wriggled and, certain the threat had been vanquished, Susana let her go. As soon as her feet hit the ground, she bounded over to Andrew and stared up at him with shining eyes. "That was brilliant!" she crowed, holding wide her arms and spinning around.

He chuckled and patted her on the head. Then he knelt before her and let her examine his sword. She expressed disappointment that there was no blood and they both laughed.

Susana's chest ached, seeing them like that, their heads together in the afternoon sunlight. Their so-similar faces. Their matching dimples.

Ach, far too painful. She had to look away. Her gaze tangled with Hamish's and she winced, reminded that he had noticed the similarities as well.

Then again, what soul with eyes could not see the truth of it?

Andrew seemed to be the only one who remained oblivious.

Which was fine and good.

She didn't know why it pained her heart so.

CHAPTER FOURTEEN

Andrew seethed as he and Hamish bound the captured men and tossed them over their horses. He'd known in his heart these woods were dangerous. He should have insisted on increasing the patrols sooner.

That Isobel had been at risk chilled him to the bone.

And with his rage, a question whirled in his mind.

Why?

Why attack a small girl? She had nothing of value to steal.

Various possibilities barraged him, each chilling his blood more than the last. Were they just villains grasping at any opportunity for malice and mayhem? Had they intended to kidnap her for ransom? Was there something far more sinister happening here? The worst part was not knowing. If he understood a threat, he would meet it, conquer it. This was nothing but a perplexing mystery.

When they arrived at the castle, Keir met them. His frown darkened as he noted the two bound men.

"What has happened?" he asked.

"Isobel was attacked by the loch," Susana said, tossing herself from her mount. "We caught these two in the act." She frowned and glanced at Andrew and Hamish. "They did."

"There were four more that escaped. We need to send patrols out to find them. And we need to interrogate this lot," Hamish said, grabbing one man by his belt and tugging him from the steed. He landed on the dirt with an *oof.*

"Of course. At once." Keir nodded.

"And then we should lock them in the dungeon," Susana said.

Andrew's head jerked around. Surely she was jesting? But no. She was not. Hell hath no fury like a mother facing a threat to her child. "You have a dungeon?" he asked.

"It's ancient. And rarely used for anything but storage," she said. "But it has cells that will hold them." He considered himself lucky that she hadn't decided to house his company there.

Her eyes burned with ferocity. For the sake of these men, he certainly hoped there were no torture devices in that dungeon. He glared at the bastards, recalling what they'd done. Well, at least, not very many torture devices. His pulse still thrummed at the memory of Isobel in peril. He wasn't sure why this ignited the fire in his belly so, but it did.

"Let's take them down there at once, but before we talk to them, I'd like to talk to Isobel first, while her memory is fresh. Maybe she has some insight on what they hoped to achieve in this." He sent Susana a questing look. When she nodded, he knelt before the girl. While she was still pale and shaking, her chin jutted with determination "How are you doing?"

"Fine." Her nose wrinkled. "But I forgot my bow."

"No worries. We'll send someone back for it." He leveled a speaking look at Hamish, who nodded and spun on his heel. Not only would he fetch Isobel's bow, he would rally the troops to scour the woods for the other miscreants. He refocused on Isobel. "Do you feel up to a chat?"

"A-Aye."

Her gaze locked on his. Her eyes were wide and pooling with a dampness she would likely deny. Still, he brushed the tears away. "Shall we go inside . . . where it's safe?"

Her chin wobbled, but she nodded. Damn, but he hated to see her so vulnerable. When he took her hand, she threaded her fingers through his and allowed him to lead her into the castle. His heart ached for her, the poor wee thing. What a fright she must have had. He hadn't realized how much he'd come to adore that little girl. Aye, she was rebellious and mouthy and far too stubborn for her own good, but she was also plucky and clever and skilled.

"I was verra proud of you," he said as the made their way to the parlor. He chose that room because it was the closest, and of all the rooms on the ground floor, it had a calm ambience.

"Proud of me?"

"Aye," he said. "You were verra brave."

Her lips tweaked and a little of her élan returned. He led her to a comfortable chair and when she was seated, he sat across from her. Susana stood at his side. She probably wasn't aware that her hand rested on his shoulder, or that her fingers tangled in his hair.

He ignored that and focused on Isobel. "Can you tell me what happened?"

Her lashes flickered. "I went hunting . . ."

"With Siobhan?" Susana asked sharply. Andrew shot her a quelling glance.

Isobel pinkened. She wound her fingers. "Nae. He dinna want to go."

"Peiter?"

Isobel snorted. Clearly she'd divined that her mother had set a guard and lost him posthaste.

"Ah," Andrew said softly. "So you went alone?"

"Aye." She peeped at her mother. "I'm sorry. I should have obeyed you."

"Doona worry about that now, darling. I'm just relieved you're all right."

Ironically, Isobel seemed to relax, as though she was much more concerned with her mother's displeasure than the fact that she'd been attacked. Although judging from Susana's tone, and her judicious use of the word *now*, this wasn't the last she would hear of it.

Andrew edged closer. "Can you tell me what happened while you were out hunting?"

She shrugged. "They just surrounded me." Her eyes narrowed. "They were laughing. Like I was stupid."

"You're no' stupid."

"I'm not. I shot one when he said something nasty about Mama and then they stopped laughing." She shuddered. "But then they got mean."

"What did they want?" Susana asked.

"I doona know what they wanted. One of them said, get the girl. She's the one he wants." She sniffed. "He's the one I shot with an arrow."

"He?" Susana frowned at Andrew. "He who?"

Isobel shrugged. "They dinna say."

"Is there anything else you can tell me?"

She shrugged again. "Nae."

Andrew and Susana exchanged a glance. They both knew, if there was anything more to be learned, it would have to be from the men they'd captured. With any luck, Hamish and his team would track down the others.

Maybe there were torture devices in the dungeon. At the moment he was totally fine with it if Susana decided to use them.

"Well, thank you for telling us, Isobel," he said. "And you were verra brave."

She glowed with his praise.

"It might be a good idea to stay indoors until we discover what those blackhearts wanted. What do you think?"

Her chin tipped up. "Are you asking me, or telling me?"

"I'm asking you what you think is the wise course."

Though Susana's fingers had tightened imperceptibly in his hair—or perhaps perceptibly—she seemed to understand and agree with his approach. Giving Isobel the decision would go much farther in gaining her cooperation than ordering her to obey. And try though they might, short of locking her in the dungeon as well, the girl would do as she pleased.

Fortunately, her lashes flickered and her rebellious expression melted. "It was rather alarming," she admitted.

He stroked her hand. "I can imagine so. I was scared for you."

"As was I."

Isobel ignored her mother. She narrowed her gaze on Andrew. "You were scared?"

"Verra scared."

"You doona seem like you are afraid of anything."

"I was verra afraid that you would be hurt, Isobel. That nearly scared me to death. It does"—he winked—"each and every time."

"Well . . ." She drummed her fingers on her knee. "I doona want to scare you . . . So perhaps it is better if I stay inside. For the time being." She studied her mother to assess her reaction. Susana, to her credit, forced a very blasé smile. But her grip on his hair was brutal.

"Verra good choice, Isobel," Andrew said. He sat forward, surely not in an attempt to free his hair. "You are growing up into a verra wise young lady."

Her eyes widened. "Do you mean it?"

"I absolutely do. I know it's not always easy making the

smart choice. Giving up things you want to do in exchange for prudence. Or to protect people you care about from worry and fear. But it is something a wise young lady does."

She tipped her head to the side. "Aye. It is. I suppose."

He grinned. "I'm verra proud of you for making the wise choice, Isobel."

Good God. Her smile slayed him. Brilliant and hopeful and tremulous. Such joy. Such delight. Such pride. In that smile he had a glimpse of the woman she would become and it gored him in the gut. Eviscerated him.

For some reason, it filled him with a restless want, a desire to be there, so see her grow up, to mature, to wed.

But he wouldn't be here. Not then.

He was here to do his mission and then leave.

Why did he have the sense that walking away from Dounreay Castle would break his heart?

∞

Oh, lord.

Susana turned away from the scene of Andrew smiling at Isobel, and Isobel beaming back. She swiped the tears from her eyes. He was so good with her. So patient and certainly more disciplined a parent than she'd ever been.

How wrong was it that she was keeping them apart? How unfair to them both?

"Susana?" His arms came around her, warm and strong. He pulled her close. "Are you all right."

"I'm f-f-f-fine," she snuffled.

His hold tightened and she allowed herself to be cradled there, if just for a moment. The comfort was far too sweet.

"Mama? Why are you crying?"

She couldn't respond, other than a shrug. She couldn't even look at her daughter.

"She was verra worried, too," Andrew said. His low voice rumbled around her. "Your mama loves you verra much and sometimes it's a heavy load to bear, worrying about a daughter. Surely you understand."

"Aye, I understand." Isobel's eyes narrowed. "But I wouldna *cry* about it."

Andrew's chest shook as he tried to hold back a chuckle. It incited one from Susana. As inappropriate and ironic as it was to laugh at that moment, she couldn't stop. Her tears turned from those of frustration and regret to those of joy.

She fell to her knees and tugged Isobel close and hugged her. "I love you so much, darling," she whispered.

"I know." After a moment, Isobel wiggled for release. Susana did not allow it.

"I love you. I love you. I love you."

"I *know*. Stop squeezing me."

"I never will. When you're an old woman I shall still squeeze you."

Isobel broke free and fixed her mother with an appalled moue. "You'll be really old then."

And once again, Susana barked a laugh.

Isobel peeped up at Andrew. "Can I go now?"

Susana's pulse stuttered. She didn't want her daughter out of her sight, ever again. Also, Isobel had directed the question to Andrew. Susana didn't know why that caused a ping in her chest.

He nodded. "Of course. But . . . Where are you going?"

Isobel tipped her head to the side. "I was thinking the kitchen." She gusted a heavy sigh. "After what I've been through, I think I need a cake."

"An excellent idea." He nodded. "Do you want me to come with you?"

Isobel rolled her eyes. "So you can eat my cakes? I think not."

"Do have fun. And give Saundra my regards."

Susana stood as Isobel barreled out of the room and into the grand foyer. She stared after her with her heart in her throat. She was so relieved that Isobel wasn't harmed, but until they discovered the who and the why of this attack, she was still very much at risk.

Andrew seemed to sense her disquiet. He settled an arm around her shoulders and nuzzled her brow. "Susana. It will be fine."

"Aye." The word held no conviction.

"We will keep her safe."

"Aye."

"Susana." He turned her to face him, tipped up her chin, and kissed her. "It will be fine. I promise."

"Andrew, someone wants my daughter."

His expression firmed. "Aye. Do you have any idea why?"

She spread her hands. "No clue."

"I suggest we keep her under guard until we can figure this out. One of my men *and* one of yours. Watching her. At all times."

"I agree. But she willna like that."

"Probably not. But I think even *she* realizes what a close call she's had. If we play it right, she willna mind." He was good at that, she realized, convincing Isobel to see reason. Much better than she'd ever been.

She frowned. "I'm a horrible mother."

He gaped at her. "What? No, you're not."

"You're so good with her. The way you explained things to her. Gave her a choice . . ."

"Manipulated her?" He grinned.

"You wrapped her around your little finger." It occurred to her that he was very practiced at that, too. And for some reason, the realization didn't annoy her.

"I helped her see the Isobel she wants to be."

She sighed. "I'm glad it worked."

"I hope it worked." He chucked her chin. "It's her safety that matters. God, Susana. Whatever works."

"I was frightened to death."

"As was I. We must do whatever we can to keep her safe."

"Aye." Susana firmed her spine. "And we must discover what those men know." She glanced in the direction of the kitchen, torn. On the one hand, she desperately wanted to be present for the interrogations of these bastards. On the other, she really wanted nothing more than to hover at her daughter's side.

Andrew kissed her on the forehead. "Go to her," he whispered.

When she looked up at him it was through a sheen of tears. "But . . ."

"Go to her. Hamish and I will see to the interrogations. We will find out what these men know. I promise."

He kissed her again, this time on the lips, infusing the embrace with warmth and comfort and bolstering courage. She knew he would keep Isobel safe. He would do everything in his power.

It was difficult tearing herself from his arms and heading for the kitchens, because more than anything, she wanted to stay right there.

But Isobel needed her.

༄

The interrogations did not go well. By the time Andrew got there, Keir had already begun, but neither of the men seemed inclined to say a word. In fact, with each query, their features closed up even more.

It truly was a pity there were no torture devices in the

moldy old cellar. Not even a one. But there were cells with creaky hinges and rusted bars. Maybe after a night on a stone ledge with a diet of bread and water, the bastards would be more disposed to share who sent them.

Andrew's frustration increased when Hamish and the men they'd sent to scour the woods returned, empty-handed.

Hamish came down the stairs holding Isobel's bow. It was incongruously tiny in his hands. "Anything?" he asked in an undertone as Keir berated one of the men across the room.

"Nothing." Andrew frowned. "They're certainly tight-lipped."

Hamish nibbled his lip. "What are you thinking?"

"Could be a number of scenarios."

"Such as?"

Andrew blew out a breath and muttered the name that had been humming in his brain for hours. "Stafford."

"Aye." Hamish scrubbed his face with a palm. "The most likely suspect." It was no secret that the marquess lusted after Reay lands. No secret that some of the recent attacks had been perpetrated by his men. "But the lands belong to Alexander now. How would kidnapping Isobel benefit him?"

"It wouldna. Unless he has some other kind of plan in place." A certain suspicion bubbled through him; acid churned.

"What kind of plan?" Hamish stilled. His expression darkened. "What happens to the land if something untoward were to befall your brother?"

Andrew shot a dark look at his friend. It was frightening how much they thought alike. "Nothing. Because they are Hannah's lands. But if something happened to the two of them . . ." The churning acid spat.

"Then what?"

"The lands revert to Magnus."

"And if something happened to him?"

Aye. The crux of the matter. "To Susana."

"We should notify Alexander immediately."

Andrew nodded. "My thought exactly. And with something of this import, we should send the messenger via the sea." A ship was much quicker than an overland route.

"I suggest we send more than one messenger," Hamish said, watching Keir in action. He truly was fierce in his interrogation, but nothing he said made the man he was questioning bat so much as a lash.

"Aye. We may be wrong in this, but it doesna hurt to err on the side of caution. Alexander needs to be prepared for the worst."

"As does Susana."

His gut clenched. Aye. Both Susana and Magnus needed to be told of their suspicions at once. "Regardless of whether or not we're right, I think we need to launch into our battle plan. At once."

Hamish's frown was grim. "Agreed."

It made sense to ratchet up their fortifications. This incident made one thing crystal clear. Though the perpetrators were too cowardly to come at them straight-on, preferring to skulk and strike from the shadows, Dounreay was under attack.

CHAPTER FIFTEEN

Dinner that night was a subdued event. While Isobel seemed to have weathered her ordeal with striking aplomb, even she was not her usual garrulous self. Magnus, with whom Hamish and Andrew had spoken earlier in the day, was dour at best, although he did eschew his whisky and that might have been the cause. Keir was moody as he picked at his dinner, and Susana was somber.

Their gazes met often, but the playfulness of the evening before was missing.

Then again, it didn't belong here.

Shortly after the meal ended, Susana and Isobel went up to bed. Susana made it a point to mention that Isobel would be sleeping in her room tonight.

It was said for all to hear, but Andrew knew the message was for him, and for all that he desperately needed to hold her again, and ached to spend the night with her, Isobel needed the comfort her mother could offer. So when she met his eye, he sent her a knowing glance and nodded. The relief and gratitude on her face was palpable.

With the frustrations of the day, Andrew had no expectation of falling asleep, but he did.

He wasn't surprised to wake in the morning with a weight on his chest. His first thought, folly though it was, was that it was Susana, come to wake him. But once he gathered his wayward thoughts, he realized the weight was far too light. And Susana would probably not be exploring his nostril with a plump finger.

Isobel.

Thank God he'd slept in his tunic.

He cracked open an eye and surveyed her.

She grinned.

"How did you know where my room is?" he asked.

She shrugged. "I know everything."

"Everything?" Now, there was a truly terrifying thought.

"Everything that I want to know."

No doubt she did.

"You really shouldna be here."

She tipped her head to the side. "You say that to me a lot."

"Because it's true." He eased her back a bit and levered up into a sitting position where he didn't feel so . . . vulnerable. They had a habit of making him feel vulnerable, these Dounreay women. "Did you sleep well?"

"Aye."

"And how are you feeling? After yesterday?"

"Better."

"I'm glad."

"Mama's still fretting, but I'm not. I have an idea."

She didn't elaborate, and he didn't ask. Indeed, he didn't dare.

"Your mama is fretting?" His brow furrowed. The thought of Susana being upset concerned him.

"Aye. She tossed and turned and mumbled in her sleep all night." Isobel closed one eye and peered at him, much the way Magnus often did. "Why do you suppose she said your name?"

"I . . . ah. I wouldna have a clue."

"Do you think she was dreaming of you?"

Now, there was a lovely thought. "I am a rather impressive man."

Why she broke into peals of laughter and rolled about on the bed was a mystery.

He put out a lip. "Do you no' think I'm impressive?"

"Och, aye." She patted his shoulder, but he could tell it was a patronizing pat. She glanced at his sword, on the table beside the bed. "I thought you were verra splendid yesterday. The way you fought. Your swordplay was brilliant."

Coming from her, that was fine praise indeed. "Thank you."

"Mama was impressed, too." She sat up and studied him for a moment before saying, in a low voice, "I saw you kissing her."

He stilled. Oh, bluidy hell. What did one say to that? Sorry? He certainly wasn't sorry. "I did kiss her."

"Do you like it?"

"Verra much."

Isobel gusted a sigh. "Are you going to ask her to marry you?"

Andrew flinched. He didn't mean to, but her words caught him by surprise. *Marry her?* The thought flooded him with an unexpected thrill, an excitement unlike anything he'd felt in a very long time. It was a bit early for thoughts like that, but he couldn't excise the notion. Wouldn't it be wonderful having a woman like that all to himself? Wouldn't it be wonderful to sleep with her each and every night? To have the right to kiss her when and where he wanted?

Of course, she didn't want a husband. She averred she didn't need a man. In all likelihood, if he were foolish enough to ask such a question, she would, at best, laugh in his face. At worst, he'd walk away with an arrow in his arse. But Isobel was staring at him, eyes wide and expectant, awaiting his answer. He couldn't lie. "If I were going to ask any woman to marry me, it would be your mama."

She sighed again, this time rolling her eyes.

Disappointment scalded him. "Do you no' . . . um . . . do you no' like that idea?" Why her opinion mattered to him so much was a mystery. But it did. And not just because if he ever—at some point in a very vast future— scraped together the courage and fortitude to ask Susana for her hand, and if she should accept, he would want Isobel's blessing. That she mocked the prospect bothered him more than it should.

Again she patted him in that patronizing manner. "I like it fine." She tipped her head to the side. "But I doona want you to get shot. She does shoot them, you know. In the arse."

He swallowed heavily. Aye. She did. "She might not shoot *me*." Was that a forlorn hope tingeing his tone?

"She's shot all the others."

"True." He fell silent for a moment and then added, because he should, "Well, it hardly signifies. It was only a kiss." A lie. "And we've only just met."

Isobel nodded. "Aye." She closed one eye and studied him again. "I've never seen her kiss a man before. I couldna help thinking . . ."

Something in her expression touched him. That frail hope, a longing perhaps. "Do you want her to marry?"

"I doona care if she does marry or not. But I would like a father. A girl should have a father." This she said with an incongruous maturity.

"Did you hear that from your grandfather?"

"Aye. But it's true." She bounced on the bed a little.

"Not just any father, though. Some of Mama's suitors were mean to me. I wouldna want a father like that."

"Aye. I never knew my father, but I had an uncle that was verra mean. I would rather have had no one."

She leaned against his chest, propping her chin on her folded hands, and gazed up at him. "Did your father die? Like mine?"

"Aye. When I was too young to remember him."

"I canna remember mine much, either."

"Your grandfather told me he was a good man."

"Aye. Everyone says that. That, and he would have been a fine father." She frowned. "I think you would make a fine father."

His pulse stalled. "Do you?"

"Aye. You are strong and smart and verra handsome."

"Do you think I'm handsome?"

She fluttered her lashes. "Verra. And Mama must like you if she let you kiss her. Aside from that, you could protect me and teach me things." She glanced at his sword once more. "Give me things."

A riffle of unease walked through him. Something to do with ominous glint in her eye. He hoped she wasn't playing him like a fiddle, but he suspected she was. She was far too charming when she wanted to be. "What . . . kinds of things?"

"I've always wanted to have a sword."

He blinked. "You're five." She couldn't even *lift* his sword.

"I was thinking I could start with a small one. That's what the boys do. They learn how to fence with wooden sticks and then they get small swords."

"Should you no' be talking to your mother about this?"

A fat lip came out. "She willna let me have a sword. She says bows are more ladylike."

Andrew nearly laughed. Neither was truly ladylike. But he wasn't going to be the one to suggest this to Susana. Or Isobel. "Well, I'm not giving you my sword."

"I'm not asking for *your* sword. But I would like you to give me lessons."

"Lessons?" He gaped at her. "You want me to teach a five-year-old girl how to wield a sword?" Ah, to what depths had he descended?

"Aye."

"And when would you want to begin?"

"Now."

He chuckled. "Surely not now. I need to dress. Breakfast would be nice."

"This morning then? After breakfast?"

Her smile was hopeful. It sparked something in him . . . an idea. A devilish idea.

"If I do agree to teach you . . ."

"Aye?"

"If I do show you how to defend yourself with a sword, what will you do for me in return?"

She narrowed her eyes. "What do you want?"

What did he want? Her mother. In his bed. Well, not this bed, obviously, but some bed. However, he could hardly tell her that. "Will you advise me on how to woo your mama?"

Her eyes widened. "Ooh. I should like that."

Aye. He thought she might.

"Then I would be happy to teach you what I know, but . . ."

She squinted at him. "But what?"

"But doona tell your mother."

Her brow puckered. "About which thing? The lessons or the wooing?"

"Both."

Apparently the prospect of such subterfuge delighted her. Her laughter rippled through the room.

∽

No one was in the breakfast room when Susana descended. She didn't know why disappointment flooded her. Surely she wasn't hoping to find Andrew there.

She'd thought about him all night. Ached for him.

She'd even thought about sneaking from her room to his, but if Isobel had woken to find her gone, she might have worried. After her ordeal, her daughter needed the security of knowing her mother was by her side. Night and day.

On that note, how vexing was it to wake and find her gone?

A niggle of unease had prodded her, prompting her to rise and dress at once, even though she very much wanted to lounge in bed. It was perhaps irrational, this urge to know exactly where her daughter was and what she was doing at any given moment, but considering recent events, it was probably understandable.

It didn't help to see that the cakes on the sideboard had been ravaged. That meant Isobel was up and about and God knew where. Susana didn't revel in the idea of spending the morning hunting for her, but her protective instincts were in a frenzy.

She grabbed a scone and turned to head out to launch a search when a movement outside the window caught her attention. She blinked and then stepped closer, peering past the drapes.

A large man and a small girl—both with silver hair— faced each other in the garden. They both held small wooden swords. In his hand, the weapon was laughable, but the scene, the import of it, was not.

Her heart swelled as Andrew showed Isobel a series of steps, and then parries and lunges. Her daughter focused on each one and copied it with excruciating accuracy.

Before yesterday, she would have been furious. For one thing, she'd told Isobel in no uncertain terms that she wasn't getting a sword, despite the fact that her daughter begged incessantly. Swords were far too sharp and dangerous.

But after yesterday, her thinking had shifted. Isobel needed to have every advantage if such an occurrence happened again. And to see Andrew teaching her warmed something in the region of her chest.

He was patient and very methodical as he walked her through the basics, and Isobel hung on every word. There wasn't a hint of recalcitrance in her expression. Nae. But there was a shining admiration. Reverence perhaps.

It was clear to her that Isobel adored Andrew. And that Andrew felt the same for her.

Susana swallowed a sob.

Ah, God. She needed to tell him.

She had to tell him.

It was a pity she didn't know how.

"Susana."

She whirled around at Keir's sharp bark, her tender thoughts shattered by his tone.

"Aye?" Something in his expression raked her. "What's wrong?"

He wiped his face with a palm. "We have a problem."

"A problem?"

"The men who attacked Isobel . . ."

"Aye?"

"The ones we were holding in the dungeon?"

"Aye?"

"They escaped last night."

Her stomach plunged. Acid crawled up her throat. "What? Weren't they guarded?"

"Aye. We had two men posted. Both were knocked out. Someone forced open the cell doors and the men are gone."

Susana glanced out the window, just to reassure herself that Isobel was safe. And aye, she and Andrew were still playing swordsmen. "We need to launch a search. Let's gather the men."

"Aye." Keir's gaze narrowed. "I canna help wondering . . ."

"Wondering? What?"

"Someone helped them. You know it wasna *our* men. It couldna have been."

"Of course not."

He nocked his head toward the window, where Andrew was patting Isobel on the head. "So if it wasn't our men, who was it?"

He let the question linger. It hung on the air in an ominous rumble. His implication was clear. It had to be one of Andrew's men.

Susana's fists tightened. She couldn't believe Andrew would order his men to attack Isobel. Not judging from the way he smiled at her. Not judging from what she knew about him.

Oh, aye, he'd betrayed her when she was a girl, and aye, she still carried some resentment from that. But this was different. That had been the thoughtless, lustful act of a young boy. This was a willful betrayal, one that could have devastating consequences to her family and her people.

She didn't think him capable of such a thing.

One of his men, however . . .

Keir leaned closer. "We need to be careful of them," he whispered. "We doona know them. Not really. We canna trust them. We canna trust anyone."

Susana sent him a contemplative glance. Keir was right, to some extent. There was a traitor in their midst, and until she discovered who it was, no one could be trusted. But she knew—knew in her heart—the traitor was not Andrew.

If it was, it would destroy her.

~∾~

After finishing his first fencing lesson with Isobel, Andrew left her with Magnus and Peiter in the library before setting off to begin the day's work. He didn't need to warn Isobel not to wander off. She seemed to have accepted the gravity of the situation and was happy to remain in the castle when she wasn't accompanied by an adult.

He'd been surprised and pleased at how adept she already was with a sword. Though she was extraordinarily young for such lessons, she'd caught on with astounding ease. He'd trained grown men who hadn't come so far in one lesson. It was as though she'd been born to wield such a weapon.

With that thought, he stopped to chat with the blacksmith about forging a real sword for her. Likely Susana wouldn't approve, but Andrew knew he would feel better if the girl had another weapon with which to defend herself should the need arise.

It occurred to him that he should probably tell Susana about the lessons. He cringed at the thought, but he hoped she would understand why he felt it was necessary. She was Isobel's mother. She would want to know.

A pity he didn't know how to broach the subject.

He found her in the study, reviewing the maps they'd drawn up, with a pensive expression on her face. She was alone, which sent pleasure skittering through him. He'd been thinking about holding her, kissing her again. He'd been dreaming about getting her alone. It had been far too long since they'd touched.

He kicked the door shut with his heel and, as a precaution, latched it.

When the thud echoed through the room, she whipped around, her eyes wide. She clutched her bodice. "Oh, Andrew. You frightened me."

He frowned. "I frightened you?" He didn't like that at all. He stepped closer, studied her expression. Something was wrong. All thoughts of kissing her evaporated.

Well, perhaps not all. But most.

"What's wrong, Susana?"

She stepped into his arms and he closed his hold on her. Ah, God, how he loved the feel of her.

He tipped up her chin and studied her face. He couldn't resist a kiss, but it was a small one. "What's wrong?"

"The men in the dungeon escaped."

He stilled. His muscles bunched. "What the hell? They were under guard. In a dungeon, for pity's sake."

"I know." She stepped away; he missed her warmth. She threaded her fingers and paced the room. "Someone helped them. The guards were knocked out and the doors pried open." She sucked in a deep breath and faced him. "Keir thinks it was one of your men."

His gut lurched. "Nae."

"It couldna be one of ours."

"It wasna one of mine. I'd stake my life on it."

"Andrew." She set her hand on his arm. "You could be gambling with just that. Or mine. Or Isobel's. How well do you know your men?"

"Verra well. Each and every one of them." They'd all grown up together. Trained together. Fought together. He pulled back and studied her. As gently as he could, he said,

"And consider this, Susana. There were traitors here in Dounreay before we arrived."

Her lashes fluttered and she nodded as she accepted this truth. The disturbing truth that it very well could be one of her men. "I'm so worried, Andrew. For Isobel. For Papa. I doona know who to trust."

"You can trust me." He set his palm on his chest. "I swear on all that is holy, I will never betray you or Isobel or Dounreay."

His vow was cold and clear and came from the heart.

He didn't expect her to respond by taking his cheeks in her soft hands and pulling him down for a kiss. He didn't expect the kiss to linger as it did.

He certainly didn't expect it to flare out of control, but it did, and quickly. Like a wildfire racing through summer tinder, it consumed them both. It was as though her fear and his frustration came together in a perfect conflagration of hunger, lust, and need. Need for reassurance, need for a tender touch, need for each other.

She pressed herself against him and deepened the kiss, raking her fingers through his hair, clutching him close. She made a sound, something like a whimper. It entered his mouth with her tongue and lit a flame within him.

He wanted her, more than he could say, and here she was, in his arms. And they were alone. Aye, it was folly to take her here, in this room, frequented by many men. They could be interrupted at any moment. His desire overrode his prudence. "We'll have to be quick," he whispered.

"Aye," she whispered back. "Quick."

He pushed her onto the table, unmindful of the papers and quills that fell to the floor. He kissed her neck, her cheek, her shoulder in a frenzy of passion. She responded in kind, tugging his tunic free and reaching for his breeks.

He yanked up her hem, baring her legs, reveling in the

softness of her body, her skin. He found her core and stroked it and she whimpered. "Andrew," she murmured against his neck, and then she bit him. It was a tiny nip, but impassioned, and her teeth were sharp. It sent a snarl of sensation through him, and with it, a surge of seething ardor.

"Susana," he huffed as, without hesitation, he thrust two fingers into her—there was no time for foreplay. He was desperate to touch her, feel her, have her again.

Her body seized around him; she whipped up her head and stared at him with a ferocity that burned. "Aye," she growled, urging him on. "Aye."

He fucked her with his fingers. Preparing her, opening her, spreading her creamy arousal over her swollen lips. With his other hand, he fumbled with the placket of his breeks. When he wasn't fast enough, she pushed him out of the way and did it herself. She sighed as she freed his cock, tall and rampant and ready. She held it in her hands and sighed. And then she leaned back and guided him home.

He groaned as he touched her entrance, shuddered as he eased the tip in.

He'd wanted this, needed this, ached for this for far too many hours. Gripping the firm flesh of her thighs, he thrust. Glory consumed him at the hot kiss of her sheath. Heat scuttled up his spine and a knot formed at the base of his balls.

She leaned back to give him room to maneuver, spreading her legs and wrapping them around his waist. She arched her hips to meet his every thrust, grunting and moaning as he held her still and pounded into her.

Her body tightened. Her breaths came in pants. Her eyes widened as he shifted position and hit her from another angle, and yet another. "Oh, aye," she huffed. "Aye, aye aye," in time to each reckless plunge. Goading him, tormenting him, leading him on.

She was, indeed, a perfect woman.

He knew she was close to release. He could see it in the taut lines of her face, feel it in the shivers of her flesh. He was close, too. A raging fire whipped though his veins, a scalding need burned in his soul. His thrusts became shorter, faster, harder. More desperate, more demanding. More savage.

And then she stiffened. She arched her back and closed on him with a heinous fist. Sensation screamed through him and his tightly leashed control snapped. He came. Erupted. Filled her.

Glory.

And glorious.

He threaded his fingers through her wild hair and pulled her up for a kiss, melding his mouth with hers as he reveled in the lingering lick of bliss. Then he eased from her body.

When he released her she collapsed on the table. "I needed that," she said.

He couldn't help lapping at her sweat-beaded brow. "So did I."

He turned his attention to refastening his breeks, but she lay there, staring at the ceiling with a small smile playing on her lips, reveling in the moment. Once his warrior was safely tucked away, he resettled her skirt, which was pooled about her waist. It wouldn't do for one of their men to wander in and find her splayed so, though he quite enjoyed the view.

She sat up and edged off the table. She smiled teasingly and stroked him, inciting his interest again, but just then, someone jiggled the door.

"Susana?" Keir's voice drifted through the wood. "Are you in there? Is everything all right?"

She shot the offending door a dark look, but forced a

cheery tone. "Aye. Everything is fine." When she passed him to open the door, Andrew caught her arm.

"Will Isobel be sleeping with you again tonight?"

Her lashes flickered. "I doona know." She caught his frown and responded with a wicked grin. "Doona fash yerself, Andrew. We'll work something out."

Well, thank God. Because even though he'd just had her, his ardor was rising once more. He didn't think he could bear another night without her.

Her grin became even more wicked. "Perhaps we can meet in the kennels."

CHAPTER SIXTEEN

Susana opened the door to Keir and he entered. His nostrils flared. Hopefully he couldn't smell what had just happened here.

But likely he could. His brow furrowed.

"I thought you would like to know," he said in a clipped tone. "You have a visitor."

Susana stepped farther away from Andrew, though there was clearly no need to try to hide what they'd been doing. Keir's gaze flicked from one to the other and his jaw clenched.

Her body still trembled from the force of their passion; bliss still bubbled through her. She smoothed down her skirts and surreptitiously checked that her bodice was in place. "Who is it?"

"Laird Scrabster, my lady."

Her head shot up. Her stomach heaved. Her face formed an automatic grimace, the reaction she always had to that name. "What the bluidy hell does he want?"

Keir lifted a shoulder. "Perhaps to offer for you again?"

Aye, that was usually why he made the day-long journey to Dounreay. He always left unfulfilled. He always would.

Andrew stiffened. A tiny growl emanated from him. "I doona think I like this man," he muttered.

Her glance was a tad derisive. "Just wait till you meet him," she whispered.

As they made their way down to the parlor, Keir didn't say a word. But then, his glares spoke for him. Susana knew it was because he worried about Andrew and his men; he was convinced the traitor was in *their* midst, but Susana wasn't so sure.

She didn't know how to reassure Keir that the men from Dunnet hadn't been the ones who had betrayed Dounreay, but they would need to have that conversation. She didn't like having the two men at odds like this. It was not productive.

That the traitor was probably one of his men would be difficult for Keir to swallow, because he had hired every man in their forces. It meant one of *his* men had turned against them. Once they had dealt with Scrabster, she would meet with Andrew and Keir, and together they would devise a plan to flush out the traitor. And they needed to do so at once.

Her impatience to deal with this pressing issue made Scrabster's visit even more annoying, which was surprising. His visits were, in and of themselves, annoying enough. He tended to be long-winded and pompous and overstay his welcome.

She and Andrew entered the parlor, though Keir remained at the door. Scrabster was seated with Papa and he had a whisky in his hand, though Papa's expression made clear that sharing his whisky with Scrabster—no matter what propriety demanded—was a burden.

Andrew wandered over to lean against the mantel, her silent supporter, but Scrabster ignored him, as he ignored Keir. He ignored almost everyone. Except her. He set his tumbler on the side table and leaped to his feet as he saw her. He was a smallish man, reedy and thin, with an unpleasant arrangement of features. His nose was long and hooked and his eyes had a birdlike glint. It was his fingers that repulsed her the most, bony and knobby. That and the whine in his voice. "Susana, my dear," he said, coming across the room to take her hands in his.

She winced and detangled as quickly as she could. His skin was clammy and his grip far too avaricious. He leaned in to kiss her cheek and she whirled away.

Though she normally didn't partake of whisky—especially in the afternoon—she felt the need for a dram now. She poured herself a drink and motioned to Andrew to do the same. He declined with an almost imperceptible wave of his hand. Though he appeared to be relaxed, his muscles were taut; he hummed with tension.

Surely it couldn't be jealousy. Anyone with eyes in their head could see that Scrabster was no threat to his claim on her.

Not that he had one.

Not that he wanted one.

This was a blissful fling for him. Of this she had no doubt.

It was a blissful fling for her as well.

She ripped her focus from the man who seemed to capture every ort of her interest and turned to their visitor. "To what do we owe this . . . honor?"

Scrabster retook his seat and pinned her with a beady stare. "Susana, my dearest." She shuddered. "I'm so sorry. I came as soon as I heard that you've been having troubles."

She sat on the divan and glanced at her father. Surely *he* had not notified Scrabster of their recent problems. With a shake of his head he confirmed it.

"I'm sure I doona know what you are talking about."

Scrabster *tsk*ed. His lip curled. It was almost a smile. He drummed his bony fingers on his knee. "The raids? The burned-out crofts? Why, I heard the brigands even tried to kidnap your daughter."

Susana almost bit her tongue, she clamped her teeth so hard. "Where did you hear that?" It had happened *yesterday*, for Christ's sake.

Scrabster's eyes flickered about the room. He cleared his throat. "I, ah, have my sources."

Her skin prickled. If Scrabster had "his sources," that meant only one thing. The traitor in their midst was working with him. Andrew had realized the same. His features tautened. A muscle ticked in his cheek.

"Regardless of where I heard this distressing news, it is verra clear, your people, your family, your *daughter* are not safe. And I have come to save you," he announced in a benevolent tone.

"Save me?"

"Offer you my . . . protection." That he said this in a lurid hiss didn't calm the churning in her gut.

"That is verra generous of you—"

His stubby lashes flickered. His smile was smug. "I know—"

"But we doona need your help."

Scrabster blinked.

"Dunnet has sent men."

Scrabster blew out a dismissive snort. "Bah. Dunnet. You canna count on him in the long term."

Susana bristled. She noticed Andrew did as well. "Of course I can count on him. He's family. He's married to my sister."

"Aye. But rumor has it, he will not be laird much longer."

She didn't like the glimmer in his eye, or the glee with which he imparted such news. "What do you mean?"

"Rumor has it, he has run afoul of the Duke of Caithness and will soon lose his barony."

"You hear a lot of rumors," Andrew said.

Scrabster's attention swung to him. His long nose twisted. "And who the bluidy hell are you?"

Andrew straightened, drawing himself up to his full height. "Dunnet's brother."

It was gratifying to see Scrabster pale. His Adam's apple made the long journey up and down his skinny neck.

Papa grinned, clearly pleased with Scrabster's discomfort and willing to incite more. "This is Andrew Lochlannach. He is leading the defenses at Dounreay." He leaned in and grinned. "A damn fine warrior."

"And mark my words," Andrew said in a cold clear voice, "we willna show mercy to the enemies of Dounreay."

Oooh. She liked the way he said that.

Scrabster did not. His face puddled up as though he'd just eaten something sour. "I am not an enemy of Dounreay." That he felt the need to make the statement bespoke his guilt.

"I certainly hope not." Susana shivered at the menace in Andrew's tone, even though it wasn't directed at her; it certainly took Scrabster aback. His eyes widened and his nostrils quivered. He tore his gaze from Andrew's fierce visage and focused on her.

"Susana. I must speak to you . . . alone."

A ripple ran over her skin. The last thing she wanted was to be alone with him. "There is no need for privacy. Anything you have to say to me can be said before my father and my . . . and Andrew."

Scrabster frowned. His gaze flicked from one man to the other. Andrew responded with a narrowing of his eyes,

and Papa with a wide grin; he took a slurp of his drink.
"But this is a delicate matter," Scrabster said in a wheedling tone.

Susana deplored wheedling tones. She crossed her
arms and glowered at him. "What is it?"

His lips worked. He adjusted his waistcoat. Cleared his
throat. "Susana, you know I hold you in the highest es-
teem."

Oh, bluidy hell. Not this again.

"I ask that you reconsider my suit."

"I have told you countless times, I willna marry you."

"But we're so well matched."

Where on earth had he gotten that idea? "Are we?" She
glanced at Andrew. She didn't know why. Surely it wasn't
to compare the two men, to consider, perhaps, how well
matched she was with one of them.

"Our lands share a border."

"These are not my lands."

He flushed. "No, of course not. I meant to say, we share
common interests. Common people."

"Those are hardly good reasons for a marriage." Aside
from which, she didn't want him and she never would. She
didn't even *like* him.

Scrabster forced a smile. It was a patronizing smile. Another thing she hated. "You have to marry sometime."

"Do I?"

His eyes narrowed. "Of course you do. You're a woman."

How that signified, she didn't know. But it certainly
made clear his opinion of the fairer sex. They were nothing, worthless without a man, in his opinion. If she had
ever been interested in him—and she had not—that alone
would have soured her.

She stood and brushed out her skirts in a very deliber-
ate manner. "I believe this interview is over."

"Nonsense. We have much to discuss. Recent events have proven that Dunnet cannot protect you." He fixed Andrew with a disdainful glare. "You need a man to keep you and your family safe. If you marry me, I will keep you safe."

"Where is my bow?"

Scrabster's nostrils flared. It was no secret she'd sent more than one suitor packing with an arrow in his hind-quarters. Scrabster might not be so fortunate. She was vexed enough to aim for far more tender territory.

"I believe you left it in the foyer," Andrew said. His lips twitched. "Would you like me to fetch it for you?"

"Yes, please."

"I can shoot him," a small voice piped up. Susana whirled to see Isobel at the door next to Keir with her bow in hand.

A wave of satisfaction and delight and, perhaps, a tinge of pride wafted through her. "If you'd like, darling."

Isobel lifted her bow and narrowed her eyes. "I haven't shot anything yet today."

Scrabster scuttled to his feet. He glared at her and then he glared at Papa and Andrew and then Isobel in turn. "There is no need for violence. I was simply coming to visit a neighbor. To offer my assistance in these difficult times."

"Ah." Susana crossed her arms. "Is that why you have men massing at our borders?"

His eyes narrowed, but he forced a smile. "Men to come to your rescue, my dear."

Why did she not believe him?

Andrew bristled. "If those men so much as step a toe across that border, we will consider it an act of aggression and will deal with it summarily."

Scrabster pulled himself up to his full height, which

wasn't much. He barely reached Andrew's chin. "There is no need to be rude."

"Is it rude to state the truth?" Andrew said through clenched teeth. "And it is the truth. Any threat to Dounreay will be answered with lethal force." Andrew fingered the hilt of his sword.

Scrabster's narrow eyes flared. He stepped back and back again, until he found himself at the door.

It was heartwarming that Isobel's arrow tracked his every move. When he noticed, he flinched. His lip curled then and he stepped closer to Isobel, running his fingers through her hair. Susana's stomach heaved. "Such a pretty girl," he said. He affected an oily smile. "It would be a pity if anything should happen to her because you rejected my offer to protect you."

Even as rage flooded her, Isobel hauled off and kicked him in the shins; Scrabster grabbed his leg and howled an invective at her, his eyes snapping with anger.

Susana bristled. The last thing she needed was Isobel learning more bad words.

"Why, you . . ." the bastard growled, and he reached for Isobel, but she scampered out of reach and across the room, throwing herself onto the sofa at Papa's side.

Papa curled one arm around her in a protective manner, and then brushed at her hair, as though hoping to remove any remnant of Scrabster's touch.

"I think it's time you left," Andrew suggested in a frosty tone, and when Scrabster snarled at him, he drew his sword. The steel hissed as it left the scabbard.

"I agree," Susana said. "Keir, will you see Laird Scrabster out?"

Keir nodded and took Scrabster's arm. As he tugged him into the hall, Scrabster warbled, "Mark my words, girlie. You will regret this."

He continued to bellow his outrage as Keir led him from the castle. When his voice had faded, Susana whirled on Andrew. "I cannot stand that man."

"I concur." He sheathed his sword.

"Imagine the gall. Coming here. Threatening me. Intimating that without a husband I canna protect my daughter."

Papa grunted; Susana frowned at him. "You agree with Scrabster?"

"Nae. I doona. But you must admit, if you had a husband, he would probably stop offering for you."

Well, that silenced her impending tirade. It was true. No doubt it was true. She flicked a look at Andrew and then refocused her attention on her father. "A woman doesna marry for those reasons."

Papa sighed. "And for what reason does a woman marry? Because I've been wondering."

Isobel kicked her legs. "A woman marries when she falls in love."

"Nonsense." There was no such thing as love.

Isobel ignored her. She continued ticking reasons off on her fingers. "A woman marries when she finds a man she likes to kiss. A woman marries when she wants to have babies. A woman marries when she doesna want to be alone anymore . . ."

Susana ignored the fact that all those reasons applied to herself.

"A woman marries when the right man asks her."

She rubbed at her face. "Isobel, isn't there something you'd rather be doing?"

"Aye. But I canna go outside by myself."

Papa grinned at her. "What do you say to a visit to the library?" His gaze flickered to her bow in a meaningful way and Isobel's grin blossomed. He winked at Susana as he led her daughter away. Lord knew what mischief the two of them might get up to, but at least Isobel would be in safe hands. And she seemed to have accepted her restrictions.

"Are you all right?" Andrew asked. His hand was warm, comforting as he stroked her back. She leaned into his strength.

"Aye. But that man is so . . ."

"Aggravating?"

"That's one word for it. Can you believe the nerve of that man?"

"Indeed. As though you would marry *him*."

She rather liked the way he spat that. "I was talking about his veiled threats. That without him, my people are no' safe. My daughter isna safe. And did you see the way he touched her?"

"If you like, I could follow him and chop off the offending hand."

She peeped up at him. "Would you do that? For me?"

He chuckled. "Indeed, I would."

"How romantic." She nestled closer, enjoying their banter. Somehow, it calmed her. Of course, that could be the weight of his arms around her, or the drugging skim of his palm on her back.

"I would do anything to keep you safe, Susana. I'm here to protect you and Isobel, no matter what."

She didn't respond. Couldn't. Something clogged her throat.

It might have been her heart.

෧෨

Andrew sprawled on his bed, staring up at the ceiling and aching. With the recent threats to Isobel, he knew he wouldn't have a chance to be with Susana for the fore-seeable future, unless they met for trysts like the one in the study today. That had been incredible. As he thought of it, it didn't take long for his hand to drift down under the covers and start stroking his cock.

He closed his eyes and thought about her—her eyes, her hair, her tempting thighs—as his hand moved in a familiar rhythm.

With his passion high and his release nigh, the knock on the door was inconvenient.

He considered ignoring it, but only for a moment. Something could have happened. Susana might need him.

The knock came again, more insistently.

"One moment," he called as he tugged on his breeks.

Whoever it was, was not patient. Another series of raps issued forth before he could cross the room. He flung open the door. "What is it—?"

His words stalled in his throat. Susana, draped in a cloak, hovered in the hallway.

He gaped at her.

She was the last person he'd expected. Tonight. In a cloak.

Inexplicably, she glared at him as she slipped into the room and shut the door behind her. Her brow furrowed. "Well, for pity's sake, what took you so long? I could have been seen." Her voice was sharp. Sharper than it should have been for a late-night visit like this.

He waved at the bed. "I was . . . um . . . Susana? What are you doing here?"

"I needed to see you." She untied her cloak and swung it off, draping it over a chair.

"Why did you wear a cloak?" Indoors?

"I was skulking."

He couldn't stop his lips from tweaking. "Skulking?"

"Aye. I needed to see you."

"What's wrong?"

"Nothing." Her smile was wicked. Ah. There it was. "I *needed* to see you."

God, he needed to see her, too. But he didn't sweep her into his arms as he wanted to. Not yet. "And Isobel?" For some reason, he needed the reassurance that she was all right before he could relax.

"She's fine. She's sleeping. She insisted on staying in her own room tonight."

"That is promising."

"Aye."

"But we should set a guard."

"I already have. One of yours and one of mine, in fact." She stepped into his arms and tipped back her head so she could smile at him. When her groin nudged his, she frowned and wriggled against him. "What is this?"

"Do you no' know?"

"I have an idea." Her brows furrowed. "Why are you so hard?"

He considered his options—and the interest in her eyes—and decided he should tell her the truth. "I was thinking of you."

Her lashes fluttered. "Are you always hard when you think of me?"

"Usually."

"I want to see." Though he protested, she pushed him back toward the chair by the fire. He sat with a thud and she knelt between his knees. Now, he should have stopped her—indeed, he intended to—but she reached for the placket of his breeks, opened them, and found his cock. And when she took it in her hands and stroked it as she studied it, he found himself unable to protest at all.

"It's verra hard."

He shuddered as she drew a questing finger around the thick head and then traced the fat vein along his length.

"And verra soft." He shivered as she wrapped her hand around him and gave him a tentative pump.

"Ah, Susana. You'd better not," he said.

Her enthusiastic expression crumpled. "Do you no' like this?"

"I like it verra much, but I'm . . . God, doona do that." He lurched as she began tickling his balls.

"Why not?"

He took her by the shoulders and then, upon second thought, caged her wrists. "Because I have been *thinking* about you," he said meaningfully. "For a while."

Her eyes went wide, as though she didn't understand. He sighed. "Didn't your husband . . . touch himself sometimes?"

She blinked up at him. "I . . . I doona know." She glanced at his lap. "Were you touching yourself?"

He ignored her question. "You doona *know*?" How could a wife not know? Especially if she and Gilley had shared a bed . . . *If* they'd shared a bed. He narrowed his gaze on her. For a woman who had been married, she did seem rather ignorant of the ways of men.

Her chin firmed. She took hold of him again and countered with, "Were you touching yourself?"

"Aye."

"I want to see."

He gaped at her. "Susana . . ."

"Please, Andrew. Show me. I want to see."

Heat crawled up his neck. He wasn't sure if it was a result of his embarrassment or his desire. Or if it mattered in the least. "Susana, I want to make love to you."

"Show me first."

He sighed. "If I show you, it may be the end of me. I willna be able to make love to you . . . and I'd really rather make love to you."

She issued a snort. "Do you no' have any self-control?"

He snorted right back. "Nae." Not with her, he didn't. "You are a verra beautiful woman, Susana. I find myself lacking in any kind of control around you."

Her lips curled. "I'm sure you can hold back."

"I doona know from where you have acquired this foolish confidence in me."

"Just show me a little."

"All right." He closed his eyes—because looking at her would surely incite disaster—and began to polish his knob. He did it slowly, because he couldn't bear to move quickly.

He flinched when a whisper skated over the head of his cock. His eyes flew open and he *eep*ed. *No! Please God, no!*

That something was her breath, warm and damp.

He hissed as her mouth closed over him. Of their own accord his eyes closed, his head fell back. Heaven and hell rained down on him as she sucked the tip of his cock. "Susana. *Please.*"

She released him with a plop. "You can hold back," she whispered. "You're a big, strong man," She punctuated each word with a heinous pump.

"I canna."

"You can. And you will." The words were infused with an imperious tone that sent shivers through him. Her fist began moving faster, her mouth retook him, sucking him in.

Agony coiled at the base of his balls. Need rose within him, blinding and savage.

"Susana." A plea.

She only tightened her grip. She added a little twist to each pass. Took him deeper, until her hand met her mouth, until she had him fully encased in one or the other. And then she sucked.

Insanity swelled. Bliss and glory and excruciating pleasure exploded within him, flooded his heart and mind and soul, as he released into her mouth.

He didn't intend to, God help him he didn't intend to, but she was far more woman than he could ever resist.

He gazed down at her as she lapped at her lips—and damned if that didn't stir his ardor again. "Why did you do that?" he asked. He was certain there was no petulance in his tone.

Her smile was as satisfied as the cat that got the cream. "Because I wanted to know."

"Know what?"

"Know what you taste like."

A thousand questions spun in his head—including the most prominent: *Had she ever done that for Gilley?*—but he settled for, "What did you think?"

"What did I think?"

"Aye." He swallowed heavily, waiting for her response on bated breath. Though this was not what he'd intended to happen, he had enjoyed it immensely.

"I think you are delicious." Her expression lit a flame in his belly. "And I think I would verra much like to do that again sometime."

Though she'd drained him utterly, his cock stirred.

God help him.

CHAPTER SEVENTEEN

The scorching look in Andrew's eyes stole Susana's breath. He closed the placket of his breeks and took her hand. He helped her to her feet and then stood beside her, staring down at her face. His attention locked on her lips, and he kissed her. It was a slow, sweet, delicious kiss that made her knees shake.

"Come." He tugged her hand, leading her to the bed.

"I should go," she said, but only because she thought she should.

He chuckled. The sound rounded the room. "Do you really think I'm going to let you go? After that?"

"But . . ." What more could they do? She had finished him.

"Hush." He threaded his fingers through her hair and cupped her face. His thumb traced her mouth in a warm trail. "Hush."

When he guided her down onto the mattress, she allowed it. His expression made clear he had plans for her, plans she would greatly enjoy. But he didn't join her. Instead, he did what he'd done once before, easing off one slipper and then the other. A memory, a shudder racked her.

He sat on the bed at her feet and nibbled on her toes, her ankle, her calf. He licked his way up her thighs, nudging up her skirts as he moved. He did it slowly, with an agonizing thoroughness, not missing so much as a spot.

It seemed to take forever for him to reach the nubbin throbbing between her legs. She stiffened as he touched her, but he did it so lightly, it made her want to scream.

"What are you doing?" she asked, surely not with impatience.

"What do you think?" He opened her, gazed down at her, blew on her with a soft breath.

The juxtaposition of his cool breath and the heat of her core sent sensation and arousal careening through her. She was already damp. Already ready for him, but his slow seduction ratcheted up her tension. She wriggled a little, hoping to encourage him to move more quickly.

He did not.

He dipped his head—she caught her breath—but it was only to place a soft kiss on the inside of her thigh. His hands, broad and warm, skimmed across her hip, sending ripples over her skin.

She spread her legs, just slightly, and only to encourage him.

He pushed her hem up farther and kissed her stomach. All the while he toyed with her curls, almost touching her—almost really touching her—but not quite.

She arched up into his caress and he pulled back with a smile.

"Stop teasing me."

"It's only fair."

She frowned at him. "I doona tease you."

"You tease me every moment of every day. With each glance and every smile."

"I most certainly do not."

"You do, Susana. You do."

To her dismay, he sat up. She was about to complain, but before she could make her mouth form the words, he said, "I want you naked."

She swallowed. "N-Naked?"

"I've never seen you naked, Susana."

The thought thrilled her, even as it frightened her. She had no idea why it frightened her. She trusted him. She wanted him.

Ah. That was likely the source of the fear. How *much* she wanted him.

"You first."

Without pause, he whipped off his tunic. His body was sheer perfection, carved from stone and perfectly formed from the bulging biceps of his arms to the hard planes of his abdomen. His muscles rippled in the dim glow of the lamp. As she stared at him, saliva pooling in her mouth, aching to explore, he grinned. His expression was one of confidence, not arrogance, which she appreciated. Though he had every right to be arrogant. He was, in a word, beautiful.

"The breeks, too."

His gaze warmed as he slowly unfastened the placket and let his breeks fall.

Her heart pattered in her chest.

Och. Jesus, Mary, and Joseph!

She'd seen his cock. Touched it, tasted it, been filled by it. But she'd never seen it like this.

A magnificent man stood proudly before her. Naked. Aroused.

His face was perfection, handsome, adorable. His hair flowed over his shoulders in a silver shimmer. And those shoulders, broad and thick and strong. His chest, slabs of muscle covered by tanned skin. His belly flat and hard. His legs as thick as tree trunks and between them, his cock . . . Heavy and full, it rose from its nest, though the weight of it tipped it to the side. Even as she stared, it stirred.

His grin was dimpled, naughty. "Susana . . ." A warning tone. "Your turn."

Quivering, she slid off the bed and stood before him. She worked the buttons of her kirtle and let it fall until she stood in nothing but her thin chemise. He watched with avid attention as she fumbled for the hem and lifted it.

He hissed a breath as she bared her hips, her stomach, and her abdomen. His tongue peeped out as she lifted it higher, to show her breasts.

They were just breasts, and just hers, but his reaction when she exposed herself was delicious.

He swallowed. His fingers twitched. He made a little noise, something wistful and aching. His cock rose to full attention, a slow slick slide along his belly, a glistening pearl at the tip.

Ah. He liked her breasts. It was gratifying.

She whipped off the chemise, because she'd become impatient with that reveal. When he stepped toward her, palms cupped, as though he would test their weight, she held up a finger. "Ah, ah, ah."

He stopped. Blinked. Opened his mouth, to protest, perhaps.

Her smile was fiendish. "Not just yet," she purred. And then she cupped herself.

They were just breasts and just hers, but it was astounding how sensual they felt in her hands as she stroked them, rubbed them, played with them . . . for him.

His features went taut, though his mouth went slack, which was, she found, an amusing combination. "Och," she murmured. "So soft." She nudged a nipple, circled it, reveling in the wave of sensation her own touch sent through her body, straight to the nub at her core.

"Susana." A whisper. A hiss. A plea.

"Oh, Andrew. This feels so good."

"Susana."

His muscles were locked. His jaw clenched. His nostrils flared. He trembled as she stroked her body before him. When her hand eased down, over her stomach, to the nest between her legs, he made a strangled sound.

"Ohh," she purred as she stroked herself. Her crease was creamy, sensitive, the button hidden within the folds, hard and hungry. And aye, she would have much preferred having him touch her, but holding him captive like this was far more scintillating.

Also, he was a tease. When he touched her, she writhed in frustration. When she touched herself, she found, there was no wandering road to passion. It was direct, and intense, and immediate.

Her breath caught as she found a rhythm, a pressure, a rotation that pleased her. Desire rose like a bonfire within her. She moved faster, harder, with far more desperation than she'd ever felt. Her body tightened from the outside in.

He stared, lips damp, eyes glittering, hands clenched in furious fists.

When she broke, he caught her. When the ecstasy washed over her like a raging tide and her knees locked and her body succumbed, he caught her and laid her gently on the bed.

But that was his last moment of gentility.

Once she was on her back, he thrust her legs apart with his knees and wrenched her arms above her head, holding on to her wrists with one hand. He hovered over her, leaning on one side as, with his free hand, he fisted his cock and guided it home. "Susana," he growled, "you drive me wild with need." And he thrust in.

The glory, which had not yet abated, flared again, this time winging her to higher heights, to a pinnacle of bliss she'd never experienced. It stole her breath. Her heart pounded madly. Her mind spun, her body sang.

He filled her with his beautiful cock, shoving in like an enraged beast, stretching her, invigorating her, stoking her fire with each maddened thrust.

As he moved over her and in her, he scraped her sanity. The annoying rub of his fat head against a bundle of nerves at her core drove her wild. The hairs of his chest abraded her nipples with each lunge. Each time he seated himself, their groins met and ground together in an agonizingly brief kiss.

It didn't take long for her to succumb again. Her orgasm was a beautiful flower, unfolding within her, nudged incessantly by his movements. But he, though maddened as he was, lasted much longer.

He lifted her legs and held her up and pounded into her at a new angle, which sent drizzles of pleasure showering through her. As he worked her, slamming into her with hard thrusts, he stared at her breasts, bounding with each lunge. Unable to resist, he leaned down and seized them, licking, lapping, stroking—even pinching—as his hips continued to move.

The sensations drove her mad and though it was beyond belief, beyond sanity, she felt her body tighten again. She was close. So close. She clutched at him, raking her fingers over his back, yanking on his hair, howling her need as her crisis neared.

To her astonishment, he yanked out just as she was about to crest.

He ignored her warble of protest—it was all she could manage at the moment—and flipped her over onto her belly. Confusion ripped through her and she glanced at him over her shoulder. His expression—hard, hot, intent, and savage—eviscerated her.

God, he was a remarkable man.

He took hold of her hips with hard fingers and levered her onto her knees and then, with no warning, took her from behind, plowing into her with a mind-bending plunge. The intensity of his incursion unhinged her. She lost all control and spun into some ethereal realm where bodies and souls were wreathed in heavenly light and song and absolute rapture.

Her release seemed to inspire him. Though he continued moving, she could feel his tension mount. His groans and grunts twined with her moans. The slap of flesh against flesh rocketed around the room as he pummeled her. His cock swelled, his intensity peaked. And then he went stiff, around her and in her.

A great surge of heat filled her. And another. And another. His cry was one of triumph but also, one of submission. He thrust again, and again, but each more gentle than the last until his movements were nothing more than the gentle rocking of his hips as he released his hold on heaven.

He eased from her and collapsed by her side, pulling her along with him, cupping her with his body. He murmured something, something garbled that might have been her name, though it was difficult to tell through the pants of his breath. He took her breast, claiming it as his own, and pulled her closer.

Susana nestled back, loving the feel of his body around hers, the lingering ripples of delight, the knowledge she had power over this powerful man. She felt so safe in his arms. So protected and adored. It was the most rapturous feeling she'd ever known.

She probably should not have closed her eyes, because once she did, she drifted off to sleep.

෨෨

Andrew held Susana through the night, barely sleeping a wink. He couldn't bear to miss a moment. She felt splendid in his arms, soft and sweet and fragrant. He loved the way she curled around him and nuzzled him and stroked his skin in her sleep. He loved the feel of her bare body melded to his.

Aye, his passion rose again as he stroked her, exploring the curves and valleys of her body in the shadows of night, but he didn't wake her. There was time for passion later. At the moment, this closeness, this intimacy, was far too sweet. Too raw. Too precious to shatter.

He was still awake when dawn began to lighten the sky, lying on his back with Susana's soft weight on his chest, reveling in her warmth, the huff of her breath, her delicate snores. Each one made him smile. Made his heart swell with some indefinable emotion. Tenderness for her, love perhaps, made his chest ache.

As the sunlight stretched into the room, her body was lit in a soft pink glow. He couldn't resist tracking the lines of her form again, studying her curves as they were revealed to him. He scudded a palm over her shoulder, down her arm, and to the enticing lift of her hip.

God, she was exquisite.

His hand froze as he spotted something on her thigh.

He eased her from his chest and onto the pillow. She settled there with a sleepy snuffle but didn't wake. He leaned closer to study it.

It was a birthmark, almost a heart, with a wedge missing.

His breath caught. His gut rippled. He'd seen this birthmark before.

With a trembling finger he traced it, the mark he'd never forgotten, the mark he couldn't thrust from his dreams. Mairi had had such a mark.

It hit him hard and fast then. Why Susana reminded him

of the young girl he'd once seduced, once loved and lost all those years ago. Why his heart pounded when he touched her. Why his soul sang when they kissed.

Susana *was* Mairi.

The realization stunned him. For six years he'd been tormented by the knowledge that Mairi had died—because of him. Or at least that was what Kirstie Gunn had told him. But here was proof that she had not died.

He stared at Susana as the rising sun revealed her features. In her sleep, with all her usual tension banished, she looked younger, like the carefree girl he had so adored. One who had captured his heart with a kiss.

How could he not have seen it? How could he not have known?

Barely able to breathe, he eased back down beside her and lifted her into his arms again, staring at her in awe and trepidation. He pulled her closer, reveled in the fact that she nestled in. Wrapping his arms around her, he held her. She was a warm weight on his chest, one he'd yearned for, for far too long.

Mairi.

She was his Mairi. Here in his arms once again.

He wanted to weep, but could not.

It ate at him that, for some reason, she'd hidden her identity from him. For some reason, she hadn't wanted him to know who she was.

But he now did. Now everything had changed.

Though he risked ruining all, he knew he had to confront her with his discovery. He needed to know . . . why.

She stirred and he stilled. She glanced up at him, her eyes alight. Her lips tweaked.

He couldn't help kissing them. "Good morning," he said.

"Mmm." She tucked her head against his shoulder once more. "Is it morning? Already?"

He kissed her brow. "It is." *Mairi. Mairi.*

"I shouldna have stayed."

"I'm verra glad you did." He stroked her, running his palm over the velvety skin of her back. "Last night was wonderful."

"Mmm." Her fingers trickled over his chest, riffling through his hair, rousing his passion. He caught her hand and threaded his fingers in hers. Aye, he'd woken wanting her—it was rare when he wasn't roused by her presence— but they had little time before they would have to rise for the day and he didn't know when he would have such a moment alone with her again. As much as he would have loved to take her again, in the light of day, as much as he didn't want to spoil this fragile intimacy, his curiosity consumed him.

They needed to talk.

Trouble was, he wasn't sure how to broach the subject. He decided on a roundabout approach.

"Susana?"

"Aye?"

"I was wondering . . ."

"Aye?"

"About your husband."

She stiffened in his arms. He caressed her neck, her shoulders, her arms, until she relaxed. "What about him?"

"Did you love him?"

Her glance was shadowed, hidden beneath her lashes. "Of course I loved him."

His stomach plummeted. Had he expected another answer?

"He was a verra good man."

"I'm sorry you . . . lost him." He knew the pain of losing a loved one to death. It was devastating. World ending. Soul crushing.

She peeped up at him, frowned, and traced the lines on his face. He tried to release the tension in his features, but could not. The memory of that day, the day he'd learned his love had left the world, haunted him. "Have *you* ever been in love?" she asked.

Ah, yes. The opening he needed. He hoped this revelation didn't shatter their tender connection, but he couldn't go on, pretending he didn't know who she was. Still, he couldn't meet her intense gaze. He set his chin on her hair, drew in her scent. "Once."

She stiffened again, and again, he soothed her.

"I met her long ago, when I was a boy. At first look, I knew I had to have her. At first kiss, I knew I loved her."

She pulled back, forced him to meet her eye. "That seems verra impetuous."

"Do you no' believe in love at first sight?"

Her brow rumpled. "I used to."

"You fell in love at first sight?"

"Once."

"Was it Gilley?"

A flush rose on her cheeks. "Nae. It wasna Gilley." She sighed. "It was long ago, when I was verra young." Why she frowned at him, he didn't know. "He broke my heart."

"Aye," he said. "Mairi broke my heart as well."

This time when she stiffened, he could not soothe her.

"Mairi?" She studied him, nibbling on her lip. It was very distracting. But he waited to see her reaction, though the tension nearly killed him. "Tell me about her."

He let out his breath and tucked her back into his arms, although he was sure she did not want to be tucked.

"She was perfect," he said.

Susana *hmph*ed.

He tried not to chuckle. "She had silken red hair and soft, alabaster skin." His palm skated over her hair, her cheek. "Glorious green eyes." He tipped up her chin and looked into those eyes. "Ripe, red lips." He kissed those lips. "A tantalizing dent on her chin." He kissed that, too. "And a birthmark." His hand skated to her hip. "Here. The shape of a heart, split in two."

Her lashes fluttered. Her throat worked. What could have been a guilty expression flitted over her features. "What happened to her? This perfect girl? The girl you loved?"

He cupped her face so she couldn't turn away. "They told me she died."

Her eyes went wide. "She died?"

"Killed in a carriage accident. That was what I was told. For years I mourned her. Years, Susana. I ached for her. Wept for her. And worse of all, I blamed myself for her death."

She pushed away and sat up, covering herself with the blanket. Making it a point to cover her hip. "Why would her death be your fault?"

"Because she was running from me."

She narrowed her eyes. "Why would she run from a valiant man like you?"

"There was a misunderstanding . . . She thought I had betrayed her. But she was wrong." His gaze bore into hers. She didn't seem inclined to take the weight of it. She looked away.

"That is a shame."

"It was a tragedy. I dinna realize at the time that we had both been lied to. But now," he said, "I see."

Her head snapped up. Her frown became a glare.

"When first I saw you, you reminded me of her."

"How flattering."

"Susana. We both know why. Do we no'?"

She pressed her lips together mulishly.

"You were in Perth six years ago, weren't you?"

Her shoulder lifted.

"You canna deny it. You were that girl. You were my Mairi."

She flinched when he spoke her name.

"When I kissed you, I knew I'd tasted you before. I was flooded with such joy, such redemption. Such relief. I didn't understand it then, but I do now."

She pushed away, levered off the bed, and hunted for her chemise. Without a word, she pulled it on. He understood her need to cover herself. He felt vulnerable as well. "Andrew . . . I doona want to talk about this."

He stood and grabbed her wrist as she reached for her discarded kirtle. "We have to, Susana. We need to."

Her eyes glimmered as she stared at him. "I am not that girl."

"You were."

She opened her mouth as though to respond, but she didn't. She yanked her hand free and dressed quickly. "I need to go."

"Susana . . ."

"Isobel will be looking for me."

"Susana . . ." Her frown silenced him and he stepped back, releasing all hold on her. His hope deflated, dried up, and gusted away on a whipping breeze.

He should have said nothing. She didn't want to face the truth of their past. She didn't want to acknowledge what had happened between them, what had been. For some reason she was afraid.

He wouldn't press her. Not now.

He would give her time to release the past, to come to her own decisions about the undeniable connection burning between them.

He could only hope she would accept it for what it was. Accept him.

He couldn't bear losing her again.

Especially now.

CHAPTER EIGHTEEN

Susana stumbled as she made her way through the hall to her rooms.

He knew who she was.

She didn't know whether to be relieved or horrified. The truth was, she needed some time—away from his distracting presence—to work through her emotions, so she'd fled. His expression had been too raw, her heart too tender.

For six years she'd hated him and resented him and reviled him. He'd seduced her so callously and professed his love. She'd succumbed to his charms, only to find him in the arms of another woman. In a rage, she'd left. She'd been foolish enough to hope he would follow her when she fled Perth, but he had not. She'd assumed his disinclination to do so was a confirmation that he hadn't meant a thing he'd said.

But now, the revelation that he'd thought she'd *died*? That he had loved her?

He'd said they'd both been lied to. He'd been told she perished. She'd been told he was faithless, that he and Kirstie were having an affair—the truth of which she'd seen with her own eyes. But what had she really seen? A boy and a girl in an embrace. A kiss. Then Kirstie's expression when she'd glanced back at Susana's stricken cry. It hadn't been one of guilt or passion. It had been . . . triumph.

Susana had known Kirstie wanted Andrew for herself. She just hadn't realized how far her friend would go to win him. She shouldn't have been so trusting.

It could be true what he said. She owed him a chance to explain what had happened, from his point of view.

Aside from that, now that she'd had him again, now that she'd been in his arms with nothing between them, she didn't think she could bear to push him away.

She rounded the corner and saw Rory leaning back on a chair set before Isobel's room; the other chair was empty. His snore rumbled through the hall. Exasperation raked her. He was supposed to be guarding Isobel, not napping. She stormed to his side and kicked the legs of the chair and he tumbled to the ground with a yelp.

She stood over him, arms akimbo, and glared. "What are you doing?" she growled.

He scrambled to his feet and straightened his tunic. "I . . . I . . . I . . ."

"Oh, bother." She pushed past him into Isobel's room and stopped, stock-still. The bed was rumpled . . . and empty. She ran to the sitting room and peered in, and then to the closet where Isobel sometimes hid. Empty as well. Dread soured her stomach. "*Where is she?*"

Rory stood at the door, his eyes wide, his lips flapping. "I only closed my eyes for a moment. She was here. I swear she was."

"She's not here now." Her tone was acidic. Rory flinched.

She rushed across the hall to her own rooms. Her panic rose when they were empty as well. She never should have left her daughter. She never should have gone.

Sweat prickled on her brow. She whirled on Rory. "Who was sitting guard with you?"

"M-Marcus," he said. One of Andrew's men. Her blood

boiled. Her fists tightened. Had Keir been right? Was she wrong to trust the men from Dunnet after all? And had she paid a price too high?

She set her teeth and gritted through them, "Gather the men. We will search the castle from top to bottom. And for God's sake, find Marcus." She fixed her gaze on the quaking boy. He was pale and trembling but there was no mercy in her heart. He was supposed to be guarding Isobel, keeping her safe, but he'd failed. "If we doona find her, at once, I shall skin you alive," she bellowed, and then she stormed from the room.

He skittered in her wake.

God help him if anything had happened to Isobel.

And God help *her* . . .

ও৩

Andrew stared out the window of his chambers, seeing nothing.

It had been hard as hell watching Susana leave him, especially with the unanswered questions plaguing him. He knew with absolute certainty that she was his Mairi, but for some reason she didn't want to admit it.

He wouldn't understand women if he lived to be a hundred.

Although, when he thought back to the last time he'd seen her . . . he thought he might understand what had happened, and what it had looked like to her. He'd been waiting for Mairi in their usual spot in the woods when Kirstie had found him. They'd been chatting, Kirstie flirting more than usual and Andrew attempting to hold her off. And then, all of a sudden, she'd thrown herself into his arms and kissed him.

He'd been stunned and perhaps a little flattered. And

perhaps he hadn't pushed her away as quickly as he should have.

It was a mistake he would regret forever.

Mairi's cry still echoed in his soul. That moment was burned into his memory, when he'd glanced up and seen her expression. Eyes wide and filled with tears, limned with betrayal and heartbreak.

Before he'd been able to untangle from Kirstie's clinging limbs, Mairi had whirled away and disappeared. He'd tried to talk to her, to explain, but she'd refused to see him and then, the next day, she'd gone. And according to Kirstie, she'd never made it home.

By then . . . well, by then it was far too late to explain anything.

But her carriage hadn't overturned. She hadn't died.

Now, miraculously, it wasn't too late at all.

He glanced at the bed, remembering the beauty of the night they'd shared and his mood lifted. He'd made progress with Susana. They'd created an undeniable bond. He knew, with time, she would soften. She would allow him to tell her his story. And perhaps, they would have a second chance at the love they'd once known.

He dressed and made his way down the stairs, heading for the garden, where he was to meet Isobel for another fencing lesson. The little mite was coming along, picking up the basics like a man born with a sword in his hand.

"Andrew!" Susana's sharp tone cut through the foyer like a knife. His blood went cold. Had he really thought the night they'd shared had softened her?

He turned to see her rushing through the front door, followed by a few of her men, all of whom wore concerned expressions.

"Susana? What's wrong?"

She swept up to him, her expression hard. "Where is Marcus?"

He blinked. "Marcus?"

"He was supposed to be guarding Isobel. He's not at his station. And she's gone."

He frowned. "What do you mean, she's gone?"

"She's not in her room."

His gut tightened, but he forced the hint of unease away and set his hand on her shoulder. "Have you checked the garden? It's where we usually meet before breakfast."

She reared back and glared at him. "Why do you meet with my daughter before breakfast?"

Shite. He should have mentioned it earlier. He swallowed. "We, ah . . . I'm teaching her to use a sword."

"Oh. That." She brushed his confession aside. "No, she's not there. Or in the morning room." She leaned in and hissed, "No one has touched the cakes."

Something slightly acidic tickled the back of his throat. His pulse stuttered. Isobel would never miss the opportunity to have a cake. "Let's go find Marcus."

They found Marcus in the billet that had been set up for the men in the east wing. He was asleep in his bed. He appeared quite surprised when someone smacked him awake and he opened his eyes to find a fuming virago looming over him.

"Where is she?" Susana snapped.

"What?" He scrubbed his face. "Who?"

"Where is my daughter? You were supposed to be guarding her."

Marcus paled. His Adam's apple worked. He glanced at Andrew as he sat up in his bed. "I was relieved at dawn."

Tension sizzled around her in a dark cloud. "By whom?"

"By Hamish."

Susana's mouth snapped shut. Her cheeks paled. Her lips worked. She shot a reproving frown at Andrew. *"Hamish?"*

"Aye, my lady."

"Has anyone seen Hamish this morning?" Andrew asked. All the men shook their heads.

Susana teetered to the side.

He put his arm around her to steady her and, if he was being honest, to steady himself. "Doona worry, Susana. We'll find him. And we'll find Isobel." Andrew turned to his men and roared, "Come on, you lot, let's get moving."

❧

They searched all day. High and low. In every nook and cranny. But they found neither hide nor hair of Isobel or Hamish. When his friend couldn't be found, Andrew found himself racked by the sinking suspicion that he might never see him again.

He knew Hamish had had nothing to do with Isobel's disappearance, and if he was on watch when she was taken, there was no telling what could have happened to him. That Keir was also nowhere to be found was concerning, especially given the fact that Andrew didn't trust the man as far as he could throw him.

Andrew sent men out on extended patrols, focusing on the roads to the west and east; he charged Hamish's men with searching for clues—they were excellent and well trained at investigations like this, though Hamish was better. Andrew found himself sorely missing his friend, and his expertise.

They found little in Isobel's room, except for the disquieting fact that she'd left her bow behind. She would never have willingly left it behind. In her sitting room, where Hamish had been stationed, they found signs of a struggle, including a trickle of blood. His sword still lay on the table. A search of Keir's quarters turned up nothing untoward at all.

Tracks in the stable yard were impossible to follow, because there were so many, but he sent men out to search for any signs of recent passage in the woods. It was a gamble and a folly to expect they would find anything. Dounreay was a busy castle, and many souls wandered along those roads and rode through the woods.

There was a flicker of excitement when the men reported they'd found a trail of what looked like shreds of fabric on the road heading east, but then the trail disappeared.

That evening, as they gathered in the parlor to hear the dismal reports, he was beginning to fear they might not find Isobel.

Ever.

The thought sent a cold desolation blowing through him.

Susana was beside herself. Magnus was in a dither. Although Andrew was worried beyond belief—for Susana and Marcus, but mostly for Isobel and Hamish—he forced himself to remain focused. When his men issued their reports and left to continue searching, the three of them sat in silence in a suddenly dismal room.

Susana was twining her fingers and murmuring to herself and sharing desolate glances with Magnus. She was wan and pale. Her shoulders shook. Magnus didn't look any better. In fact, he seemed a shadow of his former self. A wraith.

Andrew frowned. "How long has it been since the two of you have had something to eat?"

They both glared at him.

"How long?"

Susana blew out a breath. "I doona know."

"Have you eaten at all today?" Her color was concerning. As were the dark shadows beneath her eyes.

"Nae. How could I eat?"

He turned his attention on Magnus. "How about you?"

In response, he lifted his tumbler, half filled with whisky. Hardly substantial sustenance.

Andrew motioned to Tamhas. "Have Cook bring a tray at once."

"I'm not hungry," Susana said.

Magnus curled his nose. "Neither am I."

Andrew sent a speaking look at Tamhas, who nodded and hustled away.

Susana stood and began to pace. "Why did he do it? Why would Hamish take her?"

His nape prickled. "Susana, I swear on my life, that is not what happened. Hamish would never do such a thing. And like Isobel, he would never leave his weapon behind."

"Then where is he?" Her eyes blazed with an accusatory fire.

"I can only assume they took him, too."

"Why? Who would want him, too?"

Andrew bristled. The suspicion that had been needling him would not be silenced. "Someone who wanted to make it seem as though Alexander's men were responsible for this. Do you have any explanation for why Keir would be missing?"

She frowned, then shook her head. "Nae."

"Has it occurred to you that Keir could be responsible?" he asked as gently as he could. She didn't respond, but from her expression he could tell the possibility had occurred to her.

God, she was so damn fragile. So brokenhearted. It made him want to sweep her into his arms and comfort her, but he knew she wouldn't allow it. Not right now.

"Susana, you need to rest."

She stared at him as though he'd just suggested she go jump naked into the loch. "Rest? My daughter is missing."

"It will be dark soon. There is nothing more we can do until daylight."

"I canna rest." She threaded her fingers and paced the room. "I canna. Who would take her? And why? Where is she, Andrew? Out there. Somewhere. Alone."

"My men will keep searching, Susana. They willna stop until they find her, do you understand? And if they turn something up, if we have a lead to follow, you will want to be rested tomorrow." He pulled her into his arms and stroked her, ignoring Magnus's avid attention. She allowed it, but then she pulled away, her face ashen.

"Doona," she said.

"Doona?"

"Doona touch me."

His heart clenched. He hated hearing those words from her. But he understood. This was the worst day of her life. She'd been betrayed by someone close to her. Her daughter was missing . . . But there was more to her despair. Something much darker lurking in her eyes.

"Susana, what is it?"

She glanced at Marcus—who was making love to his whisky—and then spun away. Andrew followed.

"Susana?"

Her gaze, when it met his, was tormented. It sent a lance of pain through his soul. "I shouldna have stayed with you." A whisper.

He stilled. Swallowed. "What?"

"I shouldna have stayed with you. I should have been with her. This is all my fault."

Ah, God. Nae. He wrapped her in his arms and held her, despite the fact she wanted to wriggle free, like

Isobel's bunny. Still, he held her close. "It is not your fault, Susana," he said into her hair. "Someone wanted her. Someone who had access to all our information. Someone who knew every detail of our defenses. It might not have happened last night, but it would have happened." Especially if, as he suspected, the villain was her trusted captain of the guard.

"I should have been with her."

He pulled back and stared down at her. "Has it occurred to you that if you had, they would have taken you, too?"

Her jaw firmed. "I doona care."

"I do. I need you." More than she knew. "I need you to help us find her."

"Me?"

He forced a laugh. "Susana, you are the fiercest woman I have ever met. Once we have some inkling where she is, we shall rally our troops and descend. Aside from that, when we rescue her, Isobel will need her mother. For comfort."

She put out a lip. "I'm not a very comforting person."

"You are an excellent mother. Isobel will want you there."

"Aye. I suppose." Her expression firmed. "And if we discover this is Hamish's doing—"

"It is not."

"I will delight in personally slicing him open from stem to stern."

"It wasna Hamish. I assure you." She clearly didn't believe him, but he had faith the truth would win out.

Tamhas surprised them by returning much faster than Andrew had expected. And he didn't have a tray. With a light rap, he knocked on the doorjamb.

Susana's head shot up. "Aye?"

"My lady. We found a note."

"A note?" Susana rushed over to his side and snatched it from him. Magnus hefted himself from his chair and made his way to the doorway as well. "When did it arrive?"

Tamhas frowned. "It dinna, my lady. Cook found it in the larder, propped against the flour she uses for cakes."

"Cakes!" Magnus wailed. "Isobel loves cakes."

Andrew frowned. "They wanted us to find this in the morning."

"Well, we found it now," Susana said. She ripped open the note and read it. Her face paled. Magnus peeped over her shoulder and read the note; his eyes narrowed and his jaw clenched.

"What is it?" Andrew asked.

She handed it over.

Susana, dearest. I told you that you would regret not accepting my offer. Now, in exchange for your daughter's safety, you will do me the honor of becoming my bride.

It wasn't signed, but then, it didn't need to be. All the clues were there. The scraps of fabric heading toward the east, this ominous threat, the cloying tone . . .

"Scrabster." The thought of Isobel in such dastardly clutches made Andrew's skin crawl.

Filled with a renewed rage, Susana whirled and began pacing the room. "I shall crush him like a bug. I shall smash him. I shall gut him and feed his entrails to the pigs."

Andrew reminded himself never to make her angry.

Magnus gave a heavy sigh. "At least we know where she is."

"Do we?" Andrew asked. It was a fair question. The bastard could have taken her anywhere . . .

Susana snorted.

Andrew glanced at her. "Would he be stupid enough to take her to his castle?"

She gored him with a caustic look. "It's Scrabster. He has no imagination."

"His lands are but a day's ride away," Magnus said.

"Aye." She nodded sharply. "We must leave at once."

Magnus frowned. "Susana. It's getting dark. Riding in the dark is far too dangerous . . ."

She brushed his concerns away with a wave of her hand. "Aye. It's dark. And my daughter is out there. Alone."

"She's not alone. She's with Hamish."

Susana spun on him. "We doona even know if Hamish is responsible."

"He isna." Andrew's annoyance riffled. He shouldn't have barked, but he couldn't help it. "Why would he align with a maggot like Scrabster?"

She threw up her hands. "I doona have a clue. But it hardly signifies. I'm leaving now. You can come with me if you wish." Magnus bristled, as though preparing for war. Susana set her hand on his arm. "Not you, Papa. You need to stay here."

"I doona want to!" he boomed. "She's my grand-daughter!"

"Aye." She patted him. Andrew could see Magnus was in no shape to be haring around the countryside on horse-back in the middle of the night. Likely, in his condition, he would not even be able to hold his seat—whisky and all. "We need you here," she said gently.

"You do?"

"Of course. In case any more news comes in."

Miraculously, Magnus accepted this—or likely, he knew the truth of his age and weakness—and he nodded.

It heartened Andrew to see Susana regain some of

her vigor, but he couldn't help asking, "What do you plan to do?"

She gored him with a glare. "Whatever I need to do to keep my daughter safe."

His gut tightened. "You're not marrying Scrabster," he bleated.

The glare darkened. "What do you care who I marry?"

"I care very much, damn it. Isn't that obvious?"

"Nothing is obvious where you are concerned."

"That is hardly fair—"

"Ahem." A deep voice rumbled through the room, shattering their mutual pique.

Susana frowned at her father. "What?"

"Whatever the two of you intend to do, I suggest you do it now, and argue later."

She sent a look at Andrew, one that sliced through to his soul. "Right," she clipped.

"Right," he responded, because he really didn't know what else to say.

They wasted no time preparing to ride out, although while they were doing so, Andrew made Susana eat. He couldn't stop her from coming along, indeed, he wouldn't dare try, but he didn't want her fainting halfway there.

Their plans were fluid; they decided to plot along the way. All they wanted to do now was get moving. It would take hours to reach Scrabster's land; indeed, they would need to ride straight through to have a chance of reaching the castle by morning. If the villains had taken a coach, which the evidence suggested, they might even catch up with them.

Still, they needed to be cautious. This whole debacle could be a ploy to lure them away and leave the castle unguarded, so Andrew left men posted at the gates and had them close up tight when they rode out. He took as many men as he could spare without leaving Dounreay vulnerable.

They pounded toward Scrabster's stronghold with all haste. In Andrew's opinion, they had no time to lose. Oh, Isobel would be safe. Scrabster wouldn't dare harm a hair on her head, not if he wanted to win Susana's hand. But if Keir had planned this, and taken Hamish along to pin the blame on someone else, there was only one thing that could happen to Hamish for his plan to work.

Hamish would have to die.

CHAPTER NINETEEN

The carriage jostled and, because her hands and feet were bound, Isobel jostled with it. It was uncomfortable, because she and Hamish had been crammed in the foot well and there wasn't much room. And he was hard.

She'd worried for a while that he was dead. She'd seen the blood on his head and he was very still. But when she stared at his chest in the waning light through the windows, she could see he was breathing.

It was a mystery, what those filthy men in black hoods had planned for them, but judging from the few things she'd heard, and the ferocity with which they'd tied her, it couldn't be good. She very much wished she had her bow. She would skewer them all and then they'd be sorry.

It had been a long and boring day, tied up in a carriage. She entertained herself ripping scraps from the trim of her chemise and shoving them through a small hole in the floor of the carriage. She had no clue if they were indeed falling to the ground below, or if they were collecting in the boot, but she kept it up . . . until she ran out of trim.

Perhaps she should have made smaller pieces.

Mama would be appalled at the damage she'd done, but Isobel found it oddly satisfying. Little else was. She was hungry and thirsty and every bone ached.

The worst part of all was the fact that she'd been good. She'd been good and done everything everyone had asked of her. She hadn't gone out to play by herself. She hadn't climbed any towers. She hadn't even gone to visit the bunny in the garden.

She hadn't done any of it, and they'd snatched her anyway.

From her bed.

Shoved a rag in her mouth and wrapped her in a blanket and carted her away like she was a carpet.

It was truly infuriating being small.

However, she vowed she'd get them back. She'd make them pay. Somehow. She just needed to watch for her chance.

She dozed as the carriage continued to lug along. She had no idea where they were or where they were going, but the road was decidedly bumpy. With a frown, she peered out the window. From her position on the floor, she could only see the sky. But when she focused and tried to be clever, she could tell from the angle of the setting sun that they were heading east. Then she realized they must be following the coast, because she could smell the brine in the air. She imagined the map of Caithness County Mama had made her memorize, and her nose wrinkled. Scrabster lived to the east along the coast. She hated Scrabster.

A wayward thought made her grin. If she were to rain vengeance down on any man, he was as good a target as any.

And Mama probably wouldn't even scold her.

Beneath her, Hamish stirred. Then he winced and groaned. His eyes fluttered open and he blinked.

"Hullo there," she said, because it seemed the polite thing to do.

He licked his lips. She wished she had some water to give him but she didn't. And she was thirsty, too. She would probably have drunk it all by now. "Is-Isobel? What happened?"

She smiled. She tried to make it as brave a smile as she could. "We've been kidnapped."

"Kidnapped?" He shook his head and winced again. "Why?"

She lifted a shoulder. "I doona know. But we're heading east, so I'm pretty certain it was Scrabster." She wrinkled her nose. "He's a worm."

"Scrabster?" Something flickered across his brow. It might have been concern. "How—How long have we been traveling?"

She sighed. "Hours. All day." She sighed. "It's going verra slowly."

He smiled, though it was a wobbly effort. "These things do."

She tipped her head. "You're bleeding."

"They coshed me on the head."

Her interest flickered. "Were you fighting them?"

He frowned. "I was guarding you."

"I was sleeping." They sat in silence for a moment, swaying with the movement of the coach. He didn't look very comfortable at all. "Why do you think they brought *you*?" she asked.

He shrugged. "I doona know. But I'm glad they did."

"You are?"

"Aye. I wouldna want you to be here all alone. Perhaps I can rescue you."

Had her hands not been tied, she would have patted him. It was very sweet that he wanted to rescue her. And though he was very old, he was valiant.

Of course, it was more likely she would rescue him than the other way around—given his age—but she didn't mention it because Mama had always taught her to try to be respectful of her elders. She'd never really excelled at being respectful, but she did like Hamish a lot. Though it was clear now, he would not make as good a father as Andrew. There was something about Andrew that made her feel safe and cared for and protected. It didn't hurt that his hair was the same color as hers. That was easily as important a consideration as the fact that both Mama and Hamish were gingers.

And Mama had let Andrew *kiss* her.

Mama had never let any man kiss her before.

Ah, poor Hamish.

She reached over and patted him anyway.

The coach slowed and took a corner, then the vibrations changed, as though they had turned onto a cobbled road. Through the window Isobel caught a glimpse of a tall tower. "I think we're almost there," she whispered.

"Isobel. I have a dirk in my boot. Can you reach it?"

She frowned. "I canna take your dirk."

"When we reach wherever we are going, they will probably separate us and I would feel better if you had a weapon."

"Why would they separate us?" Trepidation flickered through her. She very much did not want to lose his company.

He didn't answer, but his frown darkened.

"Why would they separate us?"

The carriage slowed to a halt. "Isobel. There isn't much time. See if you can reach my dirk."

She sighed and shifted around until she could touch the hilt of his knife in his boot. It was awkward trying to reach something with her hands tied together in front of her, but she got it. She levered away as she pulled it out and gazed at it in awe. It was not a dirk. It was practically a sword.

"Careful. It's verra sharp."

She blew out a breath. "I'll be careful." It was indeed sharp and long. It glinted in the waning light. She cautiously slipped it into the deep pocket of her nightgown.

"Be judicious," Hamish whispered. "Doona use it until you are certain you can escape."

"Aye," she sniffed. As though she didn't know that much.

"And pretend to be asleep," he suggested.

"Asleep?"

"Perhaps we can learn more about their plans for us that way." He winked. "Men tend to talk when they doona think you are listening."

"Good to know." He was very clever indeed. And as sneaky as she was. A pity he wouldn't be her father, but she had decided she liked Andrew best. Still and all, she liked him very much. Obediently, she closed her eyes and flopped down on him, just as the door to the carriage whipped open.

"Hell. They're both unconscious," a dark voice drawled. It was a little familiar, but Isobel couldn't place it and she didn't dare open her eyes just yet.

"I told ya we should ha' stopped to give them water."

"There wasna time."

The man with the dark voice snorted. "Come on. I'll get the girl. You lot get the man."

Whoever he was, he lifted her very gently, for which Isobel was thankful. As he carried her away from the carriage, she braved a peep at his face. How disappointing that it was still covered with the black hood.

It was difficult to close her eyes all the way after that, because she really was curious about where they were and where they were taking her, so she squinted them until she could see through the fringe of her lashes.

The man with the hood carried her up the stairs into a castle she'd never seen before, but she knew without a doubt it was Scrabster's, especially when the laird himself leaped up from a table by the hearth as they entered the great room. The castle was very old and hadn't been updated from its ancient layout, so the great room was an enormous, booming hall with a stone staircase curving up one side. At the moment, it was filled with Scrabster's men who were having dinner. The smell of roasted chicken tickled her nose and made her mouth water.

But still, she didn't rouse. Hamish's words hummed in her brain.

"Did you get her?" Scrabster asked.

"Aye," the man holding her said.

Scrabster lifted her hand and let it drop. "Is she dead?"

"She's asleep. We brought one of Dunnet's men as well."

"Excellent. Take him to the dungeons."

"The dungeons are not in good repair."

Scrabster chuckled. "It willna be for long."

"Aye, my laird. And the girl?"

"Take her to the dungeons as well," Scrabster said.

The man holding her stiffened. "She's a girl."

"And?"

"My laird . . ." His tone was much like Mama's when she was trying to be reasonable when she really wanted to bellow. "You canna toss her in the dungeon."

"Can I not?"

A sigh. "I guarantee you, once she finds our note, her mother will arrive with all haste to accede to your demands."

"So you said."

"Can you imagine her reaction if she arrives to find her darling daughter . . . in the dungeon? She would probably shoot you."

Scrabster made a sour noise. "I'm a baron. She canna shoot me." But there was a hint of doubt in his tone.

Isobel nearly snorted. Because if it had flesh in its arse, and it annoyed her, Mama would probably shoot it.

"If you want to win her mother, I suggest you take another tack."

Oh, bother. That was what this was about? Isobel nearly blew out a breath but then remembered she was pretending to be asleep. To that effect, she gave a little snore.

"Put her in the solar then. The door locks. She canna escape. And she's a tiny thing." Scrabster barked a laugh. It took everything in Isobel not to stab him now.

As the man carrying her mounted the stairs, Isobel dared a peek at the direction they were dragging Hamish. She didn't know what they meant when they said he wouldn't be in the dungeon for long, but she didn't like the tone in which it was said. She didn't like it at all.

The idiots locked her in Scrabster's solar and left her there alone. Mercifully, they brought her a tray of food and water, which they set on the desk. Once they left, it took her less than a minute to slice through her bonds and pick the lock with Hamish's knife, but when she crept out into the hall and peered over the landing to scout the area, she saw that the great room of the old castle was crawling with men. She couldn't attempt an escape with so many guards about. But it was evening. They had to go to sleep at some point.

She made her way back into the solar and occupied her time eating, drinking, and exploring Scrabster's study. It was mostly very boring things like papers and maps, but she did find a lovely bow hanging on the wall. The bow was quite large for her, but she'd practiced with Mama's— when she wasn't looking—so Isobel was certain she could handle it. She also found a chest that was very interesting indeed. The lock was harder to work than the one on the door, but she had plenty of time.

It was a great disappointment to find the chest wasn't filled with gold and jewels—just letters—though there was one very beautiful chunk of gold with mysterious inscriptions on it that captured her attention. She tucked it into her pocket. She was sure Scrabster wouldn't mind. Or maybe he would. She didn't care. At the very least it was payment for her inconvenience. She took the letters, too, but only because they were important enough for him to lock in a chest.

There were lots of other papers in the room. These she piled on the desk.

She peeped out to check the great room every now and again, and each time, there were fewer and fewer men. When finally, she saw that the hall was empty, she lit the papers on fire with the lamp and slipped out the door. It was great fun skulking through the shadows with Hamish's knife in her hand and the bow and quiver over her shoulder. She almost hoped someone would come upon her so she could skewer them. But sadly, they did not.

Silently, stealthily, she made her way down the curving staircase and through the hall, then to the stone stairs leading to the cellars. She was greatly relieved, however, to find there were only two men in the dungeons, guarding Hamish who was locked in a grungy old cell. One of the men was cutting a radish and eating it slice by slice, but the other was asleep.

Hamish saw her creeping down the stairs and his eyes widened. She shot him a grin. Tiptoeing through the room, she picked up a cauldron, likely used for some manner of heinous torture, and stepped behind the radish man. Without hesitation she bonked him over the head. He fell to the side with a groan.

It was quite fun, so she bonked the other man, even though he was already asleep.

Pleased with her work, she skipped over to Hamish.

"What are you doing?" he hissed.

She fluttered her lashes. "Saving you." She pulled out his knife and quickly worked the lock. The cell door opened with a grating whine.

He stepped out and stared at her in bewilderment. "Are you certain you're a child?" he asked.

She laughed at his joke. Surely it was a joke. Then she tugged on his arm. "We must hurry. They will find it soon."

"Find what?"

But ah. It was too late. From above stairs, shouts echoed through the castle.

"Where is she?" Scrabster's voice bellowed. "Find her at once! Susana or not, I am going to kill that girl!"

❧

Andrew signaled for a halt as the company topped the ridge overlooking Scrabster's castle. It wouldn't do to barrel in without a plan. They'd ridden hard all night and though it was early morning, they needed a rest. Pity there wasn't time for that.

He slid from Breacher's saddle and hunkered down, surveying the lay of the land. Susana followed suit. Her eyes widened as she took in the devastation.

Indeed, this wasn't what they had expected to find. In the wee hours of the morning, the castle and the land surrounding it should have been quiet, peaceful. It was not. Men poured from the portcullis with weapons, and some had already fanned out into the lea surrounding the fortress. Their shouts and calls echoed in the breeze. More disturbing was the fact that smoke poured from the structure.

One of the walls had crumbled. It looked as though it had been under siege.

"Oh, dear God," Susana breathed. "My baby."

Andrew rubbed her shoulder to calm her, though his own heart nearly pounded from his chest. "I'm sure she's fine." An absolute lie.

She didn't believe him, judging from the way she gaped at him. "My baby is in there," she hissed. "We need to get her out."

"Aye. We will. Doona fash yerself." Andrew turned back to the scene, his mind awhirl. Options on how to proceed flitted through his mind. They could simply ride into the castle, in which case Susana would no doubt be claimed by Scrabster at once. They could attempt an attack, but the men milling about far outnumbered the ones he'd brought. They could wait until dark and attempt a covert infiltration, but he worried that, if his suspicions were correct, Hamish didn't have that kind of time. Another option would be to create a diversion at the front of the castle and send men in through the back, but Andrew didn't know the layout of the castle well enough to guarantee success.

As he was weighing these options—ignoring his roiling stomach—a flash of movement in the woods below caught his attention. He narrowed his focus on it and his breath caught. Two figures, hunkered low and using the cover of brush to conceal themselves from detection, were slowly making their way up the hill. One of them was tiny and had white-blond hair. The other was a ginger.

His pulse launched into a rapid patter. He touched Susana's arm and then pointed. When she cried out and made a move to leap to her feet, he tugged her back down and set his finger to his lips. "We doona want to give them away," he murmured.

Her features tightened, but she nodded.

Then he let go a low whistle, one that might be mistaken for a birdcall. Hamish stilled, and glanced up. When he spotted Andrew, his taut expression broke into a grin. He sent Andrew a quick salute, murmured something to Isobel, and changed direction, heading straight for their position on the crest of the hill.

It seemed to take forever for them to make their way through the brush, and several times Andrew lost sight of them, but Hamish was being cautious, and he was a master of stealth when he needed to be. All the while, Andrew kept an eye on the men who were, it was apparent now, searching for them down below. It stood to reason there would be men scouring the woods as well.

He ordered his company to be on their guard for any such persons and to make themselves as unobtrusive as possible. But they were a large company, with horses. Still, Hamish and Isobel were nearly here. They would grab them, mount immediately, and hie away as quickly as possible, putting as much distance between them and Scrabster's men as they could.

As Hamish and Isobel neared—the latter tugging an incongruously large bow and quiver—he and Susana scuttled back down the ridge. When they reached a point where they couldn't be seen from the lookouts in the castle, Susana rushed over to Isobel and wrenched her into a ferocious hug. There was weeping—Susana, not Isobel. Isobel merely rolled her eyes and suffered her mother's attentions.

Andrew, overwhelmed with relief to see his friend alive and hale, hugged him as well, and while there may have been a prickling in his eyes, the embrace was far more manly and not nearly as demonstrative. They clapped each other on the back, as men do.

"Damn, I'm glad to see you," he said, though his voice threatened to fail him.

"Not as happy as I am to see you," Hamish said. "I was worrying how we would make it all the way back to Dounreay on foot." He forced a laugh, but Andrew could tell it was an effort.

Andrew smiled. "It's a nice day for a walk."

"Aye. But I am glad I doona need to." He glanced over his shoulder. "We should go. They're looking for us. Their men are crawling all over these woods."

"Aye. At once." Andrew signaled to his company and they all mounted up. He headed for Breacher as well, but as he did, Isobel broke away from Susana and threw herself into his arms. Though his tension ran high, and he desperately wanted to leave this place, he couldn't break the embrace. It was likely his hug was as fierce as her mother's had been. It was such a relief to know she was safe. Such a relief to hold her slight body in his arms. To feel her arms close around his neck.

She pulled back before he did, but it was to set her forehead on his, as she had the day they'd met. She stared into his eyes—hers crossing slightly at the propinquity. "You came for us," she gusted.

"Of course we did." His pulse thudded and he had to hug her again.

"We should go," Susana said.

"Aye. At once." Andrew pulled back and brushed Isobel's hair from her face. He thumbed at a smudge on her cheek. While she looked sallow and wan, and terribly bedraggled, a customary mischievous light danced in her eye. He was gratified that this ordeal had not broken her spirit.

Andrew stood and headed for Breacher, but Isobel tugged on his tunic. "I want to ride with you," she said.

He glanced at Susana, noting her slightly put-out expression, but she nodded, so he lifted Isobel up onto Breacher's back and mounted behind her. Susana rode with Hamish, which he found bothersome, but the fact that Isobel had chosen him warmed his heart. He couldn't resist wrapping his arms around her as the rode back down the road to the west. The first town they would hit once they left Scrabster's lands was Brims. He intended to halt there and give everyone the rest they so desperately needed. Scrabster wouldn't dare follow them there.

Andrew sidled up to Hamish and Susana so they could chat as they rode. "So tell me," he asked. "What happened?"

Isobel glanced at him over her shoulder. Her expression was uncharacteristically innocent. "Nothing. I didn't do anything. I swear."

Hamish laughed. "You did, too, you little minx. For one thing, she rescued me from certain death."

Susana frowned. "Certain death?"

"Aye," Hamish muttered. "They planned to kill me and blame this all on you."

"On me?"

"On Alexander, to be precise. Scrabster was planning to use this incident in his campaign to discredit your brother."

Andrew's eyes narrowed. *Hell.* Just as he'd suspected. Sometimes he hated always being right.

"How do you know this?" Susana asked.

Isobel fluttered her lashes. "Men are notoriously loose-lipped when they think you canna hear them. I learned a lot . . . just pretending to be asleep." It occurred to Andrew that this was a tactic she might use again in the future and considered himself forewarned.

"I'm sorry to say, Keir was working with them," Hamish said. "He wore a black hood, but I recognized his voice."

"Oh, aye," Isobel said. "That was him." She sent her mother a repentant look. "He might have been one of the men I stabbed."

Susana's eyes widened. "Might have been?" And then. "You *stabbed* someone?"

Isobel shrugged. "He grabbed me. I dinna want to be grabbed."

"Good for you, darling." Susana's chin firmed. "You should always stab a man who grabs you when you doona want to be grabbed."

"Aye." Isobel nodded. "That was my thinking."

Andrew chuckled. He wasn't sure why. He frequently had urges to grab Susana. "Would you mind starting from the beginning? So we get the whole story?"

Hamish and Isobel exchanged glances. At some unspoken accord, Hamish began. "I was stationed in Isobel's sitting room. The door opened behind me and as I turned to see who it was, someone coshed me on the head."

"He was coshed," Isobel added with far too much enthusiasm. "There was blood everywhere."

"Oh, dear lord," Susana muttered.

"I woke up in the carriage, bound hand and foot. When we reached the castle, they separated us," Hamish said. "They put me in the dungeon."

"And they put me in Scrabster's solar." Why Isobel grinned was a mystery.

"She escaped and came down to rescue me."

"Oh, holy God." Susana clutched her chest.

Hamish patted her shoulder. It didn't seem to calm her. "Isobel was really verra clever—"

"Thank you."

"She created a diversion—"

"I started a fire."

Susana made a sound, something strangled. "Lord have mercy."

Isobel's eyes widened with innocence. "I dinna know they kept their munitions storage *in* the solar."

"Half the castle blew up. We were able to sneak out during the tumult."

"I stabbed the men who tried to grab me and . . ." Isobel stared at her mother and fluttered her lashes. "I might have shot someone, too."

"She found a bow."

"Someone just left it lying there. What was I supposed to do?"

Hamish sent Andrew a skeptical look. "I really doona think she's five," he murmured in an aside.

"Well," Susana gusted. "I'm just verra relieved you're all right—both of you—and that we now know who was behind all this. That was one of the worst things . . . not knowing. I'm so angry at Keir I could spit nails."

"Apparently, he's been working with Scrabster all along," Hamish said sympathetically. "Although some of the things he said made me wonder—"

What, exactly, Hamish had wondered was lost as a cry of warning went up among the men riding behind them. "They're coming!"

Hamish glanced at Andrew and with no hesitation, they both set their heels and their mounts sprang forward. Aye, they could stay and fight, but with Susana and Isobel with them, he wouldn't dare it. Better to run for the border and seek asylum with the Baron of Brims.

At full tilt, they rounded a corner . . . and found themselves facing a battery of Scrabster's men blocking the road. Though they were all on foot, they held weapons—everything from swords and arrows to pistols. Andrew had no choice but to slow down and come to a halt. The trees in this wood were thick—too thick to ride through without risking injury—but there was a small clearing to the left. Andrew analyzed the situation and quickly realized that position was their best bet when facing a threat from the front and rear. It would force their attackers to assemble before them. Aye, they would be cornered. But his men were some of the best-trained warriors he knew. Scrabster's men seemed to be conscriped farmers and merchants, and many of them were nervous to boot.

The men chasing them wheeled up on their mounts and circled their position, but held steady.

Given Scrabster's goal of claiming Susana, it didn't surprise Andrew that the men didn't attack, they merely held his company there as they waited . . . for something. What that something was, he had no clue and didn't care.

He signaled to his men to dismount and prepare to fight. On horseback, they were far too easy a target. He slipped from Breacher's saddle and helped Isobel down as Hamish did the same with Susana, nudging them both to the middle of the company, so they were shielded from any stray shots. And then he unsheathed his sword.

Silence hummed in the clearing as the two forces faced off. Andrew's men bristled with tension, poised to defend their position. The moments ticked away, measured by the beat of his heart. The only sound was the drone of bees and the occasional call of a gull.

That silence broke with the rumble of carriage wheels. All heads turned. A dark, unmarked coach rolled up and Scrabster levered out, followed by Keir.

That Keir's hand was bound—clearly where Isobel had stabbed him—wasn't as satisfying as it should have been. She should have aimed for parts south, in Andrew's opinion.

"Susana!" Scrabster's reedy voice warbled, flecked with rage. He pushed through the crowd of his men and limped forward. There was an arrow lodged in his thigh and his hair was singed. But it was the pistol in his hand that caught Andrew's attention. It was pointed at Susana.

Without thought, Andrew stepped in front of her holding his weapon aloft.

She didn't cooperate with his protection. She pushed past him and snarled, "You bastard. I'll see you hang for this."

Scrabster laughed. "Is that any way to speak to your intended?"

"I will not bluidy marry you."

"Oh, you will." His eyes narrowed; his gaze flickered over their company and landed on Isobel. "You will, if you want your daughter to live."

With something akin to horror, Andrew watched as the pistol veered toward Isobel. He shifted his position and nudged her behind him. It vexed him that she, like her mother, wouldn't stay shielded. She poked her head out and announced, "You're a bad man. My mama will never marry you."

Scrabster's ratlike face scrunched up into a moue of fury. "You set my castle on fire, you little fiend. Blew it up! You're the devil's spawn."

"*You're* the devil's spawn," Isobel retorted.

Susana shushed her and turned her vehemence back on Scrabster. "She's a girl. And you kidnapped her. You got what you deserved. And as for you lot . . ." She whirled on Scrabster's men, pinning them with a fierce glare. "You are all going to hang for this. Ask yourself if your loyalty to this wretched laird is worth your life, because a magistrate willna take your loyalty into account when he sentences you to die."

This seemed to have some effect on the men surrounding them, the farmers and merchants especially. They began to murmur and shift their feet.

Unaccountably, Scrabster chuckled. "Be reasonable, Susana. I will have my way. And if you doona marry me, you will force me to take what I want by other means."

Susana stiffened. "Such as?"

His smile was reptilian. "I believe you have one more unmarried sister. She will do just as well for my needs."

"Leave Lana out of this."

"Aye," Isobel said. "Leave Lana out of this."

Scrabster turned his glare on Isobel; his expression sent a chill down Andrew's spine. "Be silent, you monster."

"She's not a monster," Susana bellowed.

"She shot me." There was a hint of petulance in his tone as he gestured at his leg.

Isobel stepped forward, peering at the wound. "You really should have that arrow out," she suggested.

It was a logical suggestion. No telling why it enraged Scrabster as it did. "Enough," he howled. "I'm going to kill you. I'm going to kill you all." His gaze wavered back to Isobel. "Starting with you."

Several things happened at the same time.

First, Andrew was aware of Susana's growl and her movement by his side as she lifted her bow. Second was the terror at the tinge of deranged determination in Scrabster's eye and the tightening of his finger on the trigger. Next was the burning determination that this bastard would *not* hurt Isobel, not if Andrew could help it. He launched himself to the right, throwing himself between the pistol and the girl.

And finally, he was aware of a loud explosion and a searing pain in his chest.

And then, of course, there was nothing.

CHAPTER TWENTY

Horror curled through Susana as Scrabster held his weapon on Isobel. Horror and anger. She knew, in the seconds before he fired, that Isobel, having stepped out into full view, was too far away for her to shield. But if she could hit Scrabster before he could fire, she could protect her daughter. With seething resolve, she lifted her bow and shot, without even aiming. There was no time to aim; she had to trust her instinct and pray the arrow would fly true.

She was a fraction of a second too late. Even as the arrow thudded in his chest and a bolt of satisfaction whipped through her, he squeezed the trigger. A cloud of smoke erupted from the pistol and a heart-stopping boom echoed through the clearing.

Susana didn't even wait for Scrabster to fall. She whirled toward her daughter and . . .

Her heart stopped. Stopped right there in her chest, a cold dead lump of flesh.

Oh, Isobel was fine. She stood her ground, whole and uninjured, but there was an expression of shock on her face as she stared down at Andrew's body, lying on the ground. He did not move. A red stain blossomed on his snowy shirt.

To Susana, it felt like a dream. A bad one. As though walking through a thick fog, she made her way to his side. Isobel dropped to her knees and shook him, crying his name, although it seemed from very far away.

"Wake up," Isobel commanded. "Wake up!" She was used to being obeyed. She was used to being able to demand what she wanted, but in this she was denied. Andrew didn't stir. He was deathly pale.

The confusion on Isobel's face, the tears on her chubby cheeks, the grief in her eyes when she looked up, devastated Susana. Or perhaps it was something more that scored her soul. "Mama, he willna wake up."

Numbly, Susana fell to her knees at her daughter's side. The hard, handsome face she loved was ashen, lifeless.

Her pulse seized. Her breath stalled. Prickles of sweat blossomed on her brow.

Panic, agony, and pain screamed through her, body and soul.

He could not. He could not be dead.

She couldn't bear to live without him.

A shout to her side broke through the curtain of misery, reminding her that they were all still in danger. In fact, Scrabster's men—Keir among them—were advancing on their position with swords drawn.

That Andrew's men hurried to surround the three of them did not signify.

Ferocity slashed through her. She could grieve later. Now she needed to assure her daughter's safety. More than that, she wanted to make them pay, each and every one. In the most painful way possible. She stood in a cold rage and faced the advancing men. Fury seethed in her veins as she whipped an arrow from her quiver and lifted her bow. She searched for a target. Found one.

He had betrayed her. Her family and her home.

He had kidnapped her daughter and perhaps caused the death of the only man she'd ever loved. The man she did love, and would love until the day she died.

There would be no mercy for him.

Keir's eyes flared as he realized her arrow was trained on him. He was close enough to see the determination on her face. And he knew her. He knew her well.

Her gaze narrowed as she pulled back the string.

"Oh, *shite*," he yelped, and then he turned tail and ran for cover. He could not escape her wrath so easily. She would mark him but good. It was with great satisfaction that she watched her arrow find its home in the fleshy globes of his arse. He stumbled and, with a howl, fell to his knees.

The advancing men faltered, realizing they'd lost their laird and their leader, but then they continued to advance. Susana grabbed another arrow.

A movement at her right caught her attention and pride swelled her chest as she saw her daughter, with a bow that was far too large for her person, nocking her arrow as well. Together, mother and daughter, took aim and let fly.

Susana tried not to be disappointed when Isobel's arrow went wide and flew into the trees behind the men blocking them in. The bow was very large for her and . . .

But oh.

Perhaps she hadn't been aiming for the men.

Isobel's arrow flew into the trees and with unerring accuracy severed a large beehive nestled in the branches. The hive plummeted to the ground.

The bees were not pleased.

They swarmed over Scrabster's men. With howls and bellows, they scattered, running back down the road, swatting at the angry insects, dragging Scrabster's body behind them. The bees, attracted by their frenetic movements, followed.

"Excellent shot," Susana said, trying very hard not to crow.

Isobel grinned. "Thank you."

Though the men were in retreat, Susana didn't let up on her barrage. She let fly, arrow after arrow, taking out one arse after another.

She would have kept shooting, but Hamish set his warm hand on hers. "They're retreating," he said softly. "Let's see to Andrew. And then we will need to leave this place with all haste."

It took a moment for Susana to slough off the passion of the battle; her blood was high and her ire still prickled, but she knew Hamish was right. Isobel's safety was everything now. Now that Andrew was gone.

Her chest ached at the thought.

She turned back to the spot where Andrew lay. The red tide on his chest had spread. Isobel threw herself over him, weeping with an anguish that broke her heart . . . even more.

Hamish barked some orders to his men and they all whipped into motion—Susana had no idea what he'd said. The fog had returned, carrying with it a fresh tide of grief.

What she wouldn't do to have him back.

In a daze, she fell to her knees beside her daughter, and stroked her hair. Hair so like his.

It was a crime he had died not knowing Isobel was his. And the crime was on her shoulders. It was a heavy weight.

She should have told him. She should have told him everything when she had the chance. She'd robbed him of a daughter, and Isobel of a father.

She was a terrible, selfish, petulant person.

She would give anything to go back in time and change things. She would do anything for a second chance.

It was agonizing that, through her tears, Isobel was still talking to him, imploring him, commanding him to wake up. As though her fierceness could bring him back from the dead.

Though, if anyone could command such a thing, it would be Isobel.

She patted him on the cheek, tugged his hair, fit her finger into his nostril.

Susana flinched. It was not respectful to probe the nostril of a dead man. She was about to tell Isobel to come away when his nose twitched.

Susana's pulse stuttered. She leaned closer and narrowed her eyes, staring at his chest. A rise. A small one, but movement.

An unimaginable joy rose within her. He wasn't dead! He wasn't dead!

Isobel propped her elbow on his chest and he groaned.

Aye, he wasn't dead . . . yet.

"Isobel, darling, come away," she said.

"I doona want to. I want him to wake up." She smacked him dead center and he groaned again.

"Darling. Doona hurt him." She eased her daughter back and wrapped her arms around her and held her. They both watched Andrew's face with bated breath. Was his color returning? Was his breath stronger? Was there hope?

She glanced up at Hamish as he approached. "He's not dead," she whispered. "He's not dead."

Unaccountably, Hamish grinned. "Of course he's not dead," he said. "He's far too stubborn for that. Besides"—he winked—"he's a Lochlannach."

◈

They stole Scrabster's carriage, although technically it wasn't theft. Or at least, that was Isobel's suggestion. Merely payment for their inconvenience. They laid boards across the seat and Hamish and his men lifted Andrew in. He still had not woken, but Susana knew they needed to get him some medical help at once.

Susana and Isobel sat by his side as the carriage headed toward Brims, the nearest town along the coast. Susana winced with every jostle and jerk.

"Will he be all right, Mama?" Isobel asked. Her voice was small, afraid. Susana did not like this diminishment in the slightest.

She stiffened her spine. "Of course he will. Did you not hear Hamish? He's far too stubborn to die."

Isobel put out a lip. "I like him, Mama."

"I know, darling," she said, pulling her daughter into her embrace. "I like him, too." She stared down at him over her daughter's head.

Like was not the word for it.

Love was not the word for it.

Somehow there was no word for it, this feeling of adoration, devotion, and, aye, need. She needed him more than breath in her body. Not his touch, though that was very fine indeed. But his presence. His smile. His laugh. His regard. Something far beyond desire—an *ache* for him—flooded her veins, sang in her soul, whispered in her heart.

She wanted him, required him in her life.

She had no idea if he loved her—though he'd intimated he once had. Perhaps he could love her again.

Isobel was his daughter.

They belonged together. The three of them.

When he woke up—if he woke up—she would find the courage to bare her soul. To tell him everything. And to hope he felt the same.

It was the most frightening thing she'd ever contemplated. As fearless as she was, this was terrifying indeed.

∽

They settled in the inn in Brims, although there wasn't enough room for all their men and some had to stay in the loft above the stables. Susana suggested sending them back to Dounreay, but they didn't want to leave. Hamish mentioned it would be wise to keep the company for protection. He did, however, send two men back with word of what had happened and another messenger to Dunnet, to let Alexander know his brother had been wounded, and the depth of Scrabster's perfidy.

When the doctor came to see Andrew, he tried to shoo Susana from the room, but she wouldn't leave. In turn, Susana tried to shoo Isobel, with the same result. They both watched—Isobel with a grisly fascination—as the doctor removed the ball from Andrew's shoulder and bound the wound. The amount of blood the surgery produced was concerning. He assured Susana that Andrew would survive, but she wasn't so sure. Worry for him raked her.

Though Hamish tried to convince her to take Isobel to their room and rest—it felt as though it had been days since she'd slept—she couldn't leave. If only he would wake up. If only she could see his eyes, that rakish smile once more . . .

She fell asleep, deep in prayer that she had not lost the best thing that had ever happened to her. Without him, her life would be a dreary prison, with her shambling pointlessly from day to day.

She didn't think she could bear it.

Andrew woke with a weight on his chest and a searing pain in his shoulder. He grimaced and shifted, but the weight didn't lessen and it only made his shoulder throb more. He cracked open an eye. He wasn't surprised to see a familiar shock of silver-blond hair spread out over his person. More than once, since he'd arrived in Reay, he'd woken to find Isobel draped over him. It was a surprise, however, to see that adorable, wee moue puckered in sleep.

A delicate snore to his left caught his attention and he turned his head—though slowly, as it sent pings shooting through his neck. Susana was slumped in the chair by the window, also asleep.

While he didn't mind waking to either face—he truly loved them both—it confused him. Then he remembered the scene in Scrabster's woods. The shot that had downed him.

He glanced at his shoulder to find it bare and bandaged and he winced. Bluidy hell. The bastard had *shot* him.

And worse . . . he'd been aiming for Isobel.

A blinding rage, unlike any he'd ever known, scalded him. His muscles bunched as his mind whirled. He would kill the bastard. Eviscerate him with a spoon.

How dare he point a pistol at a child? This child? *His* child?

He stilled. Shock stole his breath as the realization, certainty, flooded him. His gaze whipped back to Isobel and he studied her features.

In this light—and in light of the revelations about Mairi—it was undeniable.

Aye, he knew. Somehow, he'd always known.

From the hair that was too much like his for it to be a coincidence, to the fierce glower that so often reminded him of his brother, to the eyes that were far too familiar. She was his.

But it went far beyond the physical likeness they shared.

It was an affinity of spirit. The day he'd met her, he'd *known* her. Felt some tenuous connection. He'd adored her nearly from the start.

With a trembling hand he stroked her hair. Some emotion welled within him; it filled his heart until it hurt.

It was probably love, but there was some fear twined within it.

He recalled that day on the tower when she'd nearly plunged to her death, and the incident where she'd teetered on the railing in the library, and this last debacle where someone had crept into her room and stolen her in her sleep.

Within moments of knowing the joy that he was a parent, he was poleaxed and paralyzed by the sheer clawing terror of it.

She could have been killed or injured any one of those times.

He could have lost her.

Dear God. He didn't know if he had the fortitude for parenthood. He didn't know if he had the strength. It was horrifying. Petrifying.

And then she opened her eyes. Their gazes met and melded; she smiled. Dimples sprouted on her cheeks, dimples so like his. And he knew. It didn't matter. It didn't matter how frightened this made him, how vulnerable he felt. It didn't matter if he was strong enough to face the challenge. He would.

Because he loved her.

"Good morning," he tried to say, but it came out as a croak.

"Good morning," she whispered, patting his cheek.

"I'm verra glad you are safe." It was all he could manage and to his mortification, it was almost a wail.

Her smile broadened. "I'm verra glad you're not dead."

He chuckled, though it hurt. "Me too."

"Mama shot him, in case you were wondering."

"Shot him? Who?"

"Scrabster." And then, as an afterthought, "Oh, and Keir, too. In the arse."

He chuckled, then winced. "Ah. I'm verra glad to hear it."

"They willna be bothering us again."

"I'm verra glad to hear that, too." He glanced around the strange room. "Where are we?"

"Brims." She wrinkled her nose. "It's boring here, but Mama wanted to stay until you were better. She hasna left your side for days."

"Has it been days?"

She rolled her eyes. "Forever, practically. Did I mention it's boring here? But now that you're better, we'll be going home."

Home. The word made prickles rise on his skin. He'd thought of Dunnet as his home for the entirety of his life. He'd planned to live out his days within the walls of Loch-lannach Castle. Now he wasn't so sure that was where he wanted to be. It seemed empty and hollow. Without her.

Susana was lovely in the soft light of dawn, with her mouth slightly agape in her sleep. Though it seemed there was no room in his chest whatsoever, his heart swelled more. How he loved her. How he always had. He loved them both. Beyond bearing.

Funny how painful it was.

Not as painful as when Isobel leaned her elbow on his chest, though. He winced and she shifted off his wound. She was nothing if not sensitive, his Isobel. She sent him a look beneath unnaturally long lashes. "Are you going to leave us now? Now that Scrabster has been defeated?"

Pain and determination lanced him.

Not if he could help it.

"Dounreay still needs defenses." Was that a hopeful note in his tone? "Your mama needs a new captain of the guard . . ."

"Do you want to stay?" Isobel asked, for some reason, in a whisper.

Andrew glanced at Susana and nodded. "I do." In fact, a growing resolution rose within him. He would not be leaving. Even if he was wrong and she didn't have tender feelings for him, no one and nothing could make him leave her—leave them—again. He would stay here forever, even if she didn't want him, just so he could be close. Just so he could keep her safe. Just so he could watch Isobel grow.

At that thought, he couldn't help but reach out and trace her cheek. Her skin was soft and tender. Her expression innocent and sweet. There was so much he could teach her. So many ways he could guide her as she became the woman she was meant to be. It humbled him that he might have the chance. In her features he saw himself and Susana combined. That did something strange to his soul. Something beautiful.

She nibbled on her lip, much the way Susana might when she was contemplating mischief. "I've been thinking," she said.

Something skirled in his gut. It was always concerning when Isobel had been thinking. "What?"

"Do you still like her?"

"Och, aye. I do."

"Do you want to marry her?"

A nod. He couldn't manage the word.

Isobel grinned. It was one of her impish grins, but because it was apparently for his benefit, he didn't worry so very much. "If you like her and want to marry her, you should probably kidnap her."

He blinked. "I . . . what?"

"Kid-nap-her. It's what Scotsmen do when they want to woo a difficult woman."

"Wherever did you get an idea like that?"

"I read it in a book."

"One of the books you skewered?"

Her smile was crooked, but she didn't answer, other than to issue a heinous chuckle.

"Do you really think I should kidnap her?"

"There's a nice island in the loch. It has a hut. That's where all the lads take their kidnapped ladies."

"All the lads . . ." he sputtered. It was concerning to have a daughter with such knowledge. And she was only five. He could only imagine her at fifteen. At the same time the thought confounded him, it created a queer warmth in his belly. She would be a beauty. No doubt. Men would buzz around her like bees. He should probably begin sharpening his sword now. "How do you know these things?"

Impatience simmered in her glare. "I listen. But that is beside the point."

He sighed. "Was there a point?"

"Aye. You should kidnap her. Make her marry you."

"No one makes Susana Dounreay do anything she does not want to do. Have you noticed? Aside from which"—he indicated his shoulder—"I'm hardly in the condition to kidnap anyone."

Isobel glanced at his wound. "That is true. You should probably wait until you are better."

Andrew frowned. He didn't want to wait. He didn't want to wait to claim her.

Isobel grabbed his ears and forced him to meet her eye. "I should verra much like to have you as a father."

Something lurched, shifted within him.

She wanted him as her father. Not because they were flesh and blood, but because she wanted him. He grinned. "Not Hamish?"

She blew out a breath. "Hamish is a fine man. He would

be a fine father. But I like you best. And Mama doesna like Hamish."

"She doesna? How do you know?"

She blew out a breath. Her hair riffled. "When she looks at him . . . it's not there."

"What's not there?"

Isobel shrugged. "I doona know what you call it. But when she looks at you, it's there. Also, when Hamish kissed her, she pushed him away."

What? He jerked up; pain screamed through him. Probably because of his wound. Or not. "Hamish kissed her?"

"Aye."

"When?"

"Ages ago."

And then, "You were watching?"

"I'm always watching."

Oh, good lord. That was a warning if there ever was one. Disquiet trickled through him. "What . . . else have you seen?"

She tipped her head to the side. "Is there anything else? Other than kissing?"

"No." One word. Hard and fast. Just . . . no.

Isobel put out a lip, as though she didn't believe him. Heaven help him. Heaven help them all.

CHAPTER TWENTY-ONE

Susana woke to find Andrew awake and talking softly with Isobel. The sight warmed her heart. Not just because he was awake, but because she very much delighted in the sight of their heads so close together. That, and the expression of complete adoration in his eyes.

He would be an excellent father. If he chose to accept her proposal.

And aye, over the past few days, she'd come to the blinding realization that the past was the past. She needed him, wanted him in her life forever.

And Isobel did need a father. She was far too undisciplined. Andrew would be just the influence she required.

But if she was being honest, it wasn't Isobel's desires that drove her, it was her own.

She watched the two whisper away, in some intense and earnest conversation that she wasn't a part of, and she wanted to laugh and sing. They had come through this, all of them, whole.

They would have their second chance.

Andrew glanced at her and stalled mid-whisper. His Adam's apple worked. "Susana," he said in a rough voice. "You're awake."

Isobel sprang away and sent her a guilt-ridden frown.

Oh, lord. What had those two been plotting? She could only imagine.

He held out his hand to her and she rose and took it,

gloried in the fact that it was warm and vibrant. "How are you holding up?" he asked and she nearly snorted. *She* hadn't been shot.

"I'm fine. How do *you* feel?"

His grin was entrancing. "As well as can be expected." His thumb traced her skin, sending a shiver rippling over her nerve endings.

"Isobel," she said softly. "Will you go tell Hamish that Andrew is awake? He needs food and water, too. Can you see to that?"

Isobel frowned. "I doona want to leave. You go."

Annoyance riffled through her, but before she could repeat her command, Andrew set his hand to Isobel's shoulder. "I am verra hungry. And . . . your mother and I need to talk." This he said in a meaningful tone with a speaking look.

Isobel's expression tightened, then she nodded with a sigh. "All right. But I'll be back."

She edged off the bed and to the door. Before she left she shook her finger at them and said, in a warning tone, "You two behave."

Once they were alone, Susana suddenly didn't know what to say. She had no idea why tears sprang to her eyes. "I'm glad you are all right," she said, though the words hardly did justice to the emotions raging within her.

He tried to tug her down beside him, but she resisted. "Sit." A command.

"I doona want to hurt you."

His eyes glimmered. "You could never hurt me. And we do need to talk."

Aye. They did. She sat gingerly at his side, trying very hard not to jostle him. She was aware of his attention on her face; it burned her. There was so much to be said, but she didn't know where to start.

"Susana," he said.

"Andrew."

"I need a kiss." He put out a lip. "I've had a bad week."

"Nothing compared with mine," she said, "I assure you." But she leaned in and kissed him tenderly. His scent filled her. His taste inflamed her. She fisted her fingers in the covers to hold back, to keep from sinking in. She'd missed this so. Needed this so. She'd despaired she would never know this bliss again. "God," she huffed, pulling away and setting her forehead on his chest. She was careful to avoid his wound. She loved that his arm came around her, holding her close.

"I've missed you," he said, kissing the top of her head.

"You were unconscious." A warble.

"My dreams were lonely. Susana . . . There's something I need to ask you."

Her stomach tightened. He'd realized the truth about Isobel. She knew it in her heart. Nae. Nae. She couldn't allow him to ask. She owed him the courtesy of telling him first. She sat up and put a finger to his lips. "Before you do, there's something I need to tell you."

"But—"

"Please, Andrew. Let me tell you."

He fixed his gaze on her and nodded.

Ah, lord. Where to begin?

"I was verra young and foolish when I was in Perth."

"It wasna so verra long ago . . ."

She frowned at him. "Nevertheless, I was young and foolish and verra much in love." His lashes flickered at that, but she continued on. There was much to tell and she couldn't allow herself to be distracted. "When I saw you kissing Kirstie, I shouldna have run."

"I dinna kiss Kirstie Gunn."

She stilled. "I saw you."

"*She* kissed *me*. I was horrified when you saw that. I knew you'd thought . . . I tried to find you. Tried to explain, but Kirstie said you dinna want to see me."

She blew out a breath. "I dinna." That, at least, was true. She had refused to see him.

"And then you left." There was a woebegone thread in his tone at that. "You were gone. Really gone. Forever, gone."

She sighed. "Kirstie and I were friends. Or I thought we were. After I saw you in the woods, she told me you and she . . ."

"Aye?"

"That you were lovers. That the two of you were laughing about what a fool I'd made of myself over you—"

His face went red. "That was a lie."

"I realize that now." She forced a smile. "Did I mention how naive I was back then? Far too gullible." She swallowed. "Who told you Mairi died?"

"Kirstie."

Though somehow she already knew the answer, confirmation made rage walk through her. She clenched her fists. "Kirstie was a liar."

"She lied to both of us, Susana."

She had. And oh, how it had cost them.

But it wasn't too late.

"Andrew . . . There's something else."

"Aye?"

"On my way back home I realized . . ."

"Aye?"

She swallowed and looked away. She couldn't bear to see his face. But he tipped her gaze back to him and waited patiently. Tension hummed between them. "I realized I was with child." Though she whispered, he heard.

"Isobel?"

Susana nodded. "She's your daughter."

He smiled. It was tender and sweet. "I know."

Cold prickles crawled over her skin, and then they turned uncomfortably warm. "I thought you might have figured it out. I . . . How do you feel about it?"

"I love her verra much." He touched his chest. "I love her so much it hurts."

Ah, she knew the feeling.

"She adores you, too."

"Susana . . . You realize I canna leave Dounreay. Not knowing I have a daughter here. Not having found you again."

Her heart thudded. "Do you . . . Are we . . . Can we . . ."

Ach! Frustration racked her. Why could she not just ask?

He tipped his head to the side. "Can we start again?"

Aye! That was it. "Would you . . . like to?"

"I would like to verra much. I never stopped loving you, Susana."

"Nor I, you."

He stared at her, his eyes alight and glistening with something that might have been tears. His lips parted, as though to respond, but no words came out. She knew. She knew the feeling. No words were necessary, just this glorious welling connection between them.

She couldn't help it. She had to kiss him. His wound be damned. When the kiss ended, he continued.

"I know I'm not perfect. I know I'm a tad too arrogant—"

"A tad?"

"And I know I have much to learn about being a father. But, Susana, I would verra much like to . . . woo you."

"Woo me?"

"Isobel suggested I kidnap you and take you to the island in the loch."

"Is that what you two were conspiring about?"

"That and other things." He frowned. "Did you really kiss Hamish?"

"Hamish kissed *me*."

He issued a snort.

She couldn't resist teasing him, just a bit more. Her lips tweaked. "Hamish is verra handsome. It was a nice kiss."

"Nice?"

She shrugged. "But not as nice as kissing you."

"I am gratified to hear it." His arms came around her in a possessive manner. She quite liked it.

"Did you really kiss Lana?"

He went pink to his ears. His lips flapped. His expression was so amusing, she laughed, although it wasn't funny in the slightest. But his chagrin was so pained, she decided to show him mercy.

"I was thinking Hamish might be a good match for Lana."

Why Andrew frowned was a mystery. "I doona think Hamish is right for your sister," he grumbled.

Susana blinked. "I thought he was your friend."

"He is. But . . . he's far too charming. Far too feckless. He seduces anything in skirts."

"And you do no'?"

Andrew narrowed his gaze on her. "I've been with one woman in six years."

Her pulse stuttered. "O-One."

"Only one. I want no one else."

Her frown darkened. "I thought the two of you had a bet to see who could kiss one hundred girls first."

He flinched. "Who told you that?"

She sent him a wicked grin. "I listen. Did you have such a bet?"

"Ach. Aye. I'm not proud of it. But a kiss is only a kiss."

"Sometimes a kiss is more than a kiss."

"Aye, but it is not a seduction. And there's been only you . . ."

His words warmed her and she relaxed against him with a sigh. She sent him a mischievous smile. "Did you at least win the bet?"

He grinned. "I did."

She sniffed. "Do you remember the name of the hundredth girl?"

"I do." He leaned closer. Cupped her cheek. "Her name was Susana Dounreay. And with any luck, she will also be the last." He kissed her again, this time for a long, lingering while. Then he leaned back, he stared at her. "So, Susana Dounreay, my question . . ."

"Aye?

"May I woo you?"

Why her heart dropped was a mystery. Surely she hadn't expected a proposal or something quite so rash. Though they'd known each other, lived in each other's hearts for six years, they'd only been reunited for a month or so and most of that time they had been at odds. It made sense to get to know each other better before they made a lifelong commitment, but truth be known, she was ready now.

Still, she didn't want to rush him.

He needed to know this was what he wanted, what he chose.

He needed to be certain he wanted to accept her and her daughter and be a part of their lives forever.

So, though she wanted more, she forced a smile and a nod and said, simply, "Aye."

His grin was recompense enough for her restraint. But then he winked and asked, "And you promise you willna shoot me in the arse?"

She patted him gently on the shoulder. "My darling,"

she said with a roguish grin. "There are no promises in life."

And he gulped.

~⟡~

Andrew couldn't help staring at Susana as the carriage made the final leg back to Dounreay. They'd been gone a little over two weeks and he was anxious to get back. Not just because he couldn't wait to begin wooing Susana, but because he wanted to be home.

And that was how he thought of the beautiful rose-colored castle. Home.

If all went well with her—and he had every expectation it would, judging from her glances and smiles—he would be spending the rest of his life there. With her. And Isobel. And God willing, one day, a son.

The thought of making one burned in him.

Getting Susana alone was the thought paramount in his mind. The whole time they'd been at the inn in Brims, he'd been surrounded by people. Doctors, Hamish, Isobel. He'd had very little time alone with Susana. Barely a chance to steal a kiss, much less something more. It had been aggravating to wait until his body was ready to travel again, but Susana had insisted.

It was a relief to be on their way . . . to their new life.

She smiled at him across the carriage and he grinned back. When her foot nudged his, a ripple of excitement threaded through him. He knew he wasn't up to anything strenuous, but his imagination bubbled with ideas. He didn't have to risk his injury to have her. In fact, he rather liked the idea of her riding him as he lay beneath her on the bed.

Perhaps his expression betrayed his thoughts, for she blushed.

Isobel, who was hanging out the window, gave a whoop and pulled herself back in. "We're almost there," she announced, her eyes alight. "I canna wait to tell Grandpapa about our adventures."

"I'm sure he will be enthralled," Susana said drily.

"Of course he will," Isobel said. "It was verra exciting!"

"Indeed it was," Andrew murmured. He held out his arm and his daughter came to him and nestled in. He kissed the top of her head. "You were verra brave."

She nodded. "And clever."

"Aye." He chuckled.

Susana's lips twisted. "And you learned about the dangers of gunpowder."

Isobel tipped her head to the side. "*Scrabster* learned about the dangers of gunpowder," she corrected.

"Puir Scrabster," Susana murmured, although there wasn't a hint of mercy in her tone.

"Do you think he survived?" Isobel asked. There was a bloodthirsty gleam in her eye.

"Most likely." Susana sighed. "I aimed for his heart, but the arrow skewed to the right."

"You missed a shot?" Andrew asked in a teasing tone.

She frowned at him. "There was a gust," she said crisply, "Aside from which, I was preoccupied by the fact that he had a gun pointed at my daughter."

"But you saved me." Isobel gazed up at Andrew adoringly and petted his beard.

Susana's focus flicked from one to the other. She sighed. "We're going to have to tell her," she said with a meaningful glance.

"Aye. We will."

"Tell me what?" Isobel asked.

Andrew swallowed painfully. His lips worked. Susana

took his hand and squeezed it with a nod. So bolstered, he burbled, "Isobel . . . I . . . I'm your father."

She wrinkled her nose and blew out a dismissive breath. "Is that it? Your big announcement?"

"Are you . . . not surprised?"

"Of course not. I already knew it."

Susana blinked. "How did you know?"

Isobel rolled her eyes. "I *listen*."

Of course.

Andrew's Adam's apple worked. "I . . . ah . . . And . . . how do you feel about it?"

She shrugged. "All right, I guess." Something out the window captured her attention.

"You guess?"

"I already decided you were better than Hamish," she muttered.

Well, thank heaven for small mercies.

"You have a bigger sword."

There was no call for Susana to snort a laugh. He frowned at her and then turned back to Isobel, but before he could interrogate her further on just *how* he was better than Hamish—other than the sword situation, which was absolutely true . . . in every possible respect—she wrenched from his hold and peered out the window once more. "Whose carriage is that?"

Andrew glanced at Susana, whose brow furrowed. A visiting carriage meant only one thing. Someone of substance had come to call—only barons or lairds could afford to keep them. Trepidation swirled in his gut as the possibilities flickered through his mind. None of them good.

He leaned forward to see and his jaw tightened.

It was a very fancy equipage indeed, one worthy of the

king . . . or a duke. And he knew the seal on the carriage door. He'd seen it on a threatening letter his brother had received.

"Caithness."

Susana hissed in a breath. "What on earth is he doing here?"

"Who is Caithness?" Isobel asked. "And why do you say his name like he is a disease? Is he a bad man, too?"

"Hush, darling." Susana licked her lips as she stared at the carriage. Her gaze flicked to Andrew's and they shared a moment of concern. Caithness, the duke and their over-lord, had been absent from the parish for years, decades. Upon his return, he'd begun encouraging and then ordering barons to clear their land.

It appeared his quest for gold had finally brought him to the hinterlands.

This interview would not be a pleasant one. And very probably, a disaster.

Andrew forced a smile, though it wasn't terribly sincere. "Shall we go and greet him?"

Susana's eyes narrowed. She picked up her bow. Deter-mination flickered over her features. "Aye," she said. "Let us go and greet the Duke of Caithness."

He was certain that was what she said, but her expres-sion said something else entirely. Something such as, *Let us go and gore him.*

CHAPTER TWENTY-TWO

They found their visitor in the parlor, having tea with Papa, which was a surprise because Papa, as a rule, did not drink tea. But there were more surprises in store for Susana as she entered the room.

First was the fact that Caithness was not what she expected. Rather than a wormy, skinny Englishman, she found him quite handsome in his traditional Sinclair kilt. And he was rather enormous. He was perched on the delicate Chippendale, looking as though at any moment he might crush it. He had a dainty cup of tea in one hand and a plate of cakes in the other.

The other surprise was that Alexander, Laird of Dunnet, Andrew's brother and Hannah's new husband, was with the duke. Susana had seen him months ago at the fair in Barrogill and she recognized his harsh features, but it wasn't until now that she saw Andrew in his face and bearing as well. And for that matter, there was a bit of Isobel in there as well.

Concern shafted through her, because Dunnet was here, and Hannah was not.

Dunnet and Caithness nearly filled the room with their presences, but Andrew pushed in and, with a cry, made his way to his brother's side. Hamish followed, joining a triad of hugs and back slapping.

"Andrew!" Dunnet boomed, wrapping him into a fierce embrace. Andrew winced.

"Have a care," Susana snapped, rushing to Andrew's side and examining his shoulder. The wound still bled on occasion and it wouldn't do for this big oaf to open it again. She glared at Dunnet. "He's been shot."

Dunnet's eyes widened. His attention whipped to Andrew. "Shot?"

"He was saving me," Isobel said. She flounced into the room and studied the plate of cakes, selecting one with care and licking it. She was oblivious to the fact that Dunnet was gaping at her. His gaze flicked from Isobel to Andrew and back again. He swallowed.

"Why . . . ah . . . why was he saving you?"

Isobel leaned against the table and crossed her ankles and shrugged. "There was a bad man," she said as though this were an everyday occurrence. No doubt the incessant retelling of her story bored her by this point.

Andrew blew out a breath and eased himself into a chair. Susana flinched. She should have remembered he was still weak. She hurried to pour him a cup of tea. Isobel brought him a cake and crawled up into his lap. She even allowed him to take a bite before she ate it herself.

Dunnet continued to stare. And indeed, it was a scintillating sight. The two blond heads, the identical smiles. The dimples. He shook his head and huffed a laugh. "Well, Andrew. I see you've been . . . busy." He leveled a presumptuous glance on Susana and she glared him down. He blinked and tore his gaze away. "Ah, may I introduce you to Lachlan Sinclair, Duke of Caithness?"

The duke, who had been watching this interaction with a hint of a smile, nodded. When Andrew moved to stand, as formality required, the duke waved him back down. "No need for that," he said with a chuckle. "You've got your hands full."

Andrew laughed. "You doona know the half of it."

Susana stepped forward, loath to interrupt this scene of male bonding, but Dunnet's appearance here in Dounreay was concerning. "Is Hannah all right?" she asked.

He smiled at her. Smiled like a loon. Absolute adoration wreathed his expression. "Hannah is fine."

"She most certainly is not fine," the duke said with a chuckle.

Susana turned her glower on him and his chuckle evaporated. He might have paled. "What do you mean, she's not fine?"

"I . . . ah . . . Only that she's ruined my boots." He glanced down at his—not-so-pristine—Hessians and wiggled his toes.

"She was ill all the way here." Dunnet's grin broadened.

Susana frowned. "She's been ill all the way here?" And then . . . *oh, heavens.* "She's here?"

Papa nodded with a smile.

"Hurray," said Isobel, brandishing a cake like a well-glazed sword.

"Why didn't you tell me? Is Lana with her?"

"Aye."

"Where are they?"

"We're here."

Susana spun around and stilled. Two dear, familiar faces stared back at her. Hannah and Lana, her two sisters. Home. Delight and relief and exultation washed through her.

As they had come from different mothers, the three of them had always been very different in temperament and physical appearance—Hannah had long dark hair and Lana was a blonde—but there was one thing in which they did not differ. Their absolute adoration for one another.

Hannah seemed pale, yet she also seemed to glow,

though that could have been the brilliance of her smile, her obvious joy to be home. Lana, as always, looked so beautiful it made Susana's chest hurt.

Without a word she opened her arms and ran to them, pulling them both into a fierce, three-sistered embrace.

"Aunt Hannah! Aunt Lana!" Isobel warbled. Andrew *oof*ed as she elbowed her way off his lap and launched herself at her aunts, throwing herself into their arms and wiping sticky fingers on their skirts.

What followed was a flurry of hugs and kisses and tears. It was so wonderful having everyone together once more.

"Dunnet said you've been ill," Susana murmured to Hannah, once all the greetings had been dispensed with.

Hannah's grin looked very much like Dunnet's. "Aye."

"How is this good news?"

"It's the best news," Hannah said. "I'm with child."

Susana's heart soared, sang. "Oh, Hannah! That is wonderful!" Her sister had so wanted children one day, although she'd sorely resisted taking the husband who might be helpful in begetting one. But now her long-held dreams were coming true.

"I'm so happy," Hannah said, glancing at Isobel, who had crawled up into Andrew's lap once more. Her gaze stalled on the two of them, as so many had. She blinked. "Oh, my," she said. "I knew he'd seemed familiar." She sent Susana an accusatory frown. "Why didn't you tell me?"

Susana frowned. "I dinna know."

Lana frowned and whispered in an undertone, "How could you not have *known*?"

"I dinna know he was a Lochlannach."

There was no call for Hannah to laugh. "You're the one who advised me to marry Alexander."

"I'm aware of that."

Hannah patted her hand. "For that, I owe you a debt of gratitude."

"You are happy with him?"

Hannah turned to her husband. A soft sheen filled her eyes. "Verra."

Lana shook her head. "I still canna believe you dinna know who he was. I mean, after . . ."

Thank the lord she trailed off. The last thing Susana wanted was to air her dirty laundry in front of a duke.

"As though you dinna know," Susana said beneath her breath. "*You* could have warned me." With Lana's second sight, it was simply rude that she had not warned Susana that Andrew was coming back into her life. It would have helped to be prepared.

"I doona know everything." Lana's gaze flicked to Hannah's belly, and then to Susana's. "Although I do know some things." Her smile was mysterious.

"Come." Susana hooked arms with Hannah and Lana and led them to the divan. "I want to hear everything that has happened since you left for Dunnet."

"Surely not everything," Hannah laughed.

"I want to hear what's been happening here." Lana said.

Susana snorted. "Surely not everything . . ."

The sisters shared a grin.

They all took their seats. For some reason, when Hamish greeted Lana effusively and sat next to her, it made the duke scowl.

"Lachlan," Dunnet said once they'd all settled. "Do you no' have an announcement you'd like to make?"

The Duke of Caithness cleared his throat and Susana stiffened. Here it was. The news they'd been dreading—the duke's formal request that they clear the land and import sheep. Susana's fingers tightened into a fist. She hid them in her skirts as she stared at the duke, waiting for him to speak. Why Hannah and Lana fixed smiles on their faces at this moment of doom was a mystery.

"I, ah, yes. I do have an announcement." He glanced around the assemblage; his gaze seemed to linger on Lana. She, in turn, flushed. "I have decided against Improvements for the time being."

Susana stilled as a trill of excitement and relief washed through her. "What?"

Caithness nodded. "Alexander and Hannah have convinced me that there are other options to clearing the land. Options that are far better for the people in the county."

"That is excellent," Papa gusted, clapping his hands together. "I think this calls for a drink." Susana rolled her eyes but didn't protest as Tamhas rounded the room, presenting a tumbler to each of the men. The ladies, of course, took tea, though in truth Susana would have much preferred something stronger. This had been a trying few weeks. Thank God it was all over and everyone was safe and together again.

On that note she gave Hannah's shoulder a quick squeeze. Hannah beamed back at her.

They chatted for a while about Hannah and Lana's adventures in Dunnet, and then the conversation turned to recent events. As Andrew and Hamish sketched out the details of the kidnapping, along with their suspicion that Scrabster's plans ran far deeper than they'd thought, the duke's frown darkened. "I am stunned," he said when they finished. "While I met Scrabster, and did not like him in the slightest, I would not have suspected him of such vile acts."

"He's a verra bad man," Isobel said.

The duke fixed his attention on her, nestled in Andrew's lap as she was. "I can see that."

Isobel paused in the licking of her cake. Her nose wrinkled. "He called me a fiend."

"I do apologize for that. I am certain you are not a fiend."

She tipped her head to the side. "Why would you apologize? It wasna you who called me that."

"As duke it is my responsibility to protect you. To keep bad men from bothering you."

She peeped up at Andrew. "I thought it was your job."

He patted her shoulder. "It is his job, too. If a man threatens Dounreay, he threatens Caithness as well."

"Exactly." Caithness nodded. "As duke it is my responsibility to keep bad men from bothering you. And I failed you in that."

Isobel considered this for a moment and then nodded. Her estimation of the duke warmed.

As did Susana's. She appreciated that he was speaking to Isobel as though she were an equal. Most men would have ignored her completely and directed their comments only to the other men.

"I hope you will accept my most sincere apologies for being absent and not providing you the protection you required." Though he spoke to Isobel, the words were directed to them all. That he was man enough to admit he'd made mistakes, and man enough to fix them where he could, spoke volumes about his character.

Susana decided she liked him very much indeed.

Except, of course, for the hungry looks he kept sending in Lana's direction.

Isobel surveyed the duke solemnly, nibbling her lip and considering his words. And then she nodded. "Aye. I accept your 'pology. But it doesna matter anymore."

The duke's brow quirked. "Does it not?"

"Scrabster doesna matter anymore, at least," she said, bringing down disaster as only an innocent child could. "Because my mama shot him."

Oh, dear. Perhaps he should have directed his comments to the men.

The duke's head whipped around and his sharp gaze landed on her, causing heat to prickle on her neck. "You . . . shot him?"

"Good show." Papa lifted his glass.

Susana set her teeth and forced herself to stare the duke down. "He had a pistol pointed at my daughter."

"Doona forget, he'd kidnapped Isobel to force Susana to marry him," Andrew added. It sounded like a complaint.

"Aye." She nodded crisply. "There was that, too."

"Never forget, he planned to murder us all. And then turn his attentions to Lana," Hamish said.

This caused the duke's brows to bristle and Lana to pale. "Me?" she squeaked. She glanced at Susana and made a face. "I think I may be ill."

"You are the next in line for the lands he wanted," Hamish explained.

Dunnet bristled. "But those are Hannah's lands . . ."

"Exactly." Andrew's brow darkened. "We believe his plan was to take out everyone and anyone who stood in his way. Hence the attempt on Magnus."

"What is *take out*?" Isobel asked.

Andrew petted her hair. "He wanted to kill everyone."

Isobel's face scrunched into a furious moue. She glared at the duke. "See. I told you he was a bad man." Then with the quixotic moods of the very young, her features shifted into a blindingly ingenuous mien. She smiled sweetly and batted her lashes. "It's not my fault his castle blew up. Really. It's not."

"His . . . castle blew up?" Dunnet squeaked.

Andrew widened his eyes and nodded, nibbling away an inappropriate smirk.

Papa's guffaw rounded the room.

As for Lana, Hannah, and the duke, they merely gaped.

Isobel, sensing no impending scold, shrugged. "It was his own fault."

Caithness's brow rippled. "How so?"

Isobel blinked. "He locked me in the wrong room." She leaned closer and whispered, "There might have been a fire."

"I . . . see." The duke tried to hide his smile but could not.

No doubt Isobel took it as encouragement. She leaped down from Andrew's lap and crawled onto his instead. He seemed surprised but set his teacup on the small table at his side to hold her.

It amused Susana that Andrew seemed put out.

Isobel stared up at the duke, her eyes alight. She was thrilled with the attention. "It was a verra exciting adventure."

"I am certain it was."

"Look."

The duke blanched as Isobel reached into the pocket of her gown and pulled out a very long blade. Susana flinched. Why hadn't she *known* Isobel had a knife?

"Where did you get that?" she and Andrew squawked at the same time. They shared a horrified glance.

"Hamish gave it to me."

Susana glared at the miscreant and he shrugged.

"It was in his boot. I used it to unlock the doors." Isobel waved the knife around until the duke took it from her under the pretense of studying it. Then he set it very carefully on the table next to his teacup. "It was verra handy. I used it to open his chest, too."

The duke's nostrils flared. "I . . . ah . . . his chest? Whose chest?"

"Scrabster's."

Caithness turned to Susana. "I thought you said you shot him." Clearly he was of the opinion that all the Dounreay women were deranged.

Isobel trilled a laugh as though the duke had told a joke. "Not that kind of chest. It was a treasure chest." She put out a lip. "Although there wasn't much treasure in it. Just these stupid letters." She pulled a sheaf of papers from her pocket and waved them around until the duke confiscated them as well. As there was no more room on the little table, he handed them to Alexander, who began flipping through them. "Oh, and this." She reached in and pulled out a gold trinket.

"What else do you have in that pocket?" Andrew asked.

Isobel grinned. "That's all. I was hoping for treasure but he didn't have any. He did have papers, though. Lots and lots of papers." She beamed at Caithness, who appeared to be in a befuddled trance. Then again, Susana was rather befuddled as well. "Papers burn verra well," Isobel confided.

"I'm sure they do," Andrew said. "It's probably best if we doona start any fires here. What do you think, Isobel?"

She appeared to think this over. For far too long.

"Isobel—" Susana said warningly.

Andrew sent her a speaking look and she swallowed her scold.

"Just think of what it did to Scrabster's castle," Andrew said in a calm tone. Isobel grinned. "Would you want that to happen here?"

The grin faded. She nibbled her lip and shook her head.

"So, no fires?"

"Oh, all right."

"A wise decision." He smiled at her and she smiled back. Astonishingly, Susana had the sense there would, indeed, be no fires.

It was practically a miracle.

Aye, he would make a wonderful father. Exactly what Isobel needed, to be sure.

The duke, who had been silent throughout this exchange, silent and staring at the hunk of gold Isobel held in her hand, cleared his throat. "Do you mind if I look at this?" he asked, his hand hovering over the trinket.

Isobel handed it to him and he studied it at length, turning it this way and that.

His scrutiny was intense. Susana didn't understand the sudden tension in the room.

"Lachlan?" Lana said, and Susana's head whipped around. She gaped at her sister. The tone in which she had addressed the duke was unlike any she'd heard from Lana before. It was far too familiar. And she'd used his given name. "Is it . . . ?"

He glanced up at her with an odd expression on his face. "It is."

"It is what?" Isobel asked, taking the precaution of snatching it back and dropping it into her pocket.

The duke drew in a breath. "It is a treasure, Isobel. One I've been searching for a long time. You say you found it in Scrabster's castle?"

"Aye."

Lana's eyes glowed. "That makes sense. Both Dounreay and Scrabster are along the coast."

How on earth did that signify?

But the duke nodded. "Aye. No doubt, sometime during the past five centuries, they washed up on shore or were caught in nets."

Lana nodded. "Likely, the people who found them dinna realize what they'd really discovered."

"Would someone like to explain what you are all talking about?" Hamish asked peevishly. Though to be honest, there had been a peevish expression on his face since Lana had called the duke *Lachlan*.

"Och, it's a wonderful story," Lana said. "Involving a curse and a magic relic and the future of all Scotland."

Isobel's eyes went wide. "Really?"

"Come here and I'll tell you."

Isobel loved Lana's stories, so she hopped down from Caithness's lap and made her way to Lana's. Stopping, of course, for another cake. When she was settled in—between Lana and Hamish, much to Hamish's chagrin—Lana began.

"Long long ago there was a verra greedy man. He wanted more power than he had, so he betrayed his kin to the evil king Edward Longshanks. Do you remember him from your lessons, Isobel?"

"Of course."

"Verra good, my darling. You're so clever." Lana kissed her brow. "In those days, England and Scotland were at war because Edward wanted to take all our lands for himself."

"That wasn't verra nice."

"Nae. It wasna. There were many bluidy battles. Treachery and betrayal abounded."

Isobel's eyes glittered. She leaned closer.

"Now, the greedy man, the Baron of Rosslyn, wanted more wealth and power, so he aligned with Longshanks, the enemy of all Scots and betrayed his kin. Legend has it, the baron gave the English king the MacAlpin Cross, the magical talisman that has protected Scotland through the ages."

"Why did he do that?"

"Because he wasna happy being a baron, my darling. He wanted to be a duke."

Isobel frowned at Caithness, who shifted in his seat.

"The brutal English king smashed the relic, the heart of all that is Scotland, and tossed it into the sea, ushering in centuries of poverty, torment, and strife for all clans."

Isobel toyed with the twill on Lana's traveling gown. "I doona like that king."

"No one did," Dunnet snorted. Hannah shushed him.

Even Lana frowned at him. "Anyway, the Keeper of the Cross—some say she was a witch—"

"You dinna mention a witch."

"I'm verra sure she was a witch, and with her dying breath, she levied a deadly curse on the new duke and all his descendants."

Isobel put out a lip. "Well, good."

"But it's not so good, darling. Because, according to the curse, none of them will live past their twenty-ninth year."

Isobel snorted. "That's pretty old."

Lana snuffled a laugh. "Aye. Verra old." The duke seemed very put out indeed. "But some men want to live that long. Longer even."

Isobel's brow rumpled. "I canna imagine it."

"Now, see here," Magnus grumbled.

Isobel rolled her eyes. "But you're a *grandfather*."

"A man must live past thirty to become a grandfather," Lana explained. And somehow, Isobel accepted this at face value. "At any rate, throughout the years, all of the duke's firstborn sons have died before their thirtieth birthday."

Isobel nodded. "That seems fair. They did betray their kin."

Lana's eyes widened. "Ah. But did they? The first duke did, to be sure. And he was already old when this happened. It was his sons and his son's sons who paid the price." She swallowed. "And the people who loved them."

Susana didn't miss the look Lana sent Lachlan, nor his yearning glance in return. Suspicion began to bubble.

"How would you like to be punished for something Siobhan has done? Or your mama? Or grandpapa?"

"I havena done anything," Papa grumbled when Isobel gored him with an accusing frown.

"How would you like to pay the price for a sin you had nothing to do with?"

"I *wouldna* like that at all."

"Aye. I feel the same. Well, Lachlan is one of those descendants. He is doomed to die if he canna break the curse."

"Can anything break the curse?" Isobel stared at Lana, her eyes wide.

"One thing only."

"What is it?"

"He must reunite the MacAlpin Cross. We think the piece you found is a part of the relic."

The duke shifted under Isobel's regard. There almost seemed to be a sympathetic flicker in her expression. Almost. "But it's *my* treasure."

"It means quite a lot to me," he said gently.

Isobel frowned. "Do you believe in curses?" she asked Lana, apparently convinced that, with her aunt's occasional glimpses into unseen worlds, she of all people would know.

Lana smiled sadly. "I'm not sure if curses are real. But I do know I doona want Lachlan to die."

Ah. Suspicion confirmed. Lana was, indeed, besotted with the doomed duke. Susana's heart twisted.

Isobel studied the duke. "He is verra handsome."

"Aye. He is."

She pulled the trinket from her pocket and fondled it. "But it's a verra beautiful treasure."

"Perhaps I could offer you a trade?" The duke's voice was a low thrum.

Isobel turned to him with interest glinting in her eyes. "A trade? What do you have?"

He tugged on his plaid. "What do you want?"

"A sword."

Susana frowned. A pulse ticked in her left eye.

Caithness blinked. His jaw dropped. "A . . . sword?"

"I really want a sword." Isobel fluttered her lashes. "But not a big one. Yet."

The duke sent a questing glance to Susana. She nibbled at her lip and glanced, in turn, at Andrew. He nodded and she couldn't help but relent. Andrew had been teaching Isobel. He would know if she were ready for a real sword.

But dear lord in heaven above. Preserve them all from the mayhem Isobel could incite with a real sword . . .

At her assent, the duke smiled. "I am certain that can be arranged."

"My mama willna like it," Isobel whispered, as though no one else were in the room. As though no one else could hear if she whispered.

The duke winked. "Leave your mama to me."

The whole exchange annoyed Susana mightily, so she huffed out a breath. "I doona know. It is quite a sacrifice. Isobel giving up a treasure that could possibly save your life . . . merely for a sword."

Isobel shot her a frown.

Susana bit back a smile and added, "I think we should get something more out of this agreement."

The duke narrowed his eyes. "Like what?"

"A title?" This, she said teasingly, but the duke took her seriously.

He blinked. His lips worked. He looked around the room, but no one seemed willing to help him out. In fact, Papa even snorted a laugh. At length, he said, "Dukes don't convey titles. Only the Crown can convey titles and . . ."

"And?"

"With due respect, my lady, not even the Crown could convey a title upon . . ." He flushed. "Well, a woman."

Irritating that, but true. "I wasn't thinking of myself. I was thinking of Andrew."

"What?" Andrew squawked, straightening in his chair. "I doona want a bluidy title."

"Hush," she said. "I'm negotiating."

Caithness flushed. "Madam. I do not have titles to hand out like candies."

"Mmm." Isobel licked her lips. "I like candy, too."

Andrew put out a lip. "I doona want a bluidy title."

Susana glared him silent. "Lands then." It had begun as a jest, but now it didn't seem so funny. If Andrew was going to marry her—if he ever got around to wooing her, that was—he needed something to call his own.

The duke turned out his pockets. "No lands here, either."

A cough to the duke's right caught his attention. It caught everyone's attention and all eyes turned to Dunnet who had been silent up until now, reading through the papers Isobel had pilfered. His eyes were wide with disbelief. As he read, he shook his head and his lip curled. "Unbelievable," he muttered, turning the page.

"What is it?" the duke asked.

Dunnet frowned. "If these letters are any indication, Scrabster has been robbing the Crown blind for years. There is reference to bribing the tax man and two pages of gloating about how much he's stolen from the Regent."

Caithness stilled. His fingers closed. "Prinny won't like that."

"And I canna tell for sure, but it appears he's been plotting against you as well."

"What?"

Dunnet handed a letter to the duke, and he scanned it. His jaw tightened. "That rotter." He read on until he came to a part that made his muscles bunch. "Bloody hell. Look at this." Dunnet came to read over his shoulder as Caithness pointed to a line. Both men became very somber indeed.

"What the hell is it?" Papa asked.

Dunnet scrubbed his face with a palm. "Scrabster wasna working alone." He shared a glance with his brother. "It doesna say who . . . but I have my suspicions."

Nae. He didn't need to give a name. They were all fairly certain, given the fact that their two neighbors had both been unrelenting in their quest for this land.

It had to be Stafford. The bastard.

Caithness sat back and blew out a heavy sigh. He offered Susana a tight smile. "It seems as though I may have a title to spare after all," he said in a ragged tone.

Her stomach revolted at the thought. "Oh, no. Not *that* title."

The duke narrowed his eyes. "You did ask for a title."

"I wasn't serious. Besides, I doona want to be married to *Scrabster*. What an execrable name to give my sons."

Dunnet gaped at her. "Married?"

Andrew straightened in his chair. "Did you say, *married*?"

"Yes, of course married."

"Hurray," Isobel crowed.

Susana ignored this, and the reaction rocketing around

the room, and frowned at Andrew. "What do you think wooing is for?"

"But I dinna ask you to marry me."

She stilled. Her stomach lurched. Mortification rippled through her. "Are you . . . are you saying you . . . doona want to marry me?"

Remorse flickered over his features and he leaped to his feet and crossed to her. And though everyone was watching, he knelt before her, took her hands, and kissed her. "I'm saying nothing of the sort. I verra much want to marry you," he murmured. "But I would like to woo you first."

Annoyance riffled. She was far too impatient for wooing. She wanted him now. "How long will this bluidy wooing take?"

"Not long." He kissed her again and again until Isobel blew out a sigh that rounded the room.

In tandem, they turned to her and she shook her head, disgust written on her delicate features. "I told you to kidnap her," she said. "It's much quicker."

Susana held back a snort. No doubt it would be.

CHAPTER TWENTY-THREE

After tea was over, Caithness begged to be excused to rest up after his journey and, for some reason, Lana offered to show him to his rooms. He agreed with alacrity. Isobel hopped off Andrew's lap and went with them, much to the duke's consternation. She threaded her fingers through his and gazed up at him with glowing admiration, most likely because he'd offered to give her a sword.

Andrew and Hamish left as well, to debrief the men and see to their mounts, though Susana could tell Andrew was reluctant to leave her. With a kiss to her forehead, he murmured, "I'll be back soon." His eyes glimmered as he added. "You and I need to have a conversation."

Aye. They did, but she much appreciated this time with Hannah and Papa. And Dunnet, of course. They all remained in the parlor, chattering and catching up, and Susana found she really enjoyed Dunnet's company. Though he wasn't a man of many words, when he spoke it was with a clever observation and sharp wit. He had her holding her sides more than once, especially when he told the tale of when his hound Brùid met Lana's cat.

Tamhas interrupted their guffaws with a scratch at the door. "My laird," he said to Papa. "You have a visitor."

Papa blew out a laugh. "This is the day for it," he said. "Who is it, my boy?"

Tamhas's throat worked. "The Marquess of Stafford."

Dunnet stiffened. His features became rather fierce and

his hand clenched into a fist. No doubt he was remembering the fact that Stafford had once had designs on his wife.
Beyond that, all here suspected Stafford of much greater
perfidy. "I'm going to get Lachlan," he said. "Hannah, darling, come with me."

Hannah glanced at Susana, clearly torn between the
desire to avoid this interview with a man she found repul-
sive and her disinclination to leave Susana and Papa alone
with a snake.

"Do go, darling," Susana said, patting her hand. "We
shall be fine."

"All right," she said. "But if he steps one toe out of
line . . ." She eyed the small table where Hamish's knife
still lay.

Susana's lips curled into a smile. "Aye," she said. When
Dunnet and Hannah left, Susana turned to Papa. "What
the bluidy hell does *he* want?" she muttered.

"Only one way to find out, my girl." He waved to Tamhas. "Show him in."

Her nerves riffled as Stafford strode into the room. He
was a tall man and, but for his piggy eyes, could be considered good looking. But his features were set in an arrogant expression and his lips curled in a constant sneer she
couldn't like. Add to that the disdain with which he'd
treated Papa over the years and the way his every word and
deed seemed to underscore his belief that he was better
than everyone else, and he became very unattractive
indeed. His son, the one he'd wanted to marry to Hannah,
was no better.

He had dressed in formal attire for such a casual, un-
announced visit, turned out in the uniform of a British lord
rather than in a Highland laird. Which was telling.

"Ah, Magnus!" he gusted, as though they were old
friends; they were not. "So good to see you."

Papa rose to his feet and affected a bow, but it was short and curt. "Stafford. Welcome. Tamhas. Whisky, please."

"Ah. And your daughter." His gaze flicked over Susana in a far-too-assessing manner and her blood went cold. The man was a reptile.

He took her hand and kissed it. She nearly retched.

"To what do we owe this unexpected pleasure?" she asked. Surely that wasn't contempt dripping from her words.

Stafford stilled over her hand; his features arranged themselves into something of a smirk. "Just a neighborly visit."

"Dounreay is hardly in your neighborhood," Papa observed.

Stafford frowned but didn't reply. He took the seat next to Papa and then accepted a whisky from the tray Tamhas proffered.

"Nae. But I heard of your recent troubles and I wanted to come by and see if I could be of assistance." His tone was incredibly sincere. If she didn't know better, she might have believed him.

Papa smiled. It was not a genuine smile in the slightest. "I doona know what you mean. Everything is fine here."

"Come now, Magnus. There have been countless attacks on your lands. Why, I even heard your granddaughter was stolen from her bed." He *tsk*ed.

Susana's eyes narrowed. There was no way Stafford could know such things unless he'd been working with Scrabster. Unless the two of them had planned all this together.

She opened her mouth to vent her wrath, but Papa shot her a warning glance. "Aye. That was worrisome indeed."

Stafford looked around the room. "I do hope she's all right?" His simper was galling.

"She's fine," Susana snapped. No thanks to him.

His eyes widened. "Really? I'd heard she'd been kidnapped. I hadna heard she'd been returned."

Papa's fingers played on the fabric of his chair. "You do seem to hear many things."

"Of course." Stafford put out his chest. "I make it a point to know what is happening within my aegis."

Annoyance riffled. This was *not* his aegis.

His attention flicked to Susana. "I understand your sister has married Dunnet."

"Aye," she said through her teeth.

Stafford sighed and sipped his drink. "A pity that."

He let this tidbit linger until Papa responded. It took a while for Papa to respond. "A pity?"

"Aye. I've heard tell Dunnet willna be a baron much longer."

Papa's jaw bunched. "Have you?"

"Aye."

"And where did you hear that?"

Stafford smiled slickly. "I have my sources."

"Is that a threat against my daughter's husband?" Papa asked with matching slickness.

"Och, never say it." Stafford's expression belied his words. But then, it often did. "I've simply heard that the duke isna pleased with him and will soon have him removed from his offices."

Susana's blood began to boil. This was nearly identical to the load of tripe Scrabster had spewed. Oh, where was Caithness? He needed to hear this rot. She looked over her shoulder and stilled. For Caithness stood in the doorway, leaning against the jamb. From his position, Stafford couldn't see him.

Stafford *tsk*ed again. "Where will you be then? Who will protect Dounreay when Dunnet no longer can?"

Papa pressed his lips together and leaned forward, rolling his tumbler between his palms. "I see what you mean. That is concerning."

Stafford sat back with a gusted sigh. "Aye, it is."

Closing one eye, Papa studied the marquess. "So tell me, Stafford. What would you propose? To keep us safe?"

"Isn't it obvious? If we were family, if I had some claim on this land, of course I would dedicate my forces to keeping you all safe. The solution is as simple as an alliance between your daughter and my son."

"An alliance?" Heat prickled Susana's neck. Acid churned in her belly.

Stafford offered her an avuncular smile. "A marriage."

"But Hannah is already married," Papa said.

"Aye." His lip curled. Probably at the thought of his failure to win her for his son. "But you have two other daughters, both unwed. Give one to Scrabster in marriage, and the other to me. Between the two of us, we will assure the safety of your lands and peoples from the east and the west."

"Give my daughter to Scrabster?" Papa barked a laugh and Susana smiled as well. Stafford was clearly behind on recent events.

The marquess frowned. "Why do you scoff? Scrabster is a baron. Hardly a title to turn up your nose at. And if we're being honest here . . ." Were they? Were they being honest? "Your daughters have a reputation of being . . ."

"Being what?" Susana couldn't hold her tongue. Not if her life depended on it.

Stafford pressed his lips together. "Being . . . difficult."

The man had no idea. Susana cast about for her bow before she remembered she'd left it in the foyer. *Blast.*

"Title or not," Papa said, "Scrabster is the man who kidnapped Isobel. And . . ." He flicked a look at Susana. "I doona think he's in any condition to take a wife."

The marquess stilled. He glanced at Susana as well. She offered him a wide grin. One with teeth. "What can I say?" she gritted. "He was being . . . *difficult*."

"I . . . ah . . ." Stafford paled slightly and ripped his gaze back to Papa. "It hardly signifies. I will still honor my promise to protect you from the west. If, of course, your daughter marries my son."

"Which daughter?"

"It doesna matter." He smiled, and behind his eyes Susana saw a flicker of avarice.

The whole plot turned her stomach. The land was Hannah's. And Dunnet's. The only way Stafford would have any claim on it was if something should happen to them. And Papa. And possibly herself or Lana.

How far would he go to claim this strip of land?

But she didn't interrupt, because clearly Papa was fishing for information. If this conversation went the way she thought it might go—and considering the fact that Caithness was listening to every word—a splendid confrontation was in the offing. Anticipation bubbled.

"And if I refuse to give you my daughter? *Any* daughter since it appears you doona have a preference?"

Stafford shrugged. "There's no telling what could happen to Dounreay. A land with no overlord—"

"We have an overlord. Caithness—"

"Caithness doesna care what happens to you," Stafford said. "He's left you unprotected for decades."

"But he *is* our overlord." Papa smiled. "Technically, all the land in Caithness County is his. We are his stewards."

"Ah, but you see . . . It doesna have to be that way." Stafford shifted forward to the edge of his chair and focused on Papa as though there were no one else in the room. As though the woman sitting across from him didn't signify in the slightest. Then again, to a man like him, women did not. They were merely chattel, chess pieces to be moved about on a whim. Her stomach roiled. She deplored men like this.

"What do you mean?" Papa leaned forward as well.

"I have received official word from the Prince Regent himself that he is verra pleased with my Improvements to the land."

"I see." It was impressive the way Papa hid his sneer. Susana knew full well how he felt about the Improvements that had ravaged Stafford's land. Refugees from his crofts had flooded into Dounreay as he cleared the farmers from his holdings.

"There is word he may be considering making me a duke myself." This Stafford said with a jut of his chest. "No doubt he could be convinced to give me these lands once Caithness is . . . gone."

"Gone?"

Stafford snorted. "Trust me. He willna be around for long."

Susana stiffened. Was that what she thought it was? A threat against the duke's life?

The gall of the man, to admit it so brashly. It was a challenge to hold her tongue, but she didn't want to interrupt these revelations. They were far too interesting.

"What do you mean?" Papa asked, thumbing his beard.

"Doona fash yerself, Magnus." Stafford patted his hand and Papa nearly cringed. "You willna be suspected. No one will."

"Suspected? Of what?"

Stafford's only response was an oily smile.

"I thought the duke was a friend of the prince."

"Bah." Stafford waved away this triviality. "Prinny is easy to manipulate. Aside from that, everyone knows none of the Caithness dukes reach their thirtieth birthday. It will be no surprise when Lachlan Sinclair expires before his time."

Papa had had enough. "I canna be a party to murder."

"Ah, but that's the beauty of it. It isna murder . . . it's a curse." Stafford grinned as though mightily pleased with himself. "And what do you stand to lose?"

"A daughter?"

Stafford ignored him. "You will gain my support as your patron . . . and lose a laird who doesna care about you or your lands."

"I do care, actually," A deep, ducal voice rumbled from the door.

Stafford whipped around. His jaw went slack. He bounded to his feet. "Lachlan . . . I . . . We . . . We were just talking about you."

"Yes," the duke said in a crisp tone. "I heard."

Stafford's lips wobbled. He sent a reproachful frown at Papa, who shrugged and rubbed his lips to hide his grin, but it was visible in his eyes.

"This is not what it seems," Stafford protested.

"Isn't it? Because it sounded an awful lot like a plot to do me in."

"Nonsense!" The beads of sweat on Stafford's brow belied his calm tone.

"I think it's time for you to leave," Caithness said coldly. "And believe you me, Prinny will hear of this. This and the treason you were planning with Scrabster." His eyes glittered as he stared down the marquess. He was bluffing, but Stafford didn't know that. "Aye," he said when Stafford broke first, glancing around the room with a panicked gaze, searching for escape, perhaps. "We found some very interesting letters in Scrabster's strongbox. Before we blew up his castle, of course."

"You . . . you . . . blew up his castle?"

"Your informants dinna tell you that?" Susana couldn't keep from saying.

Caithness tipped his head to the side and shrugged. "*Someone* blew up his castle. I couldn't say who. I cannot help wondering whose castle might be next." He smiled slowly. "If indeed you have one after the prince hears of what the two of you had planned."

"Lies. It's all lies. Scrabster was a liar!" Stafford bellowed.

"And what I just heard? Your threats on my life? Were those lies, too?"

"I'm sure I have no idea what you are talking about," he sputtered with an innocence Susana might have believed if she hadn't been sitting right here throughout a very damning conversation.

The man was unconscionable.

"I suggest you see to your accounts, Stafford. Good day." The duke's tone was beyond dismissive. As the marquess rushed past him, in something of a dither, Caithness murmured, under his breath, "And good luck."

Andrew and his brother met in the library before dinner. With the kerfuffle of Stafford's visit, and the revelations of Scrabster's purloined letters, they hadn't yet had a moment alone, so sitting before the fire with a tumbler of whiskey together was wonderful. So much like old times, it made his chest hurt. Still, unease skirled in Andrew's gut; he knew there were unaddressed issues between them, and this seemed as good a time as any to tackle them.

He cleared his throat and Alexander glanced at him, but Andrew was unsure where to begin.

Alexander took the lead from him. "So . . ." he said. "Isobel."

Andrew tried not to flinch. There was no reason to flinch, surely. "Aye."

"Is she your daughter?"

"Aye. She is."

"But you've never been to Dounreay. Why did you not tell me you knew Hannah's sister?"

Andrew gazed down at the swirling whisky. "When I was in Perth, I met a girl named Mairi. I fell in love with her. She . . . died."

Alexander's lips tightened. "I'm so sorry. I dinna know that. You never mentioned her—"

"Nae. I couldna bear to."

"I wondered why . . ."

"Why, what?"

"You were . . . different when you returned."

"I was mourning. I never forgot her. Never stopped . . . loving her. I kissed a hundred women searching for . . . that."

Alexander snorted a laugh. "You kissed Lana."

"I have wondered . . ."

His brother glanced up at his dark tone. Frowned. "Wondered what?"

"If you sent me away because of that."

Alexander gaped at him. "I chose you for this mission because you were the best. And frankly, the man I trusted most. And as I suspected, you handled things beautifully. Not only did you protect my wife's land and her family, you uncovered a plot that could reach to the highest levels of the land."

Andrew turned back to the fire. "I only wanted to make you proud."

Alexander shook his head. "Make me proud?"

"Aye. To pay you back, if only in some small way, for all you've sacrificed, all you've given to me."

Without a word, Alexander stood and came to his chair, yanked him up, and folded him into a huge hug. Then he set his palms on either side of Andrew's face and stared him in the eye. "Andrew, you've always made me proud. Prouder than you can ever know. You never had to prove yourself to me. Not ever. And as far as paying me back? What nonsense."

Andrew frowned. It wasn't nonsense. It was—

"You're my brother. My family. My heart. I would have done anything and everything to keep you safe. Because I love you."

"I love you, too." He hated that his voice caught on the words. Or maybe not.

Alexander clapped him on the back and then retook his seat. "With that out of the way—" He shot a quizzical look at Andrew. "It is out of the way, isn't it?"

"Aye." Finally. Thank God. It was like a weight off his soul.

"I'm dying to hear the rest of this story."

"This story?"

"Isobel," Alexander reminded him. "You met a girl in Perth who died . . . I fail to see how the two connect."

"Ah. But they do. When I arrived here, I discovered she hadn't died. Mairi and Susana are the same girl. She left Perth carrying my child."

"Holy fook."

"She wasna happy to see me." He cringed. "Especially when she thought I dinna remember her."

Surely there was no call for Alexander to throw back his head and laugh as he did. When he finally reclaimed control of his errant humor, he asked, wiping the tears from his eyes, "So what are your plans now? I assume you intend to stay?"

"Aye. I do. I love Susana. I love Isobel. I canna envision my life without them."

"And this wooing?"

"Shall take place with all haste."

"A good plan. I have met Susana Dounreay. When she wants something, it is a good idea to give it to her without delay."

They both chuckled, and then Alexander sobered. "I shall miss you."

"And I you."

"Dounreay is not so verra far."

"Less than a day by sea."

Andrew swiped at the tears pricking his eyes. He loved his brother very much. He would hate being so far apart. But there were others he loved as well, and he felt torn. It was a decidedly maudlin moment.

It was interrupted when an arrow whizzed past his head and landed in the spine of a tome in the mathematics section. He whirled around to see his daughter standing in the doorway, tidied up and looking practically domesticated in a frilly blue dress. Her hair was braided into an intricate coif, which was topped with a lace bow. The effect was ruined by the bow in her hand.

"*Isobel Mairi MacBean!*" he bellowed. "What on God's green earth are you thinking?"

She grinned and sauntered into the room. "I was thinking I should probably do something drastic to stop you from crying."

"I wasn't crying." A warbled assertion.

"You were, too."

"How, exactly, would being shot with an arrow stop him from crying?" Alexander asked, clearly bemused.

Isobel lifted a shoulder and blew out a breath. "I dinna hit him, did I?"

"Were you trying?"

"Nae." She surveyed the shelf. "I never liked that book."

Andrew sighed. "Did you come in here with the sole intent of peppering us with arrows?" It was hard to keep the humor from his tone.

"Of course not," she said. "Mama sent me to tell you dinner is ready."

With an exchanged glance, the two men rose and, with Isobel between them, headed for the dining room. Andrew took the precaution of confiscating her bow.

"Well, one thing is for certain," Alexander said.

"What's that?"

"With that aim, she's definitely your daughter."

"Aye," Andrew said, something warm blossoming in his chest. "She is."

§

Over dinner, it became very clear to Andrew that Hamish didn't have a chance in hell of winning Lana. She and the duke sat across from each other at the table and neither added much to the conversation. They did, however, have a conversation of their own. It involved steamy glances and, perhaps, the occasional touch of a toe.

Andrew knew this because occasionally Caithness missed his mark and found *his* foot instead.

Having been in a similar situation himself, and given the fact the duke was his overlord, when the man met his eye and went pink right to the tips of his ears, Andrew hardly smirked very much at all.

While Hamish was clearly put out, it occurred to Andrew that Lana and the duke were well suited. It appeared a Dounreay sister wasn't in the cards for his friend. Ah, well. One day he would find the woman of his dreams. There were many other fish in the sea, including the indomitable Saundra who, when she served dessert, eschewed protocol and served Hamish before the duke. Fortunately, Caithness was not paying attention.

He did pay attention, however—everyone did—when Susana shared the story of Andrew's arrival in Reay, rather gleefully revealing the fact that Andrew had mistaken her for a cattle thief. By the time her tale was finished, she had everyone around the table howling with laughter, even Andrew.

He countered with her resistance to his admittedly superior expertise in managing the defenses and their resultant feuds—including their duel. Although he did leave some bits out.

As the meal wound down, Andrew stood and, on a prearranged signal, Tamhas came to his side, carrying a long thin package wrapped in cloth. "Ahem," he said. "I have a presentation to make. Isobel, can you come here, please?"

His daughter narrowed her eyes, but slipped from her chair and padded around the table. He knelt before her and stared into her eyes, struck again at how much they were like his. "I made you a promise, Isobel, and I want you to know, going forward, I always keep my promises." He pulled back the cloth, revealing a small sword in a miniature sheath, complete with a leather belt that would fit around her waist.

Her breath caught; her eyes shone. She put out a hand and traced the line of the weapon with trembling fingers. "Is it . . . is this mine?"

"All yours."

The look she sent him nearly liquefied hm. He'd never seen such delight. Never made one person so happy. He was glad he'd been able to do it for her.

"Do you . . . like it?"

"Och, aye." She gently wrapped her arms around him—he was holding a sword, after all—and pressed a kiss to his cheek. "I love it. Thank you."

"What is it?" Hannah, on the other side of the table, asked.

In response, Isobel took hold of the hilt, unsheathed her new weapon, and held it high.

"Oh, dear God." Hannah paled. "You weren't serious about giving her a sword?"

"Of course."

"She's a *child*."

"She's verra skilled. And verra wise." He turned to Isobel. "Do you remember the rules?"

Solemnly, she nodded. "No weapons at the table."

He blinked. "Ah, aye," he sputtered. "That is an excellent rule. But I meant, do you remember the safety rules?"

"Aye." Her attention fixed on the blade. "Always keep it sheathed unless it's being used." With great care and respect, she did just that.

"Excellent."

"Always keep the blade lowered and turned away so I doona cut myself."

"Very good. And?"

"And never point it at someone unless I am prepared to skewer them."

The duke, who had just taken a sip of wine, spewed it across the table.

Hannah shook her head. She stared at Susana. "You canna be serious."

For her part, Susana was beaming with something Andrew could only interpret as pride. "Verra serious."

"B-B-But a sword?"

Susana sent him an adoring glance. At least, it seemed adoring. "Andrew has been giving her lessons."

Isobel fixed a frown on her mother. "How did you find out about our lessons? It was supposed to be a secret."

A flush rose on Susana's cheeks. Her lashes flickered. "I saw you."

"You saw us?" He tried not to squeak.

"It was adorable," she gushed.

"Adorable?" Hannah again. She gaped at her husband and threw up her hands. Alexander shrugged.

"She's quite good," Andrew assured her.

Isobel preened. "He did it in exchange for advice on how to woo Mama."

Susana blinked. Her gaze on him warmed. "You did?"

"Aye."

"What kind of advice did you offer?" Lana asked with a smile.

"I advised him to kidnap her. It's what Scotsmen do, after all."

"Do they?" the duke asked with a contemplative glance at Lana, one that made her blush.

"Of course they do," Isobel snorted.

Lana forced back a laugh. She fixed her focus on Susana. "And, um, did he? Kidnap you?"

"No," Susana said.

Andrew did not imagine the petulance in her tone.

∽

He didn't kidnap her.

She kidnapped him.

She waited until after dinner—until everyone had found

their beds. She waited until the dark shadows of the night had crept over Dounreay Castle, and she kidnapped him.

Granted, he was a willing participant in the escapade, but it was still a kidnapping.

She came to his room dressed in the cloak she'd worn before and took him prisoner—although to be fair, she'd simply told him to come with her and he'd obeyed. He would obey her every command, especially when issued in that tone.

"Come along, my prisoner," she said, tugging him down the hall.

"Am I your prisoner?" He grinned at her.

"Aye. I willna release you until you succumb to my demands."

That was promising.

He grinned at her. "And, madam kidnapper, what are your demands?"

He expected her to say something flippant or saucy. She did not. Her expression was fierce as she said, "Marry me."

He stopped, stock-still, and gaped at her. "Are you proposing? To me?" Why a shaft of annoyance lanced him, he had no idea. Other than the fact that *he* had expected to be the one to propose to *her*.

She shrugged. "You doona seem inclined to do so." The slight pout on her face was undeniable.

And oh, he was. He was inclined. "I *told* you I would woo you."

"Wooing takes far too long. Isobel is right. Kidnapping is better."

"So you intend to hold me prisoner until I give in to your evil desires?"

Her grin was wicked.

Excellent.

He planned to hold out as long as he could.

He followed her up the stone staircase to the third floor, to a room in a hall that was unoccupied. Unoccupied, aye, but not unprepared.

There was a large bed made up with fresh linens and a fire in the grate and a tray on the table. She'd thought of everything.

With a naughty expression, she pushed him into the room . . . and locked the door. Her eyes twinkled. "We doona want any witnesses," she said, and he couldn't hold back a laugh. "Isobel does see all, you know."

He blanched and glanced about the room. "I . . . ah . . . Where is Isobel?"

"Isobel is sleeping with Lana tonight," Susana purred. "She doesna even know where we are. We have the whole night all to ourselves."

Thank God for small favors. He wanted no witnesses for what he had in mind. But . . .

"My wound?"

Her eyes glimmered. "Doona fash yerself, Lochlannach. I'll be gentle." She led him to the chair by the fire and sat him down. "I've missed you," she said as she knelt beside him.

He threaded his fingers in her hair. "I've been here all along."

She reached for the placket of his breeks. "You know what I mean."

While he really liked where she was heading, he stilled her hands. "Susana . . ."

She peeped up at him. "Aye?"

"We should talk."

Her frown was fierce. "We've already talked it all out."

"Have we?"

"Aye. We've both accepted the past and let it go. We

both want to be together . . ." She eyed him. "We do want
to be together, do we no'?"

"More than you know."

"So what more is there to discuss?"

"I wanted to tell you I love you."

"You told me." She was relentless with his placket. And
his cock, so long denied, was rising. Still . . .

"Not in so many words."

"Well, for heaven's sake, then say it."

"I love you."

"Excellent." She released the fastenings and took his
cock in her hands. "Mmm," she murmured, bending close
for a taste.

Though his heart—and his cock—pulsed in anticipation, he stopped her once more. His deeper need was far too
essential to deny. He tipped up her chin so he could see
her face. "But Susana . . ."

"What?" she said, perhaps a little impatiently.

"*You* havena said it." It was a measure of his true inse-
curity that he needed the words, but he did. He ached to
hear them.

Though he'd come into himself on this journey—proved
himself to Alexander, proved himself to himself, proved
himself to *her*—he very much needed this confirmation.

She sighed gustily. "Oh, all right. Andrew Lochlannach," she said, staring into his eyes. "I love you. More
than anything—"

"More than your bow?"

Susana stilled. She appeared to think about this. For far
too long.

"Susana?" A warning tone.

She sent him a smile that was both mocking and sincere. "Aye, Andrew, my darling. I do love you, even more
than my bow," she said.

"And will you marry me?" *And be my love? My life? My everything?*

"Aye, Andrew. I will."

He pulled her up for a long and lingering kiss that he was loath to end. But when he released her, she gazed adoringly at him for a moment . . . and then bent her head and took him in her mouth.

This time, he didn't stop her.

Why on earth would he?

Read on for an excerpt from Sabrina York's next book

LANA *and the* LAIRD

Available in June 2016 from St. Martin's Paperbacks

Lachlan collapsed on his pillow, gasping for breath. He hated these visits.

They always occurred deep in the night, waking him from a sound sleep, leaving Lachlan mentally exhausted and physically drained, as though the spirits had taken their energy from him and left him but an empty husk. He knew he would not fall asleep again. He rarely did.

He didn't know why the spirit kept tormenting him. He'd come. He was in Scotland. Attempting to do what his father asked, even though it was probably an impossible task. He was determined to try, even with the little time he had left.

He threw back his covers and set his feet on the floor. He had to wait until he stopped shaking to stand, and even then, his legs were limp. When he could, he stumbled to the wardrobe and found a pair of breeches and a simple shirt. After a fright like this, he needed to walk, to clear his mind, his soul, of the terror.

He didn't wake Dougal. He never did. It was unfair to ask his cousin to bear the onus of his curse. Lachlan made his way through the deserted halls of Lochlannach Castle, down the grand staircase, and headed for the terrace that overlooked the crashing sea below. There was a moon tonight. The view of Dunnet Bay would calm his soul. And if it did not, there was always the option of stepping over the edge and into oblivion.

But as he emerged into the cool velvet night, it wasn't oblivion that awaited him.

It was Lana Dounreay.

She sat on the seawall staring out at his coveted view, dressed in a diaphanous froth that had to be her night-dress. Her hair, turned silver by the night, hung down over her shoulders, glimmering in the moonlight.

His heart pattered, but for a very different reason.

She was so lovely, so serene, it made his breath catch.

He came to stand beside her without a word, tucking his hands in his pockets and staring at the sea. She glanced up at him, but without surprise, as though she had expected him. Together they gazed out at the dark ripples of the water, the shards of light dancing over the surface of the blackness.

A gentle breeze wafted by, bringing with it her scent. It made him dizzy.

Ah, how he wished . . .

He wished he were another man. A man not cursed. A man not haunted. A man not doomed to an early death.

A man who could have kissed her once.

How magnificent would that have been?

He must have sighed because she put her hand on his arm. It was warm. Soft. Alluring.

"Can you no' sleep?" she asked in a soothing timbre.

He glanced at her and his gaze was snared. Her eyes were so wide, so blue, so deep. He wanted to drown in them. "No. I . . . had a visitor."

Her brow rumpled. "A visitor?"

"Yes." He turned back to the sea. Though he was loath to discuss this with anyone, lest they think him mad, he knew she would understand. "My father."

"Ah. I see. Does he visit you often?"

Lachlan snorted a laugh, but it was really not one. "Too often."

Lana tipped her head to the side. "You . . . doona enjoy his visits?"

"I do not. They are . . . terrifying."

Why this puzzled her was a mystery. Ghosts *were* terrifying.

"Can you describe the visit?"

Something in her tone caught his attention. He sat beside her on the wall, listening to the waves crash below. It took a while for him to collect his thoughts. "He is always dour. Pained. There is wailing and—"

"Wailing?"

"Yes. But it is the chains that are the most perturbing."

Lana blinked. "Chains?"

"Yes. He's draped in them. Bound by them. It is his eternal torment. Because of the curse."

"How odd. None of the ghosts I know wear chains."

"They are probably not cursed."

"Probably not." Her lips quirked as she murmured, "As there are no such things as curses."

His heart lurched. Would that that were true. He studied her face. Beautiful as it was, that hint of amusement pricked at him. "Do you find this funny?"

"Nae. Not a bit of it." She patted his hand. Her heat lingered. " 'Tis just . . . odd."

"What is odd?" Was he really asking? This whole conversation was odd.

"Odd that your ghost wears chains. Chains are verra . . . of this earth after all."

"He's being punished. They are probably metaphorical."

"Most likely."

As they turned back to the vista before them, Lachlan

reflected that this was, indeed, a surreal conversation to be having. But then, with someone like Lana, it made sense.

"Your mother doesna wear chains."

His belly roiled at the thought. "I am . . . gratified to hear it."

"She seems quite at peace."

"Good to know."

"Except that she worries about you."

"Will you tell her I'm fine?"

"I canna."

He gaped at her.

She lifted a shoulder. "I willna lie to her. Besides, she knows you're no' a happy man."

A happy man? Was there such a thing?

"I am a cursed man."

"*Pffft.*"

"I am." He didn't know why he smiled. His lips just wanted to move that way.

What was it about this woman, this sprite, that made the shadows waft away? Made all his dark ruminations evaporate like mists in the sunlight? Made him *smile* after the horrific encounter he'd just had?

Ah, but it didn't seem so horrific. Not now. Not with *her* by his side.

Lana shot him a glance that warmed his heart. "She thought you looked verra fine tonight at dinner."

"Ah. The kilt."

"Aye." Her lashes fluttered. "I thought you looked verra fine as well."

Now that stirred something in him. Something illicit and naughty. "Did you?"

"Aye."

"Was I manly?" He was teasing, perhaps, but when she flicked a glance at him, with that expression—one of hunger and admiration and . . . heat—all his playfulness withered, scorched by the blazing flare of his lust.

There was something about the cloak of night, the refreshing scent of the sea, the fragrance of her perfume, the way her hair riffled in the breeze. Or maybe it was his churning need to wipe the memory of his father's visit from his mind, or the suddenly clawing desire to be a man he could never be . . . but Lachlan had to kiss her. Everything in him ached for it.

And so he did.

Though it was foolish and injudicious and wildly inappropriate of him, he did.

He leaned closer, slowly so as not to startle her, threaded his fingers in the silk of her hair, cupped her nape, and set his lips on hers.

It was sublime. She was warm and willing. Her mouth was mobile beneath his as she explored him as gently as he explored her.

Excitement welled, desire roared.

She made a sound, a murmur, a moan, and it incited him to further madness. He deepened the kiss, pulled her closer, eased his tongue into the cavern of her mouth. A shudder racked him as she pressed closer. Her breasts, tender and soft, pressed into his chest. His mind spun. His body shook. Need possessed him.